PENGUIN BOOKS
THE BIOSCOPE MAN

Indrajit Hazra is the author of the novels *The Burnt Forehead of Max Saul* and *The Garden of Earthly Delights*, both of which have also been published in French. He is a journalist with the *Hindustan Times*, where he also writes the popular weekly column Red Herring.

# the bioscope man

INDRAJIT HAZRA

PENGUIN BOOKS

PENGUIN BOOKS
Published by the Penguin Group
Penguin Books India Pvt. Ltd, 11 Community Centre, Panchsheel Park,
New Delhi 110 017, India
Penguin Group (USA) Inc., 375 Hudson Street, New York, New York 10014, USA
Penguin Group (Canada), 90 Eglinton Avenue East, Suite 700, Toronto,
Ontario, M4P 2Y3, Canada (a division of Pearson Penguin Canada Inc.)
Penguin Books Ltd, 80 Strand, London WC2R 0RL, England
Penguin Ireland, 25 St Stephen's Green, Dublin 2, Ireland
(a division of Penguin Books Ltd)
Penguin Group (Australia), 250 Camberwell Road, Camberwell,
Victoria 3124, Australia (a division of Pearson Australia Group Pty Ltd)
Penguin Group (NZ), 67 Apollo Drive, Rosedale, North Shore 0632,
New Zealand (a division of Pearson New Zealand Ltd)
Penguin Group (South Africa) (Pty) Ltd, 24 Sturdee Avenue, Rosebank,
Johannesburg 2196, South Africa

Penguin Books Ltd, Registered Offices: 80 Strand, London WC2R 0RL, England

First published by Penguin Books India 2008

Copyright © Indrajit Hazra 2008

All rights reserved

10 9 8 7 6 5 4 3 2 1

ISBN 9780143101741

Typeset in *PalmSprings* by SÜRYA, New Delhi
Printed at Baba Barkhanath Printers, New Delhi

*To my mother*
*the patron saint of good food and white lies*

Last night, I was in the Kingdom of Shadows ...

Without noise, the foliage, grey as cinder, is agitated by the wind and the grey silhouettes—of people condemned to a perpetual silence, cruelly punished by the privation of all the colours of life—these silhouettes glide in silence over the grey ground. Their movements are full of vital energy and so rapid that you scarcely see them, but their smiles have no life in them. You see their facial muscles contract but their laugh cannot be heard. A life is born before you, a life deprived of sound and the spectre of colour—a grey and noiseless life—a wan and cut-rate life.

—Maxim Gorky,
a news report for *Nijegorodskilistok*, 1896

—

There is no me. I do not exist. There used to be a me, but I had it surgically removed.

—Peter Sellers

# contents

# train in vain

On an especially humid afternoon in the summer of 1906, Tarini Chatterjee committed an act that would mark a violent turning point in his family's history.

The occasion was the inauguration of the spanking new Haora Station building—red brick and iron, very neat and English. Being responsible for both the morning and evening schedules of trains plying the Chord Line via Patna, Tarini was one of the seventy-odd dignitaries and senior employees of the East Indian Railway gathered in an area where, till the other day, there had only been a gaggle of tin sheds, narrow platforms and makeshift households of seventeen nondescript families.

It had started off fine, which is how these sorts of things always do. The quietly proud clerks and officers of the East Indian Railway looked on as their superiors raised their glasses, toasting a fine piece of architecture that had been under construction for the last five years. They looked on, too, as their superiors' superiors made tidy, understated speeches that showcased their wit just a little more than the pains they had taken to hammer their syntax into a final, sturdy shape.

On the platform, a separate stall had been erected away from the main dais. And it was here that Tarini, along with several others—all colleagues, only some of them friends—was taking part in a side-celebration of piping hot tea (no champagne for them), not-too-hard-crusted shingaras and jilipis, the last item bearing a resemblance to miniature French horns fit for an orchestra of midgets. The sub-dignitaries didn't have the luxury their bosses had of taking time over the titbits, as they had no speeches to make and it would have been silly to make toasts by raising cups of tea. Therefore, not to delay proceedings—which involved making a small symbolic journey from the new Haora Station to the nearest station a few miles away—Tarini and his fellowmen tried to consume as many edibles and sippables as possible in the shortest span of time.

That, as it would turn out, was a bad idea.

Tarini first chomped on a few shingaras. The volcanic pieces of potato jumped about on his tongue, leaving it temporarily numb. Then, he carefully transferred some jilipis from hand to mouth as dexterously as possible, without dropping any of their life-giving syrup on his greying white shirt, and deftly sucked his fingers clean. Finally, he bit off the head of another dough-pyramid.

No one, least of all Tarini, was counting, but it had been his seventh shingara. Looking around, he realized that if he did not want to miss the real ceremony, he would have to eat the few leftover jilipis briskly. The man blowing ripples on his saucerful of tea had finished. The grey-black smoke that, till then, was quietly coming out of the engine's smokestack had started puffing in a rhythm totally out of beat with the surroundings. Passengers were already boarding. The women, hiding their discomfort under their parasols, were the first, helped on to the carriages not so much by their important husbands as by the liveried train staff. In that blinding flurry of white cloth under a yellow sun, Tarini found a few precious seconds to pour some water on his hands—quickly, for now the important men themselves were boarding.

'Thank you for providing me this honour of being part of an historic occasion,' he had practiced in front of the bedroom-cupboard mirror in the morning. His wife had tittered to find him speaking to himself, that too in English, and this had irritated Tarini. 'It would suffice to say that I am grateful also for the opportunity to be an employee of the East Indian Railway, which, if I may be bold enough to add, has no rival in India, and that includes the so-called "Great" Indian Peninsula Railway.' Even as he ran his little speech in his head, he wasn't quite clear to whom it would be targeted, considering that his boss, Mr Edward Quested, had already boarded the train.

The ear-piercing whistle drowned out the band. It scattered a mob of crows, who began cawing their black diabolical heads off at a safe distance. Tarini smoothened his shirt front, flattened the sides of his trousers and entered the train.

He sat next to a window, its lace curtains neatly parted at the centre, as on a miniature stage. People were still settling down. Where were the others? Any moment now the train would start moving and he couldn't see Bardhan, Mukherjee or Sanyal in the compartment. Looking out of the window, he couldn't see them on the platform either. *Auld Lang Syne*, bloated and blown out of the brass band, was bending in and out of tune as if approaching a tight curve on a narrow line. But it was the chatter from inside the compartment that gave Tarini a faint idea that something was not right.

He couldn't unbutton his top shirt-button lest his vest showed. A European with a moustache—a sight getting rarer with Curzon having made the bare lip all the rage—and an air of practised authority walked past Tarini, taking a quick look at him. Tarini didn't stare back.

The teak interiors of the compartment had been varnished for the occasion. If Tarini looked carefully, he could see the contours of his face reflected above the red leather seat where the wood was the shiniest. He could just about make out the parts of his face that suddenly curved in to hold his large, slightly protruding eyes. The shine on the dark wood reminded him of the desk in Mr Quested's office. Tarini had been summoned there five years ago to make copies of some additional paperwork regarding contracts for water tanks in Patna. As he patiently stood before Mr Quested, who was going one last time through the tenders before placing them in a file marked 'Patna NE', he had noted the symmetrically arranged paperweights and the carefully scattered paper knives on the table, each object reflected by the polished table.

He had also noticed other things in Mr Quested's room. Directly in the line of vision of the King Emperor, whose hand-painted photograph adorned a wall shared by a map of locomotived India and two large clocks that told London and Calcutta time, there was a framed crochet-work that spelt in a loving cursive style, 'Blessed is he whose transgression is forgiven, whose sin is covered.' He had never been inside Mr Quested's office since that day.

A furious, long toot followed by a shudder announced the train pulling away from the station. And now Tarini stopped pretending to be blasé about sitting there among people he did not recognize, without any of his colleagues—Bardhan, Mukherjee, Sanyal—who were to travel with him. The band had moved to another tune, one that he couldn't quite place. In any case, with the train whistle blowing at tiny intervals and the agitated crows filling up the gaps, no one was really paying attention to the band.

Where *was* he? What place was this? Tarini began to feel a little breathless.

It is difficult for me to speak about somebody's inability to grasp reality. I too have found myself in situations, on more than one occasion, refusing to doubt and disbelieve until it was too late. But it was exceedingly odd that Tarini took so long to realize that the compartment he was in was occupied only by Europeans.

'Is there anyone sitting here?'

Tarini tried to reply, but no sound came out. The lady smiled and sat down facing him. She was actually a girl, not more than fifteen, trying her best to carry herself off as a young woman. She was in a white dress and a hat that curved downwards at the edges. Despite her valiant attempts at womanhood, there was something—that tight-lipped smile? those inquisitive green eyes? that voice?—that gave the game away. Tarini tried not to look directly at her; he focused hard on her hat. It was not unlike the sheaf of saffron cloth worn around the head like a stopper by travelling mendicants of a kind inhabiting north Bengal. In her case, of course, it was white and totally in line with the latest fashion.

'Adela, have you found a seat?'

Tarini recognized Mr Quested's voice, that mixture of a gurgle and a baritone. In it, now, was also a mix of authority and concern.

'Yes, father. I've got a window seat,' announced the girl as she deftly hopped out of and back into her corner to reassure the invisible Mr Quested. Tarini gulped and felt the pit of his stomach shift its centre of gravity.

'My father thinks that this station will one day be as famous as Paddington,' the girl said, her voice rising an octave. 'He's the head of the train company, you know.'

By now the train had picked up enough speed for the ground close to the train to turn into a blur. The new Haora building had given way to the old gummy landscape, half-built mud walls with dung cakes plastered on them and clusters of people gaping and cheering.

'Yes,' he said, noticing a few boys in the distance jumping up and down to catch their notice.

The girl looked at Tarini, a little confused. But she was brighter than her age would suggest and she quickly realized that the man in front of her had just responded to the comment she had made some minutes ago.

Should Tarini ask the European girl, Mr Quested's daughter, whether this was Coach A3? Or would that be too bold? And what if, as it now seemed clear to him, a little late in the day, he was on the wrong coach? Should he get up and proceed to the right one? Or should he just let matters be? But would letting matters be be wise? It was one thing to be in the wrong coach. It was quite another to be in the coach that Mr Edward Quested and his daughter—and dozens of other Europeans— were in. He wasn't supposed to be sharing carriage space with these people. Fear gripped him. It took a physical form as he realized that this was the compartment in which the Lt. Governor would also be sitting.

The phantoms of many shingaras jostled below his chin area, the part of the body that plays the role of a table for the face. Tarini started to sweat, despite the train-wind bouncing off his face. The girl in front of him kept talking, but he had stopped listening. Hurtling through his food-pipe was a sticky, syrupy torrent, and the remnants of a deep-fried past. Thankfully, it stopped somewhere between his neck and chest, just as his mouth, which he usually made sure was closed in polite company, flapped open. He had heard—but never given it any thought before this afternoon—that letting more air into your mouth will correct the loss of equilibrium within the rest of you. Later, he would tell people that this was superstitious nonsense.

The girl had stopped speaking briefly and was looking out of the window. But when she started again—'My aunt thinks that Papa has done some mighty fine work in this country and it's not been a week since she's arrived from Bath'—Tarini stepped in.

'Thank you for providing me this honour of being part of an historic occasion. It would suffice to say that I am grateful also for the opportunity to be an employee of the East Indian Railway, which, if I may be bold enough to add, has no rival in India, and that includes the so-called "Great" Indian Peninsula Railway.'

And that dip in 'Great'—so full of irony, so full of cleverness—undid all the good work of his life in one rushing, rising stream that was so strong that, even though he was sitting against the flow of the train, the gush reached its destination in one low, tight parabolic trajectory.

Miss Adela Quested, of course, had had no inkling of what the man in front of her had been going through. And now, with the greyish-green sludge still descending on her white dress—worn only once six months ago during Christmas in faraway Manchester—and forming an unnatural lake in the depression of her lap, she let out a shriek so loud, so high-pitched, that it pierced the cumulative noise of chuckles and polite banter about India and Home, the combing sound of the train passing through air and the accompanying cardiac cough of escaping smoke, and—why, even the train whistle that went off at that exact moment, drowning the rolling-away world outside with its own shrill articulation of terror.

It was a marvel that the glass of the windows did not shatter.

Miss Quested's scream reverberated inside Coach A1, bouncing manically off those frail lace curtains, tearing up any lingering cheroot smoke and even scraping the polished woodwork above the red leather seats. And everyone inside the carriage turned to the source of the incredible sound which was consequence and proof, clearly, of a terrible event.

—

Adela was different from all other girls, or even women, of her age. Even as she screamed and witnessed through her narrowed-to-a-slit eyes the man opposite her throw out the last remnants of all that he had ingested, she remembered what her father had told her about how too many people, Englishmen in England in particular, were under the mistaken impression that the Romans, in all their decadent splendour, constructed giant rooms in which gentlemen of the town would congregate and vomit.

That was, of course, rubbish. Why would Romans, the builders of an empire that straddled half the world, behave in a manner that defied civilization, not to mention table manners? The Roman vomitorium—from the Latin *vomitus*, past participle of *vomere*, to vomit—she would explain painstakingly to as many people as possible if the subject came up in a conversation, was *not* a room set aside by the ancient Romans to throw up in. That disgusting story was probably cooked up by the Pope to give pagan culture—not to mention the Anglican Church—a scandalous reputation.

The vomitorium, she had explained even to Mirmai, the ayah, as the latter folded bedclothes, was a passageway in a

Roman amphitheatre that opened into a tier of seats from below or behind. There was even a sentence in the *Caldridge History of Imperial Rome* that she had looked up in her father's not-too-modest library in her untiring and unladylike pursuit of knowledge:

> *The vomitoria of the Colosseum were so well designed that the immense venue, which seated at least 50,000, could be fully occupied in a quarter of an hour. There were eighty entrances at the ground level, seventy-six for ordinary spectators and four for the imperial family. The vomitoria deposited mobs of people into their seats and afterwards disgorged them in equal time onto the streets.*

It's another matter that Mr Quested kept another book—among a few others—under lock and key and outside his motherless daughter's reach so that his scientifically inclined and historically inquisitive Adela, whom he was terribly proud of, would not be upset. But years later, when Miss Quested—by then Mrs Adela Heaslop—did find the book and came across the sentence '*Cum ad cenandum discubuimus alias sputa deterget, alius reliquias temulentorum subditus colligit*', she wasn't appalled by Seneca's announcement. Instead, she was puzzled, confused and struck with the feeling that someone, either her father or Seneca, had been lying. For there it was clearly written in that small but heavy-ochred Latin script, the translation of which was eminently simple: 'When we recline at a banquet, one wipes up the spittle, another, situated beneath, collects the leavings of the drunks.'

All this crashed through Adela's head as Tarini ungorged himself onto her lap that late humid afternoon.

—

One would have thought that Tarini Chatterjee's head, while he vomited on an English girl in a carriage that he was not supposed to be on, would be completely blank. But like Adela Quested in front of him, Tarini Chatterjee too was protected by recollections so strong that his appalling act had become, for that short while, secondary to an overpowering, long-standing and completely unexplainable sadness.

Tarini Chatterjee's mind had gone back to his father, the long dead Bholanath Chatterjee.

The very week his father died, prematurely old, after complaining bitterly and loudly about stomach cramps, Tarini had given up a daily habit that had been forced upon him from the time that he was four till he turned twenty. It had meant rising at some horribly early hour, much before the sun came awake, and heating up water. Well, that was just the beginning.

Bholanath had shown his young son how to fan the glowing pile of coals under the container just enough for the water to reach body temperature—'not less, not more'—and then how to pour the water into a glass and add a pinch of salt in it. Then, sitting completely still, they would drink from their respective tumblers a litre each of the lukewarm saline liquid that to Tarini tasted like river silt (which he had never tasted). After that litre was consumed, more water was heated, more salt was added and more of that palate-grazing liquid was made to flow down the throat.

It was only in the middle of the second instalment of the procedure that Tarini would feel his stomach turning taut like stretched goat skin. What followed was the feeling of his belly being pushed from inside, as if by some vermin that had bloated massively and now wanted to come out in time for sunrise.

By the time the first signs of day appeared, each sip seemed like climbing up the final few steps of the tallest monument in the world. Tarini would have the distinct urge to be sick.

'Not now,' Bholanath had warned him throughout the first week of his induction into the regime. 'Use your mind to hold back the water. You still have space for at least five sips. Don't be weak.'

Tarini wanted to break into tears but couldn't, simply because his four-year-old chest was being constricted by the unnaturally spherical stomach growing under it.

'One more sip, Tari.'

After which Bholanath commanded, quietly, that Tarini replicate what he was about to do. Father and son stood up slowly. There was a slight lag between their actions. Bholanath parted his legs, which were long, lanky, with a wooden quality about them. Tarini parted his, which were short, smooth and only slightly more developed than a baby's. Then the two bent down, gently folding their bodies along their oversized stomachs.

Tarini's body wanted to break and he could almost feel the serrated rip-line. He felt he would pop, the way empty newspaper packets of muri burst when they were blown into and punched, hard. He wanted to throw up now, but bending down he couldn't. What he saw his father do, however, broke whatever barrier existed between his stomach and throat.

The first day, he was standing in a large pool of his own water-vomit while his father next to him, still bent forward, with bloated stomach and glassy eyes, inserted the index, middle and ring fingers of his right hand into his mouth. Tarini would master it only in the months to come, the tricky part being when the triple point gently touched the end of the tongue where it curled in and descended into utter darkness. His eyes, for the next sixteen years, would bulge at this moment of touch, and the water inside him would come out in regular, clear, tubewell gushes.

Through this final release, the sun would come up, with the crows in the dusty trees outside looking on. When it was over, Tarini lay down staring at the ceiling for some ten minutes. Do not be weak, the sunshine would say.

Bholanath insisted that the whole process cleaned the body and the soul. Tarini could only think of his body being turned inside out like a jackfruit after it's been scooped out and the innards left to dry.

This is what went through Tarini's head, to the music of Adela's shriek, aboard the train travelling from the new Haora station to the village of Bagnan and back.

———

But while recollections and memories are all very fine—and I find nothing immoral in seeking them out for ready comfort and cheap strength—it was the present that ate through the bones of Tarini's future after the deed was done. Edward Quested, horrified by the filthy assault on his daughter by one of his own employees, simply had to take some action. Not wanting to come across as an Englishman in a position of power wreaking vengeance on a native subordinate, he, however, held himself back, helped his daughter Adela stop weeping and clean herself, and decided to take a decision about Tarini Chatterjee the next day.

The only problem with that course of temporary inaction was that such decisions cannot be made in a calm, collected manner, or be made to wait till the next day. The moment someone had pulled the chain to halt the journey, Edward Quested knew what he would do with Tarini Chatterjee, Chief Scheduler of the East Indian Railway. He was going to relocate him to the Misplaced Baggage Department. He didn't, even as he shook with shame, want to perpetuate any stereotype.

Besides, with protests against the partition of the province sprouting all over, one had to be careful these days. Why, only yesterday he had read about the president of the Barisal Conference telling a whole lot of agitated Bengalis, 'What we could not have achieved in fifty or hundred years, the great disaster, the partition of Bengal, has done for us in six months. Its fruit has been the great national movement known as the Swadeshi movement.' It would be better, thought Quested, to rein in his anger and tame his shame and not do anything rash against this Chatterjee fellow. Being a Bengali Hindu, he was, in all likelihood, dead against the very practical move to give the blighted Muslim Bengali population a province of their own.

And what was Mr Chatterjee, Mr Quested's suddenly very flawed colleague, doing? Tarini was wiping his mouth with a crumpled piece of paper. The copy of *The Statesman* that he was using for the purpose carried a news report on one of its inside pages: 'The thirty crores of people inhabiting India must raise their sixty crores of hands to stop this curse of oppression. Force must be stopped by force.' Quested, of course, would never know of this detail in the newspaper. Neither would Chatterjee.

But all this did signal the end of the rise of the Chatterjee family under the till-then able guidance of Tarinicharan Chatterjee. It also marked the moment in which Tarini, my father, turned into an unhappy man. From Bholanath to Tarini, from Tarini to Abani, it has been a broken chain. But there must have been points, unknown to all three of us, living apart in our own designated bodies and times, where the links locked, briefly, but long enough to pass on a tic, an impairment, a delusion. As I prepare to tell you about myself, it is imperative that I get that fateful afternoon out of the way.

Unknown to me, that afternoon signalled the moment when the hidden chains and pulleys of my life cranked into place to make me the motion picture actor that I would ultimately become.

# acting one's age

When you're sixteen and you're grabbed by the shoulders after having just slapped a showcard on a wall that you have no proprietorial rights over, there are two things you can do: run like the wind or start sniffling your way towards adolescent tears. Standing outside Alochhaya Theatre, I did neither. Instead, I widened my eyes, raised my brows, put on a small pout and asked, 'Something wrong?'

—

For the last one year, I had been helping my uncle, my mother's cousin Shombhunath Lahiri, to expand his horizons in the expanding world of metropolitan entertainment. Shombhu-mama had started out at the Carlton Hotel as an attendant of some sort. Eight years before I was held captive outside a theatre, when my father was still happy and working for the East Indian Railway, Shombhu had landed up from nowhere, his particular nowhere being Krishnagar in Nadia, saying that he was tired of small-town life and ready to find work in the city. Tarini had smirked—which, I was told much later, was his way of welcoming his cousin-in-law to the fold.

Not more than twenty at the time, Shombhu was yet to be

rid of the gleam associated with being too close to nature and too far from real people. He had managed to get a job within a week at the Carlton, the regular haunt of the low-heeled Anglo-Indians—still referred to as 'Eurasians' by people in England—who were tired of being held back by natural forces in this blighted country that was only technically also theirs. My mother couldn't hide her pride when Shombhu, Adam's apple bouncing, announced five days after he had unpacked his battered trunk, 'Didi, I've got a job at the Carlton!' This was, after all, her Aunt Ronu's youngest son.

So despite my father not being too impressed with having a 'waiter' in the house, members of the Chatterjee household were all treated to a special meal that weekend, the highlight of which was a fish-head on every plate, each glassy eye celebrating quietly, and some lip-smacking curd that had to be chased with the tongue as it ran down our wrists.

But Shombhu-mama didn't remain a 'waiter' for long. He became—it wouldn't be too great an exaggeration to say this—a man of the theatre.

The Carlton had made a name for itself with its 'English theatricals'. Apart from evenings that saw billowing skirts and fluttering fans on a raised stage, there was also the theatre, the difference between theatre and theatricals marked only by a subtle raising and lowering of hysterical behaviour on the stage as well as below it.

In places like Alochhaya, Trilochan and the Bengal Theatre House, people thronged to see mostly mythologicals—rotund men in gleaming costumes, their make-up runny with sweat, thundering at women with open hair wailing to everybody's pleasure. The music was loud and when the shahnais broke into their sonorous, dolorous multiple-sound, the heightened emotions were for all to feel inside the hall. The Carlton, on the other hand, was a place strictly for 'English plays'. There were neat little comedies about families gone to seed and finding salvation in the end. And dramas about couples finding and losing and finding love again with the painted sets of Covent Garden behind them. Mostly innocent stuff, though the theatrical version of Pope's *The Rape of the Lock* did create some sort of ruckus, especially after a complaint that there was an overexposure of female bosoms between Acts 4 and 5. Things quickly returned to normal after the offending women were replaced by others who were carefully selected for their 'slightly Hindustani looks'.

Vaudeville filled the gaps between the acts and, quite frequently, the performances were peppered with full-fledged dance routines. A few local favourites such as John Bonham and Jiminy Staid and Henrietta Price had, in fact, made their way into 'proper theatre' through their very successful side-acts. Henrietta, for instance, had first been a hit as The Incredible Hoop Girl. The actors were all Anglo-Indian and to all of them Drury Lane and not Barretto's Lane was the place where they would move to once their preparatory work was done. Only occasionally would there be someone visiting from Home, dropping by for a performance before returning to England.

This was the world, of small deceptions and small glamour, into which Shombhu gained entry. In his capacity as a stagehand and 'general duty boy'—moving boxes, moving sets, moving costumes, moving about—at the Carlton he contributed, in his little way, to the cultural richness of the city. He also, finally, began contributing to the family kitty, not least by utilizing his innate talent for endearing himself to total strangers.

'It's all about categorizing the use of your facial muscles

and then using them for specific encounters depending on the person and the occasion,' he would tell me over a cigarette break during his next job, that of running the projector at the Elphinstone Picture Palace. But more on that later.

One day in the winter of 1907, while taking off his white-and-maroon uniform (with the embossed letter C curling at the top to the point of resembling the letter e) and preparing to help out with the props for that evening's performance of *The Lady of the Loch*, Shombhu crashed into Faith Cooper, the powdered apparition who was, among many other things, the very successful Lady of the Loch. Faith was what was yet to be called a starlet. She had the crowds at the Carlton asking for more. Her stagecalls were legendary and her acting skills apocryphal. But what made everybody go quiet was the way she tilted her head and delivered her lines on stage. She seemed to always come into a scene sideways, like an unnatural but thoroughly pleasing mid-afternoon draught.

One of Shombhu's friends told me much later how Faith's 'alabaster skin' and 'charcoal eyes' would make him gulp and panic as he stood in the wings or behind the stage. They made his eyes turn heavy, for every blink was a sight of Faith Cooper lost. My uncle would tell me how Miss Cooper, in full costume and breathing gin, would smile at him every time they passed each other. No other actress at the Carlton did that. It was very likely that no other performer at the Carlton knew his name. The two owners, Leslie and Duncan Rosario, the senior stagehands and only a handful of others knew of Shombhu's existence. But it was Faith who made Shombhu start thinking that maybe there was something more to him than met his eyes.

Years after he had left the Carlton and entered the projection room at the Elphinstone, Shombhu would still hear her voice in his head. Faith's low voice, granular like flecks of poppy seeds and glazed with honey, would drown out the piano in the front and the racket from the audience that accompanied the early bioscope shows. It was Faith in her many forms and guises appearing on the screen far away from the projection room, and whiter than she had ever been on stage, who seemed to be speaking to him: 'Shambolics, look into my eyes and say that you love me. Say it.' There would be no sound from her giant lips on the screen, of course. But to Shombhu that was the gist of what she said, silently, in the ten-minute shorts, a few seconds before she planted her river-stopping lips on the lips of another man—an act conducted a few seconds after she appeared on the screen.

Faith had moved on to bioscopes some eight months after Shombhu's first meeting with her at the Carlton. It was she who had inspired him to try and get some work at the Elphinstone. He had overheard her telling a fellow actor after a show that she had just met a certain J.F. Madan, a man who was venturing out into the new business of motion pictures. He had been a big admirer of hers, and with some movie money coming his way, Madan had expansion plans that went beyond just making shorts. He wanted to make bioscope features, sell them to theatres and have motion picture palaces of his own to screen them in. He also wanted Faith to work only for him.

Faith thought about it for two days. On the third day, after coming off the stage for what would be the last time, she told the Rosario Brothers, who were seated in two different corners of their modest office on the top floor of the Carlton, of her decision. The brothers scoffed at the idea of moving pictures in confident unison, and Faith responded with a smile and thanked them for giving her time and space at the Carlton.

'Well, at least he's not a bloody Bengali,' said Arthur Ashton, who seemed to be still in character as Captain Roerich, a foul-tempered and perpetually sinning slave-trader who finds love and salvation after a chance meeting with the unhappy concubine of a Mysore prince.

'I don't know about that, Art dahling. But it's decent money and it's new. Margaret wrote the other day that everyone's lining up to see the pictures in the continent,' Faith replied out of Shombhu's line of vision.

That was Shombhu's great epiphany. After coming out of the storage room into which he had just tucked a serrated piece of cardboard meant to simulate a stormy sea, he stood near Faith's green room with a wig in his hand, a wig that not more than forty minutes ago had adorned the head of Arthur Ashton. Standing there, imagining Faith on the other side and perhaps not oblivious to his presence, Shombhu was shaking with an excitement he had never felt before. He would later confide to a close friend that he had quivered with what seemed to him like the warmth 'of a hundred klieg lights'.

'Art dahling,' Faith said smokily, dreamily, 'the bioscope is the future, and that's where I belong. Try and see one if you haven't gone to the pictures already.'

Half a year later, Shombhu had left the Carlton and become a Second Assistant Projectionist at the Elphinstone Picture Palace. As a pujo gift that year, he gave me an absolutely fabulous miniature magic lantern, complete with wicker in the middle and the story of the death of Kangsha fluttering all around. To see King Kangsha's decapitated head flying in a calm, straight horizontal line through space was my first real introduction to moving pictures.

Unfortunately, Shombhu never did meet Faith Cooper at

the Elphinstone. In fact, he didn't meet her anywhere again. He saw Mr Madan himself—twice, once while he, Shombhu, was waiting at the bottom of the stairs holding a can of lime and letting the great man pass, and the other time as the great man climbed into his automobile before it rolled away. He also saw the other actors and actresses at the Elphinstone, most of the time watching short features with themselves projected in giant, silent, monochromatic forms in front of them. But Faith was never to be seen. Except in projections.

With his elevation to the position of a full-fledged projectionist in two years, Shombhu-mama would encounter Faith Cooper as Damayanti, as Ratnavali, as Noor Jehan and, in one bioscope, as a dreaded bandit queen. And all the Faiths provided him with the fuel to do his job—which was to sit beside a well-maintained Pathé KOK 28 mm ciné projector and turn the handle while the pictures flowed unfolding a second-hand life in one seamless action.

By then, my life was being illuminated by Shombhu-mama and his flickering world of the Elphinstone. It was around the same time that life at home had started to simmer like overheated nitrate in a projector being cranked faster than 16 frames per second just before flaring into crinkly flames.

After my father's tragic moment inside the train compartment, his star had started to dip lower and lower. Not only was the new job at the Misplaced Baggage Department of the East Indian Railway not Tarini's idea of how things should have been at that juncture in his career, but the fact that another male member of the household earned more money than he did had also started to bother him.

And then there was my presence. That I had been around in his life for some years before the train tragedy did not provide me with any protection from his rapidly darkening days, afternoons, evenings and nights. How could it? As I grew out of infancy, I was turning out to be a full-fledged product of his life after The Downfall. And, worse, I had also started taking up too much of my mother's attention. While many would consider this particular change of focus to be the result of a sensitive woman protecting herself from an increasingly difficult husband, others (including myself) considered it a natural, maternal realignment of priorities. For my father, however, this was a fundamental betrayal: he was being denied his only audience, the only person who could appreciate his role as the misunderstood man struggling against the degenerate and seditious forces of the world.

It wasn't long before I started to associate the sweetly-sick smell that permanently hung about my father with life at home. Tarini, the historically quiet man of moderate sophistication, had turned into a loud-mouthed, inebriated oaf, whose position in life as the head of the Chatterjee family was becoming increasingly perilous. He had become warped and hateful.

'Bloody waiter-r-r-r!'

And his tongue, turned flabby from disaffection, demotion and drink, would continue to produce sharp, consonant-tripping words late into the night.

This was not the Tarini who had been Chief Scheduler of Trains; the man who had quietly smirked at his wife's cousin for being a 'jatra-party' country bumpkin; the man who had maintained a benevolent dictatorship in the land inhabited by his wife, his son and his late mother, and who had taken pride in the fact that he was firmly on the side of civilization and progress.

This was a different Tarini who sat in a corner-room of the

sprawling East Indian Railway building waiting for people to recover their suitcases, bags, trunks, hold-alls and parasols; a man whose personal schedule had changed now to include a tottering walk to bed each night, sending out a volley of insults to his wife, her cousin and her family. This was a broken Tarini Chatterjee. He was now a new man—a tiresome, flaky drunkard who, if you cared for him, made you wonder how nature allowed such change to come over him. There were evenings when I could hear my father ramble on like a train without a destination, rushing through a landscape that none of us would ever care to see.

With home becoming increasingly inhospitable even for a young boy who didn't care much for the world outside, I began to appreciate the virtues of being noticed less and less by the adults of the house. Getting the hang of it after a few months, I was leading a life that few people of my age could ever dream of. Nobody seemed to be watching, and I could do anything at all. It was like being a grown-up without any of the side-effects. Besides, over the last few years I had become acquainted with the flickering world of the bioscope, and this, too, was a defence.

Shombhu, too, with his Pathé KOK and various avatars of Faith Cooper, was left relatively unscathed by the changes at home. The one person who did, however, find herself looking down the wrong side of an unending pipeline of woes was Shabitri Chatterjee, wife of Tarini Chatterjee, my mother.

Since the day of my father's public humiliation, she had tried to make things all right by doing what she was best at: pretending that nothing was wrong. (I have never cared to investigate just how much I have inherited from Shabitri; but I will, at least, acknowledge this talent: If one pretends well enough, chances are that everything will be all right.) Her firm belief in the natural rightness of the world had not been shaken even when my father hadn't spoken for eight days after that fateful day. (This record was broken when I was seventeen and Tarini kept quiet for fifteen days.)

On that fateful day of 1906, Shabitri had greeted her husband the way she always did. She took his office bag—a leather satchel that contained a spare handkerchief, a lunch box and the day's newspaper—and spread out his evening clothes on the bed, to be worn after his evening bath. When Tarini kept sitting upright, ignoring the immediate and important matter of personal hygiene, she asked him how his big day had gone. When she received no answer, she asked him whether he would like some tea. Again, this was something she did every day while he chattered on about his colleagues and the way the country was going to seed.

With no response forthcoming, she brought him his tea anyway. She took it away some minutes later, not showing any unease at the fact that he had not touched the cup. The next morning, Shabitri woke up, told the maid to start chopping vegetables and proceeded to serve Tarini his morning cup. Cups of tea provide the illusion of variety in life when there is none and a sense of comforting routine when things are falling apart. But for Shabitri, tea had no other function but to activate that prime spot of physical and mental wakefulness: the back of the tongue.

Tarini left the house, still behaving like a man who had committed a crime and was left unhinged by his own complete lack of guilt. And Shabitri proceeded to attack the day as gently as she did any other day of her life.

To turn away from life when things are going awry is a talent not applauded or encouraged in this world. Facing up to reality, as if it is better to walk on glowing coals than to sidestep them smartly, has been so vigorously propagated as a virtue that it must surely be the biggest scam the world has ever seen. But even I can see that the dice have been already loaded in the very expression 'facing up to reality'—a short, diminutive, quivering desire cowering under the shadow of a towering, overweight, real world. And the giant does not tolerate being ignored.

Shabitri Chatterjee tricked reality on a regular basis. She simply did not give it the attention it was accorded among the rumourmongers, and let nothing unsettle her everyday routines: sipping her tea, tying her hair, fanning the oven smoke, folding her saris. It was not a defiant gesture on her part. To be defiant, one must accept and acknowledge the existence of an oppressive force. She simply denied this force any leg space.

Take the time she was all set to visit her parents, not too many months after my father's accident. Everything had been planned from months before. There were the obligatory saris bought for my aunts and for my grandmother, who had also asked her daughter to bring along a framed picture of the Kalighat Kali with her.

'Is that the Kali inside the temple?' I asked my mother. All I could make out in the small rectangular frame was an unnaturally flattened and elongated pair of eyes, thick red garlands, heaps of ornaments and an oblong heap that had to be the lady's outstretched tongue. Like the picture of the King Emperor on the wall of Edward Quested's office that I had heard my father talk about, this picture of Kali was also a hand-painted one.

As I peered into the reproduction of the widening expanse of godliness, I felt a sharp slap landing on my cheek. My mother had caught me once again digging my nose.

'Give me that, you filthy boy!'

Shabitri snatched the picture from my hand, touched it to her head and for the umpteenth time told me to refrain from digging my nose once I was in Krishnagar.

'Abani, have you wished your father?' my mother asked me after the luggage had been loaded on to the phaeton and we were climbing down the stairs.

'He isn't back from office yet.'

'Yes, well, yes, of course. All right then . . .' she let her voice trail behind me on the staircase.

Gopal was there to see us to the station. After passing on instructions to her household deputy, Abala, my mother entered the carriage, after the suitcases and me. Just before the horses started to move, she added an extra 'Dugga' to the valedictory 'Dugga-Dugga' while knocking a couple of quick pranams on her forehead. That my father had been behaving very unlike himself for the past one month and that we were leaving him behind with Abala and Gopal did not seem strange. What sounded odd was my mother's very uncharacteristic triple Duggas. Three shaliks brought bad luck. I wondered whether there was also such a rule about uttering three Duggas.

As we edged closer towards the station, the carriage slushing its way along the waterlogged streets of Cossitola and beyond, it became clear from Gopal's complaints from behind the carriage that some mysterious forces were at play trying to keep my mother away from her 'beloved Rani-di and Parama'. Sure enough, my mother had been recognized by a man who emerged from inside the station to meet and escort her and her son to the train. Even before Gopal got down to unload the suitcases and trunks, the man said, 'Terrible downpour, Mrs Chatterjee. I'm afraid all the trains have been cancelled. The train to Nadia hasn't even arrived here yet. And it was supposed to come in an hour and a half ago.'

I noticed that the man's sympathetic look from under his umbrella went beyond apologizing for the pouring rain and cancelled trains. Were it not for the fact that the rain had already wet his face, I could have sworn he was going to break into tears looking at the two of us still inside.

So we slushed our way back home, luggage, steaming horses and all.

In other families, Shabitri Chatterjee would have been considered an exceptionally patient woman, taking the world for what it was and not what it should be. But she was no stoic in a sari. It was again her genius for being in denial that made her continue that day as if nothing untoward had happened. After she had unpacked and settled down at home, she simply made herself believe that she hadn't planned the journey to Krishnagar at all.

I noted one change, though. My mother stopped noticing my continued efforts to mine my nasal passage. It turned out to be the last day she ever complained about my filthy habit.

But there are times the real world takes grievous offence when it is not even glanced at. Quite clearly, Shabitri's approach to handling calamities worked only to a point. Among other things, it did not prevent Tarini coming home from the Misplaced Luggage Department with a much whittled down fund of patience with each passing day. And she bore the brunt of it. Tarini's impatience was never directed at me. It couldn't be. For he got to see me less and less, confining himself to his room after returning from work.

The changes at home also provided me with the happy opportunity of missing school with increasing regularity until, one day, I stopped going altogether. Fantastically, once again, it was a matter of people not noticing my absence: my mother had already been told by the school that my presence in the classroom was causing a problem for other students. The changes at home, however, had some less happy consequences as well—the business, for instance, of relieving two of our three servants. Gopal and Keshto had to go. The rotund-but-reedy-voiced Abala stayed on, despite years of complaints from my mother (and, before her, my grandmother) about the quality of her clothes-washing.

It was the final descent into a semi-spartan life that would ultimately signal the next cataclysmic event in the House of Chatterjee. It had been two and a half years since my father's unfortunate metamorphosis, and while my mother tried to maintain some semblance of dignity in the house, the wear and tear had started to show. Physically. It was an old house, and now it had decided to mirror Tarini's decline.

Yet, since this is a world in which sons pick up the art of survival not from their fathers but their mothers, I continued to urinate straight into the lane overlooking my bedroom window, didn't stop digging my nose, kept hanging out with those friends of mine whose only concern seemed to be to wage war against diphtheria-friendly street cats. Nothing needed to change.

We carried on—Shombhu-mama, my mother and I—making sure that nobody was unduly crumpled by Tarini's long and rapid degeneration into something that was no longer Tarini Chatterjee. That is, until the Other Downfall. It took place on December 22nd, 1908, three days after my thirteenth birthday.

To see the most startling landscapes within our house, one had to visit the rooftop where garbage of a generation and a half had gathered in a corner, mixing up the decades as if time wasn't a clean creature that walked in an impeccable straight line but a messy, slothful beast that shifted according to its growing weight. Pieces of ancient clay ovens mingled with door frames suffering from painful skin diseases; piles of old papers curled in bulk; metallic bits of lamps of various vintage; broken limbs of dolls; and foliage—if you can call carpets of moss foliage. All busy eating each other up in a slow-motion beggar's banquet.

The other place one had to see was our bathroom. It was a cavern on the first floor, a massive room that lost any sense of being held together by a ceiling and walls the moment it was illuminated. And it was illuminated, during day as well as night, by a single kerosene lantern that threw shadows across the walls, shadows like live things made of expanding and contracting gas. The door could be shut from the inside by a heavy wooden bar whose real function was to keep natural light and humanity at bay. Closest to this door was an ever-dripping tap that kept the floor permanently wet. The walls that seemed to be lost in the distance had no distinct colour. But in the unflickering light of the lantern, they did take on a hue, and one hue only: the dark, viscous shade that colours the inside walls of old people's veins.

Each time I entered the huge wet room that ricocheted darkness, I was no longer in a world inhabited by family, friends, nose gunk, theatre, or the bioscope. This was a dark temple dedicated to the individual, a place where I stopped being anyone else but myself—that is, the chap who orders my thumb to wiggle when I want it to and it complies. I, in that bathroom of ours, had no father, mother or name. It was one stop away from being everyone else but myself.

Myself, Abani Chatterjee, could give way to any other

person—anyone I chose to be. Without a mirror in the room, it was actually easier to become Warren Hastings with a nasal voice, Lord Krishna with supple wrists, Tipu Sultan with a mechanical neck—why, even Tarini Chatterjee—than to remain myself. In that bathroom, I was other people.

At the far end of the room, attached to the wall, was an open tank where water was stored for the express purpose of bathing. How this water differed from the variety that came out of the tap, I had no idea. But no one in their right mind mixed the two. Across this tank, seemingly miles away, was The Hole.

With two dirty red bricks as pedestals, this was where one unburdened oneself. Looking into the orifice as one crouched, one would have guessed that it led to the centre of the earth. But more than connecting our surface world to a subterranean lava-spewing landscape, The Hole was a short cut to a dark, noisy underworld. As I hung on my haunches suspended between the state of being Abani and me, I would ponder about how the denizens of that underworld were already acquainted with bits that emanated from my body—forgetting, of course, that other members of the Chatterjee household also visited the bathroom.

And then there was Rajlakkhi. She came in every day to clean the two bathrooms in the house. (The smaller one was attached to Shombhu-mama's room. After my grandmother's death, that one was modernized and equipped with a chain-flush mechanism.) About a year after my father's accident, Rajlakkhi had huffed and puffed and left. She had been demanding a raise for over a year and my mother had actually agreed. But with my father's condition and my family's state, keeping the promise had been impossible. Since her departure, it had been Abala's job to do the needful. Unfortunately, despite the radical gesture of allowing the person who helped my mother in the household and the kitchen to also clean the bathrooms, Abala had never specialized in the demanding art of bathroom-cleaning. She was not from 'that kind of family'. And soon, the effects of human negligence and the lack of specialized talent and generational skill began to tell on the larger, darker bathroom.

A wet surface that sees no sunlight is the ideal place for moss to thrive and grow in. With no virile sweeping of the bathroom floor with the necessary weapons of choice—a crust-destroying coconut stick broom and liberal doses of ash—the floor of the bathroom had become a slippery, treacherous terrain. With Shabitri's mind and energy occupied elsewhere, no one noticed the danger signs.

Shabitri Chatterjee had gone into the bathroom early one morning with the same untrained confidence with which sleepwalkers walk in their sleep. She had swung the wooden bar across the door, barely hearing the regular clunk of wood on wood confirming total privacy. She was unfurling her yellow sari with the green border that was remarkably resistant to getting crushed, when she realized that she had left her keys behind in the bedroom. The bunch of keys was tied in a sari-knot, and each time she moved from one sari into another, she transferred the metal bundle. There were the rare moments when they came untied, but such separation happened only in bed, sometime between her going to sleep and waking up the next day.

Shabitri shouldn't, therefore, have felt overtly concerned about the whereabouts of her keys, for she would have known where they would be. And yet a stubborn discomfort made her re-furl her sari that morning so that she could fetch the keys and return to her routine. Of course, she needed to be covered decently first. With a tight tug and a sharp tuck-in near her waist, she walked the short distance to the bathroom door ready to unlatch the block of wood from its wooden catch.

There must have been some form of impatience in her gait that transported her up to the closed door. For, even before she fell, the back of her head rushing forward to meet the ground, she felt her body swing and rise like milk left to boil an instant too long on the coal-stove. Interestingly, what she never registered at all was her left foot landing on a grinning patch of moss. This slip, for the lack of a better word, pushed her body weight along the side of one heel and scooped her up in the manner that the air in a corridor is sucked up by a midsummer storm. What took place behind the unclasped door of the bathroom was gravity's victory over my mother's body.

In medieval Rajasthan, women would announce the arrival of the bodies of their battle-slain men with loud ululations, not unlike the tongue-clicking, full-throated sounds made in this city to announce the arrival of a bridegroom before the actual wedding ceremony takes place. The morning that Shabitri fell inside the bathroom and hit her head on the wet-yet-firm floor, there was no noise apart from a loud thud. People could have been forgiven for not paying any attention to this sound, for it was too early in the morning for either curiosity or concern. And after that thud, there was no further sound. Shabitri had passed out, and she had passed on to a dark and dry place.

It was only hours later, much after Abala had blinked herself to wide wakefulness and had stoked the cooking fire, made her first cup of tea and was taking the cup to the lady of the house, that she noticed something amiss. Shabitri would, by this time, be awake and out of the bathroom. She would have been walking about the courtyard in a new starch-nibbled sari, her hair loose. Except, she wasn't walking, sitting or standing anywhere.

Abala peeked through the grills of the half-opened bedroom window. Tarini was still sleeping, his body barely visible through the grey mist of the mosquito net. Placing the cup of tea on the balcony floor, Abala walked towards the bathroom. One small push on the door made it apparent that Shabitri was still inside.

'Didi, your tea is ready. Will you be long?' she asked.

There was no answer.

When Tarini got up, he noticed the tea meant for Shabitri waiting patiently on the floor, wrinkles shivering on its surface.

'Where's Bou-di?' he asked, as he pulled off the coir knot around the rolled copy of *The Statesman* that the newspaper man had, only a few minutes ago, hurled on to the balcony that faced the street. Tarini would leave the house in an hour. And yet, there was no sign of Shabitri.

'Oof, isn't she out yet? She was in the bathroom when I woke up. She hasn't even had her tea.' Abala went to the bathroom door again and this time, with her face pasted on the door, loudly said, 'Bou-di, your tea has gone cold. And Bor-da is up.'

No answer.

By then, I was up and, with gummy eyes, dead-walked towards the bathroom. Only to find it locked. Very soon, Abala was thumping her bangles-jangling wrists against the door. Tarini, despite what liquor and shame had done to him, was still a man whose husbandly concerns had not completely vanished.

'Listen. Open the door. Are you listening? Open the door, Shabitri!' he spoke loudly. This was the first time in my life I heard my father address my mother by her name. It was also the last.

I was told to go upstairs and tell Shombhu-mama, a late

riser, to come down. This was not going to be an ordinary day.
The fact that people were getting worried and increasingly
agitated was exciting. If there was concern, it was not shared by
me. For all I could think of was, 'This, Abani, is not an ordinary
day.' By the time I knocked on Shombhu-mama's door, I was
wide awake, bursting with an energy that made me feel as if I
was sitting watching a theatre performance being staged just for
me.

I took the opportunity of being inside Shombhu-mama's
room to empty my bladder in his twentieth-century bathroom
that, despite being easier to navigate, felt strangely out of place
in a house like ours. It was while I was still in this room, the
sound of my cascading urine hitting various inclines inside the
European-style toilet bowl, that I heard the ululation. It was
Abala's long, high-pitched tongue-scream that I had heard and
continued to hear.

The bathroom door had been forced open. (The screws that
held the brackets on which the two ends of the wooden bar had
rested from inside had been uprooted by the joint action of the
two men of the house.) And immediately afterwards Abala had
screamed. Those who have seen that famous scene in Rajat
Biswas's *Sita* at the Malcha Theatre, in which Lakshman (played
ludicrously by Balaram Saha) slices the nose of femme fatale
Surpanakha (Champa Rani), would have recognized the scream.

I buttoned my pant front and rushed downstairs, peering
through the railings of the staircase. Even at that moment on the
stairs, I was seeing myself as I would appear to a viewer. I was
playing the role of a young boy who was about to discover that
his mother had slipped in the bathroom and died.

All the people in the house seemed to be moving in too fast.
There was something comic about the whole proceedings, in

which no one was behaving like adults at all. It was only after the incoming clanging of the ambulance bells had changed to outgoing rings, long after the two men towing my mother's inert body had disappeared into the black carriage—with a white cross on either side and pulled by two hyperactive horses—that I came to know what had happened. My mother had fallen down and lost consciousness. She wasn't, as the script had had it, dead. Like after the mysterious devastation that was reported across vast tracts in Siberia six months before, life continued beyond the Chatterjee household's second major debacle.

Although no one said it out loud that day or ever after, it was quite clear that there would be a radical change in lifestyle for my mother. As with all other things, there had been a cause that had led to this effect. If you wanted to look at it in a different way, there had been an effect which, when retraced to its origin, led to a particular cause. No one had been tending to the bathroom properly since the departure of Rajlakkhi, the patron saint of bathrooms. The floor had been, for quite some time now, all set to be the venue of a tragedy. And why had Rajlakkhi left? Because she never got her promised raise. And why hadn't she been given her raise? Because in the beginning was a demoted Tarini Chatterjee.

It was odd to find myself in the quietness that had suddenly descended on our house after my mother's fall. This increasing quietness was dexterously balanced by the growing loudness outside the house in the city. Every second day there was news of some 'action' that had occurred in some part of town. The seditionists, it seemed, were becoming fearless to the point of making life for ordinary people hazardous. More than once in the stillness of my room in the evening, I had heard loud reports. Whether they were crackers being burst or gunshots being fired or bombs going off, I could not tell. They do, at a distance, sound the same.

—

The city's loudness and our household's quietness reached their individual culminations two years after my mother's accident. We got to hear on December 13—I remember the day as I was telling Bikash that I didn't want another bloody buttonless jumper from my parents for my birthday which was six days away—that it had been announced by the King Emperor at the durbar the previous day that the country's capital was upping and leaving our city for Delhi. Everyone was aghast. The city would revert to its original form—a cluster of villages and a lot of brackish river water. My father's copy of *The Statesman* had reacted with uncharacteristic rage: 'The British have gone to the city of graveyards to be buried there.' Strange, considering the paper was run by Englishmen.

The people whose presence defined my presence—Jadab, the perpetually sweating sweet-maker at the Narayan Mishtanna Bhandar; Ram Bahadur, the towering gateman at Alochhaya; Bikash and Rona, the two mates of mine with whom I spent most of my waking hours—all of them had become crabby. Already, it had started feeling like village life.

'I still don't understand what was wrong with this city,' said Shombhu-mama a few weeks later, shaking out the contents lying at the bottom of an oil-stained paper packet. So even he didn't know why the city had been given the snub. I asked him whether the move meant that this city would now turn into a mosquito-infested hick town.

'How the hell would I know?' he snapped. 'All I know is that there was a durbar and the King Emperor had come. But more importantly, Mr Charles Urban was there, in bloody Delhi, and he returned to America without setting foot in this city. Do you think I care two hoots about the King Emperor or where the Government chooses to have its offices? It's Mr Urban whom I was interested in. And now he's gone! Gone, gone, gone!'

I had no idea what he was ranting on about.

'He was supposed to come to *this* city with his spanking new Kinemacolor camera-projector. I've heard about the machine from Mr Madan himself, and if there's any truth to what's being talked about in America, the Kinemacolor will be like nothing else that's around.'

'Like what? Will his bioscope make motion pictures with songs and sound like in gramophones?' I said, hoping not only that the bioscope would catch up with the theatre on that front (how much of that three-violin, percussion and shahnai orchestra that had nothing to do with what was being played out on the screen could one take?) but also that my show of interest would make Shombhu-mama temporarily forget about his disappointment.

'No, you idiot! What do you need songs in bioscopes for? The Kinemacolor means colour! Mr Madan was excited about Gregory Mantle coming from England with his Warwick Bioscope Model B to photograph the durbar on film. Phaa! But that's because Mr Madan is more interested in doing *biz-niz* with a friend of the president of the Durbar Committee than thinking about *real* motion pictures. The real man to meet is Charles Urban who's already left the country. And I was supposed to meet him. And did I? No, I didn't. And what does that leave me with? Cranking the handle at the Elphinstone where we'll be stuck with Lumiere technology till the end of time. Hell! Maybe it is time for me to move and join Bikash Mukherjee and Bhobothesh Sinha in Bombay.'

Shombhu went on to deliver a small lecture about how the Kinemacolor, with its red and green filters and 32 frames-a-second speed, would turn picture palaces across the world into spectacles of *real* colour—'more colourful than real colour!' He had started moaning about how he had been all set to make that jump from projectionist to photographist when someone decided that the capital of the country needed shifting. Which, of course, meant important personages like the mysterious Mr Urban not bothering to drop by our city and meet my uncle Shombhunath Lahiri.

I knew that the capital was being moved because the Europeans were tired of the heat, the wet heat, of this city that drains out the spirit from the body the way the early sun sucks out the darkness from the night sky. Even I knew, courtesy that Bengali classic about Rajputana kings, *Raj Kahini*, that North India was continuously bathed in a dry heat during summers and a dry chill during winters. But then, for King Emperor George, holding a durbar in the middle of scorched earth that knows no wetness in the air—and then dragging the capital there—must have been the Mughal thing to do.

But there was another debacle added to the smaller one that involved the transfer of the capital. The doctor had told my father and uncle glumly a week after my mother returned from the hospital that she wouldn't be able to walk again. In fact, barring involuntary movements inside her body, she was going to be as stationary as the head of a cauliflower lying at the bottom of a pile of cauliflowers in a Saturday wholesale market.

She had suffered a severe injury to the base of her spine, and a full-time person would have to take care of her needs night and day. The hapless Abala would be forced to add yet another responsibility to her professional life.

'It's all God's will,' Dr Talukdar had said while shutting his bag and shuffling towards the door. The doctor was a short man with round spectacles and a brush moustache. Behind the glasses were eyes that appeared to be buried miles inside his face, the way faraway trees appear to be far away. My father had seen him to the door, oblivious of the fact that the good doctor had twirled his nose after detecting the odour of something stronger than the wet moss and after-food sediments growing in the untended courtyard.

So what, you might ask—conditioned to reading those modern European novels that are so popular these days—did I feel seeing my mother now forever confined to her bed? Or, for that matter, finding my father wrap himself in an even thicker haze than before? I could tell you that my life snapped into two. Or that I was thrown into the rough sea of chop-chop misery. Or that it made me suddenly see that I was now horribly alone, left to fend for myself against a walls-collapsing-on-me world.

But why should I want to con you into believing that? In any case, that would be too arm-flailing, too throat-quaking for me. The truth is that I was liberated. It was as if the very pure relationship that I had with myself, all this while confined to the four melting walls of the cavernous bathroom, was now about to extend itself limitlessly, gobbling up everything in its path. Not only was everyone in the house too busy, too harried, too tied down—or in the case of my father, too far gone—to take notice of me, but there was also the fear of more tragedies coming that made everyone more accommodating towards one another.

I saw my mother from time to time. She would have her eyes opened and closed by Abala. Not a muscle under her sari (changed every day once in the morning before lunch and once in the evening after shondhi had been conducted with its accompanying wafts of incense) stirred. Only if you squinted your eyes and concentrated hard enough would you have been able to detect the tiniest movements of her chest. But even that was like noting the movement of the hour hand on the clockface at Maniktala crossing.

I cared for her. But I cared for her in my quiet, no-need-to-cross-her-path way. What I did feel was pity. Children don't pity their parents, not at that age. I am sure, though, that I did feel sorry for my mother. But my concern—a by-product of my unnatural sense of pity—was buttressed by the fact that life is a solitary action when it comes to the actual business of living it.

To put it less melodramatically, I suddenly found that I could do anything, anything at all that I wished. All I had to do was hide any visible signs that I was not in any one else's control any more. People don't like it when the young are not beholden to the old. That was when I understood (like my mother, you ask? well, perhaps) that pretending—and pretending well—can give one power, a power that by its very nature should not be flaunted.

Another beneficial feature of my mother's unhappy condition and my father's continuing ascent to the world of ether was that I actually got the most believable answer to why our city was no longer the country's capital. One day, I was slurping water—and listening to the slurp—after a hectic round of ruleless football, when I heard my father singing completely out of tune, '*My life flows over the riverbed . . .*', a rendition which made me snort a bit of water up my nose. I moved closer to his room, still feeling the aquatic sting in my nose and eyes, trying to see without being seen whether my new interest in my father was worth it or not. Much later, as a bioscope actor, I learnt to perform in a way that took advantage of no one else being able to see me. Of course, there were fellow actors next to me and crew members milling all around. But there wasn't any *real* viewer near me. There wasn't any ticket-paying public whose presence I would have to endure. That day, though, creeping towards a singing father, I was not yet adept in the art of turning invisible. Tarini saw me.

'Abani, is that you? What are you up to, huh? You better go and tell your mother not to wait up for me. And I've quit. No more looking after other people's bloody luggage! There may be a bloody waiter in this house, but there sure isn't a coolie! Just as well they've shifted the bloody capital. These bloody seditious fools are going to drive this city to the gutters anyway. You think that those bloody no-gooder gutterollas have anything better to do? I'll bet my last bottle of honey that that Shombhu is also in it! Isn't he? Tell me, boy, he is, isn't he? He bloody well is. You also plotting with him, eh, Abani? Eh? You want to change the world, don't you?'

I slipped out of the house, to sit on the rock where a few men were sipping tea and talking about—what else?—the transfer of the capital and the Reunification. ('It was Curzon's plan to destroy us Bengalis. Minto, and after him this Hardinge, they all knew that even before they set foot in this country.') Jadab, I could see, was twirling jilipis on to a crackling pan a few metres away, perhaps fearing that a large section of his clientele would now shift to a northern city where the sand and dust get into your teeth and eyes.

I had always planned that one day I would tell Jadab the bitter truth about the Bengali sandesh and rosogolla. What Jadab and millions of people in this city believed to be the defining creation of Bengaliness—their sweets—was actually an import, handed down to us by the Dutch architects who built the church in Bandel. German pot cheese, a coarse kind of cottage cheese, was the magic ingredient that the Dutch had handed down to Jadab's ancestors. Without them, he would still have been making sweets out of boiled sugar and we would have been munching them. I would have told him that day at the rock, after fleeing my father's song, what I had once learnt from Tarini. But I haven't ever bothered to spread the truth. So forgive me if I refrained from saying it to the owner of our local sweetshop in that gravely passionate year of 1910.

—

After weeks of suppressed curiosity and having nothing more exciting to do, I decided to pay my mother a visit. It had been quite a while since I had actually crossed the threshold of Shabitri's room. I moved quietly, believing that when a person cannot move, her thoughts and faculties become keener, magnified to the point of being able to hear the din of a fly wiping its face with its legs.

You are perfectly right to ask why, as her only child, I hadn't visited my mother more often. The only reason I can think of is the one I have mentioned in passing before: I wasn't unduly upset by her condition. Such behaviour in a boy of sixteen would strike one as unnatural. But like Shabitri, I knew that unpleasantness doesn't really go away; it needs to be quietly side-stepped. Perhaps I found it too hard to pretend that my mother was not as she had always been. Maybe I had found only one solution: not to see her. I insulated myself. That's the only explanation I can think of now to defend myself from any charge of filial unnaturalness. I didn't come up with this solution by careful, cunning planning. I was too young for such carefully wrought thinking. It came naturally, like the instinct that made me shut my eyes every time Rona playfully conducted the chupki, the classic double entendre, the traditional visual pun which suggested that it could go either way: a head-slap coming your way, or just a person smoothening his hair. But you always close your eyes.

So what made me keep my eyes open and make that journey to my mother's room that day?

'Poor, poor boy,' Rona and Bikash's mother had said as she was pouring water on my food-stained hands. I had just enjoyed a hearty Sunday breakfast and Rona had already gone upstairs to get the carrom board out from under his bed in preparation for a full-fledged, first-to-twenty-nine-points match.

'Abani, you mustn't break down now. We're all here, aren't we, Bikash?'

Her elder son was standing behind me and waiting for his turn to wash his hands. He didn't know what to say. The last match had been close with the final score being 29-23. Rona, the best carrom player among the three of us, had been one team playing both ends of the board, while Bikash and I formed the losing side. Both Bikash and I were itching for payback time. But clearly, not everyone read the stress marks on my face as a keenness for revenge on the matchboard.

'Shabitri was . . . is a fine woman. Finding a mother like that is so difficult. But what's happened has already happened. It's fate . . .' she said before she turned away from us.

'Ma, will you pour the water please?'

The breakfast had not lulled Bikash into forgetting the earlier defeat.

As I wiped my hands dry on the end of Bikash's mother's sari, I felt that maybe there was something on my face that suggested a sorrow that I didn't acknowledge, a secret that was leaking despite what I thought I thought. I touched my mouth to check whether there was some freak tug of nerves pulling my face downwards. It felt normal—cheeks that had not yet lost their puppy fat, lips that were growing thicker because of my excessive whistling and two rows of teeth that fitted each other only when I consciously closed my mouth and thereby forced myself to breath through the nose.

Which is when I felt that maybe—just maybe—there was something not right in me behaving as if nothing had happened. It didn't matter what I really felt—or in this case, did not feel. It would be right for me to *behave* a bit differently. It was time to bring on the sadness. If nothing else, I would just go to see how she looked and come out again like circulating air.

So after the carrom match (we lost again) and before dropping by Shombhu-mama's room in the evening, I went into my room and in front of the mirror attached to the almirah practised the look I should have when I visited my vegetable mother. My eyes, bulbous, just short of being goitrous, needed to glisten and look the part. The eyes are, after all, the windows to the soul, the veranda of the heart, the courtyard of the spleen, the attic of the bile, the collapsible gate of dreams. As Valentino knew best, the eyes have it.

It is actually quite hard to make one's eyes water. This was something I hadn't reckoned with until that moment. But how hard could it be? All I had to do was stare long enough without blinking. But that wouldn't do. I had to look the part when I was inside my mother's room.

I approached the room, already feeling a medium-sized wave of sorrow riding upwards. It was that time of the day when the afternoon spills over to the evening—the crows crowing, the sky growing pale, a more accessible version of dawn. It was that time when everyone's guard is down, whatever one's guard of choice is.

There was someone else apart from my mother in the room. It wasn't Abala. Standing at the door behind the curtain-partition that had seemed pointless till that moment, I could see a short man with round spectacles and a brush moustache. He was facing my mother who was lying there and staring up at the ceiling. His face flashed once before me as he turned to shut his bag in the same manner he would have if asked to snap the mouth of a crocodile shut. Behind his glasses were eyes that appeared to be miles inside his face, the way faraway trees appear to be far away.

I stood behind the curtain and the door, choosing a vertical pathway of sight to see Dr Talukdar bend over my mother's face, pull himself up again, quickly look towards the door and then run his healthy pink stub of a tongue across my mother's cheek and mouth. He did it slowly once. The second time it was faster, a lizard in slow motion. Barring parts of her face subsiding and rising again in the wake of the pressure applied by the doctor, not a muscle or bone moved in Shabitri's body.

My heart shrank and was instantly travelling in my blood stream. I didn't know how to react to my mother being suddenly a part of somebody else's physical life. I crossed over and went into my room and waited for the man to leave. I heard him call for Abala, and after not more than five minutes, he was seen to the main door—which wasn't really a door at all but a gate that pretended to keep the outside away from the inside, and the Chatterjee household from spoiling the world outside.

I then found myself sitting next to my mother, Shabitri Chatterjee, her face uniformly moist from the general but mild heat. This act of sitting beside her strangely provided me relief as I looked at the jumble of cans and bottles of medication that sat there next to the lamp on the bedside table. Looking beyond the twin-framed picture of Ramakrishna-Ma Sharada that had been thoughtfully placed near my mother, I looked at her.

Then I found it—the look of being stricken with sadness. Gently he came, the negligent son, the uncaring offspring, the only child who was prancing about town kicking a football, flicking carrom pieces while his mother couldn't even wiggle a mosquito away if it sat on her cheek and drained her of blood.

My mother kept breathing as she had been breathing since that day in the bathroom—so invisibly that one would mistake her for dead. I sat there for some fifteen minutes and then returned to being the Abani Chatterjee I was more accustomed to being. I spoke not a word about Dr Talukdar to anyone, not even Shombhu-mama, whom I listened to with rapt attention as he earnestly talked about using the motion pictures to show things that could never be shown elsewhere.

'People and things moving, appearing, disappearing, dissolving in ways that can't be *seen* anywhere else but just imagined.'

Listening to Shombhu, it didn't sound like the bioscope would quickly become a fantastic form of theatrical performance. It sounded like the bioscope was going to be the fantasy.

# my fair ladies

The bioscope caught me by the scruff of my neck long before I even cared for it. Being born in the same year as the motion pictures, I always looked upon it as a kind of sibling with our accompanying rivalry. I was impressed, more by Shombhu-mama's bioscope stories (Faith Cooper, cameras, how to count when you're shooting, apertures, drying rooms, the latest motor-driven Debrie perforators, etc.) than by the actual experience of sitting with a hallful of people watching the phantoms in front and half-hearing the whirring from the back.

But in a way that I still find hard to explain, the bioscope started to turn into something new, something that was becoming more and more young as it got older. It was so different from everything else that was there. I knew that the public pretended very successfully that theatre and jatra transported them to a heightened world, where people spoke in a ridiculous way and shouted when they had to speak, shrieked when they had to shout. This was considered to be absolutely normal, the abnormality of it all.

As the years rolled by, the bioscope started becoming something more than just a sophisticated version of picture shows in travelling tents. It went beyond watching the black-and-white moving images of places where one would never go, of occasions that one could never witness. Beyond the goggle of it all was something else that the 'Living Photographic Wonder' provided for me: enactments that couldn't be real were it not for the fact that we were actually seeing these impossible actions. And, above all, as we became more familiar with the bioscope, the bioscope became more and more *modern*.

Even a crusty, middle-aged, hydrocele-affected ogre like Nirmal-babu next door couldn't help but change into something quite un-Nirmal-babu-like when he returned from the bioscope after seeing a decapitation, followed by the severed head floating mid-air, supported simply by the sheer slow gush of a dark gas coming out of the neck. The dark gas was bioscope blood.

He had gone to the Athena three days in a row, watching the same scene and dropping his jaw each time during the momentous sequence. I was there sitting between his two sons the second time Nirmal-babu watched the climactic scene of *The Death of Kangsha*. The flying disc that sped across the scene was wobbling. But the levitating head was the most precise, steady movement I had seen in the world. It was far more remarkable than the scene of Kangsha losing his head in the magic lantern that Shombhu-mama had gifted me not long before this.

*The Death of Kangsha* is not considered to be the first feature made in this country simply because it was made by a German along with Indians trained in art direction, stage production and the motion picture science in Berlin. The British wouldn't allow a German to go down in the record books as the man who made the first Indian bioscope. That honour would have to go to some Bombay stooge with whom the authorities did business and would later ask for help in their numerous propaganda exercises. The fact that no print of *The Death of Kangsha* has survived tells its own story. As does the fact that no biography or book or magazine on cinema has any mention of Shombhunath Lahiri. Even as an adolescent I could make out that there were many more sinister things taking place in the country than the shifting of a capital.

If it weren't for Shombhu Lahiri's chest-first dive into the world of bioscopes, I would have been, at best, an enthusiastic clapper, hooter, cheerer, ruckus-meister joining in with the rest of them in a dark room bisected by a widening sliver of silver that was constantly being fed by cigarette smoke, freed from the usual constraints of babble from a theatre stage and captured by the spectacle before us. This spectacle was far too real to have come from this world.

As real as Shombhu-mama was in my life *and* in the world of bioscopes. And yet, I admit that it is odd, odd to the point of worry, how I don't have a single picture of his. I do recall seeing his face, gaunt and moustached, in group photographs. But where are those pictures? If I didn't know better, I would excuse you for thinking he didn't even exist. But as I said, I do know better, and Shombhu-mama was there at the beginning. It's the end—and any real signs of his presence—that's missing. Who knows, maybe you'll come up with something and let me know.

But back then at the picture place I was led to stare at the appearance of dancing girls out of the blue over a grey-and-white fire; frantically read the fleeting title cards explaining why a girl was silently shrieking as she was being bricked away from the world outside; follow each phantom frame of raging battle scenes where being impaled didn't mean gaudy actors sticking spear-ends into the hollows of their armpits and giving out comic death-sighs. I was made to see with wonder a man who, on realizing that he can't afford the cake he has just consumed, proceeds to bring it out one spoon at a time and place the de-eaten cake back on the plate to be taken back by a dainty, slightly cross waitress.

As we aged with the bioscope, both Rona and Bikash saw quite a few of those longer features depicting the lives of nationalist criminals, mythological brawlers and the heroes of our time, Khudiram Bose, Prafulla Chaki and the rest of them. These bioscopes were, of course, never mentioned in the programme lists lest the censors make an appearance. Instead, they were tucked in between Fatty Arbuckle, Mack Sennett, Buster Keaton and Charlie Chaplin shorts; or after a bioscope about a train ride through a tunnel (in which a very proper lady is seen sitting next to a gentleman before the screen goes black for a few seconds, and then is seen all ruffled up and improper when the train and the audience pull out of the darkness again); or right at the end of moving pictures depicting the 'adventures' of far-flung lands like Egypt, Russia and Greenland. But after the few times of seeing them, these clandestine features turned out to be thoroughly boring.

For me were the raucous Babylonian orgies (with tigers lolling about the frame like arrogant servants); the 'informative movie pictures' depicting the various stages of drunkenness captured in five fade-ins and five fade-outs; the bioscopes about bandits and demon kings; and, of course, shorts depicting the various ways in which a body can behave outside the realm of the real world (a favourite: a girl looking straight at us and inviting us to follow her on her trek along the walls and ceiling of a room).

Like the jatra people, the figures inhabiting this flickering, heavy-black-heavier-white world were not of this world. But this was a place that the world *should* have been, rather than the apologetic version that we inhabited. It was a world that I should have been inhabiting: a physically real dream that didn't fill itself up with silly day-to-day details like accompanying Abala to the market, or waiting for the bathroom to be free, or spending minutes answering pointless questions asked by Rona and Bikash's inquisitive mother. Ordinary life killed.

'You think that all this is what really happens when we have bad dreams?' Bikash had once asked after we returned from an afternoon show. In the feature, a disturbed sleeper in front of a bedroom mirror splits into four women—one, her prone body lying blissfully as if she was dead; two, the reflection of her prone body in the mirror, tossing and turning as if she was possessed; three, a translucent twin above the resting figure floating and swaying like some white seaweed in sea; four, the reflection of this floating phantom looking straight at the audience, leaving my blood frozen in my veins.

'Of course not,' I had replied. In my head I had added, 'But that's why the world is so b-o-r-i-n-g.'

I have to admit that by 'the world' at the time I did mean what was, by default, home.

Talking of home, I wonder if I have misled you—it is important that we get the setting—the location, the backdrop—just right. If I have given you the impression that the Chatterjee household was an old-world mansion that became increasingly decrepit only after my father's swift slide into a different kind of other-world than depicted in bioscopes, then I have presented a flawed picture. For one, there was not a single mansion on the lane where the Chatterjee house stood with its many legs spread out. This was no Jorasanko or Marble Palace. Not unless you had the impressive imagination to convert an essentially badly lit and honeycombed construction, with small plants growing out of its brick-corners and inhabited by four sets of families, into a mansion with rooms, sub-rooms, elongated corners, zigzagging stairs and high ceilings.

The gaslight at the mouth of the lane, not yet changed to new electric lamps like in some other parts of the city, was incapable of keeping the darkness from our main door. But it did throw up its own shadows right on to the weakening wood of the 'Chatterjee Gate'. It was the kind of streetlight that, if it could speak, would have said, 'Psst, here's a bit of light. You won't get it cheaper anywhere else. Take it or leave it.' Unlike the bright spillage that shone forth from a burning piece of lime inside Shombhu's Elphinstone projection box like some formless divinity, this asthmatic spectacle had nothing to show or tell. It was just darkness dolled up.

There wasn't anything remotely grand about our house either—despite the moulding courtyard in the middle that I would much later find bearing a strong resemblance to the Great Bath in Mohenjo-Daro as depicted in those speckled pictures in the papers. This was a courtyard where I would occasionally assault a prowling cat in search of after-meal fishbones; where the tireless Abala washed and scraped the piles of dishes, pots and pans with ash and tamarind, all the while muttering about her general bad fortune and the state of her corns; where my mother, during her days of mobility, would check to see that the clothes hung out to dry on the first-floor railing hadn't wafted downstairs; where we all came down to brush our teeth, rinsing our mouths on a perpetually wet and bleached spot next to a temperamental tap.

This large rectangle of semi-solid housescape was shared by four other families, one of which was the Moitra family who occupied the two rooms and a half overlooking ours on the first floor. Nirmal Moitra's two sons, Rona and Bikash, were, apart from being constant companions, my direct link with the outside world.

'So you won't be coming to school at all?' Bikash had asked me one day while the three of us were urinating from the window on to the darkening evening lane, too lazy to make the trek to our respective family bathrooms. This was in the days when my mother was still consciously mobile.

'That's right. Mother said that I'll be going to another school from next summer.'

'It's because your father drinks, isn't it?' Rona asked after buttoning his shorts front.

'You mad or what? What's that got to do with me? It's not that. It's because parents have complained that they don't want a boy from a nationalist's family to go to school with their sons.'

Bikash chortled, 'What, Tarini-kaka a nationalist? He with his bound copies of *The Statesman* and working at the rail company? They should just come and have a look at his Brahma-Vishnu-Maheshwar. He still has those framed pictures of Victoria, Edward and George in his room, doesn't he?'

'Shut up, Bikash! Ever since that Haora day, some folks do think that he carried out an action.'

'What, by throwing up on his boss's wife? Quite an Aurobindo Ghose, eh?' It was now Rona's turn to chortle.

These were the days when crude bombs were being made by sons and nephews in the rooftop rooms of unsuspecting fathers' and uncles' houses. Most of these bombs never reached their intended targets. These inactions were called actions.

'It wasn't his wife, idiot! It was his daughter. Anyway, some people like Jatin-master believe my father—'

'But isn't Jatin-master a bit of a nationalist himself?' Bikash interrupted me. 'I mean, remember how he came into class one day not in his baggy jacket and trousers and with his "Hail to thee blithe spirit!" but in a panjabi and dhuti and a "Bande Mataram", and then proceeded to tell us how the Muslim League was a pack of jackals in league with the British?'

Jatin-master aka Jatindranath Mallik was our young school headmaster. In fact, the youngest in the history of the Romesh Dutt Comprehensive. He had apparently taught English, history and logic for a while at Sanskrit College at the 'remarkable' age of twenty-eight. After a brief stint at the David Hare School, he turned his attention and talent to imparting quality education to boys from aspiring Bengali households. For seven years, he had sat at the feet of the immortal giants of the European Enlightenment and the terribly clever Romantics, drinking just a bit from the fount of their knowledge and rinsing out the rest into the mouths of Dutt Comprehensive students and teachers alike. All of a sudden, he switched positions and went nationalist. That's what people said, but I was never sure.

'Jatin-master is no nationalist. And he's an idiot!' I snapped at Bikash. 'He's the one who came over last week to tell mother about the complaints and how he was left with no choice but to ask that I be taken out of the school.'

'So are you feeling rotten about it? I know I am,' said Rona sincerely.

'Phaa! No, why should I? My mother's talked to your mother about me going over to your place thrice a week to catch up on whatever I'll be missing out on. There's some talk of me going to that Ahiritolla school two stops away. However it goes, it's fine. What does it matter to me?' I let out a fake, crooked smile that was as fake as it was crooked.

So that became the routine—not the Ahiritolla school that was two stops away, but the rest. Every Monday, Tuesday and

Friday—barring special days that included pujos, birthdays and ceremonies—I would land up at the Moitras'. This amounted to crossing the corridor and peering through the Moitra household's door curtain and then entering. I was being educated at home, a bit like Rabindranath, really, if you come think of it. But my education was to be a couple of notches more radical than the one doled out at the Jorasanko household. I had one great advantage over young, impressionable Rabi Thakur: for me, Abani Chatterjee, the bioscope was close at hand.

To see moving images—of men and women, of elephants and horses, of cities and landscapes, of breaking waves and creeping fires, of made-up objects and creatures—projected on a flat, white screen or wall (which disappears the moment it's put to use) is a confusion of the senses. The bioscope pictures arrived as a miracle that took place on a regular basis at some improvised space near us.

Whether it was inside converted playhouses or within the gelatinous walls of those travelling tents whose holes and rips required regular stitching, we knew that this was something different. Something beyond a simple projection of light depicting things we knew we weren't going to see when we stepped out of those old, rudimentary motion picture theatres. And yet, the phantom people on the screen, drained dry of speech and colour, weren't complete strangers to us. And it turned out we weren't complete strangers to those phantom people either.

—

So on that particular evening when I, a sixteen-year-old, by now moderately appreciative of things cinematographic, was caught wet-handed plastering a showcard that proclaimed an evening's

entertainment at the Elphinstone Picture Palace on the walls of
the Alochhaya Theatre, I had my future in the pictures already
flickering before my eyes.

And why shouldn't I? *The Great Performing Life of Abani
Chatterjee* had been running day after day, night after night, in
the smoky and raucous picture palace of my head for quite
some time. Apart from the fantastic Emile Cohl (I had watched
his *Nothing Is Impossible for Man* six times one year, twice from
behind the projector), George Méliès and Roscoe Arbuckle,
people like Amritlal Bose were becoming proper proper nouns
for me. The last name belonged to a local self-styled 'player,
playwright and actor-manager' whom Shombhu-mama had seen
visiting the Elphinstone, successfully pushing Mr Madan to
screen his biopics, *The Death of Nelson*, *Queen Victoria's Diamond
Jubilee* and *Gladstone's Funeral Procession*, short features that
weren't quite as bad as their elegiac tone might suggest.

Years later, I heard about how the first bioscope audience in
Paris had swerved and screamed and ducked when a
cinematographic train rushed towards them during the screening
of the Lumieres' *The Arrival of a Train*. The crowd here reacted
very differently the day the motion pictures came to town. This
Shombhu-mama had overheard Amritlal-babu telling Mr Madan
in the office room at the Elphinstone, so it couldn't have been
just a rumour.

'As Nelson's carriage creaked along the cobbled streets of
London . . . by creaked, of course, I mean that you could *see* the
creaking . . . everyone started clapping, whistling, shouting. It
was all absolutely spontaneous . . . although I did recommend
having one or two members of the staff start the proceedings
and letting everyone take it from there. The stalls at the Star
went wild.'

Madan heard him out, listening to the details, calculating ticket prices if and when Elphinstone were to show bioscope shorts between two, maximum three 'live' acts—as if motion pictures were apparitions that needed to be quarantined from live acts. While the early bioscopes were shown in between a play and a stage performance, it was now becoming increasingly clear that moving pictures were going to be the main attraction and, very soon, the primary draw. If, at the turn of the century, two shorts ran after a brief comic drama about effeminate husbands and before a rousing performance by Miss Nelly Mountcastle who danced for twenty minutes with her pet python, by the time Shombhu-mama was chief projectionist at the Elphinstone, the bioscope provided the longest segment of the evening's entertainment.

With theatre in this city becoming increasingly unfit for family consumption, more and more entrepreneurs started to look towards the moving pictures as a substitute rather than a supplement to theatre. The initial razzle-dazzle and mindless hurrahs never vanished, of course. But slowly and surely, the bioscope became less of a carnival and more of a gummy mixture of vaudeville and art. Which was around the time I unofficially joined the Elphinstone Picture Palace as a part-time publicist, thanks to Shombhu-mama.

When the burly Ram Bahadur caught me by the scruff of my neck pasting Elphinstone showcards on Alochhaya walls, I had, for some bowel-churning moments, thought that my reel had finally snapped. With no schoolgoer's halo to provide me some middle-class relief, an alcohol-soaked father who, for many, was in league with the city's seditionists fighting a low-intensity war against a well-meaning ruling class, and a mother who was being regularly tasted by a physician, I was ready for the worst. As Ram Bahadur held on to my shirt, I started to think of ways I could get out of the mess. I could play up the fact that my father and mother were a drunkard and an invalid respectively. But that would have been facts already known to Ram Bahadur and the Alochhaya management. And the burly gatekeeper was not paid to show pity.

The other ploy was to blame the seditionists. 'A man had come to our house and told my uncle that if I didn't put up these posters on the walls of all the theatres in the city, he would make life very difficult for all of us.' The only problem with that approach was that neither *Pundalik* nor *A Dead Man's Child* that were being advertised on the showcards was remotely seditious and therefore worth any vague sympathy.

Ram Bahadur didn't speak a word as he lifted me and carried me around the main entrance of Alochhaya and entered a narrow passageway on the side of the theatre that was so dark that I thought that we had entered a bioscope show. Even at this hour, the entrance was as deserted as a midday village. A door creaked open and I was deposited inside a room that was illuminated just enough for the people inside to conduct basic activities like counting ticket sales and talking about such activities.

A clean-shaven man, who seemed to have his eyes propped up by hoods from below, looked up from his desk as the door opened. A few seconds later, as my eyes had adjusted to the light, I noticed a thin line of hair running between his nose and upper lip.

'Yes, Ram Bahadur. What is it?'

I staggered into the light, opening my eyes wide and at the same time keeping my eyelids taut enough to give the impression that I was an innocent boy who had been mistakenly hauled up for some petty, silly thing by a mindless ex-wrestler.

'You're Tarini Chatterjee's son, aren't you?' he said, pointing the nib of a pen straight towards me.

He knew who I was. That immediately put me at a disadvantage.

'I caught him putting up bioscope posters on our walls. This isn't the first time he's tried to do something like that. The last time round, I let him off with a warning. You remember, when the mem had come and people were giving speeches. But this time, you've got to deal with him to teach those bioscope people a lesson!'

Ram Bahadur certainly got his facts right, although I thought he was exaggerating the whole affair of 'the last time'.

'So, Abani? Is your uncle still cranking the handle at the Elphinstone?' Mahesh Bhowmick, the owner of Alochhaya, asked me calmly. A remarkably innocuous question, I thought with relief.

—

My first entry into Alochhaya was prompted neither by theatre nor by bioscope. It was Bikash who had first caught a glimpse of the showcard as we were taking our usual roundabout way back home from school. I was still going to school then. Alochhaya was not on the way home. But if one wished to delay things a little and hang out for a while after school, there was the triple choice of the pond, the Bohra Muslim cemetery and the Alochhaya theatre.

It wasn't just one showcard. There were scores of the same poster slapped around all over the area, some pointlessly pasted over others on light poles, walls, postboxes and shopfronts. *The Demand for Home Rule*, it read. But what caught our eye was the darkened-to-toast lithographic picture of a lady who stood there in the centre of the showcard, oblivious to all the letters swirling like a pathetically made noose around her. She wore a black dress with frills running down the front, and her hair was done in such a fashion that it could have been mistaken for the frills on her dress.

Her eyes looked away from the viewer. In fact, it wasn't as if she was looking at anyone or anything at all. Instead, she seemed to be lost looking at an idea, her eyes taking on that slightly unbalanced look of a Lakkhi Owl, a bored but arrogant look that said nothing about what she was seeing. She looked as if she was *over*looking rather than looking. But most peculiarly, her left hand (with a large, dark ring on her finger) was raised up to her right breast, a bit higher actually. And that was what made her look so other-worldly and, dare I say, desirable to a sixteen-year-old boy with no real knowledge of the fluttering, flapping inflammatory world of women.

'It says "All welcome",' Rona pointed out.

I couldn't say anything. I was transfixed by her pose. She looked like one of those divinities whose picture comes attached to a wall calendar that marks not only the days of the week, but also the special days of the year. The mem, however, was prettier, warmer, more approachable than any calendar goddess, and this despite the fact that each and every calendar woman flashes a coquettish smile.

'If it says everyone is welcome, then we can go in ...' I trailed off as I noticed her curled fingers.

The show was slated for late afternoon. So we came back, Rona and Bikash fabricating some story about going out to watch an annual procession as it passed through the main crossing. (Their parents always seemed to need an explanation for their actions.) The show was not scheduled for the usual theatre hours. Which meant that this would be more than just the usual theatrical performance that we sneaked into from time to time. Alochhaya didn't show bioscopes. Which meant that *The Demand for Home Rule* could be—going by its protagonist— a foreign dance drama.

Dance dramas, at least those I had the misfortune of witnessing, left me mentally shivering like a malaria patient. People sang, writhed and pitter-pattered in and out of the stage with the musicians croaking along on their instruments. How this could entertain anyone but the very, very lonely eluded me. But this show promised to be somewhat different. It had a European lady in it and, anticipating a free show at Alochhaya, we hoped for the best. Usually, European actors played in the European theatres. But if Alochhaya had managed to get one, this was bound to be something special that the papers would write about later that week. The woman, I guessed, couldn't be less than world famous. After all, she didn't look Anglo; she looked the mem she was.

When children are moderately old enough, they have more than a vague idea of the kind of person they will fall in love with. This image stays with them until one gives up waiting (the duration of waiting being different for different people). I had the image of such a person lodged inside my head. Unfortunately, I still have it at this doddering age. It was the woman on the showcard.

Walking towards Alochhaya, I grew more and more agitated. I was worried that something so alluring would culminate in something toweringly disappointing—like the disappointment that crushes you when you find yourself seated next to an ugly woman. But the poster-woman seemed to be more flesh, more blood than the women whom I had seen either cooking, swabbing, lying prone like death or performing hysterically on stage. This woman could only be of the bioscopes.

'Are you sure this is open to everyone?' asked Bikash as we approached the gate.

'Well, what do you think "All welcome" means?' snorted Rona.

But Bikash did have a point. The usual crowd going into Alochhaya was a mix of the raucous and the gentlemanly. There were those who came in a gang, loud and all excited, as if their brains had started to malfunction the closer they got to a theatre. Then there was the dignified lot, who either came alone or in a small collective, looking towards the people they considered louts and philistines with pained shame and practised derision.

Today's crowd was different. It seemed to be formed of the louts and the gentlemen as well as a third type: men who were walking with reserve as if the future of Man was tucked inside their inner pockets. These people, who formed the bulk of the crowd that was entering, walked as if they were more comfortable marching. This made them appear like gentlemen who were trying to hide the fact that they had soiled their undershorts that lay below their astoundingly white dhutis.

'Odd crowd for a musical,' said Rona.

'It's a demand, not a musical,' retorted Bikash.

'What happens in a demand?'

'I guess people ask for things and . . .'

'You think there'll be songs?'

Despite the slight confusion about what would be on offer, we walked past the heavy, old curtains in the foyer. There was nothing that suggested that there were people who had come with a purpose different from ours. Everyone else was walking in calmly, and the few ushers, usually all energetic with their torches and I-am-the-authority look, simply stood there.

Be that as it may, we did see the towering figure of Ram Bahadur standing in front of one of the two entrances that led into the hall on the ground floor. With his handle-bar moustache and trademark vest-meets-dhuti waistline, he still looked as if he was guarding the mouth of a treasure cove. In a way, it was reassuring.

'Let's wait till his end gets a bit more crowded,' I said, moving towards the side where a serious dark cloud of mosquitoes was hovering above the heads of every person passing under it.

When the right moment arrived—and it always does—we turned our shoulders sideways and melted inside. Considering that Alochhaya was noted for its 'mature' productions, this was the first time any of us had ventured into the bowels of the theatre. But I didn't let the other two know that I, too, was an Alochhaya virgin. After all, they knew that my uncle worked in the Elphinstone, and by virtue of that advantage, all theatres of entertainment, frolic and art were supposed to be familiar to me.

'Come on then, let's go to the front,' I said with mustered authority.

We quietly sat in the third row from the front, close enough from the stage that rose before us like an altar and far enough for three kids in a crowd of grown-ups to be left unnoticed. The house wasn't full. Neither was it empty. Despite the shutters on the wooden windows letting the afternoon light stream inside a place that usually favours darkness and artificial light, the scattered audience was energetic. Interspersed with coughs and some vendors making their sales pitch, there was a general hubbub that circulated around the theatre, climbing up to the high ceiling like hot air and descending like unconfirmed gossip. It was nearly half past five and the occasional office-goer was creeping in, pushing the curtain aside and settling down for some free entertainment before making his way home.

Up on the stage, the curtains had been left drawn apart. It was as if we had entered in the middle of a scene. There was a medium-sized table with two vases clogged with rajanigandha, and five chairs all lined up in a row. So at least we knew how a 'demand' looked: pitifully boring.

As we waited for the show to begin, I looked around. The gentleman next to me glanced towards us and then looked away. I saw him leisurely stub his cigarette out in the small metal drawer attached to the back of the seat in front of him. There were two men in front, the kind responsible for the future of Man, talking away. Or were they actors practising their lines before going up on stage?

'Tilak is absolutely right. How long do the Moderates expect people to wait? Last year I heard them saying that they were definitely working something out with London. Well, I'll be damned if it's ever happening.'

'But you know why Chittaranjan had to backtrack and grovel so much? Because of people like Aurobindo Ghose. It's all very well to talk of direct action and all those things he's learnt from England. But it doesn't really help when Tilak is already getting some results with the demand for Home Rule. Now Nivedita's also talking of Home Rule.'

Why were they sitting in the second row with the audience when they should be on the stage?

'The question is whether it's good for *us* to have Home Rule.'

'Well, of course, it's good. We ruling our own country, what else can anyone ask for?'

'It won't be people like you and me ruling the country, my friend. Not unless we all become paan-munching businessmen. Think about it. Who are the ones already moving in and doing the sweet talk with the Viceroy? Who are the ones who have their homes and families in the new capital? Who will benefit by Home Rule?'

'Not us?'

'No.'

At this point, he looked sideways and lowered his voice.

'The Lalas! Everything will be taken over by Marwaris! You think they're not waiting quietly in the wings for Home Rule?'

'I don't know. But tell me, how can London take Annie Besant seriously? She's into theosophy and all those notions about ectoplasm and universal suffrage. How can she seriously convince the Viceroy and the India Office that Home Rule is what is needed when she herself is from London?'

'Isn't she Irish?'

'No, she's English.'

By this time, some people had walked on to the stage purposefully. The hall, as far as theatre halls go, didn't have a very high ceiling. But that didn't in any way hinder the collective murmur around the closed space building up into a collective sound that could have easily been steam-operated. As the stage began to fill up, with one, two, three, four and finally five people, the smoke-flapping sound subsided until all one heard were staccato gunshots that were coughs mortally afraid of silence.

'I think there will be long speeches,' said Bikash nudging me with his sharpened elbow. 'God, another *Slaying of Meghnad* epic!'

I nodded, but only as an automaton nods its head. I wanted to see the lady. There was a woman sitting between a bespectacled mouse of a man and another gentleman wearing layers of linen wrapped in a short black coat. There was also an Oriental. The woman was an old, slightly corpulent Anglo lady who kept adjusting her light-rimmed glasses. What caught my eye was her white-as-cotton hair that was cut short like a widow's. But then, all old Anglo women look like widows.

It was the mouse-man who spoke first. He introduced the Oriental, a Japanese art collector whose name was Kakuzo Okakuro. I didn't like him from the moment he opened his mouth.

'I came here ten years ago, and during the year I lived here, I was amazed by the vibrant culture of this land. I expected a lot of change this time when I was here again. But nothing has changed. You are such a great and cultured race. Why do you let a handful of Englishmen trample and beat you down? Do everything you can to achieve freedom, openly as well as secretly. The Japanese people are there with you.'

This Okakuro fellow was one patronizing Oriental. All those in the hall, including the three of us, heard him telling us how we should wake up, as if it was time for school. I hoped that his role was restricted to the first act.

'Political assassinations and secret societies are the chief weapons of a powerless and disarmed people who seek their emancipation from political ills,' he continued in his cold, tinny monotone.

'I thought he was a bloody art collector in the play,' Rona whispered across the seat. Bikash quickly reminded him that this was not theatre but a demand. This sort of theatrical playfulness is *de rigueur* in demands.

Where was the lady on the showcard? Was she going to provide the entertainment after these crashing bores had done with their monologues?

It was getting bone-crushingly dull, and all that happened in front of us was just talk and more talk about achieving freedom, secret societies and the ignominy of being ruled by 'others'. It was after the man with a short moustache and a balloon of a body started speaking about the 'cowardly' shifting of capital and the failed attempt to split the province that we realized that demands were no substitute for theatrical entertainment.

The man kept talking about India as if it was a country that existed only on an atlas, a carefully plotted patch sitting in a space procured by longitude and latitude merchants—and not a place that we were sitting in right then and there, waiting with diminishing patience for the lady with the curled fingers and the dark ring to make her appearance. The brothers beside me were getting restless. When Rona suggested we go home, I was about to agree and get up.

But just then, the old Anlgo woman with the white hair stood up. Towering over one of the vases stuffed with the white flowers that signify a death in the family, she slowly raised her hand before she started to speak. Her hand hovered around the region of her chest and stayed there as she kept speaking in a sonorous but slightly wobbly voice.

She was wearing a white sari, but she was wearing it strangely. The cloth seemed one long, tied-up, messy affair that was hanging together only because it had been ordered to. But as the hand fluttered, I noticed that another face was forming on the puffy face. There was a faint shimmering, her whole face blurring as if it was travelling inwards at great speed. And then I saw that it was her. She was the woman on the poster.

'Indian men do not deserve to be free politically until they give freedom socially to Indian women,' she started. 'A bird, ladies and gentlemen, cannot fly high with one wing broken before it starts upon its flight.' There was not a single lady in the theatre, but she addressed all of us without batting an eyelid.

It was her, the silly, old woman with nothing but age in her eyes, hair and outfit. On the poster, she had seemed divine, what we used to call 'American'. It turned out that the woman in the poster had become the sea-elephant who was now lecturing us about how rotten everything and everyone had become.

There in my seat, which only a second ago I had planned to vacate, I sank deeper and deeper, fighting back waves of anger that come with the raw realization that one has been duped. The words oozing out of the old woman's mouth were weighing me down like some thick, viscous gas. She, more than anyone else, had cheated me. She had drawn me here with a monumental lie, this shape-shifter, this impostor. All these years later I have not forgotten my great disappointment.

'The British missionary in India is a snake to be crushed; the British official a fool, playing amidst smoking ruins; the Native Christian a traitor in his own land. What India needs now is the ringing cry, the passion of the multitude, the longing for death in the country's service.'

That was it. I sprang up, startling the two gentlemen in front of us, the gentleman next to me and my two friends.

'And who are you, Madam, that so longingly undertakes to set *our* house in order?' I shouted with my ears buzzing and the fuzz on my upper lip bristling like static on a dry day. My voice sounded ridiculously squeaky in that hall of elders. In response, there was the sound of fifty-odd seats creaking into attention at the same time. The silence that immediately followed was breathtaking in that it filled up the whole theatre in a matter of seconds. Even the perpetual punctures of clearing throats had stopped.

I hardly heard the waves of murmurs that arrived next. It was one messy 'gmmmmhhmm' that flew over my head and on to the stage in front of me. My ears still ringing with a new kind of disappointment, I sensed panic inside me. I ploughed my way through the legs that belonged to fellow members of the audience in my row and as we ran up the aisle—for Rona and Bikash had no choice but to run after me—every eye in that blighted theatre was on us. Most piercing of them all was the pair of eyes that I, till a few moments ago, had thought were incapable of fixing on anything particular. I felt her glare, two pin pricks boring into the back of my neck, on the spot where, after a hair-cut, the skin turns blue.

'What was all that about, Abani? I thought we were staying?' Bikash panted as we ran, ran, ran our way down the foyer, outside the gate and down the road well past the cemetery and the pond. The 'gmmmmhhmm' behind us had twined and creaked into real words and shouts when we had scampered up the interminable aisle.

At the gate, where the sound of the giant steam-operated machine could still be heard, we had seen a perturbed Ram Bahadur. The last thing we heard was the hulking figure shouting, 'Oi, you! Stop! You sons of pigs, stop!', mixing with someone else's voice in the middle of other voices shouting, 'Yes, who are you, Madam, to tell us what to do? Who are you all giving us lectures. Why don't you go back to where you came from!' Something sounded wrong with the sentences and bits of sentences that came to us from the departing Alochhaya.

By the time Ram Bahadur had stopped running, the three of

us were well out of his reach. As we entered our house, excited enough about the turn of events to have become unnaturally quiet, all I wanted to do was forget everything about the lady in the showcard who was the woman on the stage, and who had been introduced by the mousey man to the theatre mob as Annie Besant. She must have been a bloody Anglo after all. How could I have ever thought that she was a mem?

But that was then, and now was now. If my last run-in with Ram Bahadur at Alochhaya was not characterized by heart-stirring friendship, this time it was likely to be less so. I stood in front of Mahesh Bhowmick, the owner of the Alochhaya Theatre who, as far as I could tell, was even less merciful to errant kids.

'It's Shombhu who put you up to this, didn't he? Do you know that what you were doing is wrong? Do you know that defacing a private property can get you in more trouble than you can imagine?'

I locked my eyes on to my toes. I wanted him to know that I was sorry—which, of course, is never the same thing as being sorry. I quietly stood there, shaking my head ever so lightly, curling my lower lip up in the official sign for emitting shame. It had always worked before. The idea was to make the person believe that the pointless action on my part had a point—in this case, a plea to be forgiven.

'You're from a respected family, Abani, despite the sad events that have overtaken it. What would your parents think about you running about town putting bioscope posters up on the walls of other people's properties? A young boy like you getting messed up in pictures. Chhi-chhi.'

The thin line of hair on Bhowmick's upper lip gave him a

look of being sterner than he probably was. One more look at him and it became as clear as very early morning air that I had to act fast. I conjured up the image of my mother, lying there, unable to move a muscle, being told how I had been caught in some seditious act or another—hurling a bomb at a High Court judge or painting lewd words on the Government House wall—before being taken away by the authorities to be hanged. The news would enter the curl of her ears, settle down the two funnels before picking up speed and reaching her brain where it would register the same way fresh, hot dung sticks and stays on a wall facing the sun. She would be unable to even mutter a word of protest like all good mothers do even when their sons are found guilty of something that they know they are guilty of. Then I conjured up the image of my father, shaking his head slowly, looking as if he was being made to sit on a donkey, the wrong way around, with his head shaved and covered with curd, and being made to travel in that state along Chitpur Road in broad daylight. My parents came to my rescue. Forcing my eyelids to remain open also helped. A reserve of a trickle of tears was finally emitted.

'How old are you?'

'Eighteen,' I lied.

Then, before any another question could be hurled at me, I looked into Bhowmick's eyes and said in a quivering voice, 'My father's in no state to take care of us and my mother is confined to bed. I just help my uncle who works at the Elphinstone to get some money for the house. I wish my life was different, sir . . .'

I let my shoulders shudder as if I was on an especially bumpy tram-ride.

'Will Shombhu work for me?'

I looked up at him through my teary eyes.

'But . . .!' Ram Bahadur blurted out, ready to take a step forward.

'Ram Bahadur, wait outside,' Bhowmick said sternly.

The giant sulked and disappeared.

And then Bhowmick told me that if Shombhunath Lahiri, currently employed by the Elphinstone Bioscope Company, joined Alochhaya, I would be forgiven—and also be provided with some small-time job. I was to tell my uncle when he got back home that night that Alochhaya was thinking about going into the bioscope business. The plan was to first show shorts, and then move into features, making them, showing them and selling them to other theatres. If Shombhu was game, I could work as a helper.

I knew that Bhowmick let me go that day only because of Shombhu-mama and his profession. But I gave him a wide-eyed look of relief and gratitude, a gesture that would have made perfect sense in any reputed jatra performance. He didn't smile back and simply returned to the pile of tickets that was on his table.

'May I go now, sir?'

'Yes,' was all he said.


And through such a turn of events, I officially entered the world of entertainment and the moving pictures. I was still to be an appendage of my enterprising uncle who, incidentally, left Elphinstone the very next week and joined Alochhaya. But I was to become increasingly aware of myself as someone entering the still new and magical world of the pictures. I was also becoming more and more acquainted with the colourful and entertaining adulterated version of Abani Chatterjee.

Within the next few years, not only did I become the

assistant to the projectionist at Alochhaya—my job involved carrying reels, loading and unloading them, lighting the lime, perforating film stock and occasionally even cranking the projector handle—but I also started to understand bioscope as a twentieth-century medium of dreams, messages and power.

Shombhu-mama had started to hang out with some people who went one step further. These people, all of them chain-smokers, made their own bioscopes. It took a talented man to turn into a camera operator. Tagging along with him, I realized that I had started to see the fantastic creature from the inside. The rolling handle of the camera wasn't too different from that of the projector, despite newer models not performing as both camera and projector. But whether it was the same box or different ones, it was about sucking in the people and things in front of it and then spewing them out again on screens. Pieces of nitrate viewed through bright gaslight were snipped, glued and made to flow like water, like life.

This was the churning-turning-swirling world of camera positions, focused electric arc lamps, distances, faces, set design. Then there were directors like Haren Roy and Partha Mukherjee shouting out orders into their megaphones as if they were waging war; and the actors, shorn of their manic play-acting and trembling voices, ingredients for the visual soups being cooked inside the dream kitchen.

It was thanks to Shombhu-mama and his contacts that Alochhaya started to make bioscopes. Thus began the Alochhaya Theatre and Bioscope Co., which by early 1916 was advertising its creations and getting them noticed even by Europeans. The real change came when three theatre stars joined the company on a full-time basis. They were Ronobir Banerjee, Sudhabala Devi and Pobitra Basu. But it was a fourth person's entry that marked out the Alochhaya Theatre and Bioscope Co. from the rest—a lady who featured in bioscopes as Durga Devi. Her name was Felicia Miller.

During all this expansion, one couldn't help but notice that Mahesh Bhowmick's theatre business had prospered ever since I had been dragged into his dingy office. All that was now required was for me to act. To be inside the bioscopes, that is.

———

Unlike pretty much everyone else in bioscopes, I had no experience acting on the stage. Alochhaya, like most theatres in the city at that time, also continued staging plays. But increasingly, the theatre and the bioscopes had separate shows and separate audiences. The pictures were targeted more at families, what one would call these days 'households'. They would talk and prattle and pass comments over the din made by the orchestra. In other words, they weren't the ruffian, lumpen-class that formed the bulk of the theatre crowd. On a good night, one could actually see the two tiers of the city's society brush past each other—one walking out, the other marching in, like two animals once vaguely related but having evolved into different species long ago.

However, within the many-walled theatre-cum-picture palace and beyond the hubbub of the 'public', there were occasions when theatre and bioscope would meet and mingle. These occasions were prompted by a theatre production drawing in more spectators than usual and the management—essentially, Mahesh Bhowmick—deciding to capture the whole production on camera. Shombhu-mama was dead against bioscoping theatre productions. 'Even an idiot can crank a handle! A bioscope is about showing things that can't be seen. Making a bioscope out of a play is neither a play nor a bioscope. It's just bloody making a stupid copy!' He was especially hostile towards the stage directors who insisted that he photograph actors as they appeared on the stage, full length from head right down to the feet, without cutting them off at the knees—or even higher. But in the face of smarter economics, Mahesh Bhowmick and his old faithfuls could do little but grumble about 'artistic mongrelization'.

One such play drawing crowds by the droves was the Ronobir-Banerjee-starring *Prahlad*. It was clear from the very first week that this was a production that was getting noticed. No one seemed to recall who had scripted the story, but everyone knew the old tearjerker about the star-crossed father and son well enough. What Horen Ray, the director, wanted to do with this blood and gore, faith and treachery fable was to infuse it with a patriotic subtext. Nationalism had acquired some amount of radical chic, and there were ways of tapping this spirit without falling foul of the authorities. After all, it was a straightforward story from the *Puran*s.

'Prahlad is someone who, despite his circumstances, will not compromise his goodness. He is standing up for good, fighting against oppression and demanding freedom, even from his own father and elders, no matter what the older generation thinks of all this,' I heard the director tell the actors as they were going through the two-page 'script'. I never found the connection between the Prahlad story and anything that would have appealed to the Bande Mataram types. But clearly, Horen was on to something. The ticket proceeds suggested that *Prahlad* was not being received as an ordinary mythological play at all. And so it was decided that this Horen Ray production would be turned into a bioscope feature, Alochhaya's first.

There was a rerun of Hermann Haefkar's short, *Spectacles of the Earth*, playing before that day's show of *Prahlad*. Shombhu-mama had positioned the camera at a ninety-degree angle to the stage in disgust and was stubbing out one cigarette after the other, which others mistook as a sign of nervous tension. Bhowmick had even cut corners to show the Alochhaya audience *Spectacles of the Earth* well after the legal date of its exhibition had lapsed. But a legal loophole had been found. A camera recorded Haefkar's masterpiece when it had been (legally) projected for three months nearly a year before. All that was required now was to snip a few frames and change the title to *Wonders of the World*. No one complained. In any case, this was before movies were rented out or distributed. They were simply sold by the feet to bioscope theatres and once sold, the new owner-cum-exhibitor could do anything with the print, including snipping out existing frames and slipping in new ones.

With the last few frames flowing by to show a line of camels moving like office-goers in front of the Pyramids of Giza before the title card proclaimed 'The End', I was already in my usual place, getting ready to do my job as part-time prompter. Which was when I was told by Dhananjoy Guha, the resident jack-of-all trades, master of none, that Horen Roy wanted to see me immediately.

'Abani, you familiar with Prahlad's lines?'

Behind the stout, short man who asked me that question out of the blue, I could see a phalanx of people in costume, their faces caked with make-up, waiting with bated breath for my answer. The moment I told Horen that I knew nearly every line of *Prahlad* by heart—naturally, given my job as a prompter—I was quickly whisked away by more than a pair of hands into the dressing room, a room in which I had only a few minutes ago left a small bottle of brandy as required by the Prahlad-to-be Ronobir Banerjee.

It turned out that Ronobir had met with an accident. A tram car had knocked him down as he was about to negotiate an open drain. And while he was out of immediate danger, one of the horses had trampled over his right hand and he was certainly not fit to be on stage for at least a few weeks.

There was some talk of getting Barin Saha, who was playing the irascible snitch Narad, to step in as Prahlad. But that was impractical. Narad had the bulk of the songs to sing, and Barin was in the play not because of his thespian skills, but for his incredibly nasal singing voice that was quite the rage in those days. In any case, Barin, a forty-year-old man, playing the role of a boy had already been cause for some debate when the casting had first been discussed. There was no time to go into all that again.

Sitting in Ronobir's chair and propped up to the right level by a few uncomfortable pillows, I was given emergency tips by Horen and company—rules about always facing the audience and not running into the lines of other characters (a classic prompter's problem).

'There's nothing to really worry about. The main scenes are going to be carried by Palash [Palash Mitra, playing the blustering demon king Hiranyakashipu—interestingly, wearing a blond wig] and Abinash [Abinash Chatterjee, playing both the benevolent Vishnu and his sin-avenging avatar Narasingha]. They will take care of the climax. And there's Durga to carry you through most of your scenes.'

The truth was that whatever was being said into my ears didn't really register. I knew that there was indeed little to be afraid of. Today's show was primarily for the benefit of the camera, which didn't require me to say my lines anyway. Next to me, but seemingly a whole theatre hall away, was Durga Devi, staring into the mirror and, occasionally, patting her hair down in the thicket of false gold head-jewellery that she was wearing. She looked both competent and kind, and I trusted her to 'carry me through'.

Suddenly, Durga became the focus of all my attention. The make-up man told me thrice to look straight, but my head kept swivelling to take another look at her through the rest of those present in the room. She seemed transformed; I had seen her like this only once before. *Where*? I ached to remember where. And then I did. I had seen her playing the unfortunate Elokeshi in *Elokeshi & the Mahant* during a clandestine outing to the theatre with the boys.

'Don't worry too much about the lines. Just make sure you're performing right.' That was the last bit of advice Horen passed on to me before disappearing into the wings, signalling rather dramatically for the curtains to be raised.

I was not required to be on the stage for the first twenty minutes. As I kept watching the performance from the side, I could only marvel at how exquisite Durga Devi was as Kayadhu, Prahlad's mother, Hiranyakashipu's queen. Yes, there *was* something different about her tonight. There was less of that wooden movement of previous nights; more life on her face and in her eyes.

As a stage actress, Durga had yet to achieve the dizzying popularity of other ladies like Sushilabala, Basantakumari, Norisundari and Ranisundari. These were women who started their professional careers as prostitutes and courtesans—words that meant little to me then, and I was intrigued by my mother's hushed-tone condemnations when she told my still-responding father about our neighbour Nirmal-babu's 'unhealthy addiction to the theatre and those prostitutes on stage'. From what I could gather by the time I was more familiar with the entertainment world, the entry on stage of women like Ranisundari was greeted with blasts of the shahnai from the orchestra and approving hoots and whistles from the audience. This happy commotion continued through the time these ladies delivered their thunderous lines drenched in tears. Their very appearance in the middle of a play was a small theatrical phenomenon by itself.

'They're screechers. Pure and simple screechers,' Shombhu-mama would say whenever the subject of any of these actresses came up in the form of a newspaper report or part of a general discussion from behind the bioscope machine.

'But you must admit they ooze theatrical passion, Shombhu,' one of his hair-combed-back friends had said one evening, leaning against the front wall of our house just as I was about to unbutton my shorts and urinate from the second floor.

'Rubbish! It's Girish Ghosh who's made it impossible to say a word against those banshees. They were better off at Boubajar with their arm-flailing, bangle-shaking caterwauling.'

So Shombhu agreed with his sister Shabitri. These women on the stage were up to no good. I felt relieved that I was no fool to think so on my own. But Durga was different. In the few productions I had seen her from the wings, her entry would bring about a hush. Coughs from the seats could be heard suggesting a need for attention. Her beauty when mixed with her words and gestures demanded the cigarette and cheroot smoke in the whole theatre to settle down. Even the shahnai and violins heard what she had to say.

And I was going to join Durga on the stage.

'Abani, when you go out there on the stage, imagine you're underwater, where you can't see anybody and nobody can see you except the characters on the stage. There is no sound in the water. There is only the light. So all you need to do, all you have to do is be *seen*, your face and your eyes. Use the light, okay? I need you to use the light, underwater. Okay?'

I knew what Shombhu-mama was saying. In my costume of white cloth wrapped and tucked across my scrawny body, I muttered an okay. When he let go of my shoulder, he seemed to throw me into water. I turned one last time to look at him and then disappeared into the darkness of the wings and beyond.

Twenty-odd minutes later I walked onto the stage. Everything below me—those bobbing heads, those eyes, those faces, those curling smoke ribbons from the bobbing heads, the stagelight bouncing off those faces—disappeared. If I did see anything at all outside the stage it was a partially illuminated figure standing not too far behind the man with the dhol on a raised platform in the orchestra pit, who seemed to be hiding behind a camera. There was a corrugated strip of smoke curling up and breaking, curling up and breaking behind the man with the dhol and behind the inhaling camera. With Durga and I sharing the stage and Shombhu's sturdy 1913 Éclair-Gillon Grand in front I felt the glare of the shadows and light. I was speaking through the pupils of my eyes, darkened double-fold by the paleness of my face. I was no longer standing on the stageboards. I was being sucked in and faithfully etched on to nitrate to be replayed from the distance. I was underwater and Prahlad. The lines didn't matter.

*Long shot of a room. At the far end, we see a young boy tossing and turning in bed. On the other side stands a giant cupboard with a mirror and a carving of a stag's head. It is night and the only light comes from the moon that can be seen through a vast window.*

*Medium shot of the boy tossing and turning in the moonlight.*

*Close-up of the boy's face. It is crunched up with tension and a frown crunches it even more.*

*The title card reads: 'The young Prince Prahlad is having a bad night. Like every night, he is wracked with uneasy dreams.'*

*Medium shot of Prahlad's mouth opening and a white, translucent ether seeping out of it. The prince is still tossing in his bed and is completely unaware of the mist-like emissions from his mouth travelling across the room and taking shape near the cupboard. The room is bathed in a light that seems to be moonlight reflected off and refracted from the white mist.*

*Long shot shows the mist slowly taking a human form. It hovers a few feet above the floor near the cupboard. It throws no reflection on the mirror. In fact, it is forming in the mirror.*

*Medium shot of the mirror which now shows a full-formed human body still swirling into complete shape. But instead of a human face, the head solidifies into that of a lion.*

*Close-up. The lion's head blinks its lion eyes. It is calm and it ducks its head once.*

*Long shot of the room with the lion-man apparition hovering at one end and Prahlad still in his bed. The reclining figure lifts his hands up to his chest to form a pranam.*

*The lion-man lifts one of its legs, brings it up and across its waist, even as it keeps standing.*

*Close-up of Prahlad. He opens his eyes with a start.*

*Title: 'Prabhu! Save me!'*

*Long shot. Prahlad is sitting up. The moon is shining. There is no one but the boy in the room. Iris-in on the moon.*

—

Another day of storms and thunder. Another day of torment for Prahlad. It was as clear—clear as the waters that went up, down, through, under, over and out of the aqueduct that his father had installed downstairs—that it would be a terrible day. It wasn't that the rains were responsible for him feeling this way. It was the knowledge that once again he would not make the grade. Being the only son of Maharaja Hiranyakashipu sounds like a delightful thing. Heir to the throne, free of confusion that affects so many other royal houses where squabbles break out as fast and furious as the thundershowers across the kingdom. But unlike the near-perfect sewage system of the capital, Prahlad's heart was getting clogged with rising misery. He had failed his father so often, and he knew he would do so again today.

He remembered, with shame, his archery lessons. 'Hold the bow finger below your chin. It's pointless if you dangle it in front of your chest, like a woman,' Hiranyakashipu would tell him with all the patience that the Lord of the House of Dwabhuja could muster. And that was a lot, considering the stories that Prahlad had heard about his grandfather Trinayanraje. His uncle Paranjaya had once let go of the rope in a tug-of-war contest. To set an example for all the male members of the House of Dwabhuja, Trinayanraje had ordered his son to spend six weeks in a farmer's household. Paranjaya was to drag a heavy ploughshare every day, replacing two fine and relieved bullocks who tasted leisure for such a stretch after so long.

The most recent occasion when Prahlad had disappointed his father was when he had fainted at the sight of blood. The encounter had been postponed for as long as things like that can be postponed. To make matters especially humiliating, it wasn't even human blood that was spilled. At the annual festival, twelve buffaloes were sacrificed at the altar of Lord Maheshwar. It was the usual thing. But unusual for Prahlad, for Queen Kayadhu had done her bit all these years to protect her son from seeing the bloody ritual. She knew that Prahlad had an instinctive squeamishness about blood. She had almost had to call for the calming herbs—dangerous if administered to minors—when the boy had once scraped a knee playing. Red pinpricks had appeared on the damaged skin, and the sight of these droplets, rather than any pain, had made young Prahlad scream in terror and agony as if he was being crushed to death by one of the crusher elephants his father used to deliver justice. So every year close to the anointed day Kayadhu sent out the message that the prince was stricken with some contagious ailment, or had developed stomach cramps (for which one of the cooks, rather unfortunately, received ten lashes), or had dislodged his shoulder bone after a rough tumble from the royal pony.

This time, though, it was not just any old buffalo sacrifice. It was impossible for Prahlad to get out of this one. He had reached the important age of fourteen.

And after he had fainted, and recovered—forced to, by his father's mighty roar—Prahlad was told that, two days hence, he would have to undertake a much more severe task ·than blood-watching—and that his father would be close at hand to initiate him into manhood. To make matters worse, even this, like practically everything else in the world, would be initiated with another round of bloodletting.

The cutter in the hands of the man reflected the bouncing flames of the torches lighting up the hall. Beyond the hall was the newly constructed bedchamber. Hiranyakashipu was waiting, along with a hallful of elders and priests, for his son to come down from his room and take one of the most important steps in any man's life. He remembered his own case and smiled to himself. His father had led him to the chamber where the lady, decked in gold and nothing else, waited on the bed. She was blindingly beautiful, as temple ladies were required to be, but as his father saw him to the door and closed it, he was too nervous to look at her.

'Nothing to fear, Rajadhiraj,' she had said.

It was important that no kind of stimulant was taken by the virgin prince. The time and occasion would come when stimulants could be taken and would be taken. But tradition dictated that the first time it would be done, it would be done with all the senses intact. The idea was to confront and conquer the fear and nervousness that comes with ignorance.

She had patted the white spread on the bed and had gently told young Hiranyakashipu to sit next to her. What had followed was, on his part, clumsy, terrifying, pleasurable. Parts of his body were guided into parts of hers, all the while, constant motion being of utmost importance. And when he cried out—a shrill, short unmanly sound—he had gained the right to claim something new in this world.

In the end he had come out of the room wiser, in charge of his body and with the knowledge that seeking the pleasure of a woman, like seeking victory in war, needed preparation and a mindset. The woman had kissed him fully on the lips, smiled a motherly smile and had bid him goodbye. On the other side of the door, the awaiting crowd had roared in approval and, to the sound of conch shells blowing, the cutter had come down on yet another buffalo.

Today, Hiranya's son, Prahlad, was to gain that knowledge and correct the sinful blemish of being ignorant of bodily pleasures. Except he was late.

Climbing down the broad staircase, escorted by two junior priests and two royal guards, Prahlad was worried sick. His stomach had already heaved much of its contents out of his body. This, despite his mother having stayed up with him the whole of last night, trying to dispel as many fears as possible. She had even tried to make light of it by showing him parts of her own body, if only to tell her son that he would encounter them and many more in a totally different context but that finally nothing would be entirely strange. But he had shaken his head furiously till dawn, and twice broken into sobs.

It was useless, Queen Kayadhu thought, as she heard the drums beating downstairs. She prayed to her God, Lord Narayana, for some kind of help, considering she had no idea what she could specifically pray for, since she did want her son to know the pleasures of a woman—let no one doubt that she didn't.

But it was Maharaja Hiranyakashipu who was now starting to harbour unpleasant doubts. Where *was* Prahlad? Where were the two temple priests and guards who were supposed to bring him to the ceremony? By sheer force of personality and writ, he had managed to negotiate many other embarrassing moments that his only son, his heir and pride, had brought on him. He had been patient and yielding also because he wanted to be considerate to the wishes of Kayadhu. But this was getting too much. Would Prahlad now refuse to be led by him to the bedchamber that awaited him? And would that be because the boy disapproved of his father, or was it something more fundamentally abhorrent?

Hiranya sprang out of his bedecked seat and rushed upstairs himself. The whole hall went silent with only the gurgle of the aqueduct audible. He swivelled round at the black stone banister, already thundering, 'Prahlad? Prahlad!' But before he could set a foot on to the second step, there was Prahlad, flanked by his four escorts, some twenty steps above him. The son froze seeing the father. Both man and boy remained planted where they stood as if momentarily transformed to stone.

It was Prahlad who first spoke. His voice had changed from its usual whinnying tone and, for the first time in his life, Hiranyakashipu was afraid of his own, beloved son.

'Dearest father, do you not know who is king? This is the time for people—subjects and monarchs in this mortal world—to gird up their loins for the honour of the real king, the Lord who is everyone and knows everything,' said Prahlad, boring his eyes into his father's and emitting this guttural string of sentences. 'Your false rule, father, will end and the true king shall rule again. I care little about what I am to do as prince or son. For my heart and my mind are free and settled in the true king's worship. The person who calls me his son is no father of mine until he accepts this truth.'

Hiranyakashipu had started shaking with a shame that quickly transformed into rage. This was his son, his heir, his pride and joy that had spoken these words in a voice dripping with disdain. Understanding would come later. He first let out an amplified groan and turned around to rush back to the silent, dumbfounded hall. His head was throbbing with a ringing sound that, if anyone else could have heard it, would have been identified as metal on metal. As Hiranya went to grab the nearest blade that he could lay his hands on, Prahlad rushed up the stairs and barged into Kayadhu's room.

His mother was resting on the bed. She propped herself up immediately on seeing the look on her son's face. It was one of horror mixed with surprise and Kayadhu jumped up and dragged the bar across the door behind her sobbing son. He was crying, unable to hold back anything at all. His nostrils and now his face were wet with dripping mucus and he shuddered in recoil as he wept uncontrollably. Kayadhu held him and also shook with his sobs. Prahlad was momentarily blinded in the darkness of her embrace. All he heard was a muffled heart beating furiously through the silk.

As he lay there in his mother's arms, oblivious of the first thumps on the barred door, his hands felt the soft body that lay under the rustle, the world-defying contours of her waist, the cloth-like surface of her back, the cliff-drop of her shoulders. Above all, he felt the pressure of his body on her body and he felt cushioned by her breasts. He was aware of every part of her body except her hands when the thunderous shout on the other side of the door demanded that he come out.

'Come out you worm!' he heard the roar above the thudding of the battering ram against the door to his mother's room. In the overpowering silence that followed, he was in the arms of an armless woman. Raising his head a little, even as he clung to her tightly, he noticed that his running snot had formed a pattern on the cloth that covered his mother's right shoulder. And then he noticed that the shoulder belonged to a human form with the head of a lion. Prahlad awaited his fate in the folds of something that was neither here nor there, neither of this world nor of that; something that was all body, no hands and as quiet as a relic.

# tumbling upstairs

Forgetting is the key. And what can be more satisfying than to forget who one is.

In 1917, at the ripe age of twenty-one, I fell in love for the first time. With Durga, on the stage, I stopped, even if it was for a couple of hours, being the son of two bathetic figures, the friend of two pointless souls and the nephew of a man with desires that could, by their very nature, never be fulfilled.

With the real Prahlad, Ronobir Banerjee, recovering miraculously and back on stage after two weeks, Durga and I were together for only that many hours. But we had been joined together in nitrate. True, I was somebody else, she somebody else. But for those cumulative hours, detached from other scenes and other people playing other characters, we were a pair. But that wasn't the most rapturous part. The best part was that she recognized me not as Abani Chatterjee but as a *man* who was more present than a dissolve and more visible than backlight.

Despite our relationship now made permanent, I saw no point in telling Durga what I felt about her. How could I? Durga was Felicia Miller and Abani was Abani Chatterjee. And whatever may have led you to believe that love can be a battering-ram for all doors, it's not true. Love has its limitations, its garbage-blocked corridors.

*Prahlad Parameshwar*, the name given to my first bioscope, was the Alochhaya Theatre and Bioscope Co.'s first resounding moving pictures success. In fact, it made more money than Madan Theatre's *Harishchandra* and *Bilyamangal* put together. More features followed, and I was in all of them (barring that dismal failure, *The Good Son Shravana*, in which the diminishing Ronobir Banerjee played the title role). Shombhu-mama had finally convinced Mahesh Bhowmick that simply rolling the handle and sucking in a stage performance with a quiet counting of frames was not the way.

'It's so boring for the audience,' he had told Mahesh, finally talking in a language that the latter would understand.

But what also changed was the way we performed. I had told Mahesh as well as Horen Roy, both of whom had started to listen to what I had to say since *Prahlad*, that for the bioscope what mattered was how things, actors included, were *shown*. Nothing else mattered. If we had a special role to play as actors, it was what we did with our faces, our body and our eyes. If they weren't visible on the screen, then they would mean nothing. Anyone who had seen those international silent screen idols, John Barrymore, Francis X. Bushman, Rod La Rocque and, of course, Rudolph Valentino, knew that.

However, acting then, especially in this city, was ludicrous, overstated puppetry. It was just about bearable in the jatra. The ridiculous overstatements, after all, went perfectly with the ridiculously overstated atmosphere. Theatre was awash with that kind of nonsense. And those entering the bioscopes were dragging in their vocal hysterics to the new, silent medium.

Nabina Devi running her hand across her forehead in *The Kidnapping of Sita*, for instance, would have meant nothing were it not for the camera taking in the terror in her eyes and then moving on to her hand, in close-up, to show it leaving a black sindoor smudge in its wake.

So instead of recreating a dumb show, Alochhaya was pioneering something else: the theatre of the spectacle.

And the crowds, even the raucous lumpen-classes, were beginning to revel in the visible, the details, the impossible images that only the bioscope could bring. And Mahesh Bhowmick could tell the impact it was having on the public. With profits piling up, Alochhaya became the first non-European theatre to be fully electrified. Even Mahesh's dingy office room now had electric lights and a mechanical fan that initially kept blowing away all the pieces of paper on the tables. (This problem was solved after the arrival of a hook-like device with a long metal spike, curled at one end and fixed to a wooden, circular block at the other. Pieces of paper would be 'hooked' and 'speared', to be arranged like abacus balls across the length of the metal spike.) We had also become the best paid bioscope people in the country. We had become what in America they called a Studio.

But all those advantages that the bioscope had over theatre were nothing compared to the real thing that made it a wonder of the world: one didn't have to wear out one's mental and physical bones playing the same roles and characters, making and speaking the till-death-do-us-part movements and lines.

That old rascal of an actor Dhiren Chatterjee had once told me with genuine panic after a production season how his body had taken over all control.

'I was to bang my fist on the edge of the dock and shout, "Objection, m'lord!" in that courtroom scene. This I had done for the last two and a half months at the same juncture in the play, facing the same actors on stage and standing at the same spot. This time I decided to bang my fist on the left-hand corner of the cane-front that was supposed to be the dock. I wanted to change something, even if it was something as tiny as shifting the position of where I brought my hand down, if only to make that evening's performance a bit less deadening for myself. But there I was on Tuesday playing the same goddamned scene as if it was part of a ten-thousand-year-old custom. At the exact moment when I had to bring my fist down, I pounded it on the same bloody place where I had every evening for the past two and a half months. I had lost all control over my body and my mind!'

Dhiren promised himself he would shift his fist to the left for the next six days. But on every occasion his hand came down on the same wretched spot. The day he was complaining about his enslavement to the stage habit, he had a weal shaped like Ceylon running down the side of his hand. For the next three months, he found himself shouting, 'Objection, m'lord' and crashing his hand down on the same spot. That's what the stage does to you.

The bioscope, on the other hand, never numbs you. It simply doesn't have the time. And once the performance is being projected, no matter how many times one redoes the scene, the images bring the actor to life each time, and each time as if for the first.

Not only did my appearances before the camera draw out something that I had never guessed existed, but it also extracted something more than my body was capable of showing. It was much more than Abani+nitrate+light+darkness+angles+distances+other actors that came spewing out. Seeing me on the screen wasn't at all like seeing Shishir Badhuri or Ahin Chaudhuri on the stage ten years later. However competent they may have been in their day, Shishir would remain Shishir and Ahin Ahin. The theatre just couldn't lie well enough. It still can't. As for the bioscope, it makes sublime truth of deception— not just for the viewer but also for the actor. I would get transformed each time I faced the whirring camera and the sun-like lights.

I've heard many of today's actors and actresses go on and on about how the real thrill lies in acting 'live' in front of audiences. I've never understood that—unless, of course, your pleasures come solely from hearing your own voice and from looking at other people looking at you. For in the end it's not about the effort, but about the result. And in bioscopes, every gesture makes sense, even when it's not supposed to. And, and, and, before I forget, I never had to bow in the moving pictures to the vultures after every performance each night.

—

My life of love continued after *Prahlad Parameshwar*. There was *Othello*, a feature made purely as a bioscope. I had expected my bioscope self to go back to being Abani Chatterjee, after it, and Desdemona to being Durga. But we weren't back in a snap after the camera handle stopped turning and the lights had all clacked off one by one. As I removed the black paint from my face, I could still feel the Moor inside me. He remained, perhaps as he had always been inside Abani Chatterjee—in some warm pit miles below my chest.

'It's funny how anyone, English, Indian, or whatever, has to wear that make-up to play Othello,' I told Shamaresh Biswas, who was removing Iago from his own face.

'I know. But then Durga doesn't have to put much colour on, does she?'

Till Shamaresh pointed this out, I had never thought of Durga as a full-fledged Anglo. Not the way I saw Faith or Alice Kydman. She was Felicia Miller and Durga and Kayadhu and Desdemona, and nobody in between. I knew nothing, then, of Durga outside the lit-up space we shared.

In the months that I got to know Durga better in front of the cameras and sometimes onstage, I learnt—from others, of course—how she had been a convent schoolteacher in McLeodganj, a hill station somewhere in the north, before moving back here with her family. Her father, Sam Miller, had been a seaman who had sailed from Manchester and had then decided to make this city his home. At the grand age of forty-three he had married the daughter of a Scotsman working at the Soorah Jute Mill, a lady some twenty years his junior, who spoke fluent Hindustani but no Bengali at all.

Mr Miller's subsequent job at the British India Steam Navigation Company—which he had obtained through the good offices of his short-lived father-in-law—wasn't a very senior job. But he never found it odd to have his name on the rolls alongside those of Indians. He was better paid than his brown-skinned colleagues and, quite clearly, life was grander here than in bleak, grey-skinned and steam-filled Manchester. Where else would he have been able to have a bungalow filled with servants, and a social environment in which his wife and children could thrive? Imagine having an ayah for the children, a baburchi capable of fixing Sam's favourite two dishes, prawn malai curry and black pudding, at an hour's notice, and a personal servant who would do everything from fixing a hot bath to working the fan during those long summer Sundays. And Sam was a gentleman here, a member of the South Calcutta Billiards Club.

But for the last few years, things had not been going well for Sam Miller. For some buffalo reason, the government had decided to start a long-pending special programme for the 'domiciled'. In the mind of the authorities, Europeans in India should be 'setting into motion the labour of the country' and should 'develop its resources'. An increasing emphasis was being placed in the sweaty corridors of power on the fact that English prestige should be maintained to continue to achieve the 'dominion of the mind'. In other words, Mr Miller's talent in overseeing the fitting and repairing of valves and pipes and pistons on ships and cruisers was not the right way for a European to go about things in the country. Miller, for one, didn't like it one bit when two gentlemen visited his house late one Saturday afternoon advising him to move to a more agreeable place.

'For God's sake, it's not as if I'm sitting down to drink with the bloody babus, is it?' he had erupted after being exceptionally gracious to the two sinister gentlemen. 'I'm a proper gentleman, too, and you can bloody well see it for yourself!'

'We aren't here to doubt your social position, Mr Miller. It's just that the government sincerely thinks that you and many other fellow Englishmen in this city have much to gain if you consider working in new, burgeoning northern townships,' one of the frock-coated men had calmly told him while staring at the slightly chipped rim of the cup in which the tea had been served.

'Burgeoning towns, my arse! And why would I want to move to Dehrabloodydun or Mussoorie or, what's that other place you mentioned . . .'

'McLeod—'

'Whatever. I'm a city person, gentlemen, and I do an honest

living here. My children were born here, brought up here. The government and the King can't tell me to up it and leave for the bloody mountains now!'

That was their first visit and Sam Miller had not been convinced at all by their argument of a better life in the hills of the United Provinces of Agra and Oudh. But by the end of the following year, four ex-sailing men, all of them out-and-out Europeans—Bob Davis from Oldham, Bill O'Brien from Slough, John Davies from Glasgow and Sam Miller from Manchester— were politely told that their services were no longer required in the British India Steam Navigation Company. Davis, O'Brien, Davies and Miller, all bona fide members of the South Calcutta Billiards Club, never spoke a word about whether their being 'working class and all' had anything to do with their sudden retirement. They were going to get a moderate pension all right, but that still left them hanging dry. As they noisily ordered yet another round of quickly warming beer, the option of returning Home was brought up almost as if they were talking about a fatal disease that should never be named.

'I don't understand, Bob. They should be making our lives here better. Not telling us to bugger off and climb some trees in the mountains. I thought this country belongs to us,' Sam had said with an extra head of self-pity.

'Sometimes I get the feeling that they're going to give everything away to the Niggers. I mean, it's insane. I didn't make so much of a noise when that Bengali joined our division replacing Ronald Kitson, remember?' Bob replied.

'It's the bloody liberal Campbell-Bannerman government,' spoke out John about his fellow Glaswegian. The clubhouse was quiet, as it always was on weekday afternoons, and if anyone had kept his ears pricked up, he would have heard a mutter of approval from the other three.

'He's already given the Transvaal and Orange River Colony self-rule. Now he's getting ready to give it to India.'

But each time the conversation meandered its way back to any thought of returning Home, they would change the topic, or order another round of beer, or pick up their billiards cues, the tips of which they would chalk away until their hands turned white.

It was Sam's eldest daughter, Felicia, who had shown enterprise and the nuns at her school had suggested that she seriously think about a career in teaching. They thought that she would do well in the noble profession if she went on a teachers' training programme that was held every six months in McLeodganj in the United Provinces of Agra and Oudh.

'Not to McLeod you don't!'

The name rang all the wrong bells in Sam's ears.

'But Papa, the sisters want me to train there and become a teacher. Then I can come back here and teach in any school, the best schools. Sister Martha has even given me a list of where I should apply when I'm back. All I have to do is go there and complete the course.'

It was finally Mrs Miller, now fully developed into a feisty woman herself, who convinced her husband that it would be the right thing for their Felicia to do.

'You don't want her to end up like Patterson's daughter, do you?'

Of course, no one in their right minds would want their daughters to end up like Jenny Patterson who, after running away from home following an argument with her father, had ended up marrying a native Christian 'poet' and now lived in some filthy bylane on Shukhia Street teaching middle-aged Bengalis the piano. So Felicia Miller was fondly seen off by her family at the station.

Not much is known of how she got along with the nuns at the Convent of the Sacred Heart. And we shouldn't make much of the talk that did the rounds in Anglo-Indian circles in the latter half of the second decade of the new century about her mishap while visiting the St John's Church near Forsythgunj with an English gentleman. But Felicia did return to the city exactly six months and a week to the day that she had left it.

But instead of joining the well-known girls' school on Lower Circular Road as a junior teacher, as had been planned by her guardians at McLeodganj, she joined the theatre. For with a woman like Felicia Miller, too, forgetting was the key.

Felicia was careful not to take up any job in show business that meant her performing in the city's European hotels and theatres. To her family, she was still Felicia Miller who taught nice little English or Anglo-Indian girls to grow up and become nice English ladies before they returned Home. Except that she wasn't a teacher. Instead, she found happiness, solace, call it what you will, along with a modest and steady income in an up-and-coming Bengali theatre production company that was making its forays in the world of bioscopes.

It was only a year and a half ago that she had signed a full-time contract with the Alochhaya Theatre and Bioscope Company. Three hundred rupees a month was much more than she would have got as a schoolteacher. On top of it, Felicia had started to enjoy being people that she, till the other day, couldn't even dream of pretending to be. And it was here in the theatre, a couple of years after she had become a full-fledged member of the Alochhaya Theatre (and soon to be Bioscope) Co., that I met Durga Devi, and fell in love.

—

Years after my Alochhaya days, I was talking to Dhiraj Bhattacharya at the Mahajati Sadan where both of us had been invited for an especially tiresome show. (It was 1944, the centenary celebrations of that retard, Girish Ghosh.) He was telling me about his early days as an actor.

'Abani, let me tell you a story. My uncle was a clerk in a merchant office who didn't like it one bit that I had started working in the bioscope. One evening, suddenly out of nowhere he asked me, "So, Khokon, how much are they paying you?" You know how it was. I didn't want to show that I was bringing in money slower than it took me to spend an anna out of my pocket. So I told him that I was getting one hundred and fifty at the moment, and that the sum would jump to five hundred once the bioscope I was in was released. His eyes popped out of their sockets. "Five hundred!" "Yes, so? That's not so much by bioscope standards, you know," I bragged. "The bioscope's going to be really big in the next few years. I've been told a thousand rupees a month will be the going rate for any actor in another five-six years."

'Ha, Abani, you should have seen his face. This man, so much older than me, of whom I was secretly scared, was staring out of the window when he told me in a voice that had lost all its force, "What are you saying? People with BA and MA degrees consider themselves lucky if they manage to get a job that'll pay them a hundred rupees a month. And you're saying that just by dolling up your faces and rolling your hips with those women you'll be earning more?" Ho, ho, Abani, I did feel a tinge of sadness for the old man. How things have changed!'

'Things change, Dhir, things change,' I had told him before proceeding to speak into a bulbous microphone about how great a national treasure Girish was.

Back in 1918, in the months following *Prahlad Parameshwar* and then the very successful *Othello*, it had become clear that things had indeed changed. The Alochhaya Theatre and Bioscope Co. had found that there was a star in its fold. I would be on a tram, travelling from Picture Palace or Variety after an evening of enjoying Eddie Polo in *The Broken Coin*, and people would recognize me.

'Isn't that Prahlad?' or 'Shubho, look! That's Ratnakar' or 'That's the ghost of *The Ghost Who Walks*.' There would be glances, looks and gawks. Fellow commuters and neighbours would see an Aurangzeb or a murderer or a depraved lover flit past them. But it hadn't yet reached the point where people would recognize me as Abani Chatterjee, the shape-shifter, the man who could turn into one person one day and into another the next.

That would happen after the portly Lalji Hemraj Haridas entered our lives, making his first appearance in the whirligig office of the Alochhaya Theatre and Bioscope Co. The many-ringed Lalji was everything that everyone in Alochhaya was not. He had no real interest in the world of entertainment and had once walked out of a Chaplin bioscope simply because he was feeling hungry and, in his own words, 'gassed'. But the biggest difference was that his livelihood depended not on bioscopes or theatre, but on something far removed.

Lalji had come to this city from Kathiawar in the west as part of his family's rites of passage. His brother had expanded the family 'piece good' business by opening up a branch in the Burabazar area. Over the last twelve years business had been doing so well that the family—or at least part of the very large and extended Haridas family—decided to move here and make this city their home and headquarters.

For the last few months, Lalji had been trying to become the Bengal agent for Bombay's Kohinoor Film Company. And the day Mahesh Bhowmick called me over to his office, the Marwari with a perennial supply of betel juice sloshing between his teeth and tongue was explaining why he wanted to enter the bioscope business.

'Bhowmick-babu, I don't understand anything of bioscopes. And frankly, I'd rather be in the presence of baijees for an evening of entertainment than inside a dark room watching jumping shadows on the wall. But I do understand business and I understand that there is good money to be made in your bioscopes. I have been told that the bioscope is something that everybody wants these days. And if everybody *wants* to see it, everybody *will* see it. And they seem to want to see it badly enough to spend good money on it. Bhowmick-babu, I'm a businessman. So let's make money. Some paan, Mahesh-ji?'

Very little had changed in Bhowmick's office over the last few years. There was now an electric bulb hanging behind him and some fans. But the other, bigger electric light that dangled from the ceiling in the middle of the room like a Khudiram noose wasn't used except for emergencies. And during the many times I had entered this room since Ram Bahadur dragged me in the first day, I had experienced an 'emergency' only twice. (Once when a rubber stamp went missing and everyone went on their hands and knees trying to find it, and the second time when a European from France had come seeking a sales partnership.)

'Ah, Abani, come,' Bhowmick greeted me slightly nervously. 'Swapan, get another glass of lassi.'

I think I must have looked put out. You have to understand that I was still very young. Being young is having a special fluid running through the body which, in the right temperature and circumstance, reacts violently to things like quietness, mediocrity, pusillanimity and red-teethed fat men who have much more money than oneself. Lalji Haridas, at that point a complete stranger to me, greeted me more effusively than my employer ever had.

'Arre, Abani-babu. Come in, come in. I was just telling Mahesh-ji about you. My daughters and my wife thought you were a fabulous Prahlad. I have yet to see it, but I trust my family's judgement in matters related to entertainment and you can be assured that I am also a big admirer of yours. Sit, sit.'

He seemed to rub the table, his panjabi crinkling up to show a sweaty hand that started with an arrangement of heavy rings and ended midway with a ridge of creases at the elbow. His speech rhymed with his soft chewing. His undulating hair glistened in the roomlight, and a slab of flesh bulged below his hairline. Despite his unfortunate looks and uncouth ways, he had that entirely attractive, absolute confidence that comes with monetary success. As I sat down next to him in front of Bhowmick's table, I instinctively shuddered myself into attention.

'This is the man I want, Mahesh-ji. I'll come straight to the point before, as we say, the halwa gets cold. I think Abani-babu here is someone whom the public will take a liking to. Call me a man who takes risks,' he said fingering one of his rings, 'but I'd rather think of myself as a worshipper of fate. You know what I think, Bhowmick-ji? I think we should make more bioscope pictures with this young man here. He is also so talented, nah?'

Bhowmick was stunned, the way an irksome insect is when it receives a tap from human fingers. He hadn't expected Lalji to launch forth in such a forthright manner. He first looked at me, and then at the man who was sitting in front of him.

'What is it, Bhowmick-babu? It's very simple. I put money into bioscopes with Abani Chatterjee, and the Alochhaya Theatre and Bioscope Company makes them. What is in it for me? Well, I make a bit for myself from the profits, 40:60, nothing too much, for the first three pictures to be made in a year. A fair deal, I should think.'

I sank deep into my unsinkable wooden seat, not because of the gravity of the proposition I had just heard, but because I suddenly felt lightheaded and didn't want to show it. I had not expected business of such nature to be conducted in such a flash, and certainly not in front of me. But as I sat there listening to the man gush on like an open tap, I felt him transform from a fat, red-toothed Marwari, wearing ten kilos of jewellery on his hands, into a visionary who truly understood the value of the bioscope picture.

Lalji wanted to back *my* movies and he was putting his money where his paan-stained mouth was. The only other precondition he had was that the three bioscopes—*his* three bioscopes, with his name in the opening credits—should be longer than the usual two-reelers. He wanted the public to be treated to a longer story for the same ticket price, bioscope features that would run longer than just the curiosity-fulfilling, hallroom-filling fifteen or twenty minutes. Lalji was now a new addition to the set of protagonists in the Alochhaya Theatre and Bioscope Co., and he showed it.

'But he's a Marwari,' Bikash squealed when I told him about our meeting a few hours after I had signed a contract of fifteen thousand rupees for eight bioscopes in the next twelve months.

'So?' I said, sitting in a long room full of people in various stages of riot and nodding. 'He understands business and that is what is missing in the picture industry in this country today. We need a visionary, an entrepreneur. He's the person. He'll make a Star Theatre out of Alochhaya.'

'And a Girish Ghosh out of you, I suppose?'

'No, a Dranem,' I said plainly, referring to my current favourite screen actor, the neck-kerchiefed Frenchman with a pudding hat whose capers I (and Shombhu-mama) would follow in great detail.

If Lalji was just investing money in a few bioscopes, I wouldn't have been convinced about his seriousness about the whole affair. There were quite a few such characters entering and exiting the burgeoning moving pictures industry every month. But after a week of signing the deal, he brought in his family—his wife, four sons, three daughters, his brother, his brother's wife and their three sons—to see a special screening of *The Slaying of Ravana*. It was then that I figured that this was not going to be just a weekend fancy for him. Along with the Haridas family watching the special screening at eleven in the morning was the man himself, seated next to a Mahesh Bhowmick furiously chewing on the calluses on his fingers and spitting them out in the illuminated darkness of the theatre.

In *The Slaying of Ravana*, I played the role of Lord Ram, with Durga playing Sita, and Dinesh Baral as the demon king. I wasn't there at the screening, but Ram Bahadur, who was standing at the exit the whole time, narrated to me what happened.

'Oh, I haven't seen anyone in the crowd in the last twenty-five years react in such a way to a performance—theatre, jatra or bioscope. They were thrilled. Five minutes into the bioscope, one of the ladies stood up, walked towards the aisle and then in the dark hall went down on her knees, saying, 'Ram, Sia-Ram,

Sia-Ram, jai jai Ram.' The others followed. I also joined in. Both you and Durga-mem were so moving on the screen that even I forgot that you were both actors and not Ram-ji and Sita-maiya themselves.'

'What was Ram doing,' I asked, hiding my inquisitive-as-a-maid voice, 'when the lady first started praying?'

'Er, I wasn't really looking at the screen, babu. But I think it was the time when Ram-ji announced that he would go into exile . . . I think . . .'

'Go on. And then?' I said knitting my brow and taking a short drag on my cigarette, still unable to conduct the habit like a fully-fledged adult.

Okay, so it was the scene in which I, Durga and Paral (playing Lakshman) were about to change from our royal finery into our saintly robes and topknots, preparing ourselves mentally for the next fourteen years—twenty-odd bioscope minutes—in the Dandakaranya forest.

'A few minutes later, another lady went up to the front near the screen. Lalji and all the others followed, with Bhowmick-babu the only one still sitting in his seat. Towards the end, as you sat on the throne back in Ayodhya again with the petals being scattered, the whole family started throwing grains of rice at the screen. One of the ladies had already broken open a coconut right there inside the hall and lit up incense sticks. Bhowmick-babu looked quite petrified by the end but even he joined in with the lot.'

By the time I acted in *Parasuram Avatar* and *Chhatrapati Shivaji*, this would become something of a norm at the picture palaces this side of town. People would leave their shoes outside, shower the screen with flowers, rice and loose change at the right moments. And depending on which divinity or hero

I was playing, they would cry out my name—not Abani Chatterjee, of course, but that of the character I was playing. It was no longer just a spectacular circus; it was forty-five-odd minutes of epiphany, congregation and a meeting of the faithful as well.

By the end of the following year, no one could doubt that Lalji Hemraj Haridas had ushered in a new era in entertainment. Also, Lalji Hemraj Haridas had by that time bought over the bioscope division of Alochhaya. Mahesh Bhowmick was happy to get only a portion of the profits and use his rather limited talents to tend to the dwindling Alochhaya Theatre Co.

Throughout those giddy years, I kept acting in bioscopes. People were starting to know Abani Chatterjee—not in the 'Oh, now wasn't he the actor who was Karna in *The Sixth Pandav*?' way; it was more 'That's Abani Chatterjee! Remember we saw him on Thursday at the Mancha?' In all the bioscopes I starred in—barring *Birbal*—Durga was cast opposite me. Even her name, hyphenated with mine, had started to become a familiar proper noun in households. That itself brought us closer.

Then came the watershed year for the Abani Chatterjee–Durga Devi duo. It was Lalji who brought it to our notice how 'nationalism' was becoming the big cultural thing those days. We had reckoned as much when we staged and screened *Prahlad*, a bioscope whose sub-subtext had been 'nationalist'. But somehow, after that, we never tried another one of those 'symbolic' features. Maybe Bhowmick wasn't the boat-rocking, hovering-on-the-edge kind. Neither was Lalji, for that matter. But he was a genius with the box office. At a meeting, Lalji had simply announced that there was much to be gained—in terms of reputation and money—if we took a swerve towards a direction where 'nationalism' and 'self-rule' and all those fashionable ideas could be hinted at without making them too obvious to the authorities.

'Sure, it's in your face. Sure, it's banal. And sure, it's not wonderful art. But we're not in the business of social service. For that, there are books and there are sadhus. If nationalism is what the crowds want, then nationalism is what we'll give them. In any case, anyone complaining can easily be told that it's all just make-believe. It's not that we don't pay our taxes and want the English to go away. It's like reading those Bat-tala books that Dhiren is always reading without actually being unfaithful to your wife. Hah, hah!' Lalji said and laughed some more.

That was how Bankimchandra Chattopadhyay's *Anandamath* was scheduled to be turned into a one-hour-ten-minute bioscope. Horen Ray, the man behind the camera on *Prahlad Parameshwar*, was given a tell-me-what-you-want-and-I'll-give-it budget to turn the story into tangible nitrate. I was to play Jibananda, the man equally tempted by a revolutionary life and the domestic life of a husband. Durga would be Shanti, Jibananda's wife who wanted her husband's love and found it only by becoming a revolutionary herself.

The beauty of this 'nationalist' bioscope was that it couldn't possibly get into any trouble with the authorities. *Anandamath* wasn't a story about the struggle for freedom against the English. It was a rousing tale of courage and sacrifice in the face of Muslim tyranny. In fact, some lines were introduced to pad up the nice things that Bankim had said about the necessity of English rule for the country. Above all, our *Anandamath* would also be a love story. Love and fashionable politics—what else could one ask for in a non-mythological bioscope?

I stood there, inside the makeshift sets and in front of a

battery of yet-to-be-kicked-awake spotlights. The dynamos were roaring somewhere in the sprawling factory space where the sign 'M/S Lalji Hemraj Haridas & Co.' was still visible at the entrance. Along with some technicians, I was standing there alone with my make-up and costume—just a white dhuti and shawl—waiting for the director, the cameraman and the lightman to arrive. Only a few lights were required for this 'outdoor' shoot, for the roofless studio allowed the midday sunlight to generously pour in from the top.

Which is when I saw Durga, her hair loose and pouring down to her waist, black and glistening as her real hair could never hope to be. She was wearing kajol, and that made her face glow with a spirit that stays suppressed in real life. The white sari she was wearing looked like the sails of a ship wrapped around hastily so as to catch a brief gust. There she was. Shanti, my wife. Somewhere between the moment that she walked in and when the shoot started, Jibananda climbed out of the pit where all my characters—past, present and future—live.

## \<interval\>

*Long shot of a dirt trail with scrub and small trees on either side. A figure is walking briskly with something in his hands. He slows until he stops completely. He looks straight ahead for one moment and then continues to walk briskly again.*

*Close-up of the man's face. He is agitated, even worried.*

*Medium-shot of the man moving along the path which turns right to disappear from view. The dirt trail with its scrub and small trees is left behind.*

—

Jibananda had not had a proper meal for two days and it was his body's right to feel weak under the blazing summer sun. But he had been trained to keep his body in its rightful place. One thing that he wasn't trained for, though, was an unscheduled return home. Home was a door that opened to a courtyard with a low-roofed two-room house on one side, next to a mangoless mango tree. Further on, next to a lemonless lemon tree, was a hut that served, depending on the circumstances, as a spare room for spillover guests, a goat shed, a place where all the farming tools could be kept. Home was, for all that he had been through in the last year and a half, the place where he could return and pick up from where he had left things hanging. And those things now, in memory, seemed happy and comforting—both qualities associated with habit formation.

The life he had been leading the past eighteen months was a deliberate digression. A life of action; a 'revolutionary' life. Oh, he was stricken with laziness, tiredness and cowardice even now. But he stayed the course despite this because he had realized that driving out the Mussalmans—driving out smallness and banality from his own life—required much more than energy and courage, those twin over-rated qualities. What was needed, in fact, was to keep everyday life at bay for some time, to temporarily suspend it, and this state could be attained only if one created new habits. Over the last several months he had done just that. In a way, Jibananda had been picking up new habits so that he could, one day, happily collapse into the old ones.

A girl came out of the farthest room of the house and stopped to lean on the trunk of the mango tree. Jibananda's sister. He had expected her to create a ruckus in her usual loud and unbridled manner. But she kept leaning on the tree instead, staring at the bundle that her brother was carrying.

'Dada, whose child is that?'

Jibananda had practised the entry he would make, making some rehearsed 'spontaneous' remarks about how his sister had shot up since the last time he had seen her. He had imagined that after that initial exchange, he would then quickly hand the baby over to her. But he kept standing there, still outside the shadow of both the house and the mango tree, holding the infant wrapped in a flimsy red cloth and looking at Nimi. He felt awkward, deciding not to look around with pretend-nostalgia as he had earlier planned.

'He was . . . I found him left there, stranded under a tree.'

The lemon tree that his wife had planted some years ago had grown in the distance. Trees come in handy during awkward moments. He thought he would say something about the tree, but he held back. It would be pointless to talk about the lemon tree at that moment. All he saw now was his widowed sister, teenaged into maturity, taking the bundle from his hands and telling him to sit inside, in the shade. As he drank some water, his throat making the sound of a vessel bobbing out of a tankful of water, Jibananda felt the fear that he had been dreading since he started his journey. It was the fear of feeling at ease, of the awkwardness suddenly lifting. The fear of not going back to finish unfinished business and staying home.

Mussalman tyranny was far from over. In fact, apart from a few raids that had made the enemy realize that there was one force with one cause behind the attacks, the land was still firmly under the foreign yoke. A famine had led Jibananda and many other young men to recognize what had been staring at them all the while: effortless subjugation.

Jibananda quenched his thirst and hoped to look adequately changed and man-like before his sister. He would tell her to take care of the baby, not lose hope and expect his return soon. He would also tell Nimi to tell her sister-in-law, his wife, that she should not worry and that he would be back soon. That was his plan. As was the only concession that he was willing to make: giving in to her demand of carrying a knapsack with some muri moa and a small brick of gur in it. All that didn't happen. Nimi demanded that he have a proper meal at home.

It was when he was still protesting with some mumbles that Nimi called out, 'Boudi, look who's home! Dada's . . .'

Terrified, Jibananda jumped up, almost tripping himself on his dhuti front, and grabbed his suddenly prancing sister who had balanced the baby in her stick-like arms and pushed her against the lemonless lemon tree, covering her mouth with his hand. Without thinking about the consequences of what would happen if the baby slipped out of Nimi's arms, he clamped down the 'mmmmm's seeping out of his sister's arrested mouth. He kept his hand there for a brief moment, all the time it took for him to realize that his visit could not really be kept a secret from Shanti.

Even as Jibananda gave up and moved away, Nimi looked at her brother with eyes that had aged all too much all too soon. She looked down at the squalling child and then again at her bestubbled brother-stranger. Pulling the end of her white sari tightly around her while deftly balancing the baby on her hip, and facing the blazing sun, she said, 'Dada, you must see Shanti. She's your wife. I'll tell her that you're here and get you some lunch. You can then do what you want.'

Jibananda wanted to look at some more things, discover some changes as his sister walked away. But all there was to see were things that had already become familiar again in the last few minutes. If they had withheld their inherent power of evoking extreme nostalgia when Jibananda walked into the courtyard, they unleashed this power now that Nimi had uttered Shanti's name.

The house on his right was standing as neatly as it had done when he left it. The raised threshold space outside the two rooms still bore decoration marks from the last pujo—the second that Jibananda had been away from. The leaves of the mango tree did not move in the heat, which was something totally normal. The last time he had seen it bear a single fruit was when both his parents were still living. The lemon tree in the distance had grown, but a tale of fruitless growth there too. In effect, nothing had changed.

Nimi returned alone. It was as if the strained encounter between brother and sister had not taken place at all. She chirped on about the neighbours, the village, Shanti. Rakhsit had become a father four months ago, which 'actually dispelled all those rumours that he had a problem down there'; Padma had got married to this bloke from a nearby village without her father arranging any wedding ceremony; old hag Indubala had once again been driven out of Harihar Pandit's house by his wife for 'corrupting' her grand-niece, and this time she couldn't be found. Jibananda held back a sigh. His eyes were still darting about in the direction of the lemon tree and the hut next to it.

As he polished off the meal before him—dal, daalna, rice and jackfruit—he recognized the luxury of leading two lives. For the duration of his meal and Nimi's train-rattle gossip, he guiltily thanked the preoccupations of his other life—the need to raid, to plan new raids, to work at the belief, the conviction that gives structure to the most smoky and insubstantial of things. Each descent on a group of Mussalman soldiers did not result in success. But it moved his life some distance away each time from the twittering boredom and rural idiocy of Nischindipur. The public life with the Brothers made Jibananda melt into a crowd, giving him a purpose other than just reading out the scriptures, shaking a bell and thrusting out brass-handled lamps for people to stain their palms with the heat and smoke of the flames and rub it on their heads like unani ointment. The life with Shanti, with Nimi and with the never-changing trees also had a meaning. But it was the kind of meaning that the act of snoring has—air passing through a narrow passage, so make what you will of it.

He was not allowed to forget the unsaid promise he had made Nimi before his meal. Jibananda emitted a sharp, short burp while his sister poured water on to his hands at the base of the trunk of the mangoless mango tree. As he wiped the water off his face first with his hand and then with the wet gamchha tucked between the bars of the nearby window, he had no memory of the last plan sketched out by Bhabananda and the others of driving Alivardi Khan out of the country. Instead, he was completely occupied by the sight of the white-sari-clad woman emerging from the faraway hut. Her sari was not wrapped around her like Nimi's was. She was wearing it in a manner that suited a proper woman, with the right stretches and folds.

The house, the two trees, the hut and the courtyard tilted under the sun. Shanti looked older, quieter, but her dark eyes, now at the closest of quarters, gave the game away.

'Bande Mataram,' Jibananda uttered to cover his rush of breath.

She kissed him once on the lips, holding his face with both her hands as if aware of the possibility that it could dissolve any moment. And then she released him.

## starlight starbright

By the time *Anandamath* was running to packed houses, people were not only coming to various theatres specifically to watch Abani Chatterjee bioscope features, but they had also started to recognize me outside the darkened halls. It was all very wonderful. I was young, at the age when one is prepared to be loved, leading a life I could not have imagined even a year before.

The most tangible symbol of this state of being was the Model-T that I had purchased. It was a gleaming black rectangle on wheels. The driver, whom Alochhaya had hired, had previously driven an automobile owned by either Mr Samuel Bourne or Mr Charles Shepherd—of the photography firm Bourne & Shepherd—with whom Alochhaya and a few other bioscopes had business tie-ups for the purpose of publicity stills and showcard pictures. The driver, Narsingh, was a proud and scruffy Rajput, who talked so much that the motor's engine could hardly ever be heard. But because he spoke lengthy monologues in Hindustani or sentences in unintelligible Bengali, he never did bother me.

As I was being driven down Strand Road one Sunday, with the afternoon Hugli breeze taking my mind off the previous day's shooting, I decided to treat myself to a bioscope in the Chowringhee area.

I must have been the oldest person in the theatre that was filled with children and their screams and banter. The show hadn't started yet, but the orchestra in front seemed to have started the proceedings anyway by striking up one tune after another. The piano kept rising above all the din.

Experiencing silent movies was anything but a silent experience. As the reel unfolded above one's head from a half-hidden grotto, the sound of the people amassed in a hall was unmistakable. The chattering and talking were rolled into one ball and bounced off the walls. If you were sitting close to a voluble huddle, the comments sometimes having little to do with the light show going on in front, you could believe that it is possible to never be alone. Over and above the human babble, there was the music. Depending on the scene, the strings and the rhythm section of the orchestra would measure out life inside the picture palace. People may have forgotten this these days, but silent movies were never ever silent.

It was a special matinee show at the Palladium exclusively for children. The manager seemed only too happy to see me as he led me to the empty box seat next to the upper stalls. In that circus atmosphere, I could see from my perch some of the older boys below sliding down the front of their seats and chugging secretly on half-smoked cigarettes that they'd collected and straightened out.

An electric bell sounded and there was a cumulative squeal. A second metallic insect sound turned the hall dark and the monkey-noise became a frenzy—just after which the horn section announced the parting of the curtains, at the same time that the third and final bell announced that the show was starting. The screen lit up, first with a perfect house-sized white rectangle of light, which soon dimmed itself clunkily to show a distant figure walking through a park. I sank into my seat and lit a cigarette.

*The Folly of Mr Tuba* was a short animated feature in which a rodent-like man keeps trying to kill himself. Each time, though, he is thwarted by various characters that include a spineless tree, whose main branch bends and touches the ground each time Mr Tuba attempts to hang himself; a depressive dynamite stick, whose tears snuff out the charge; a paranoid bottle of poison, whose contents shrivel up along its upturned base the moment Mr Tuba up-ends it for consumption; and an overly friendly footpath that keeps rushing up to Mr Tuba from below before he can walk all the way down. The last scene shows a faceless, hooded figure with a scythe tapping cigarette ash from its skeletal fingers while Mr Tuba, having given up trying to end his life by now, leans over to kiss his finally-at-ease sweetheart in what zooms out to be a giant airship. We are left with an iris-in on the at-last-happy couple, but not before we catch a tatter of flames in one corner of the airship.

The audience woke up with a shriek of delight and I too couldn't help but smile. The lights had flicked on as suddenly as they had gone out some twenty minutes ago. Down below, I could see a few Europeans, teachers no doubt, trying to restore order among their hyperactive flock. Three bell rings later, it would be the main show: *Sunnyside*, starring Charles Chaplin.

Just a few years before, along with the Ed Porter Westerns, theatres in the city were getting crowds in with an increasing number of bioscopes from America. Even if most of the newsreels and shorts were still predominantly from England, France and Germany, the American comedy shorts and features, with their French-style hyperactive characters, were becoming more and more popular.

I had enjoyed the sheer pace of these out-of-breath comedies. I liked Mark Sennett and Marie Dressler. But Roscoe 'Fatty' Arbuckle was the best. I sincerely believed Fatty, especially in the Keystone Cops shorts, was destined to become the human face of the bioscope. For, like him, the bioscope was only about what you saw. Instead of Arbuckle, however, it was the hysterical, gag-a-shot Chaplin who went on to become the biggest draw. Talk about public taste.

Sitting in the box seat after the yellow lights had blinked off and the white light from the screen was smeared across the theatre like fine chalk dust, I recognized Chaplin playing the same character I had first seen him play four years earlier at the Athena. The young audience below me were guffawing and rolling with laughter nearly every second. The air itself was being punctured with laughter, one volley followed by another followed by another like a lunatic boy going crazy with a sharp pencil and a sheet of paper.

Chaplin in his brush moustache was an over-utilized farmhand and while his actions were hilarious, his expressions, especially with his kajol-tinted eyes exaggerating each one of them, were what made me sit up and take notice. He was almost as good as Mr Tuba, but he deserved extra credit, for he was not an animated character. I watched him, with the rest of the crowd, add milk to his coffee, milk that was taken straight from the cow's udder, and fry his breakfast eggs by holding a chicken above the frying pan. These were images doing the talking, the talking that no theatre production had ever thought of doing before.

It was a little while after Chaplin, the farmhand, had dozed off and entered a dream inhabited by nymphs that I saw one of the ushers, his face reflected by the screen light, walk up towards where I was seated.

'Sorry, Abani-babu. But could you please go downstairs to Mr Evans's office? He says it's very important.'

The usher was perhaps a couple of years older than I, if you overlooked the manner in which he addressed me with outlandish respect. I followed him down to where the door swung open for a brief moment and I was out again in the natural light of the foyer.

Eddie Evans was the manager of the Palladium and we had met for the first time only some eight or nine months ago, during the screening of a German mythological feature.

'Mr Chatterjee. I'm afraid I just got some bad news. Mahesh Bhowmick has been looking for you. The man he sent has been trying to find you for the last two hours. Someone finally recognized your automobile and chauffeur outside and came into my office.' Eddie Evans, like all the Anglos I had ever met, talked too much. But unlike in any Sennett or Chaplin bioscope, the torrent of talk made sound. There in the corner of Evans's poster-covered office room, Ram Bahadur was sitting on his haunches under a framed poster bearing two faces—one of a maliciously smiling man wearing a monocle and the other of a woman who seemed to be finding it painful to smile. Just before I looked down into Ram Bahadur's dour and nervous face, the very opposite of Chaplin's in the bioscope I had been watching only moments ago, I read the words on the showcard:

Carl Laemmle offers
Stronheim's Wonder Play
'Blind Husbands'
Universal-Jewel De Luxe Attraction
Produced by Stronheim himself

Before I could even consider recalling any scene from the motion picture I had watched wide-eyed and wide-mouthed with Shombhu-mama just last summer in this very theatre, Ram Bahadur, by this time standing up to his full height, spoke in an unrecognizable, gnarled manner: 'Tarini-babu has passed away.'

For the last few days, Tarini Chatterjee had complained of pain in his stomach. Frankly, because his words had increasingly started to sound like the fast gallop of police horses chasing off an unfriendly crowd bearing banners, nobody in the house had really understood what he had been saying. Abala, whose sense of understanding what people in the house were saying was the keenest, had found nothing abnormal in his behaviour during his last few days. Like always, she saw to it that Tarini had his meals and changed into a new set of clothes every day, even though he had long stopped even stepping out of the house.

Within a week of airing his final round of loud and unintelligible complaints, my father died. Dr Talukdar did not explain his final condition as God's will. But this neither surprised nor disappointed me. All he mentioned to those sitting around my father's cocooned body was that a poisoned liver had ended Tarini's life.

I mourned Tarini Chatterjee in a befitting manner—by polishing off one of his unfinished bottles of liquor, the contents of which had reached, I realized only then, the dangerous point of tasting like something far more corrosive than just alcohol. Seven days later, after having removed a stubble that had grown nearly as long as the one on my dead father's face, I was back in front of the camera. Under the reflectors in an open field a few miles outside the city, I was playing the role of a desperate son who bargains his soul with a demon to save the life of his father. Both Mahesh and Horen insisted that the script had been ready weeks before and that the decision to produce the short had been made only the previous Sunday. I wasn't so sure, being aware that the picture was always scheduled to be made two days after what turned out to be the day of my father's death.

Even as I played tricks with my face and eyes and crept from one angle to another, I kept thinking of only one thing: my buffer against death had been removed. After Tarini, it was my turn. This revelation lent a certain extra desperation to my character's bid to see that *his* father remained alive. The short, *The Son's Wager*, which was immediately added to the *Prahlad Parameshwar* screening, went on to become very popular indeed.

—

One would have thought that Shabitri Lahiri, because of the tender age at which she got married to Tarini Chatterjee, hardly had a childhood. Nothing could be further from the truth. Even when she turned into Shabitri Chatterjee and found herself transported from the Ruritania of Krishnagar to the huff and crackle of the city where she would spend the rest of her life, she refused to become the full-fledged woman that girls are meant to become either overnight or over years. This refusal, like her ability to sidestep awkward or untoward moments and incidents, came as naturally as sweat accompanies heat.

So while my father was only some five years older than her, Shabitri always seemed some twenty years younger than *she* was. This anomalous, stretched-out girlhood was not only reflected in her deceptively youthful looks but was also evident, as one was to find out a few days after Tarini Chatterjee's death, in the ease with which she had managed to fake her comatose state for nearly two and a half years.

Faking immobility is as difficult as faking physical pain. Or perhaps more. And Shabitri managed to pull off her performance without even Dr Talukdar, a registered physician, catching on. I wondered if her body, not always privy to her thoughts, knew of her great pretence. Her bones and muscles, lying there in one position barring for the occasional roll-over, may at some point have atrophied, innocently, by the sheer victory of gravity over her body. But what of her mind? Did she move when no one could see her? Did she move with extra vigour during the night, just to compensate her sedentary performance? One will never know.

Shabitri may well have succeeded in her pretence, her life's great game (no, I wouldn't call it deception). But her own blood betrayed her, as one's blood usually does. It was I who shattered the night-quietness with one single slingshot of disturbed air: 'Ma!'

I remember the evening the way one remembers a few-seconds-ago fall by the painful bump on one's head. I had been unable to sleep, and looking out from the balcony into the courtyard that was bathed in weak moonlight, I struck a match to light my cigarette. Suddenly, in that yellow flash of sulphur that normally travels not farther than a few millimetres, I saw an outline swiftly changing in the line of my vision. I chugged on my cigarette, briefly suspending a sequence with Durga and me in a future bioscope, and walked back into my room.

I made it a point to make my departure from the balcony a little more voluble than I normally would, and then, taking my slippers off, tiptoed back to the door of my room. Going by my instincts, it would have been any time between two-thirty and three-thirty at night. Peering from behind the door curtains of my room, I only saw the balcony railings, complete with two motionless saris hanging from them, illuminated by the aforesaid moonlight. There was no one there.

Watching bioscopes and being in them give people an extra ability to notice lines of light and shade. Light directors and cameramen notice this most keenly, but everybody in the bioscope business has the ability. Standing behind the curtain, noticing nothing but a still-life, I was quite certain I had seen someone in the tiny flare of the matchstick. I don't know what made me do it, but after some healthy minutes, I slunk out from behind the curtains, careful not to throw any shadows, tiptoed a little distance down the long balcony, and stood outside my mother's room.

During the day, Shabitri's door was kept open, with only the curtains blocking a direct view. But ever since electricity entered the Chatterjee household, the curtains would flutter like slothful moths at the wind churned up by the metal fins of the new ceiling fans. At night, the complete blockage of view was disrupted every few seconds by these sighing electric-fan-fuelled curtains. I stood outside my mother's door, making sure that beyond the tip of my nose nothing could be seen from inside.

The first thing that I thought as I fixed my limited vision on to the darkened interior was that somehow Dr Talukdar had entered my mother's room. But before I could play out what I would do once I found the doctor inside, I saw a movement. This time it was a clear and crisp movement, a vertical line of blackness cutting through the rest of the darkness and moving ever so slowly.

'Abani, is that you?'

It was my mother's voice and I was petrified. A split second later, the fear vanished, as I realized that it was my father who had died and was liable to haunt me, not my immobile but living mother.

'Abani, quiet now. Come here.' It had been her raised hand, gently waving, that I had seen earlier.

'Ma!' It was one sharp sound that came out of my throat, like a single loud clang from the nearby temple. It's remarkable how in the deepest end of the night, unless you keep on creating the sound, a loud but second-short racket can go completely unnoticed. During all the months of bombs being flung by coffee-fuelled seditionists across the city in the dead of night, no one actually reported hearing any blast. And yet, the slightest report of crackers, made somehow louder by its duration, had the ability to irritate a whole citizenry.

My quick and frantic burst of words—gibberish, really— that followed were mere hoarse whispers that melted away in the moonlit courtyardscape. Shabitri sprung up from her bed and, in a mock-stern manner that wasn't at all feeble, whispered, 'Quiet, Abani! Keep quiet and come in at once!'

In the same firm but familiar voice, she told me to shut the door behind me. As I waited for the darkness of the room to settle before me so that I wouldn't knock down objects, she was already speaking, more normally now. I even detected a girlish glee in her voice that I had long forgotten.

'Surprised? Sit here next to me and be very, very quiet.'

Even if I could only see the vaguest contours of her face, I could make out that her eyes were open and that she was smiling.

'How are you able to open your eyes? How can you move?' I was, as you would expect, flabbergasted.

In the shortest two hours of my life, I heard Shabitri Chatterjee explain how and why she had decided to stop moving in the presence of other people. And to make it absolutely credible, she had stopped moving even when she was alone. It wasn't only my father's downward spiral and the accompanying grief that had made Shabitri pretend to be immobile to perfection.

There were many other reasons which, she told me, 'you're too young to know about, Abani'.

It was only in these last few days, after news of Tarini's death had trickled up from his room to hers, that she had started to feel restless. She still didn't want to give up what she called 'the luxury of just existing and doing nothing', however, so she stirred herself out of complete immobility only briefly, and only when everyone had fallen asleep—or—as in my father's case—died.

Even as she filled me in about her twenty-six months of 'mind-wandering', talking in mirthful detail not only about the immense will power that was required to refrain from waving away mosquitoes and scratching mosquito bites, but also the discipline required to become comfortable with the horror of urinating and passing faeces in bed, all I could think of was her not intervening and putting a stop to Dr Talukdar's activities. But sons cannot ask their mothers to clear up matters such as this. So I listened quietly to her telling me about the supremacy of the mind over the body, and how when one pretends something down to its minutest details, one starts successfully lying to oneself. And that once this happens, it stops being a lie.

'And you become what you pretend to be,' she said, gripping my fingers that must have still smelt of freshly burnt tobacco.

She only said it once and that too almost as if in passing, but I figured that if she didn't want anyone to know her little secret, I wouldn't be the one to let it out. Which makes it even more awkward for me now, some thirty-five years after that night, to talk about her pretence, considering that it is also thirty-five years after her death, for only a fortnight after we talked in her room, my mother Shabitri passed away in her sleep. It was as sudden as her fall and I still think I did the right thing by not telling anyone, not Shombhu-mama, not Abala, not the pink-tongued Dr Talukdar, about her big secret. I just wish she had cleared the bit about her allowing—for it *was* an allowance—the doctor to use her body in the fashion that he had over months, and possibly years. She could have explained why in a matter-of-fact tone that may not have left me witless.

But in a way, I'm glad she didn't. For sons don't expect their mothers to shed any light on such matters. It's just not right.

—

Around this time, there was another departure. None of us at Alochhaya had expected Shombhu-mama to actually leave the city for good. He was, of course, always talking about moving to Bombay to make pictures of his own, motion pictures that wouldn't be stifled under the 'Lalji philosophy of always catering rubbish to the rabble'. It would be wrong to think, though, that Shombhu-mama didn't appreciate the public—what he called the 'audience'. After all, it was he who kept telling everyone that if there's one thing that mustn't be forgotten while producing bioscopes it's that bioscopes are made for the eyes, not for empty air. But he was deeply suspicious of Lalji clinically discussing what the public wanted—'what the public are preferring'— before venturing into a new production.

'He's racist. He has something against Bengalis, it's bloody obvious.'

Shombhu-mama was also getting increasingly frustrated stuck behind the camera and not doing some Horen-Ray-style megaphone-shouting of his own. What made him sink deeper into his own comforting puddle of pity was that he knew the craft of light exposures, camera speed, lens sizes and life in the cutting room better than anyone else at Alochhaya and yet he was still not recognized as being ready for directorship.

He had heard that J.F. Madan, his old employer, was besotted by directors from Bombay. This trend would permeate to other studios including Alochhaya and that would be the end of any chance at all of Shombhu from Krishnagar making the grade. Bombay was clearly on his mind when he burst out of an elaborate indoor set one day after the director had said that any superimpositions, double exposures or other camera trickery would 'ruin the tone of this bioscope'.

This time, in a fit of furrow-munching depression, Shombhu spared the person he believed to be the source of all his problems: Lalji Hemraj Haridas. Instead, he railed on about people I had never heard him gnash his teeth about before.

'That Tilak is a fool! Gandhi didn't get elected in the Subjects Committee of the Congress and he's bent the rules to get him in. And this Gandhi wants to make Hindustani the language of India and turn us all into Marwaris. What next? All of us turning vegetarian?'

But I don't think creative frustration alone was the reason Shombhunath Lahiri upped and left town one fine day.

One evening, after meeting up with him outside the Elphinstone, we went to the Dilkhusha for some kabiraji and mutton cutlets. Shombhu-mama, for some convoluted reason he had once given me, refused to travel in my automobile. I suspect it had something to do with his theory that 'luxuries make people soft and destroy civilizations'. So I sent Narsingh and the Model-T back, while we walked our way to the nearby Dilkhusha.

As we ate our kashundi-dipped and onion-cucumber-beet-accompanied morsels of meat, a gaggle of chattering young men sitting at the table next to us suddenly stopped talking. One of them, with thin, generously oiled hair plastered to his skull, looked intensely at me. By now, I was used to people recognizing me in public. But this stare was hostile. They looked like students—not the shirt-trousers sort, but the kind who made a point by wearing their dhutis and panjabis as if they were banners.

'You know, Abani, there's a rumour that the city is flush with Australian money. Here, I found this in my pocket after I had bought paan from the shop yesterday,' Shombhu-mama said, and took out a small quarter-anna coin and placed it on the table.

'It's a quarter-anna coin.'

'Flip it over,' he said.

The profile of George V looked familiar enough, with the beard and a tiny elephant depicting the Empire of India dangling on a chain from the royal neck. The words hugging the rim of the coin—'George V King Emperor'—also looked reassuring enough.

'Flip it,' Shombhu-mama repeated, as he crushed his cigarette into the battered ashtray that lay between us. Instead of the usual 'One Quarter Anna' and 'India 1916' below a dividing short line on the other side, the words 'One Half Penny' and 'Commonwealth of Australia 1916' was inscribed on the metal surface.

I looked up at Shombhu-mama.

'I have a feeling that the government is planning to merge all the dominions into one country.'

'But why Australia?'

'Because it's one of the biggest countries in the Empire and it's full of Englishmen. It's pretty obvious, isn't it?'

Shombhu started explaining how the coin on the table in front of us and many more like it were being made in the City Mint. He had a friend who knew someone who had a tea shack in front of the mint. He had apparently found himself with a whole stash of 'Australian' coins. According to Shombhu's friend—who knew the tea shack person—it was part of a much bigger conspiracy by the authorities to redistribute money.

'The next step is to redistribute people across the Empire,' said my uncle before starting to chew on the crumb-fried stub that forms the handle of a mutton cutlet. As he burbled on, I saw the three student-types get up and move towards the door. One of them, the one who had been staring at me, frowned. All of them left.

The Dilkhusha, for all its size, has a single tapering entrance—not a wide, open one like Niranjan or Baishakhi. Shombhu had gone to the restaurant's corner where a wash basin awaited him. As he was coming towards me, shaking his hands to dry them, and his face showing signs of the pleasure one attains after an oily, carnivorous meal, I cleared the bill. Without sitting down again, Shombhu said that we should be on our way home. It was already twenty past nine.

This was a time when the trams were moderately crowded, less full of bodies than even an hour before, but not as near-empty as they would become an hour later. A tram, unlike a train, with which the Chatterjee family was more familiar, was a benevolent vehicle. It travelled at a luxurious speed and did so without making its passengers feel that they were not part of the immediate surroundings. Its pace was like Shombhu-mama drawling 'One one thousand, two one thousand' aloud as he rotated the camera's handle, cranking things down to 14 or 16 frames a second in an even, exact speed—unless he needed to slow things down for a comic sequence.

Neither of us got a seat. The next coach was practically empty, and inviting, but being 'Ladies Only' we couldn't take up the offer. Hanging on to the wooden handles, looking like a lazy Christ with my wrists wrapped around them, I saw the city clank past me frame by frame. Some fifteen years had passed since the first electric trams had started running. Now, there were no more of those forever collapsing, constantly defecating Waler horses pulling tram cars. Like the bioscope, the tram I was travelling in was a smooth, astounding welding of technology and aesthetics.

It was time for us to get down. By the time I saw Shombhu-mama extricate himself from the tram-mouth tangle, I was already facing a familiar street.

Adjusting his shirt, Shombhu said, 'Crowded for a weekday, isn't it?'

Walking towards the mouth of the lane to our house, I was about to say something innocuous, when I saw two men with halos on their heads walking briskly towards us. A more careful glance revealed that there were no halos; their hair was simply bathed in oil and the otherwise unilluminating streetlight was bouncing off it.

That was also when I noticed the chalk mark on the back of Shombhu-mama's shirt. In the straggling hurricane lamplight from the paan shop we had just walked past, the white mark on the white shirt looked yellow. Even in the receding light, the chalk mark stood out like an ink blot.

'Shombhu-mama, there's a mark on your shirt.'

I was about to brush it off, when he walked back towards the paan shop, and turned to look at what I was talking about in the small mirror hanging in the shop. His face changed in shape as well as in quality as he did this. The blood inside its well-defined contours seemed to stop flowing. His face turned taut and pale. The barely visible scrawl on his shirt was in the shape of the figure '8'. It was only after I looked at Shombhu-mama's terror-stricken face that I recognized the sign.

—

Here I must digress. For a little history that will better explain Shombhu-mama's terror and his subsequent departure from the late Tarini's and Shabitri's household, from the city, and from my bioscope life. Sometime in 1904 when the government announced its plan to divide the province into a neat half, an anti-Partition movement began. I vaguely recall my father, then still a trusted employee of the East Indian Railway, lecturing visitors like Nirmal-babu from next door with considerable passion about how 'criminals' were on the loose, and how these lumpen Bengali youngsters were just 'pretending to do something noble and heroic, when all they are are scheming murderers and pilfering thieves'. It became apparent only much later that my father was not alone in holding such an opinion.

Pankaj Pal Chaudhuri, the head of the Pal Chaudhuri family—at whose mansion I saw one of my first bioscopes—and the driving force behind the very successful United Jute Company, received a letter in January 1910, which summed up what these 'swadeshi nationalists' were really up to:

*Respected Pal Chaudhuri-babu,*
*On the occasion of the 1st of Baishakh, we wish you a happy and prosperous year ahead. As you must be already aware, six honorary officers of our Finance Department have taken a loan of Rs 9,658-1-5 from you and have deposited the amount in the office noted above on your account to fulfil our*

*great aim. The sum has been entered in our cash book in your*
*name at 5 per cent per annum.*

*As we thank you for your generous gesture, we also*
*think it wise to remind you that the Government of the*
*United Republic of Bengal will not permit anyone in your*
*family to enjoy your enormous wealth if you were at any*
*time forced to co-operate with the Government of India*
*authorities. For it is our understanding that it would be*
*better if the rich men of the country, like your honourable*
*self, subscribe monthly, quarterly and half-yearly amounts to*
*the GURB Finance Secretariat.*

*Once again, we wish you a joyous and profitable new*
*year. Thank you for your continued support.*

*Yours sincerely,*
*Finance Secretary,*
*Government of the United Republic of Bengal (GURB)*

While this was all very dramatic, it was also baffling.
Things became clear a whole six months after the letter landed
on Pankaj-babu's desk, when six men forced their way into the
accounts department of the United Jute Company. Between
them, they had one pipe gun that hadn't looked very menacing,
but no one wanted to take a chance. Badal Biswas, the chief
accountant, was there at the United Jute Company office when
the robbers appeared. He later told Pal Chaudhuri with a wan
look, 'They were young. And they were very polite.' That was
all he could say about them.

The six had walked out with more than nine and a half
thousand rupees, threatening Biswas and others at the site of
the crime not to call the police or else . . . Pal Chaudhuri had to
go to some length to see to it that news of the robbery was not
published in the newspapers. His business depended a lot on

reputation. If anyone started to think that the United Jute Company had become a terrorist-funding operation, it could mean the end of his business. So he did what he was told to do in the letter—he kept quiet.

Such blatant criminal activities were gradually linked to violent terror actions. There were stray bombings (the handmade bombs mostly landing in ponds or puddles without going off), shootings (in which no one was shot, only ricochets ricocheted) and a general sense of foreboding in the city. This fear was not overbearing. Life went on, but unclear unrest hung in the air like the moon during daylight—present and nearly invisible. Only after an 'action' would this be turned temporarily into minor, private panic. Then it would subside again and return to being the background migraine it was. In the case of Tarini Chatterjee, the 'terrorists' just provided him with another excuse to speak bitterly about the country's youth. By the way, it was my father who had coined the term 'bhadralok loafer criminal class'. He was thrilled when it became a catchphrase in all the English newspapers.

But things quietened down considerably after 1911, partly because the partition decision was reversed, and partly because the hooligans were quite ineffective in their stated goal of bringing about 'freedom'. Also, papers like *Jugantar*, *Sandhya* and *Bande Mataram* that had, incredibly, kept on writing about the need to target Europeans (despite the fact that it was mostly Bengali businessmen, Bengali policemen and Bengali 'informers' who ended up as targets) during the worst years, also finally came under the purview of the authorities after crackdowns and raids on their one-room offices.

This retreat of the 'bhadralok loafer' nationalists hadn't happened overnight, of course. The tide had started to turn three years before 1911, the year the country's capital was shifted. In 1908, four innocent people were killed during a robbery in Muzaffarpur, two of the victims being women. Only a few weeks earlier, in the same town in Bihar, the terrorists had blundered badly. I'm not sure whether it was because it had been a moonless night or because the two terrorists, Khudiram Bose and Prafulla Chaki, were simply incompetent. But their assigned task—to blow up the transferred Presidency Magistrate D.H. Kingsford—went all wrong. The bomb didn't take out Kingsford. Instead it killed the wife and daughter of a pleader at the Muzaffarpur Bar who had nothing to do with the magistrate.

Between the shooting of the missionary Hickenbotham in 1908 and the killing of Shamsul Alam in 1910, the terrorists had killed six Bengalis. We were led to believe that during the same time, there had also been attempts on four Europeans, but all had ended in failure. Naturally, one felt that there were very incompetent, frustrated and armed people roaming about town. Anyone could be the next victim. That everyone wasn't the terrorists' target didn't comfort anyone. Nevertheless, as I said, life, that banal sideshow we all inadvertently buy tickets for, went on.

With the arrest of the ringleaders of the Muzaffarpur incident, and the hanging of Khudiram, the city was waiting to completely recover its easy, languid ways. But there were still assassinations and robberies—and, by default, Bengalis were ending up dead, maimed or extremely ruffled. I was to hear the funniest bit of news about terrorist bungling from our headmaster Jatin-master during the last month of my very-soon-to-be aborted school life.

Jatin-master had suddenly responded to the 'call for

independence and self-rule'. Looking back, there's nothing surprising in that. He was young, and he was a failure. Why else would he, supposed brilliant scholar from Sanskrit College, end up teaching snotty children of government employees, company clerks and general upstarts? His overnight transition from shirt, coat, trousers and Nesfield English to panjabi, dhuti and rousing Bengali couldn't be explained at first. But when he told us about Lieutenant-Governor Andrew Fraser and his brushes with the terrorists, we vaguely got the idea that he wanted to let all of us know—in as subtle a manner possible for a headmaster, of course—that he was a nationalist.

Fraser, thought to be one of the chief architects of the partition, had always been a prime target for assassination. Four attempts had been made on his life. In the first three instances, bombs were hurled at the train on which he was supposed to be travelling. In the first and the third attempts, the bombs didn't go off. On the second occasion, when the train was travelling through Narayanganj, the explosion shattered the rail track along with the engine. Fraser, however, was left completely unhurt. It was in the fourth attempt that Fraser came closest to meeting his maker. At a conference being held at the YMCA hall, a gangly teenager with a gun missed his mark despite shooting from point blank range. As he would explain in court later, the revolver trigger had 'got stuck'! Jatin-master told us this story with not a hint of humour or irony. He always was a bit of a fool.

So, as I've said, the blundering, overheated anti-partitionists were quietening down by 1911. But their tribe didn't entirely disappear. As a war raged in faraway Europe, a new crop of terrorists began to emerge from the woodwork. From 1916 onwards, there were fresh rumours flying off the walls and bouncing along footpaths and gutters: criminals were once again spreading terror, all in the name of 'Independence'. Life got a little complicated again, so that even a trip to the market to buy vegetables and meat or attending a travelling jatra would have a shrapnel edge to it. That year, three Bengali zamindar families were forced to ask for police protection after they received threats for conducting business with the British Crown. By 1917, it was wise for a Bengali to avoid Chowringhee, Esplanade, Ballygunj and other European areas at night. Though it wasn't always safe to stick to their own side of town either. And in any case, you couldn't sit inside your house and office all the time. But there was definite evidence of a certain fear. The Victoria Memorial, its grounds opened to the public with some fanfare six years before, was now visited by Europeans only. The handful of non-Europeans seen walking about its lawns during the day would vanish before dusk set in.

This time round, it wasn't the old 'anarchists' of the Anushilan Samiti or the Maniktala Secret Society or the Jugantar Party that were creating a ruckus. It was the turn of unnamed groups to conduct 'action'. The shadowy members of these shadowier organizations had decided to take Direct Action against people who traded in European goods and services. A few outfits went right ahead and announced that they would attack anything and anybody involved in the 'direct or indirect propagation of European civilization'. But unlike with the old boys with their toys, this time there was no hormonally charged wake-up call, just a blowpipe shower of poisoned darts.

The city was becoming home to an increasing number of gangs and private armies. And if one looked through all the noise and smoke of 'Bande Mataram' and the country-as-Goddess nonsense, they were just armies of hooligans going about their jobs the way bioscopewalas and moneylenders and doctors went about theirs.

Around this time, one began to see the figure that is the English 'eight' and also the Bengali 'four' scrawled in various places all across town, most prominently and scandalously on the corner wall of Dalhousie Square. The authorities erased the giant chalk marks twice, but they cropped up for a third time. After that, the '8's just flourished like weed throughout the city. Only the white marble of Victoria Memorial managed to protect itself from the onslaught thanks to guards put on triple shift.

The Bengali papers remained strangely quiet about the whole thing. But the *Amrita Bazar Patrika* ran a small report in one of its inside pages about a dance hall in Entally being gutted by arsonists. It was run by a Bengali lady and the clientele were Bengalis *and* Europeans (probably Anglos). After initially suspecting that the fire had been caused by a faulty electric line, the authorities realized that it was arson when a police sepoy spotted an '8' scratched on a soot-covered wall. It took a few weeks for the authorities to understand that the mark was a gang signature. The words 'Char Murti'—Gang of Four—had finally been found alongside an '8' written many times over on a showcard outside the Palladium. How someone had managed to scrawl the sign on a poster that lay behind a standard gauze net that could be opened only by the theatre's management eluded everyone, including the Palladium's nervous management.

—

It was with all this murky and phantom-like information that I looked at Shombhu-mama's shirt that bore the mark '8'.

'Get it off, Abani! Get it off. Let's get home,' Shombhu said to me, sounding just a little agitated.

I slapped him on the back, hoping that the mark would come off in powder puffs. But it stayed like a burn mark. It didn't help that Shombhu had already started moving at a furious pace towards the streetlight opposite the garbage pile. The '8', tilted—as if trying to roll over and become the mark of infinity—by the movement of Shombhu's shirt folds, became even more visible.

'Where do you think you got the mark?' I asked, running after him and looking around to see where the men with the halos were. The paan shop was still and quiet, with only the paanwala peering into the rack directly behind him. The stationery shop next to it had its shutters down. The makeshift three-brick temple under the peepul tree across the pavement had the usual bunch having their post-supper smoke and pointless chat. The clinic-cum-residence of Dr Shibnath Ghoshal, MBBS (Edin.), House Surgeon, Medical College, with the wooden blinds on its doors that opened and closed at different hours of the day in snappy, noisy blinks, dozed in the night shadow of the peepul tree.

'It must have been in the tram. I don't know,' Shombhu fumed.

As he stopped under the light, positioning himself to take his shirt off, I saw a movement from the corner of my eye. There were figures at the mouth of our lane. I wish Shombhu-mama hadn't stopped. I saw three dogs sniffing and scrounging the garbage pile that was a permanent landmark of our lane, and the toothless widow who also scrounged the same pile but was now sleeping some distance away, on the pavement. And it was clear to me that it wasn't any one of them who had triggered the sudden shift in light and shade near the mouth of the lane.

'Don't make a sound. Don't move a muscle.'

The voice was calm, and collected because of its calmness. The face was covered with a handkerchief but the light bouncing off his hair left me with no doubt as to who he was. It was the boy from the Dilkhusha, the one who had been staring at me. Another figure came up from behind and joined him.

'You're Shombhu Lahiri of Alochhaya.' It could have been a question but it wasn't.

'Yes, but ... who ... what do you want?'

'Quiet now. I can blow your brains out and just walk away. So listen carefully. And who might this be with you? The famous Abani Chatterjee, I see.'

'He's my nephew.'

'And so our friend of the uncles is a mama himself.'

The second man gave out a small grunt. I now noticed that his face, too, was covered by a handkerchief, but one that was less spotless than his companion's.

'I don't understand ...' Shombhu-mama had started to whimper, his shirt still in that indeterminate state between tucked in and taken off.

'You, Lahiri-babu, are an informer. And you have been an informer since you were at the Carlton, then at the Elphinstone and now at Alochhaya. I can understand the English. But you're the worst kind—a traitor to your own kind.'

'Nooo! You've got it all wrong. I'm just a cameraman. I work for Lalji Hemraj at Alochhaya and I don't know any Englishmen, you fools!'

'Ah, but perhaps you know an English*woman*, a mem, eh? Perhaps the name Faith Cooper rings a bell?'

'I never knew her! She was at the Carlton where I was then working.'

'And we know that you had planned a meeting with Charles Urban. Are you now going to say that you've never heard of Charles Urban, Mr Innocent Bioscope Babu?'

While Shombhu-mama frantically tried to explain that there had been a huge misunderstanding, I noted that the breath of the other man, the one without the gun, was incredibly bad. There must have been a rotting tooth or two lying somewhere inside his mouth. Perhaps he had bad gums.

'Shuren, I've seen him with that Madan chap at the Elphinstone.'

'Shut up! Shut . . . up! Haven't I told you not to call me by my name while we're working . . . TAPAN?'

Tapan breathed out from under the piece of cloth covering his face, making the handkerchief flutter and reveal a chin as shiny as his hair. So they were members of the Char Murti.

'Look, I'm Bengali. He's Bengal . . .' Shombhu-mama flubbered on.

'Yes, Shombhu-babu, you *are* Bengali. Which makes it doubly sad, doesn't it? Which is why it's also fortunate for you that you didn't actually get to meet Mr Urban.'

'But . . . but he's American. I was supposed to meet him about the Kinemacolor . . .'

'Would you call Charlie Chaplin American?'

'He lives in America, works there too . . .'

'No, no Shombhu-babu. That doesn't make him American. Does the British Minister of Munitions become an American just because his mother is American? No, Lahiri babu, Churchill is English. I guess you'll say that the Anglo actress isn't English either, eh? Now what's her name, Tapan?'

'Face Cooper,' grunted Rotten Breath.

'It's Faith Cooper. And then there are your old friends from the Carlton and Elphinstone. When was the last time a Bengali found himself working at the Carlton or working for a Bombay stooge of the English? I'm afraid we'll have to make an example of you, Lahiri-babu. But we're not impractical. You will leave the bioscope business immediately. If you're still at Alochhaya next week, Lahiri-babu, we will be disappointed. Won't we, Tapan?'

'Shuren, there's somebody coming,' Bad Breath said suddenly.

In the streetlight I could make out two figures coming our way. Shuren quickly tucked his gun away inside his shirt.

'Don't be too smart. I won't hesitate to shoot,' he added briskly.

But if anyone seemed to be acting too smart, it was Tapan. He seemed to have suddenly developed some sort of breathing problem and had started wheezing furiously. He bent over once and mumbled out something to his partner that none of us could make any sense of. Shuren pulled the handkerchiefs off both their faces and, as Tapan painfully unburdened his lungs, we all stood there, waiting for the passers-by to pass us by, which they didn't.

'Oh, look who's here! Abani, coming from the studio, eh?' It was Bikash. 'Not in your fancy motor? Shombhu-mama, hope things are fine? Rona and I are just returning from an evening of divine music. Heard of Manikarnika Tambey? She sings kheyal. Oof, terrific!'

Ever since Rona had settled down into a new, improved life of domesticity, the two brothers had been left to themselves to do what they did best—go to Bagmari and while away their evenings listening to music at a friend's.

Shombhu suddenly regained his composure. 'Arre, Bikash,

Rona, haven't seen you two for a while. Returning from the Palits, I see. So you're into kheyals these days. You don't care for our local singers any more?'

'Oh, only last week we heard this young havaldar from Karachi, Nazrul Islam. Bengali chap, actually, from Bardhaman. Used to be part of a leto group before he joined the army. You should have heard him, Abani, this kid is better than . . .'

'Nazrul Islam? Boy with glasses? Funny hair? Didn't we meet him at Nibaran-da's?' It was Dragon Breath Tapan.

His partner just stared at him, waiting for him to turn to ashes.

'We met this chap at Nibaranchandra Ghatak's place the other day where this Islam fellow had also gone for training,' Tapan informed all of us.

'You mean Nibaranchandra Ghatak the seditionist?' Rona asked looking straight at the still-wheezing man.

'He's no seditionist, mister. He's a revolutionary, isn't he, Shuren?'

'Let us go now, Tapan,' Shuren chewed the words out, staring fixedly at his friend. 'We'll see you again, Lahiri-babu. Sleep well. And all the best for your new job.'

'Sleep well,' repeated Tapan as he followed Shuren into the night.

Bikash, Rona, Shombhu-mama and I turned to walk towards the lane that ultimately led to the safe confines of the Chatterjee–Moitra household. Before we entered our respective quarters, Bikash asked my uncle about his new venture to which Shombhu concocted some lie or the other. Rona pointed out that there was a mark on Shombhu-mama's shirt. My uncle took off his shirt as he walked up the narrow wooden stairs to his room.

Not a week had passed since this night when Shombhu-mama announced that he was leaving for Bombay. This was a pity, since some twenty-five years later I discovered that Shuren and his cousin Tapan were not members of any seditious gang but lumpen elements hired by Star Theatre to scare off bioscopewalas who were affecting the theatre business badly. My uncle never told me what offer he had got, but he did say something about a man by the name of Dhundiraj Govind Phalke offering him a position in the newly formed Hindustan Cinema Films Co. in Bombay. Shombhu mentioned in passing that Phalke was apparently the first Indian to make a feature, having made *Raja Harishchandra* some four years before Madan's *Satyavadi Raja Harishchandra* and Horen Ray's *Prahlad Parameshwar*.

Initially, he would send letters once every two months describing the 'total revolution in bioscopes and bioscope audiences that is taking place here at the Hindustan Cinema Films Co.'. In one letter he wrote five pages of scribble and scrawl about the new Indian Cinematograph Act with such passion that I seriously believed the pressures of being surrounded by non-Bengalis in Bombay had finally got to him.

The letters stopped in another six months. No one heard from or of him again, till years later, when someone brought news about a certain Shombhunath Lahiri, by then 'late', who had been legendary in Bombay for complaining about how cameramen, all apparently Chitpavan Brahmans, would change the aperture setting ring from its correct position after every shot and refuse to let him touch the filter lens. In other words, he didn't achieve fame, didn't become a bioscope legend—something that I did, in the next few glorious years of my life.

## geometry of taste

Ever since Lalji Hemraj Haridas appeared on the scene, it had become apparent that this was a man who knew how to make bioscopes work. From the day he took over the Alochhaya Bioscope Company—the 'Theatre' in the name was dropped swiftly—not only did many more people start entering the theatre to watch fifteen to forty-five minutes of sheer motion pictures, but the quality of the fare, too, drastically improved.

But it was only in late 1918 that Lalji displayed his true genius. This man, who had just a few years ago struck us as being a coarse, jewellery-obsessed Marwari, called a few of us into his office—the same room in which Mahesh Bhowmick had once counted notes and coins—and showed us a diagram.

'This, my friends, will be our business strategy, our philosophy for bioscope-making and bioscope-showing from now on.' And he unrolled the rolled-up paper, and this is what we saw:

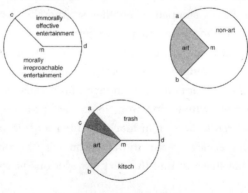

Geometry of Taste

In that room, now brighter because of the new electric light as well as a mammoth gold-plated statue of a reclining Ganesh, we all looked at the 'Geometry of Taste'. I bent my head to get a better view and waited for the lecture. Lalji beamed and slid forward in his chair, ready to explain.

'As you can see, there is an overlap of the kind of motion pictures that can be considered artful and non-artful and motion pictures that affect audiences morally and immorally. I am a family man, gentlemen, and I want us to make bioscopes that I can show my children and family. If a man goes alone to watch a bioscope, that's one ticket. If a man is comfortable enough going to a bioscope with his family, that's at least five tickets sold at the counter. But at the same time,' he said as he granted us a heavy smile that seemed to drag his jowls down, 'I want people, all kinds of people—the degenerate, the loafer class included—to come and watch our bioscopes. And people don't want to be just instructed or lectured to any more. Those days of audiences coming saucer-eyed to see photographs moving are over.'

That was true. The theatres that still insisted on showing some of those imported 'Adventures', 'Wonders of the World' and 'Brave Explorations' were losing money. Just pointing the camera at strange, unknown places and people no longer did the trick. As for the old hit shorts, such as Hiralal Sen's *Anti-Partition Demonstrations and Swadeshi Movement at the Town Hall on the 22nd September 1905*, which were still being shown in some halls trying to cash in on the Swadeshi fever, people were simply finding documentary pictures dreary. After all, how much can you get excited, some thirteen years after the event and more than a decade after a camera had stopped pointing at horses wagging their tails in a line, or dullards opening and twitching their mouths in front of a large congregation? Where was the action? Where was the story? As Horen Ray had once said, 'What will the orchestra play along with that?'

'Straight morally uplifting stories are nice. But they leave the crowds fidgeting and forgetting what they saw the moment they stand up to move towards the theatre exit. We need bioscopes that aren't part of their everyday, ordinary, bone-crushingly dreary lives, things that are impossible for real lives to experience. Partho-babu, what is the scene you remember the most in *The Sixth Pandav*?'

Partho Basak had joined Alochhaya some years earlier as art director and, although he was a tame fellow who kept to himself and his pile of books on theatre set production that he had brought back with him from Germany, over the years he had become a key player of the Alochhaya Bioscope Co.

'Well, Lalji . . . the scene in which Karna's chariot wheel is stuck in the mud and he looks at, er, Arjun approaching . . .'

'Rubbish, Partho-babu! You and your European notions of crooked angles and headache-inducing backgrounds! We all remember the scene in which Draupadi is being disrobed by the Kauravs. *You* know that, *I* know that. And it's safe. No authority will have a problem with it. And no audience will get scandalized by Tara Bibi being peeled and standing as a white blur in front of them. And you know why? I'll tell you why. Because that scene *is* already in the country's most popular story. And it's so popular that a child is regularly retold the bit without anyone breaking into rashes. It's that disrobing bit that thousands will remember. And it's not like the stage where no matter how realistic the actors are, no matter how realistic the sets are, the audience will be aware that it's not the real thing. Gentlemen, the beauty of the bioscope is that it seems real. It can actually be *more* real than the real thing!'

Lalji went on to unveil a startlingly simple plan. Carrying out this plan would make the public take to Alochhaya bioscopes the way a sinner takes to penitence. We would produce bioscopes, he explained, keeping the thin blue wedge in the 'Geometry of Taste' diagram—the slice that is 'amc' in that third circle—as our area of operation. In other words, Alochhaya bioscopes would be immorally effective entertainment that was artful at the same time.

'I have no problem with that. But what about the family crowd? You just mentioned that you want respectable people to bring their families to bioscopes too,' said Shombhu-mama, whose unscheduled departure from the city was still some months away.

'Ah, that's where we come to the second and more important aspect of bioscope-making.'

Lalji Hemraj, for all his cold business acumen, was working himself up. It was usually difficult—on account of his perpetual smile—to guess at his emotions by peering into his face. But there was an easy way in which to find out when he was truly excited about something, and that was when he began to speak Bengali, the language being drawn out of him as if by a pair of invisible horses tugging on opposite sides of individual words. The Marwari in him would then take over. As it did now:

'I've called it the Theory of Compensating Values. If virtue is always rewarded and sin is always punished, if good always triumphs over evil, and if the bad man is always punished miserably at the end of the bioscope, everyone's satisfied—the authorities, the family, the individuals. So we can show sin—and we'll have to. But all we need to ensure is that all sinners come to a bad end. Vice will be the main theme of most of our features, but in every one of them virtue will triumph. Draupadi will be shown being molested by Dushyashan but Dushyashan will then be shown to have come to a very sorry end. You know what I mean, don't you, Abani-babu?'

I nodded my head furiously. I understood what he was saying. I understood it perfectly because I knew what he was saying even before he had said it. I hadn't the words for it only because the bioscope was—I don't hesitate to say this—in my bones.

Lalji leaned to a side as if he was going to break wind but, instead, picked up a sheaf of papers from behind the table.

'Look at this.' And he read out in his limping English from an American newspaper that didn't look too dated with creases.

'Here's what the *Daily Bugle* of Chicago has written about a hit that's packing picture palaces across America. It's called *The Inside of the White Slave Traffic*. Let me just read out a line. He's the president of the American Sociological Fund, Frederick H. Robinson,' saying which Lalji peered into the paper and read as steadily as his paan-munching mouth would allow formal English to be spoken in.

'"We are glad to give *The Inside of the White Slave Traffic* our unqualified endorsement." And wait, there's another quote from the *Medical Review of Reviews*: "I consider this film to be a truthful presentation of a particularly vicious phase of life—a correct portrayal of those horrible occurrences which cannot but arouse a *tremendous public sentiment*."' Lalji looked up from the paper, shone out a smile that would have exposed any film in the darkest of rooms, and victoriously repeated the words 'tremendous public sentiment', thereby dousing them with a special, tingling significance.

This done, he banged on the bell on his table. He wanted some water. It was obvious that he knew that he was on to something novel and yet something that was also the most obvious thing in the world. But even at that point not one of us was clear about how we would put his excellent theory into practice. Would the public accept moral depravation if it was displayed on a bioscope screen? Would any one of *us* be comfortable doing the basic necessary job required in such a scheme of things even in the manipulative world of the bioscope?

I looked at the posters on the wall behind Lalji. There was *Prahlad Parameshwar* in which I was grasping Durga inside what looked like either a pyre or a thicket. It was clearly a bad sketch. There was another poster of the very successful *Anandamath* with a slightly more acceptable drawing of a band of sanyasis brandishing swords and the letters making up the title melting into dripping blood.

Lalji continued, 'Dr Pankhurst says, "Every woman should see this film exposing white slavery and its attendant horrors." And here's the line on the showcard: "This is a film with a moral; a film with a lesson; a film with a thrill." That's what I call brilliant! That, friends, is what Alochhaya needs.'

In other words, Lalji wanted bioscopes that would make audiences come into picture palaces in hordes, without feeling that there were something awry about them—just as the hordes on the other side of the world were crowding into darkened halls to see *The Inside of the White Slave Traffic,* a feature about white prostitutes in America. Real success lay in making motion pictures within that thin blue sliver that was the triumph of artistic degeneration—a repertoire that would always be accompanied by the message that sins were worthy of contempt and would always, without fail, lead to an end that was worse than death.

Bioscope-watching would not become going out for a night

at Bowbazar, or an evening of music with baijees, or cavorting with the crude entertainment of the English plays with their Anglo actresses. This was bioscope that would make people aware that the world was a wicked place and the only way to protect oneself from the wickedness was to be aware of it. And what could be a safer place to be aware of sin without the fear of committing it than the comfort of a bioscope theatre?

Lalji Hemraj was a genius.

—

Lalji's lecture made me more of a bioscope creature than any other single event that I can think of. I understood the true potential of the bioscope—its potential for spectacle, for commerce, for seduction, for honest, nuanced trickery. It felt good to be part of such intelligent mischief, and I became keenly aware of my actions as an actor. Before the beginning of any shooting, my body and I would spend a few weeks not getting along with each other. It wasn't the outcome of some crafty, clever, thought-out process, like deciding which shirt to wear for maximum impact in what kind of light conditions, or how to position one's mouth when talking and how when not talking, or indeed what words to speak. It was something more automatic, like buttoning a shirt, or swearing silently when the pretty girl in the tram is lost behind a thicket of bodies.

There is no inherent harm if, for an elongated moment, one actually starts thinking about the process of buttoning one's shirt or why one is disappointed not to be in the visible presence of beauty. But buttoning the shirt and thrilling to the sight of a pleasing form do become difficult and false. In the case of the shirt, the two opposite actions of buttoning and thinking about buttoning leave one giddy. There are some things in the world that one must pay attention to and others that shouldn't be attended to at all. Pushing each button into each slit of a shirt front, staring at a stare-worthy woman, acting that one is somebody else can only succeed if one stops thinking about the verbs attached to all three of them.

It was while I was refirming my craft in this manner, which I can now admit was more than a little self-conscious, that we heard of a version of the Black Hole of Calcutta that seemed to us to be good bioscope material. It didn't take us more than a couple of weeks to track down and get in touch with Bholanath Chandra, a landlord living in a two-room apartment in Shyambazar. The very undistinguished-looking man, scrawny as a crow's beak and as dark, dry and noisy as the bird, had unofficially proved a few decades ago that the old story about the Black Hole of Calcutta was bunkum, stating that a floor area of 267 square feet could not possibly stash 146 European, overwhelmingly male, adults within its confines.

His reasons for proving that the Black Hole story about native barbarism against European bravery was all nonsense arose not out of any nationalistic motive, but out of a more practical concern. One of his tenants had filed a case against him in the court that the rent he was dishing out entitled him to an adjoining room in addition to the terribly cramped one-room place he shared with five other members of his family. Bholanath kept the other room locked with a heavy padlock, hoping to rent it out to a bachelor in the very near future. It was his refusal to let the room be occupied by his scheming tenant that had led the latter to petition the court. The tenant had remarked in his notified complaint that Bholanath Chandra had refused his perfectly legitimate request because he was planning to make his whole family perish in that crowded, claustrophobic room the same way 'the Nawab had killed 123 Englishmen by suffocating and crushing them to death in a Fort William guard house in 1756'.

So in his bid to prove that the rent being charged was not the cut-throat amount that his disgruntled tenant was making it out to be—and that even if he wanted the tenant to clear out of the one-room place in his house on Paddopukur Road, he would surely seek bhadralok ways—Bholanath became determined to prove *not* that his tenant's floor area was much larger (and therefore worth every anna-paisa of the rent) than the complainant insisted it was, but to prove beyond any reasonable doubt that the 'Fort William prison cell comparison' had been 'wrongly made'. He would prove that the 1756 Black Hole incident was a piece of fiction.

Bholanath fenced an area of 18 feet by 15 feet with hard bamboo and crammed as many of his employees as possible— all Bengalis—into the carefully measured space. He chose a December day for the demonstration as he 'obviously didn't want anyone to collapse from heatstroke or fatigue'. The number that could fit into this area was found to be a gnarled, gnashed, limbs-atwist, heads-akimbo 44.

'And everyone knows that a Bengali's body occupies much less space than any European's,' he famously told the court after he had conducted his experiment twice, the second time in the presence of two court officials. As the never-blinking Crown's justice would have it, the tenant did win the case against Bholanath, thereby managing to permanently occupy not only the small room in which he and five other members of his family lived, but also two other rooms next to it, one of them being the padlocked room in which Bholanath had been hoping to install a tenant.

But in the process of his futile experiment, Bholanath had become a local legend. Even much later, when the nationalist papers like *Jugantar* published long, thunderous essays on the lies spread by the English in India, there would be a paragraph on the so-called 'Black Hole of Calcutta' and how Sri Bholanath Chandra had 'scientifically and effectively proved that it was yet another fabrication fuelled by London's unholy desire to feed its own people on lies and keep its tight leash on the Indian imagination'. Even an English paper in Manchester was supposed to have carried the name of 'Bolanauth Chunder' for exposing 'imperialist attempts to create a mountain out of a non-molehill'.

And it was remembering Bholanath Chandra that my fellow Alochhaya actor Dinesh Boral suggested a feature on the Black Hole, and also that the studio try and get Bholanath's support in promoting the bioscope. It was decided that a few laudatory words printed on the posters and the publicity pictures before and during the release of the bioscope, *The Black Hole of Calcutta, or Survival of the Fittest*, would do the trick for the nationalist bioscope viewer.

It had been made clear that Alochhaya couldn't afford to run foul of the authorities. To show that the Black Hole story—of 146 European prisoners being crammed into a cell measuring 18 feet by 14 feet 10 inches by Shiraj-ud-Daula's men, and only 23 coming out alive the next morning—was an exaggeration would be inviting official alarm. After all, this was still February 1919, Rowlatt lurking round the corner. Any blatant challenge, through a bioscope story or otherwise, could lead to the confiscation of the print of the motion picture, the arrest of at least Lalji Hemraj and even the closure of the Alochhaya Bioscope Co. and the Alochhaya theatre. And yet, countering London's view of history would be to ride the nationalist wave, thereby drawing in the crowds like ants to a drop of spilt malpua syrup. The answer lay in portraying the sufferings of the prisoners in bioscopic detail—but, at the same time, making the survivors the heroes of the feature.

That I was going to play my first flawed character—anti-hero if you will, villain if you won't—in *The Black Hole of Calcutta* excited me. My portrayal of Karna in *The Sixth Pandav* didn't count. He was an established borderline case, a character who comes from the alluring, rare category where goodness and badness hover over a precipice, squabbling through small body movements for sheer survival. The character of John Zepheniah Holwell was blacker and without the spring of stock sympathy that epic villains like Ravana had.

As the production day approached, I was already draining myself out so as to make space for Holwell to enter. In fact, by the time we met for our pre-production meeting, I didn't have to work at being him at all. Abani Chatterjee was oozing out, like air from a tiny tyre puncture that makes no sound. This notion of losing myself occurred from time to time even when there was no immediate acting schedule in store.

Among all these various forms and templates of humanity, I kept slipping out of me like a gas. The swift leak would continue until I told myself as lucidly as a courtroom sentence: 'I simply inhabit this body. I am a shape-shifting man who can't interact with this world on the basis of a fixed, agreed-upon-and-signed identity. But because of this body, I do not pass through the world like a hot knife does through butter. Instead, I clank through it and hear solid clank into solid even if the solids I speak of are words and actions, the two things that can be faked with practice.'

The script of *The Black Hole of Calcutta* had been hurriedly based on two separate pieces of writing, one riding on the creaky shoulders of the other. There was, of course, John Zepheniah Holwell's own account of the Black Hole as described in his 'A Genuine Narrative of the Deplorable Deaths of the English Gentlemen and others who were suffocated in the Black Hole'. This article published in the *Annual Register*, 1758 had never been seen by the two people who were given charge of coming up with the basic script, Horen Ray and myself (with additional inputs from Dinesh Boral, who was playing the role of Nawab Shiraj-ud-Daula, and from Lalji Hemraj himself). What we had carefully read was a longish entry on the Black Hole in an English encyclopedia, which heavily quoted passages from Holwell's article, and, most importantly of all, a thoroughly researched article by J.H. Little entitled 'The Black Hole: The Question of Blackwell's Veracity'.

In Little's opinion, Holwell was clearly an unreliable witness to the whole incident. The survivor of the Black Hole had, according to the scholar, creatively tampered with the truth in an attempt to pass himself off as a hero. Considering that Holwell went on to become acting Governor of Bengal, the ploy seemed to have paid off quite handsomely. Little's article had come out only four years before, and India-watchers in London had become agitated—a rather complex word that covers the various sub-feelings of being irritated, surprised and aghast to the point of disbelief—over this bit of revisionism. In India, most people hadn't even heard about the radical article, let alone the small ruckus that it caused in England.

A letter was sent to Little and permission was sought to make a fictitious account of the contentious event that occurred on June 20, 1756. A line from him, Lalji figured, would make the bioscope even more authentic. There was just the small matter of getting him to not mind the fact that in our fictionalized depiction of the historical event we would actually show 146 whited-up, European-seeming bodies crammed in a very small closed space—and the minor but necessary inclusion of a lady in the climactic scene. J.H. Little was a Liberal. So perhaps he would require some sort of incentive to lend his trust and support.

Shooting began with the scene in which Shiraj-ud-Daula gets the news that both the English and the French have started to build armed fortifications in a territory that he, as Nawab of Bengal, was given to rule after the death of his predecessor, Alivardi Khan. Even as the camera—with Shombhu-mama still turning the camera handle—was sucking the story in, telegraphic messages were stuttering between London and this city. Little, as we had feared, was adamant that his premise not be overturned even in a bioscope dramatization, which Lalji tried to explain was just an imaginative depiction of the Black Hole incident and *not* a historical documentation or recreation.

Eight days went by deciding on what constitutes a bioscope recreation and a bioscope dramatization. The uneven, twirling and inebriated type of telegrams were all kept inside a green file marked 'Little Black Hole' in Lalji's office. After a longish meeting that also involved what must have been an expensive overseas telephone call, and through which nerves were getting frayed sooner than they could be repaired, it was agreed that at no point in the motion picture should there be any mention of a fixed number of Europeans in the blighted room. (The title that would have read '145 shahebs and 1 mem all crammed inside on a blisteringly hot night!' was junked.)

But when Little finally got to know (admittedly, a little late in the day) that we also had an Englishwoman as prisoner inside *our* Black Hole, he sent a terse telegraph: 'NO STOP NEVER STOP WONT HAVE ANYTHING TO DO WITH BIOSCOP STOP'.

At that point even Lalji, ever composed and controlled, thought that he had made a blunder by getting in touch with Little in the first place. This would now inevitably lead to a ruckus even before the bioscope was finished. Just when he was about to politely ensure that the Englishman's involvement in the feature was cancelled, a message from London came three days after the explosive telegram from Little. This hinted, as much as a telegram can hint at things, that the scholar was willing to come to a compromise.

'HEARD OUT BIOSCOP SOURCES HERE STOP WILLING TO MAKE MINOR RPT MINOR CHANGES TO SCRIPT'

It took less than a week to renegotiate the 'terms of consultancy and quasi-historical approval'. Little ended up with £30 more in his kitty for willing to have his name and quote in the publicity material of *The Black Hole of Calcutta, or Survival of the Fittest*. That was, incidentally, a 15 per cent increase on his original fee.

It was a good thing that Little agreed because with his blessings and endorsement *The Black Hole of Calcutta* became the talk of the town, it drew crowds from all over the city and beyond like no other performance—theatre or bioscope—had ever drawn before, or indeed would for some years. Bholanath Chandra's approving words in the reviews and on the flyers and posters helped, of course, by getting the bhadralok crowd interested. But, only the Englishman J.H. Little—an English scholar who, naturally, knew history in the way that only English scholars do—would draw them to *The Black Hole* like beggars to a zamindar's wedding. However, it was also clear to us that what really made everyone flock to the Alochhaya theatre, and to all the other bioscope theatres across the country which had bought prints of the feature, was something else altogether: the presence of one mem among 145 men in the dungeon.

Dinesh Boral would later write accurately in his autobiography, *My Silent Years*: 'Shooting was hell. There was no way anyone could speak in the heat. Even though the routine had always been to mouth something that one felt was apt for the scene despite it being a silent film, it was just too much of an effort. Horen was the only one anyone could hear speaking out loudly, commanding us, sometimes individually, but mostly as living pieces of furniture, brandishing his tapered megaphone at anyone who needed instructions. And everyone on the field of Tala—which pretended to be the vast expanse of Laldighi—did need instructions galore.

'So in the heat, we faced the camera—one camera changing positions constantly, with the sweat-drenched Ashok Ray behind it—and acted, pretending to shout, scream, moan and speak without uttering a word. It's hard to decide which of the two made the heat really unbearable—the sunlight beating down on us like non-stop yellow sheet lightning with no gaps in between or the huge mirrors that magnified this light and directed it on to our bodies already toasting inside the costumes. The make-up came off too soon and I think you could see it in *The Black Hole*'s tremendous battle sequence.'

Initially, it had been decided that we would hire a large contingent of the 125 extras who were required to play the role of the European soldiers from the Anglo-Indian community. But just before word was about to be sent out through the media of *The Statesman* and a few handouts at places like the Carlton, there was a change of plan. Fair and sturdy Bengalis were found and the make-up artists applied just the right amount of foundation, talcum and finely grained lacto calamine (for the palish pink hue) for them to look like shahebs—which they did only remotely even in black and white. (The silly trick of applying just foundation and topping their heads with blond wigs would not do if standards were to be set.) More than a few of them looked rather odd, like photographic negatives walking about.

It was the prison scene, of course, that the crowds actually paid good money to come and see. We knew even while making the long scene that this was going to be the point on which the whole bioscope would hinge. Out of the mammoth, till then unheard-of one and a half hours of the motion picture, a whole forty minutes were devoted to this scene. It started with the European prisoners being hoarded into the black, cobbly-walled cell. It ended with the dramatic survival of a few. But the real story within the story of *The Black Hole* as a whole and the prison scene in particular was undoubtedly the passionate—and illicit—love story between the two strangers, John Zepheniah Holwell and Mary Carey, one of the few women who had been left behind in the city when it was overrun by Nawab Shiraj-ud-Daula's forces.

Durga, who played Mary, was uncomfortable before the scene. She was to partially bare herself not only in front of the people around her on the sets but also before an unending stream of people whose character, identity and proclivity towards tastefulness she would never know. Sounding almost like a flesh-and-blood version of J.H. Little's exclamatory telegraphic messages, Durga had shown signs of acute nervousness by spluttering before the day of shooting approached.

'You know Alochhaya would not do anything that isn't artful,' I had told her one day when she was on the verge of chewing up her lower lip.

'You have no idea about the risks that I face, playing an Englishman who is considered a rogue by the whole country,' I went on. 'But you know why I'm risking it? I'm risking it, Durga, because this will be big. I just know it, and these are not Lalji's words. I just know it.'

I can never be sure whether it was my small pep talk or Lalji's clever ploy that made her give in: Lalji had been the source and at the forefront of rumours doing the rounds in Alochhaya about the studio seriously considering someone else— some Nadia from Bombay—for the coveted role of Mary Carey. But who should take the credit is inconsequential. Durga agreed. Which, you must admit, was brave of her. For not only would she have to reveal more of her body than any other woman in Indian bioscopes had ever done, she would have to do this pretending that she was an eighteenth-century *European* woman too busy fighting for her life to think about her modesty.

It was a very crowded space that Durga and I entered. She was wrapped in a loose bedcover underneath which she wore a white dress that she had practised peeling off several times alone in her room as well as a few times in the trusted company of another Alochhaya regular, Bimala. I was told that she had had two large gins before coming out of her room with make-up and costume. If the gin helped, it hadn't hidden her discomfiture totally.

The awkward, slightly ridiculous, fact that there were a large number of people who didn't have to do anything but writhe about in an extremely close space was eclipsed by the more overwhelming fact that I would be in intimate physical contact with Durga. We were to be so close, so intermingled in body and limb, that I felt unsure where the pretending would end, where the loss of control begin. A man with a powder puff gave me one final powder puff and a quick flurry of dabs of thickened water faking as sweat. The powder and the water miraculously refrained from mixing and as the mirror flitted away, I caught a dour-looking old-style Englishman scowling back at me with visible derision.

There are many things that a good actor can pretend at with great conviction. Love, hate, funniness, physical pain and being unloved—these being the basic five. (Relief, thankfully, was a theatre device, and if required to be recreated in a bioscope was effectively taken care of by a pair of wide eyes and a mopping of the forehead with a white handkerchief or clothes-end.) With talent and practice these five pretend-emotions could be conjured up to inhabit the face and the rest of the body like jewellery on women. But acting is not only about conjuring up emotions and gestures that wouldn't otherwise exist. It's also about directing the flow of existing feelings, like cupping running water and redirecting into the mouth for the purpose of drinking.

Inside the narrow set, illuminated by spotlights carefully placed to stretch individual shadows to their physical limits and make them sprawl on each other, I was expected to display physical discomfort. It didn't help at all that Durga looked beautiful. She just stood there, diffident and a little vulnerable, at the edge next to the camera, waiting for the shot to be shot.

Long shot of a room with one gate. The gate is a row of stripes through which one can see a slow but constant movement. The source of the faint light is inside the room but it can't be seen. The movement is a slow churning of pale matter made extra visible in the surrounding darkness. That the room has a high ceiling can be made out by the fact that the moving pale matter inside is a high heap that continues beyond the height of the barred entrance.

A medium shot of three guards sitting on a stone platform and nodding. There are three lances resting diagonally against the wall in the corner where they are seated, at the end of a long passage. This passage is lit up by a lamp placed in a niche midway between the ground and the ceiling.

One guard scratches himself in his sleep. All three have their shirts unbuttoned and their head clothes as little mounds beside them.

Close-up of the padlock hanging from the gate. The lock is big. Behind the barred gate, one notices a shuffling form. It is actually many forms. One can focus on a hand. That soon turns into a hairless chest. Which turns into a part of a face that could be a mouth. A mouth that could be a foot. A foot that becomes a chest. Which soon turns into a hand. And so on.

*Medium aerial shot inside the room. One looks down on a hillock of bodies. The figures in the middle are less active than the ones at the edges. But the movement is more brisk, less slow, now that one is inside the room. The walls are black and shiny. It could be slime. The mass of bodies is white and shining. It could also be mould. Faces can be seen. One face is contorted and appears to be just a head with no body attached to it. Another has its eyes rolled up with only the whites showing and its mouths open. The huddle and the heap do not look Asiatic at all.*

*Medium shot of a pair of small barred windows looking out into scratchy, hazy night.*

*Long shot of a tall window set high into the wall opposite the gate. The jumble of mass of bodies is moving between the window and the gate.*

*A few faces can be seen below the window. These faces are breathing slowly.*

*On the other side, next to the gate, a body comes into view. It presses out from the inside of the giant white dough, pressing itself on to the bars of the gate. It belongs to a large man. His white shirt is unbuttoned and is translucent with sweat. His thinning hair and drooping moustache are drenched and pasted to his skin as if he has been baptized and pulled out of the water only a moment ago.*

—

John Holwell had reached the mouth of the cell once before in the last eight hours. It seemed like hours, but it probably was minutes since he had last faced the bars and negotiated frantically in bad Hindustani with the guard who insisted on speaking to him in bad English. But since the transaction involved the procurement of drinking water, and neither of the two men on either side of the gate knew the right word for water in each other's language—John had said 'penni' when the guard had expected him to say 'wetter'—it took a full twenty minutes to get the message across.

'Paani, tell him to get paani,' croaked an emerging face from behind John Holwell. It was Tyler, one of the carpenters from Writers' Row. The guard shrugged on hearing the request, looked sideways, then, extracting a promise of a grand thousand rupees immediately after the firingi's release, disappeared and returned a full quarter hour later with a large thimbleful of water. By that time, John's coordinates in the room had changed. His back was now touching the area where the metal bars ended and the damp but hot stone wall began. He had, however, somehow managed to keep his eyes glued on the entrance. He called out when the guard with his thimble came into view.

'Here man, here. Paani, paani, please.'

Announcing the nature of the transaction about to be under way was a mistake. He should have used his reason and made that extra effort to show his face fully. Instead, he had shouted out to the guard. Not too many inside the cell were as ignorant of Hindustani as John was. What followed was a small mayhem in reaction to the word 'paani'.

The two small grilled windows next to each other near the ceiling on the other side of the room had no one looking in through them. But if someone had, he would have seen very little in the one stop short of pitch darkness below. Instead, he would have registered the slow moan—a slimy polyphony, really—change to open cries of desperation and some flickering animal sounds. And his eyes would have smarted with the fumes that emanate when a crowd of bodies cling to each other, without proper desire or volition, but without complaint or disgust either, crunching and sliding the flesh and bones, the hair and sweat.

With a great effort, John bent his body into a half crouch-half stretch position in order to take the thimble-thing between his fingers. His mouth was too far from the bars to accept the water straight from the guard. In the crowd, and with three separate instalments of contortions to mediate, his hands were as steady as those of a drunkard loading a rifle. Only a few drops of the precious fluid remained in the receptacle, most of the palmful amount having fallen on the nearby bodies.

Through the hours that followed, John slipped in and out of an overheated and constricting consciousness. At one point, he found himself next to a man who was propped up by his own body on one side and someone else's on the other. The man's fingers held a tricorn cap up to the level of his chest. In the inadequate light it looked as if the man's heart, bone and tissue had been scooped out of his chest, leaving a neat, quiet hole. But it was, John saw after a long spell of disorientation, only the man's blue hat, turned black in the darkness, against his spectral white shirt. John only realized that the man with the hat had either passed out or was dead when the figure dropped away from his vision like a set of old clothes the moment he moved and stopped supporting his weight.

'Only if General Drake hadn't been so, so very stupid,' John said to himself closing his eyes. He pressed his eyes until he started seeing pinpricks of swirling colour. Perhaps, being outraged at Governor Drake's action against that scoundrel Omichand would help him through this hell.

No one messes with one of the most powerful natives in Bengal. And Drake had done just that. Omichand was a fat ball of grease who would happily sell his mother if that meant making a profit. But he was the richest man in Calcutta. And that kind of wealth brings power that can be transmutated into security, more wealth and even a lease of life. It was this Omichand that Drake had decided in his very finite wisdom to throw in jail. In fact, if John—as magistrate—remembered correctly, Drake had thrown the man into this very cell! People of Omichand's stature do business by remembering, like elephants, the behaviour of the men they do business with. And Drake had thrown him in prison.

*This* prison.

That *fool*.

The pinpricks had dissolved into the darkness of his closed eyes. Opening them again, John hoped that the general had been cut to ribbons on the steps of the council building by the Nawab's men.

The last two days had not prepared anyone now languishing in the cell for all that finally happened. Not for the cowardly departure of Manningham and Frankland on the *Dodaldy*. Not for the swarm of indigo-wrapped heads breaching the fort. Not for the dark, billowing smoke that signalled the destruction of Black Town. And definitely not for this room packed with more than one hundred able-bodied Europeans swaying between life and death and gasping to get out of this unintended, suffocating embrace.

But what John at that moment was really unprepared for was the appearance of Mary Carey next to him, with one of her breasts and half her body pressed on to the bars in front.

John had been aware of Mary's existence ever since he was introduced to her by her husband, Peter, a shipmate who doubled as a transport manager for the company. Peter was married to his job and had consequently risen up the ranks as such men sometimes do. John had helped him just a bit, guided by a tucked-away feeling that this would allow himself to be presented to Peter's young wife in a good light. No one had really asked for any explanation why John Holwell, magistrate of Calcutta, would take a special interest in the career of a young ex-sailor from Winchester. Even if they had asked for such an explanation, perhaps fuelled by spirits stronger than bourbon (which, incidentally, had been boycotted since the war in Europe), he would not have told them that he took a special interest in Peter Carey because he took a special interest in Mary Carey.

The question of how Mary had found herself in the cell with him and more than a hundred other men was swept away from John's expanding mind when he saw Mary bending her neck down. When she rose back again, she had gathered one of John's shirt sleeves between her dark lips. With her left breast positioned between two bars of the locked gate, she pressed the cloth with her lips which started to sparkle—or so John imagined—with newly discovered moisture. It was only after she had done pressing with her lips that she bit into the sweat-drenched cloth with her teeth.

If Mary had behaved in any similar manner a few days ago, she would have probably earned a different reputation from the one that she had—the devoted wife of Peter Carey. Tongues would have wagged, fans would have fluttered extra briskly. But on that hellish night inside a room that the English had built, in which their own people now found themselves heaped upon each other like cabbage left to rot, no one said a word about Mary Carey sucking and biting out the sweat from John Zepheniah Holwell's left sleeve. They were too busy surviving or perishing in what Mary's saviour would soon go on to immortalize as the Black Hole of Calcutta.

## from the state of grace

Overnight, Durga and I were forever joined together in some never-decaying couplehood. Only a few months earlier, the public had made a similar connection between Jibananda and Shanti after *Anandamath*. But with *Black Hole*, Abani and Durga had become more than bioscoped sweethearts. Mary and John had given out the signal that there was more to amorous attraction than glances, glimpses, gestures or even passionate kisses. There were no distributors those days, but theatres lined up to buy prints of *Black Hole*—European, Bengali *and* Anglo theatres.

And then they started showing the picture across the country and beyond. The Europeans and the Anglos lapped up the account of the survival of John Zepheniah Holwell and Mary Carey. The rest cut straight through the chase and stared at the more elemental side of the story as depicted by the giant, visual, more-real-than-real activities of two bodies thrown together in a cauldron seething with humanity. This was Oriental reality cleverly played out in a story about Europeans. With *The Black Hole*, the bioscope had discovered senses beyond just the visual.

In all this, I attained a stature that can only be described as something born of a mix of worship and envy. Durga, on her part, found herself swimming in a sea of male adoration that cut across race and colour. This, I would later recognize in others as stardom. But in those glorious early days, there was no word for it, not here, not in Europe, not in America.

No one, least of all Lalji Hemraj, was in doubt about what had brought the vast crowds to pay for and watch *The Black Hole of Calcutta*. But the reviews, each reviewer trying to show how clever he was in discovering and savouring nuances in the bioscope that the others had missed, hailed it as a 'bold', 'unflinching', 'educative' spectacle that 'has made the bioscope take that unthinkable leap from a plaything to our age's true form of dramatic art'.

(It is true that unless you have actually seen *The Black Hole*—and I'm glad that you have—it can sound like a production that romanticizes the Europeans who were locked up in an English guardhouse by the Nawab's men. But if you want to, you can also see it as a nationalist bioscope. Though not, I must emphasize, a crude, one-dimensional patriotic flicker like Hiralal Sen's agit-prop shorts or the even more cloying nationalist bioscopes that were simply mythologicals in disguise. Our production was subtle, sophisticated—equivocal, if you must, but is that not a quality to admire in art?

For one must understand that my John Zepheniah Holwell, a man who had come across the seven seas as a surgeon's mate, was a native-hating lout with a groin of steel but a heart of gold. In our bioscope, while he has no qualms kicking one of his servants to near-death because the poor chap's caught staring at one of his master's lady guests, and in another scene he is shown forcing himself on a nautch girl, he also has, after all, a 'civilizationing' mission in mind. Like all the other Englishmen who braved the journey to our teeming tropical lands.)

As for our moments inside the Black Hole, the crowds that

came to see it cheered every moment of our torment and pleasure, in glorious black and white detail. However, the loudest cheers and heaviest torrents of coin-throwing were unleashed each time Mary Carey bucked and shook next to me in the simulated death-heat.

The air inside bioscope theatres showing *The Black Hole* across the land was found to be heavy with sweat, cigarette smoke and something intangible after each show. The doors leading in and out of the halls were kept open extra long in between shows for the next audience to walk into a tolerably comfortable theatre. In the safety of the bioscope one witnessed, for a rupee or less, an event that was not natural even in the scheme of motion pictures make-believe.

And if my memory serves me right, when Lalji Hemraj Haridas shook me proudly by my twenty-three-year-old shoulders in the middle of a small gathering to celebrate the runaway success of *The Black Hole of Calcutta, or Survival of the Fittest*, he invented a word that would outlive my ridiculously short glory days.

'You'll now be shining as bright as a star, Abani. You're a star,' he said smiling a gleaming caterpillar smile that must have been at least two feet wide and nine reels long.

—

It was pure coincidence that the year *The Black Hole* was released also saw a dramatic change in a large section of the population.

Till then, there had been only a few oddballs here and there who, finding nothing better to do, indulged in activities that they called 'nationalistic'. How going on and on about a figure wrapped in a sari that was supposed to represent the country in fetters could be helpful in *any* manner eluded the rest of us. These oddballs were mostly oily-haired students who suddenly found themselves charged with an energy that came from nowhere and settled inside them like sediment gunk. They changed their attire, spewed slogans and catchphrases (instead of the traditional banalities directed at female and effeminate passers-by) and made noises about changing the world. At the bottom of this pile was the bhadralok loafer criminal class, breeding young people who were more terrified of becoming middle-aged and then old than living out their lives under an English administration. Infiltrating into this pile of flotsam were the pure and simple thugs, thieves and criminals. For them, 'nationalism' was an opportunity for expanding their business and getting themselves a new sympathetic image. 'Movement' clearly suggests motion. But the 'Independence Movement' was a stagnant mosquito-breeding pool that suddenly formed when many gutters coalesced.

This was boom time for 'freedom fighters' who were criminals with ambition. As for the rest of us—indifferent enough not to be caught in any slipstream of loyalty or revolt—it didn't matter one bit who was in charge as long as the trams worked, the roads were cleaned, the oil bills didn't jump, the weekend food appeared on the table and the bioscopes ran from the first reel to the last.

All this changed a few months after *The Black Hole* came out in early December 1918. No one was allowed to be indifferent any more. Fence-sitting, a very different activity from being indifferent, also could result in fatal impalement. *The Black Hole*, I must reiterate, had nothing to do with this change.

It was slightly odd that the papers reported the upsetting incident that actually pushed things off the precipice more than a month and a half after it had taken place. (The biggest news in the papers around that time was not even about India—the killing of two dangerous communists, Karl Liebknecht and Rosa Luxemburg, in faraway Germany.) It was in the last week of May 1919 that we learnt that a large gathering of people had been fired upon in Amritsar on April 13. Children and women were among the dead. Why the authorities had decided to open fire on the crowd was not mentioned in any of the reports. I had even picked up the *Jugantar* for details. None were provided.

At the Carlton, even the Anglos had become less raucous after the massacre in Punjab. Amritsar may have been as far away from our city as Belgian Congo was, but the place got closer all of a sudden. Of course, I do not mean to suggest that the earth stopped spinning. Indeed, life went on and nothing ground to a halt. As summer approached, people still bathed next to tubewells and ruptured pipelines, building up the lather as if it could be the last time they would encounter water.

Carriages still trotted up and down Esplanade, the horses automatically trotting faster when they sensed an automobile nearby. Marriages proceeded as planned, functions were hosted with the usual banal pomp (potted plants on the dais still being mandatory), lectures were attended at universities and at the Asiatic Society with necessary gravitas.

People still drank, laughed aloud, cut vegetables (the vegetables making the barely audible hiss of dying that vegetables make when put to the blade). Experienced customers still haggled; irate mothers still slapped their children; couples still quietly copulated in the other room. But everyone did whatever they did with one difference. No one could quite put their finger on this difference simply because nobody noticed it. However, there it was, a change that comes with the knowledge that people not completely unlike oneself have been permanently removed in a cool, efficient manner.

June onwards, the crowds increased to a serious torrent. More picture palaces were showing *The Black Hole* and there were also special screenings in certain theatres across the country. A German bioscope company had bought prints and was running the film in three theatres in Berlin and Paris. Here at home, it was running to packed shows, the usual catcalls and suction sounds mimicking kisses during the climactic prison scene had been replaced by raucous shouts of 'son of a pig' and other more loosely constructed expressions of easy contempt and safe rage. An earlier scene showing the European forces being cut down by the Nawab's men were greeted with enthusiastic whistles and showers of coins directed at the screen.

'Didn't I tell you, eh? Everyone loves nationalism these days,' Lalji had chuckled as Ram Bahadur and others collected coins of various denominations from the front of the screen after each show.

I attended a few screenings alone and witnessed the transformation first hand. People who earlier seemed capable of finding happiness only through a good oil-massage were now shouting expletives at a giant white face that resembled mine on the screen. When Mary Carey was dragged into the prison and became the sole lissome element in a tumble of bodies, the crowd hooted with barely hidden hormonal happiness. There was something that had been set loose the year after *The Black Hole* made me a star.

The movie became the first feature in the country to have four shows throughout the day seven days a week. Another projectionist, five more men at the ticket counters and half a dozen additional hands were added to the Alochhaya alone to keep up with the sheer jump in demand. At this point, Lalji was negotiating the purchase of two new theatres, one of them being Minerva, which had an Anglo-Indian and European clientele.

Piggybacking on *The Black Hole* was an *Anandamath* revival. So there it was—Durga and I as two couples, coming from two diametrically opposite worlds and yet conjoined by images being spurted out from the same machine.

The first couple was the estranged and then reunited husband–wife pair who used a very public struggle to repair private disaster; the second, two people with nothing in common barring their firingi stock, thrown into a tight space and finding out that between lust and love there lies an escape clause. I admit that 1919 was the most interesting year of my life. But I wouldn't know that till much later, would I?

In that whirligig, however, there was always the worry that the authorities would now find something objectionable in *The Black Hole*. Even though special banners, showcards and publicity material had been made for theatres outside our part of town, specifically for English and Anglo consumption—'A Tale of Extrao-dinary Courage and Daring in the Face of Native Savagery!', 'The Two Whom the Black Hole Could Not Consume', 'A Love That No Prison Could Contain'—we were worried. After all, it would have been foolish not to expect that the bulk of the audience response would escape the notice of the authorities. Even the papers had started mentioning *The Black Hole* and 'the tyranny of the Empire' in the same paragraphs. We had to be extra careful about the shows in the Anglo theatres. For that was where misunderstandings were likely to start.

A complaint did pop up against *The Black Hole*, *Anandamath* and, fortunately, bioscopes in general. It was in the form of a newspaper letter that was later picked up and given editorial space by *The Statesman*. The first irate letter was published in *Sandhya*, and its content would be echoed in a tirade during a protest gathering outside the Chitpur mosque. The letter was signed by a certain Shamsul Haq.

> *Dear Sir,*
>
> *I think there is much evil that has been depicted in the moving picture* The Black Hole of Calcutta, or The Survival of the Fittest. *For one, it shows Muslims of this country as bloodthirsty barbarians who take great pleasure in torturing and killing Europeans, including their women and children. This is, to put it mildly, scandalous. The Muslim community bears not the slightest ill-will against the English Government or the Crown and continues to be loyal subjects of the latter. The other picture* Anandamath *is perhaps less direct in its anti-Mussalman message, although no less damaging.*
>
> *For another, the depiction of the female body in all bioscopes, especially those dealing with Hindu mythologies and legends and portraying European ladies, is leading to an increase in immoral and lascivious behaviour throughout our society. I ask the Government in its capacity to control and contain these degenerate bioscopes. For the sake of our women and youth, this 'entertainment' should be stopped immediately.*

I read about the Chitpur gathering in a small news item in *The Statesman* the very next day and was not surprised to read that one of the speakers had been an 'S. Haq from Metiaburz'.

On the same day that Mr Haq's letter appeared in *Sandhya*, there was another letter in another newspaper whose name I can't recall. I showed it to Bikash, who by that time had become a bona fide intellectual flirting with the idea of representing the proletariat despite not quite giving up his aspirational ways. I figured that he had already seen the letter. But it turned out that he hadn't as he never read 'any of those papers catering to the bourgeoisie'. While he stirred his infusion and I sipped my late-afternoon milky brew, he read the letter in the corner of the large chattering hall opposite the fair edifice of the Presidency College.

The tone of the letter writer was agitated. At the same time it was firm in the way that observations that can't ever be refuted are. The letter itself had nothing to do with the bioscope or with the monumental nuisance of somebody's sensibilities being hurt. It just pointed out what it thought to be a writer's stupidity.

*Dear Sir,*

*It would seem to me that Mr J.J. Gambraith's article, 'Nationality and the War, with Reference to the Ethnology of Europe' that appeared on these pages is the product of the kind of thinking that is delusional at best, propaganda at worst. In his quasi-scholarly tone, he has written that the main difference between the Celtic and Teutonic races is that in the latter there is 'all the horror of disgusting and blood-embraced barbarism, the drunkenness of carnage, the disinterested taste . . . for destruction and death'; while in the former there is 'a profound sense of justice, a great height of personal pride'. I find this laughable and flying completely in the face of reality, especially since Mr Gambraith's nonsensical ideas were aired at a time when the world now knows what has taken place at the Jallianwala Bagh.*

*Mr Gambraith writes that the Celts 'seem possessed by habits of kindness and a warm sympathy with the weak'. The*

*Lt. Governor of Punjab, Sir Michael O'Dwyer, and his henchman Gen. Dyer, if I understand correctly by their surnames, both come from Celtic stock. Both of them have conspired to gun down and kill innocent people on Baishakhi Day in Amritsar and for Mr Gambraith to then insist that it is the Teuton, and not the Celt, who is 'revolting by his purposeless brutality, by a love of evil that only gives him skill and strength in the service of hatred and injury' is indeed laughable even as it is subsumed by tragedy.*

*Yours sincerely,*
*Subhas C. Bose*
*Scottish Church College*

'Hmm,' Bikash said meaningfully, before looking at me with an expression that denoted manufactured anguish. 'I'm surprised that *The Statesman* published it.'

I had started wearing powerless glasses in public by then, if only for the pretence of being a gentleman when I was moving about in the non-nitrate world. The truth was just the opposite. I was no dignified gentleman at all. Instead, I was thrilled to be fêted, to be recognized and to be occasionally stared and pointed fingers at. The more vociferous ones were to be found at the market, which I drove through, sitting in the back seat of my Model-T, hoping to be caught reading from a book that I would never actually read.

'So when's the next bioscope then, Abani?' Bikash asked. His interest in the motion pictures was tangential. What interested him was the people who had now become devotees of this new science that was trying hard to be considered an art. His question in the hall might as well have been, 'So when's the next magic show then, Abani?'

'There's some talk of a new one next month. But I think

they want to start pacing them out a bit from now on. Give us a bit of breathing space. It seems we run the danger of squeezing this lemon dry if we're not careful.'

And then he suddenly asked the question.

'This Durga Devi. How close are you to her? Isn't she an Anglo?'

So that had been what Bikash had wanted to ask all along. We had driven down to the coffee house in my motor and throughout the journey he had had a look on his face that suggested some sort of mental constipation. Unable to ask me what, how, why and other such questions that *demand* answers, that day in the motor his eyes had been restless, as if a group of very tiny creatures was running about just under the skin of his brow. I remember him having the same look just after my mother died. Till finally one day, after his brother Rona was out of sight and while we were—though no longer boys in shorts—urinating out of the window of my room, he had asked me, 'Abani, does it feel bad or does it feel good with your mother and father no longer here?'

I had mumbled a reply that was a lie—something couched in sentimentality and probably a line plucked out of context from one of those strings-searing theatre productions. I had then buttoned my pants and that had been it. The matter of my (happy) orphanhood was never raised again.

And now, sitting in a hallful of slurping, chattering people, Bikash had asked another awkward question. And yet, I recognized it for what it was: a question that I myself had never asked, afraid of answering it correctly.

'Oh, you mean Felicia? Hah, Bikash! She's nothing but an Anglo airhead who's ugly to boot! Give me more credit, will you?' Just to drive the message home, I let out a very believable snigger, shaking my head in bioscope mirth. But a gramophone needle skidded across inside me. Felicia Miller was anything but an Anglo to me. She was, at the time, the only object that could leave me exposed, like a filmed reel left outside its canister, like a target running about on a ground with no cover and no choice but to dive into a dry, deep well, like a liar whose lie had been caught, like a neck whose purpose can only be to be caressed or snapped.

It only made sense, therefore, to defend myself against charges of having any feelings for Felicia Miller.

Acting is not about pretending to be someone else. It's about peeling the swathes of people wrapped around one's body and exposing whichever person suits the occasion. Sometimes while walking down a street, careful not to bump into passers-by, I watch my feet. They've become slower now, but the basic concept remains the same. Left foot, right foot, siblings who know each other so well that they don't have to talk to drag my body forward. The body that they transport—whether from this room to that or along longer, far more complicated routes—is a bundle of muscles and bones that have no history, except for time-serving banalities like diseases or injuries. All the actor does in a bioscope is take control of this body, deny it its zombie-life for the duration of the performance.

Effectively, nothing is allowed to be automatic for the actor. And yet, consummate performer that I had become by then, feted for my ability to control every visible part of my body for the camera to record, I lost all control and broke into splinters the day I heard that Durga Devi had quit the Alochhaya Bioscope Co.

—

Ronny Heaslop had been a tea estate man before he expanded into coal transportation. It was only after he realized that a steady pile of money was being made without him having to even lift, let alone shuffle, a finger did he notice that being a young, successful and rich Anglo-Indian had made very little difference to his social standing among the Europeans in the country. It was wonderfully different when someone was arriving from Home for the first time. He had valuable tips to give and his presence was appreciated with invitations and social meetings. But after a few months, even these green-horns from England would stop short of being too familiar and would restrict their dealings with him to the strictly professional.

Perhaps this was something Heaslop imagined. Or perhaps it was something real. But the Lucknow boy couldn't shake off the feeling that in any gathering of import there were whispered conversations exchanged whenever he was just out of earshot— and those inaudible sentences were invariably about his balmy pedigree. He tried his best not to show that such rumours, which he may have circulated in the confines of his head, bothered him. But the fact of the matter was that Ronny Heaslop wasn't happy despite his success and riches. He wanted something more.

It was through his ventures in coal that he had first met Edward Quested, formerly of the East Indian Railway. And it was through Mr Quested that he would get introduced to and then acquainted with his charming daughter, Adela Quested.

Adela had been a resident of this country for more than seventeen years and had picked up, among other habits, more than just a smattering of Hindustani, some local habits and a tropical imagination. But because of her birth and subsequent years in the therapeutic English town of Bath, she was never clubbed in the same league as the other ladies that Heaslop had come to know during his bachelorhood. That, however, could not be the sole reason why he started courting Adela with the determination of an Assam rhino. A subliminal desire to rise through the ranks of society may well have played a small part in his romance, and Ronny was honest enough to admit that to himself.

The association with Quested had started working soon enough. After his application for membership to the Bengal Club had been rejected twice (officially for 'not providing adequate information about his recommendees' and unofficially for having been 'a regular customer at the Carlton Hotel & Theatre in the past' and 'having no permanent residency in the English mainland'), it took one glowing recommendation from the general secretary of the Asiatic Society and former head of the East Indian Railway to get him in this time. That Ronny Heaslop was now engaged to the general secretary's daughter must have quickened things up considerably.

Ronny's new-found confidence also translated into his desire to put his money into something a bit more glamorous than tea and coal and poker—like in the burgeoning moving pictures business. Through an acquaintance of Edward Quested's fellow Asiatic man Douglas J. Smith, a man who had as keen an interest in the new technology of bioscope cinema as he had in ancient Pali inscriptions and seals, a dinner party had been arranged at the Bengal Club in which senior members of the Alochhaya Bioscope Co. had also been invited. It was also a chance for Quested to show that he was not the kind of insufferably hidebound Englishman who was uncomfortable with Indians and Anglo-Indians.

Lalji Hemraj Haridas was pleased as rum punch to be

invited by the Questeds. Before setting off, he had refrained from munching on a mandatory before-dinner paan, opting instead to douse the high collars of his black jacket with his wife's perfume. Lalji and the rest of us who were invited were obviously not allowed inside the Bengal Club building. But Quested had thoughtfully arranged a garden party and shamiana dinner just outside the main premises. This he had managed after reading the club rules and convincing George Godfrey, the club president, that the Europeans-only rule was applicable only within the polygonal walls of the Bengal Club building. The food and drinks ordered would officially be for the consumption of the European guests at the party, of course. The others who would join in would be 'invisible'—not totally unlike the gnats and mosquitoes that inevitably hover around their human guests.

'And that's the thing, Mr Hemraj . . .'

'Call me, Lalji, please, Mr Heaslop.'

'Ah, and that's the thing, Lalji-ji, the bioscope *is* universal. You don't have to learn another language to follow what's happening in the story. I mean, apart from a few title cards, the *pictures* are the language—a Bengali, a Frenchman, an Englishman, a Marwari, they all understand what's going on. Like when I saw an Alochhaya picture two days after I had seen a Griffith film. It could have been made by the same man from the same studio and the audience wouldn't have known the difference.'

Heaslop was visibly excited. He had plans and was all asweat. The news of Indian bioscopes had filtered back Home, but apart from a few public screenings in Europe, Britain was still an untapped market. He was planning to use his proficient coal–tea network to export Indian features. Or was it a plan to *import* Indian bioscopes?—considering that somewhere not-too-deep inside his head, Home was still the cabbage-smelling place his grandfather Gregory A. Heaslop had come from as a pale young man to this country that fights paleness. He would ultimately bring the bioscope from the East to picture houses across England. Instead of selling the prints outright to European picture houses as Hemraj and every other bioscope man in town had been doing, distributing them and renting out the prints would make more capital sense. And Heaslop would be the distributor. Over a glass of brandy, he told Lalji that he would be going to England the next month and it would make incredible good sense to take stocks of *The Black Hole, Prahlad* and a few other Alochhaya films with him.

'England is waiting for your pictures, Lalji-ji.'

'Not Lalji-ji, Mr Heaslop,' Lalji reminded him with a smile, 'just Lalji.'

'Yes, yes. I have business partners in London, Manchester, Liverpool and Edinburgh who have already shown interest. The Elphinstone people and another Bombay bioscope company are already keen about this. But to tell you honestly, Lalji-ji, it's the Alochhaya bioscopes that I'm impressed with. They've been . . .' Heaslop cocked his head back as if he was an army man on night duty creaking his neck all around, waiting for it to snap into place, and emptied his glass in an eye-blink that could have been deemed as dereliction of duty.

It was at this point that I had walked into the Club lawns. Lalji caught me by his eye and gestured me to join him. That, however, was easier gestured than done. As soon as I helped myself to a drink from an exaggeratedly turbaned waiter whose job was to waft by everyone like a ghost with a silver tray, I was approached by a small swarm of people that included ladies in silk saris and gowns and men in bow ties with cigarettes. Minutes passed by with me telling admiring strangers about the 'gruelling prison scene, where the camera was almost on us', about the various trick shots in which I was made to stand or sit in carefully selected positions that would later be translated into 'impossible actions and images', about my plans and about Durga Devi's acting prowess.

It was finally Ronny Heaslop and Lalji who crept up to me.

'Ah, Mr Chatterjee, I hope you're having a good time?' asked Ronny as he hopped back a few steps to widen the circle that till then had comprised no one I knew. 'I hope our star actor is not getting bored.'

Lalji introduced me to Ronny. We shook hands. I saw Ronny Heaslop as a large man who used his largeness as an introduction in a gathering. I saw, too, that he was clearly awkward meeting me. Even as he spoke, his booming voice spreading like just-burst pollen, I could see by the regular bobbing of his head that he had rehearsed this moment at least a few times. He was keen on making a good first impression on me as an investment.

'No, not at all. It's quite delightful here, thank you, Mr Heaslop. Lalji, I don't see Durga. Won't she be coming?'

It was my idea of a conversation-changer. It would, I had figured, give Lalji the necessary time and space to do whatever he had intended to do when he first caught my eye as I walked in. Lalji muttered a hurried 'excuse me' and gently guided me towards a giant pedestal fan that looked more like a caged bird forced to flutter for a living.

'Abani-ji, about Durga Devi, there's been a slight development. It was all very sudden so I couldn't announce it to anyone at the office. I would have told you first in any case.

It's just that . . .' He had taken out his handkerchief and was dabbing at his bumpy forehead the way he did each opening week as he waited for the ticket receipts to come in. 'Durga Devi has left the country.'

Half my face was inside the glass of brandy, so if I managed to hide my splutter—and in any case, I had, by then some years of professional and amateur pretending behind me. I looked up and waited for Lalji to continue.

One clear-cut symptom of adulthood is that everything quietens down in a nice, underwater fashion. If it's bad news, it drops like a spanner in a lake, heavily, but without the ferocity of a fall on the ground. As for experiencing joy, that too is stunted by adulthood, watered down and served as polite grog. Something on the Bengal Club lawn splintered into pieces and the giant rotor fan was simply blowing the pieces away, silently.

Because of who I was in that titterful, chattering garden, I was able to conduct myself during the first half-hour or so of that evening as Abani Chatterjee, a particularly famous bioscope actor in a composite world created a bit from here and a bit from there. Yet, when I heard Lalji say the words 'Durga Devi has left the country', the words and pretty much everything else exploded without a sound. In the evening air lit up by lights that were being fed by those old-style generators that lay far enough not to be heard, objects floated about like dust in the sunbeam. 'Durga', 'Devi', 'has left', 'the', 'country'. Splintered words seeped into the people all around me. They were soaked in the drink I was downing.

It was a surprise. I had not expected Durga's absence to shock me, in so cinematic a fashion, with emotion. How much, after all, had we to do with each other? She was not the first thought I had every morning, nor the last every night. Her presence, next to me, affected me, her touch when we performed for the camera moved me to conscious feeling, and that much I could understand. But the intensity of what rose and spread inside me, like a mushroom cloud, that evening when Lalji spoke those words left me bemused and startled. I hadn't the means to understand or deal appropriately with it. My instinct was to duck; to smoke a cigarette.

It was necessary to say something entirely natural in a completely natural manner. With Lalji having done his bit, it was my turn to speak. 'Some more ice, please,' I told the waiter who was floating by like a giant insect. I had switched to whisky, and after Lalji had convinced himself that I had taken the news of Durga's departure well enough (I had simply asked, 'Oh, has she left for another studio?', to which Lalji had replied, 'No, she's left for Australia . . . family reasons'), I made the same waiter pour me another double.

It was an hour or so since I had joined the party and the gnarling sensation I had felt earlier in the evening had vanished like a scene that never made it alive out of the cutting room. People were talking all the while, some of them talking to me. I could hear snatches of conversation erupt around me. And I entered one conversation and slipped into another like a trapeze artist swinging from one pair of hands to another.

'Darjeeling, I'm afraid, is getting increasingly crowded by the day,' I heard a familiar face tell a man whose ruddy cheeks had started getting redder even as I stood staring at them. 'I honestly think it's better to go off to one of the hill stations in the Central Provinces for some peace of mind. I went to Dalhousie last year. I think I'll go there again. Been there, John? Or to Mussoorie?'

Then there were two Englishmen talking bioscope.

'Comedy is still an avenue that needs to be explored in the motion pictures here. I saw a splendid American short a few years ago called *A Lucky Dog*. Oh, it was hilarious! The two actors, Oliver Hardy and Arthur Jefferson, should seriously pair up for more movies. But I don't know, do people have a sense of humour here?'

I moved about for a bit in the crowd gathered in the garden, the tables of food forming the border of this artificially lit picture in motion. Then I positioned myself, glass in hand, next to a stairwell. Lighting up a cigarette, I heard an important-looking man in a cravat tell Heaslop: 'If measures for educating these children are not promptly and vigorously encouraged and aided by the government, we shall soon find ourselves embarrassed in the large towns with a large floating population of Indianized English. These people, I must tell you, Ronny, are loosely brought up, and exhibit most of the worst qualities of both the races.'

He seemed completely unaware of Heaslop blanching and blinking uncomfortably, for he continued, 'This Indianized English population, already so numerous that the means of education offered to it are quite inadequate, will increase more rapidly than ever. Frankly, I can hardly imagine a more profitless, unmanageable community. It might be long before it grows into what one would officially call a "class dangerous to the State", but it'll only take a few years, if neglected, to make it a glaring problem for this government. Mark my words, Ronny, mark my words.'

'I can't agree more with you, sir,' Heaslop replied with a sad attempt to replicate gusto.

'Ah, Mr Quested, so what new findings from the Society will you educate us about tonight?' asked the tipsy gentleman who had, till now, been busy giving a lecture on social engineering to the now visibly relieved Heaslop. Someone else had joined them, a man with a scholar's voice.

'I could tell you about the latest paper by Rakhal Banerjee about Harappan sites, but why don't you ask him yourself next week, Mr Allen?'

Quested. Quested? Had I heard the blubbering man right? Considering that the chance of too many Questeds walking about town was fairly slim, could this Quested be Tarini's Quested? As if on cue, Heaslop swung his future father-in-law and the other man towards me just as I was wondering whether the next sip should be a gulp or a sip.

'Mr Quested, let me introduce you to the man who is *the* face of Indian cinema and whose talent I intend to showcase in England: Abani Chatterjee. Mr Chatterjee, this is Mr Edward Quested.'

'A pleasure to meet you, Mr Chatterjee,' said the elderly but not old gentleman, whose kind horse-like eyes immediately made a favourable impression on me. 'Both Ronny here and my daughter have told me about you and your excellent skills. Unfortunately, I must admit, I haven't seen enough of you. Just the *The Black Hole of Calcutta* and *Anandamath*.' A friendly laugh emanated all around and, just for a moment, I thought that they were laughing at me. Alcohol does obstruct clear judgement.

'Yes, I thought you were splendid in *Anandamath*. "India's Valentino" is how my daughter describes you. I must introduce you to her. She'll be thrilled,' Quested spoke with breakneck speed. But instead of bringing the admiring Adela to my attention, the troika of Heaslop, Quested and Justice Allen— joined intermittently by others who fluttered in and out like pigeons landing on ledges during sundown—continued their peripatetic exchanges. These exchanges included the matter of a particular snail population from Africa wreaking havoc in a few tea plantations in Assam, the British Conservative Party's shape-shifting (and therefore 'comic') imperial policy, Adela Quested's weakness for the many historical artefacts of this land, the 'excellently argued and packed with telling facts' leader in *The Statesman* about the need for a separate goods-train-only rail network between the major industrial cities . . .

But regardless of what fleeting subject was being lobbed about in our tight but easily breachable circle, the conversation kept skidding back to motion pictures. It was either part of a sinister plan to get me to talk about something they needed me to talk about. Or it was just one of those English conversational tricks that ensured that there were no uncomfortable spells of blank silence within the conversations. My presence could have been utilized for the purpose of furthering business plans as well as filling awkward silences. I, on my part, was becoming increasingly quiet and drunk.

The next whisky was waiting for me. The fluid turned opaque and Lalji's distant figure was blocked out as I tilted the glass to my mouth. When I lowered my glass, I saw Lalji transport a few pieces of spiced-up cucumbers into his stain-free mouth near the giant rubber plant. Conducting the bottoms-up routine, I walked up to him before he got stuck to another round of small talk.

'Lalji, so this Heaslop fellow will be taking our movies abroad?'

'Ah, Abani, yes, it's all been worked out. It could mean America, my friend, America! Try some of those shami kebabs, I believe they're really good.'

'So why has Durga gone?'

I slipped in the question as if I was asking something about distribution rights or about the next film we were planning on the life of Tipu Sultan.

'Oh, Durga Devi? Well, I tried to explain things to her father. But he was very upset for some reason.'

Durga's father, Sam Miller, had stormed into Lalji's Alochhaya office a week ago. He was terribly agitated, to the point of being flushed and furious. As he shouted his ruddy face off, Lalji could make no sense of what he was saying. And it sometimes *was* quite impossible to understand what a European was saying, especially if he was blabbering on in white rage.

In between more cucumber and other vegetarian delights, Lalji told me how Sam Miller, 'all smelling of liquor and tobacco', had barged into his office and told him that his daughter was not 'a fooking nautch girl' and that he was not going to stay quiet while Felicia had any sort of association with 'the fooking Bengalis of the Alochhaya Bioscope Company', or for that matter any bioscope company in the country. Before Lalji could explain that not everybody at Alochhaya merited the tag of 'fooking Bengali', Sam banged his fist on the table, scattered the betel nuts that were till then resting in a small silver box all over the cheap wooden surface, and announced that he and his family were moving to Australia.

Still calm, Lalji tried to get a word in about 'Miss Miller's contractual obligations', at which Sam stared at him like a Victoria Terminus gargoyle for a few seconds. By this time, Ram Bahadur had appeared behind him, but Lalji's eyes told the hulk to stay where he was.

'She's not coming back here,' Sam said bristling all over. After looking beyond Lalji at the posters depicting his daughter in various forms, he looked at the man sitting again, let out some more spit and stormed out of the room leaving a few more blasphemies hanging in the Alochhaya air.

It transpired that Sam had gone to the Carlton with his mates Bob Davis from Oldham, Bill O'Brien from Slough and John Davies from Glasgow, for the ostensible purpose of 'celebrating' O'Brien's decision to move to McLeodganj where he had been offered a pretty respectable job as an overseer of something—no one was quite sure exactly what. It transpired that they had proceeded to go and see *The Black Hole of Calcutta, or Survival of the Fittest* at the Athena. Less than halfway into the film, poor Sam was horrified to see his daughter being held half-naked, and on display for the hundreds of others in the hall. Things only got worse as the bioscope rolled on to a hallful of hoots and applause that kept drowning out the orchestra in the front.

That was how Sam Miller realized that Durga Devi, a name that he was moderately familiar with in the papers and the publicity posters, was none other than his sweet daughter from the convent, Felicia. Till then, he had been resisting the offers made by well-meaning authorities helping him to relocate from this city to somewhere more genteel. The two gentlemen who had come twice to his house, trying to convince him to move to a hill station in the United Provinces, had finally come up with an inviting proposition for the Millers to move to Australia, where a man of Sam's talent and fortitude could make a more decent living and have more than a decent life.

Sam had planned to turn this offer down as usual. He had given out the usual signs of polite rejection to the two frock-coated-in-June gentlemen. The pursing of the lips, the tilting of the head in fake apologia, the quiet shaking of his head while he smiled—he had done all this when the gents had presented him with the 'McLeodganj option'. He knew that they knew that he was going to also turn down Australia.

'Let's face it,' he had said to the turbaned bar man at the South Calcutta Billiards Club, 'Australia is on the fooking edge of the world.'

This edge hurtled to the centre after he saw Felicia cavorting shamelessly on screen. It took him less than two hours to seek out the frock-coated governmenters, thrash Felicia without uttering a word and land up on Lalji Hemraj Haridas's doorstep. Ten days later, he had boarded *The Baltimore* with his wife and daughter, looking forward to starting a new life in the windy town of Perth.

The cucumber-consuming Lalji continued, 'I haven't seen Durga Devi since. I had sent Ram Bahadur over to her place with some money and to return her things. Technically, she was breaking the contract, so I needn't have sent Ram Bahadur. But Abani-babu, she has been part of the Alochhaya family for so long. I liked her, I respected her. But Ram Bahadur found a lock hanging on their door. They had already upped and left.'

As Lalji spoke, I felt abandoned and desolate—both emotions that came unnaturally to me. Standing on the lawn, ostensibly celebrating my prowess as an actor, I contemplated the reaction that my leading lady's abrupt and permanent departure was having on my body.

There were people, strangers really, who were coming up to talk to me, shake my hand or simply say hello while looking into my eyes. They were all sparrows, moving about friskily, stop-motion fashion.

The effects of alcohol are difficult to put in words. For the man getting progressively drunk, it's like sitting in a boat which has sprung a leak and the hole is allowed to grow unchecked.

As I sloshed back another gulp, not emptying my glass but leaving enough in it for another instalment, I pushed back my coat and shirt sleeve to see my arm. The whisky must have already been well into its looped journey, conducting circuitous turns around the bends of my arteries. And in all its wisdom, the alcohol in me was unaware of what was going on in my head. Everything had become amplified. The words ricocheting around me, the clutter of the forks and plates, the luscious chewing sound that seemed to come from the mouths around me. But exaggerated above everything else was the hammer sound of dejection and disappointment I felt just under my chest, above my belly. As I saw each point of light, each blob of face quiver into many, the fact that Durga had departed without a word became harder, sharper.

The best replication of inebriation I have come across was in a short French feature I had recently seen. In the short, the effects of liquor were shown as if it was a study of the seasons. Instead of a landscape changing its light and foliage, it was the changing man's face that was being shown in seamless detail on the screen. There were changes that were taking place in his gait, posture and behaviour. But it was the shape-shifting face of the actor that had left an impression on me. He was so good, plotting the incremental change with every bottle, every glass, every sip, that it was like watching the hour hand of a clock move in minutes. I still believe that he wasn't acting and it was deft work in the cutting room that had expertly kept out the genuinely unsavoury parts of the trajectory of his induced oblivion.

But no one drinks to replicate the visual effects of heavy drinking. Why, then, you could ask. I haven't bothered to find out and ruin my drink. I leave that to the zealots. I only know that there's a familiar place I reach after my fifth drink, or the seventh. There is in cinema, in life a landscape that lies outside what can be shown and seen—not a large tract of land, I admit, but a landscape nonetheless. And it was in this territory that I found myself that evening when Mr Edward Quested and his son-in-law-to-be Ronny Heaslop had thoughtfully thrown a dinner party.

'Could you tell me where the washroom is?' I asked the turbaned angel flitting by with a tray of ice-box-tongs-and-glasses.

'Straight down the corridor and right, sir. It'll be on your left, sir.' He spoke without emotion.

Ploughing through the gaseous swirl of people, I made my way inside the Club building, its architecture slipping and sliding before me with its flotsam of potted plants, framed watercolours and ominously dignified lights in tow.

A woman was on a ship bound for Australia, that slab of land floating on the Sea of Forgetfulness. If she hadn't already reached Australia, she was probably holding on to her hat, trying to prevent it from being blown out into the great wide open, and looking at the bald expanse of evening sea. This was Felicia shorn of being Durga, but it was the same woman whose face was known by countless people in its various forms. She was now returning to what she was before she joined the bioscopes, before she became a household name and the more adored half of the silent era's most famous couple.

As I swam through the cool passageway, careful not to swing too close to the watercolours presenting the city in various phases of its life, I caught a form moving and vanishing in one swift frame. From afar, all I could make out was a figure in a burgundy dress. As I turned left after spelling out the letters C-L-O-A-K-R-O-O-M with considerable difficulty, I imagined a dark pair of eyes, lined with kajol, staring back at me. As I entered the bathroom, I realized that it was a mixture of drink and imagination that made me see those eyes, for in that considerably large and bright room, I was alone.

This bathroom inside the bowels of the European-only Bengal Club was a far cry from the abomination that had, until only a few years ago, existed in my house. There was a green settee next to a glass table with a single, squat vase on it that was pretty because it was so out of place. I thought of sitting on the green velvet-like material, but I wanted to first splash water on my face so as to snap myself out of uncontrol. The white basins sparkled like the water they were supposed to catch and let go of. I smudged my way in front of one of the basins, suddenly catching my face in the mirror above it.

A drunken man looking into the mirror looks at a never-ending stretch of reflections reflecting reflections. My eyes were red, but more than their colour, what struck me about them was how heavy they were. And it wasn't only the eyes. Looking at my face, I also looked into it. Was that face that was slipping in and out of solidness a confirmation that I inhabited my body?

'Abani,' I said slowly, watching my mouth conduct itself in perfect synchronization with the sound that came out. I smiled and noticed myself smile back at me. I uttered my name again, this time in a normal fashion, barely noticing the intricate mechanical workings of my mouth. I turned the tap on. I had turned it on too much and the water gushed out in a violent rush. I had sprayed the first instalment of liquid refreshedness on my face and was cupping my hands to catch the next, when I registered a brief but sharp click, the sort that a projector makes when the film reel jumps from one spool to another. A woman in a burgundy dress with ruffles around the collar and down the front came out of nowhere. She hadn't finished pressing down her dress when her eyes locked on to mine and, for that brief moment, both of us seemed to have been thrown into a vacuum from where all air had been utterly drained.

It would have helped me if that really had been the case. But there could be no doubt that the room was not only blessed with plentiful of air but also had splendid acoustics. For as soon as the time-stopping moment of us staring at each other passed, the woman in burgundy let out a scream that overpowered the loud sound of gushing tap water and the pleasant silence that had surrounded it. Her body, wrapped as it was in ruffles and fabric, shook for minutes like a single leaf held out of a window in a storm. It was actually a series of screams, long ones punctuated by the smallest of breaks, that left her face quivering in a manner that made me fear it would split along that short, sharp nose of hers.

I panicked. Instead of turning the tap off and proceeding to explain matters, I tried to move away from and towards her at the same time. In the process, one of my legs caught the other and I fell on her like a lizard that had just lost its grip on the ceiling. As I lay on her, my head foaming with smashed-to-smithereens thoughts of self-preservation, her scream continued, this time directly into my ears. I don't know how long it took for everyone to rush into the Club's north wing L-A-D-I-E-S Cloakroom, but by the time Ronny Heaslop's fiancée, that is Edward Quested's daughter, Adela Quested, was extricated from under my weight, the deed had been done.

If I recall correctly, I was pulled up by my collar and pelted with blows that fell like wide and blunt rain. What abuse was hurled at me, I could not make out then, so I cannot recollect now. But I did register the very odd presence of Lalji, who was standing behind the green settee along with a huddle of others. He stared at me, his mouth ajar the whole while I was being dragged out of the bathroom, out of the Club building, out of the premises of the Bengal Club, out on to Chowringhee overlooking the Maidan, and out of the world in which, only a few hours ago, I had been graciously fêted. Adela Quested lay there on the settee, spreading distressed burgundy on green, being fanned furiously by the shocked but understanding guests.

But what really lay there was my future in tatters. My one single tumble was much more real than the one that my mother had concocted. And what made it more real was that it turned me overnight from bioscope's top talent and draw into an industry leper, a member of the bhadralok loafer-criminal class. It was as if I had been transported to the edge of the world. It was like being shipped to Australia.

# hello, operators

It wasn't the ageing that I minded. Clocks live long, people settle into themselves. What gnawed away at my innards during those lost years was the fact that I was doing nothing. By nothing, of course, different people mean different things. I ventured out of the house, I watched bioscopes, I took pointless drives up and down Chowringhee, I mingled with a handful of people. And I drank. But my five-odd years doing nothing meant being away. Acting had once again been confined to private pretending, driving me perilously to the brink of ordinariness.

The fall, in more ways than one, made me Tarini Chatterjee's son, to the marrow of my bones; the inheritor of Tarini's blood, fate and boredom. Abani Chatterjee. This was the truly rotten part of being driven out of paradise—that I was now forever stuck being me. As the typical day ended, it would be a horribly short time before the typical day started all over again. Abala's tea would come; I would unroll the coir from the day's newspaper like a garter off a leg; I would proceed to open a book and drag my eyes through it as if they were my feet walking through some monsoon-village slush. I would even set out, aimlessly, in my car, stopping to eat somewhere, hoping that the driver, hired for just the day, wouldn't catch on that I was eating alone. Sometimes Rona dropped by and we talked only about politics, and drank till it was a reasonable enough hour for him to leave, and then I went to sleep while flipping the latest issue of *Photoplay* in bed. I started hating doing nothing and there was nothing I could do about it.

All this happened quite naturally, of course, and in the end it was even bearable. For, the truth is that like pretty much everything before and pretty much everything after, I was filling in for someone else, the someone else being the Abani-like me. And then, nearly as swiftly as I had driven myself off the rails, my life returned to its original trajectory on a scandalously ordinary morning.

The day was marked by an incessant, droning kind of rain, nothing more than a sprinkle. It was such a sham; if one paid close attention, one would have noticed that a large part of the rain never actually reached the ground. There was no sign, for instance, of the streets or footpaths taking on a darker sheen of grey as they should have under the circumstances. And yet, it was raining, a spittle visible enough to mark the railing outside with speckle-points. I was staring out of the window into the fake outdoorness of the courtyard when the phone rang.

Considering that over the last few years I had been walking deeper and deeper into an increasingly dense outgrowth of gloom, the fact that I was noticing inconsequential things like the limpness of the day's rain wasn't surprising. But at the same time, one could see in my ability to hold on to the value of earthly details a sign that I was not totally defeated. I had been inoculated against failure thanks to my ability to keep pretending that I was still a success. But for an actor sitting idle for half a decade, away from the props of other pretenders and enthusiasts, the risk of slipping into the cycle of charmless routine was a genuine risk. Forced abstinence can break the strongest. So when the telephone instrument rang with a clang, I was expecting nothing.

I placed the glass, half emptied of its Haig's Dimple Scotch, on the tabletop next to the phone, and let the clanging continue just a bit longer. All the while, my Adam's apple bobbed up and down like a castaway raft on the Arabian Sea.

Before I describe the telephonic exchange that followed, however, let me be frank about the reason I had come to distrust telephone calls. Since my banishment into the wilderness, there had been calls from people telling me through coughs and splutters that they wanted me to work with them in their bioscopes.

'Abani-babu, it's a perfect role for you. I think you should seriously consider the job.'

The voice would go on to tell me the names of the other actors who would be in the bioscope, and how all of them insisted that I be in it.

'Dhiren-babu will have no one else as Baren, the zamindar's youngest brother. And let me tell you how critical Baren's role in the whole story is.'

The character of Baren Banerjee, I would find out within twenty minutes of battery-cranked conversation, was that of a whoring, drinking wastrel who falls victim to a blood-lusting, class-despising ghoul that was ravaging landowners throughout the land. A six-minute bit role in a ninety-minute feature consumed by the middle-aged ham-ster Dhiren Sarkar who was making inroads into the bioscope industry. It would be the same story every time: Abani Chatterjee as the perfect endearing uncle, Abani Chatterjee the perfect level-headed vizier, Abani Chatterjee the perfect meditating sage or, worst of them all, Abani Chatterjee the tragic hero's perfectly comic friend.

There were a few occasions in the early days when I asked whether my name would at least be on equal billing with the leading man. Extra deference would accompany more coughs and splutters. In other words, there was no role worth considering. All because of the notion that Abani Chatterjee had pounced on a European lady in the sacred confines of a European club.

My calls to Lalji were never returned. The other studio bosses wouldn't come on the line. As for the public—the same public that had applauded my giant image on the screen, cut out my photos published in the papers and pointed me out with great excitement each time I passed them—had turned me invisible as if by the flicking of a switch. Even the approving murmur that had accompanied my father's fall from grace was absent. It was one thing, it seemed, to carry out a nationalist action against the English, and quite another to 'assault' an Englishwoman at her engagement party. I was deemed the lowest of the low, the hormone-reeking sleazeball who gave the people of this genteel town a bad name.

The Natyamancha had even run the very successful *Mr Banik, Master Actor* to a pretty decent crowd for a season. I never saw *Mr Banik*, but I did read the papers, and they had described the play as a 'powerful re-enactment of a recent scandal that exposes the filth invading our arts and entertainment industry through the medium of bioscopes.' Shuren Gupta, our old acquaintance from the (Son of/Sort of) Char Murti Gang, played Chandra Banik, the star actor turned universal scoundrel with his special fetish for Englishwomen. More than one paper noted that Banik's manner of speech was 'quite extraordinarily like the discredited Mr Chatterjee's'. Considering that I had been an actor in a medium that allowed me no speech, I marvelled at this bit of public knowledge.

So don't judge me when I say that I took my time picking up the phone the day it was raining spittle. I let the phone ring a few more times, allowing myself to water my lips with another quick ebb and tide of the Haig's. The drink would help me maintain my dignity come what may.

'Could I please speak to Mr Chatterjee?' said the voice that seemed to echo from under at least two layers of blankets.

'Who is this calling?' I answered in my 'secretary' voice that I had mastered over the years.

'Ah, Abani, this is Charu, Charu Ray. We had met at the Corinthians a year ago.'

I answered in my own voice. I was never a mimic-man anyway.

'Yes, of course, Charu. So how have the pictures been treating you?'

'Fine, Abani. Good, quite good actually. Haven't seen you around for a while. Working on something?'

'Well, actually . . .'

I would have managed to come up with something. But he cut me off.

'I must say that there's been a lot of change in the industry over the last two years or so. I couldn't call before because I was travelling. Bombay mainly. But things have been moving in a different direction since these Bombay studios started elbowing in after Bolu Sarkar's disappearance.'

I gave him the quiet uh-huh.

'Abani, I'll cut through the chase. I think the best time to be in movies is just round the corner. It won't be a lead. But it's an international production. And the director—he's a top-notch German—is keen on having you for the role. I think you should take it.'

I sensed over the phone line and under the aftertaste of the Haig's that there was more to his calling me up than a friendly nudge. Just because one sees a plain expanse of green doesn't mean that there are no rows of artillery behind the trees.

'So what's this about, Charu?'

There was the framed photograph of me with Lord Chelmsforth just after the premiere of *Ratnakar* at Alochhaya. Standing on its cardboard clubfoot, the picture looked quaintly confident in between the telephone instrument and the now-empty glass. I was smiling, unknown to everyone else in the picture, at Chelmsforth's undulating side curls. Fortunately, my smile came across as joyful pride. I poured another round of Haig's halfway down the glass and emptied it in one devouring go.

—

The last time I heard the words 'international production', they had sprung from the thick and dark lips of Balendranath Sarkar. I was one of the last people, if not the last, who had seen Balendra Sarkar aka Bolu-babu before he vanished from the face of the Earth. I couldn't detect anything in Charu's voice that suggested that he thought I was in any way linked to his disappearance. And why would he, some four years after the man's disappearance? But one could never tell over telephone lines. Maybe they wanted to completely bury me, see me beyond the pale and available only in the black-and-white form of backlighting on the screen.

Those were funny days. Everything, from witty remarks about that Machiavellian Gandhi to urinating against an Esplanade wall, everything could be construed as a seditious activity—and they probably were. The terrorists had all vanished like bioscopes in sunlight. Or they had found some sort of dodgy spiritual solace and turned inwards and become saints. In their place had appeared the new variety of nationalists, who worked increasingly in the open, chatting and laughing with the authorities inside buildings and cooking up long-winded, metaphor-ridden speeches against it outside.

But Bolu-babu's sudden disappearance was, in many circles, being interpreted as the handiwork of the last of the bhadralok-loafer criminal class of weekend terrorists holding out against the increasingly more fashionable nationalist movement. Bolu-babu had been known to be too close to the authorities. And more importantly, after my tumble, there had been much speculation linking me either with the authorities or with the remnants of the Maniktala Secret Society. The fact that I could be neither was never an option. With the chainmail of fame no longer protecting me, I was well within my right to be paranoid.

Those were also paranoid days. Gandhi was making all the noises he was capable of ('independence by a year' and other fruity delights); Tagore did the clever thing by going off to Japan, the United States and Argentina; and the authorities had been quivering with nervous activity when the Prince of Wales dropped by to see how the Jewel in the Crown was holding up to the light. All this while, as I rotted outside the frames of the motion pictures, there were reports about community problems, mainly Hindu–Muslim in nature, gathering force. The force with which nearly everyone's fingers were hard-tapping those days could be gauged by the high-pitched voice with which Lord Birkenhead kept stating everywhere that self-rule was a 'ghoul'. If one concentrated hard enough, one could even hear his tinny voice washing out this noise-infected town with 'Ghoul, ghoul, ghoul, ghoul'.

Bolu Sarkar called one day.

'Abani, we need to meet. It's something I can't really tell you over the phone. You're definitely going to find this very, very interesting.'

'Bolu-babu, I'm a bit tied up now. What is this about?'

'What else could it be about, Abani-babu! It's about the biggest bioscope this country has ever seen. And only you will be able to . . .'

'It's not one of your shorts, is it? I thought you already have that chap mimicking Chaplin . . .'

'Ah, Dhiren Ganguli? No, no, nothing of that sort, Abani. This is an international project. I need to talk to you.'

There's no point denying it. The word 'international' did raise my interest by an octave.

'Who's doing it?'

Producer extraordinaire that he was, Bolu recognized the distinct sound of a mouth latching on to a bait when he heard one.

'Ah, Abani-babu. All in good time. Could we meet later today? I'll be able to tell you everything. Maybe at your place around . . .'

I had quickly recovered. What was I doing? Had things got that desperate that I was going to have Balendra Sarkar puckering his lips and giving me the kiss of death by landing up in my house? Not if I could help it.

'I'm a bit tied up today at the studio,' I lied.

'At Alochhaya?'

I couldn't believe his gall. This was Bolu Sarkar, real estate scum turned cloth'n'garment pirate who was now asking me about my engagements, knowing fully well that I hadn't entered Alochhaya for over four years.

'I'll be busy till the day after. Maybe we could meet at the Tea Room on Park Street. I have to meet someone there in the morning. Come over at noon.'

There was a small sparrow-dip of silence on the other end. This was followed by his characteristic heh-heh.

'Sure. The Tea Room, I know the Tea Room. Wednesday at noon then, Abani-babu. It'll be . . .'

'Goodbye,' I said. Bolu-babu simply didn't know when to stop a conversation. It was always someone else who did the hanging up.

It was a hasty call on my part to agree to meet him so easily. For in case there was any doubt over the matter, this was Balendranath Sarkar, and not any old bioscope production man. Rumour, that raspy-voiced bird with flapping wings, had it that Bolu Sarkar had first come into a good deal of money by getting close to the city council authorities. He had apparently provided them with useful information about the activities of some of the youthful members of a few big families in this city. The authorities, fed with information from Bolu-babu and his men, had proceeded to make official 'entreaties' to the heads of these families, asking them to rein in their wards before things got out of hand. So if the Jorasanko household and other families hadn't ended up having a single member on the wrong side of the law, one could thank Balendranath Sarkar for his contributions towards minimizing law and order problems in the city.

Playing model citizen, Bolu-babu had done well for himself. But he had bigger ideas, showing quite a talent in the area of real estate, winning over land in and around the Tiretti Bazaar area. No one found anything suspicious about his acquisition spree as the lottery system in place to make the process of public land sales tamper-proof had been around for some two hundred years. So what if dignified nostrils twitched with indignation as Bolu went on to become the biggest owner of property and land outside the European quarters.

If that was all there was to it, then Bolu-babu wouldn't have been any different from the half a dozen other heavy-pocketed fellows cotton-elbowing their way into the motion pictures business. But there were more pungent rumours circulating since Gandhi and other such comedians had called for the boycott of English goods. The noise about Bolu Sarkar using political clout to make money started to grow louder. And this time round, it was the nationalist demand for *self-rule* that was making him money that was as good as—if not better than—the pile he had made earlier with the help of the authorities!

The word out on the street was that Bolu had made quite a lot of money by 'converting' Manchester cotton into homespun cloth. Who could have been behind all those tiny production plants remaking dhutis, saris and all other 'made-from-Indian-cotton' items? Why hadn't the authorities shut these plants, or been so quiet about Gandhi's latest call to boycott English goods? One will never know. There were dhutis at the Bagbazar shops with the name 'Khudiram Bose' woven along the border. Those were Manchester cloth turned into value-added dhutis and Bolu Sarkar was somehow stitched to the whole operation. Was he, then, a 'double agent'? So you see, I had my reasons for not risking his presence in my house. I had had enough of paying for sins I had never intended to commit, and would not have known how to, except perhaps at gunpoint.

But when Bolu-babu called again that evening to confirm our meeting at Park Street, I was desperate to step out of my cupboard and return to the real world that I knew so well. The words 'international project' had briefly convinced me that the theory about Balendranath Sarkar being close to the authorities while seeming to be a supporter of the nationalists was just a theory.

I told myself that he was just another businessman, doing things that businessmen do to make their business run like molten ghee. So what if a hopeless actress like Renee Smith had made a smooth transition from nothingness to bioscope big time as Sita Devi thanks to Bolu Sarkar? At a time when half a dozen theatres in the city had been forced to roll down their shutters for 'exhibiting profane, indecent and obscene representations to the annoyance of inhabitants or personages'—exactly at the same time that four theatre palaces had opened in the north, the biggest one at Tiretti Bazaar itself—bioscope people could do with friends like Bolu-babu.

So Wednesday came and I found myself sitting inside the Tea Room and staring at a cup of swirling black coffee. Twirling my spoon and making white ribbon lines in my cup, I was a man waiting. In the span of some twenty minutes under the slow, slicing rotation of a Tea Room ceiling fan, I kept involuntarily creaking my head to the right every few seconds. In that period of waiting, I wanted to hear that crack of my neck as many times as possible.

I was sitting next to a monstrous tank inhabited by three comatose fish and one ceramic mermaid. The only real activity I could gauge in the fish tank was that of the bubbles coming out of the end of a small plastic pipe, and the twitching brown tendrils from the bottom of a perforated test-tube device. As I looked at this crushed mass of worms that managed to fiercely retain the individuality of its many components, I couldn't help but think of Durga. She had struggled with me once, cheek-to-cheek, limb-to-limb, inside artificial and close confines too.

'Abani-babu, waiting long?'

Bolu Sarkar was early. It seemed as if he was addressing me from across the room. He was actually standing right in front of me. Why he had to talk so loudly remains a mystery. I had been turning a newspaper page after wasting precious seconds of my life reading a news report about workers of the Assam Bengal Railway Company joining the 'Non-Cooperation Movement' to show their solidarity with mistreated workers of Chandpur's tea gardens and a long advertisement for gripe water under a picture of a Baby Krishna. That was when Bolu-baba made his entrance.

'I hope that's good news you're reading. Everybody's humming on about self-rule these days. Tiring stuff. Fired up by Jibananda in *Anandamath* you reckon? Ha, ha.'

He had started on a bad note. The high chuckle that rippled down his white clothes settling somewhere down on his black turned-up shoes could have made a large puddle. But I had already looked up at his face and my eyes were now locked to his. I welcomed him the way the family welcomes bad news from a doctor.

'Well, you know how it is,' I smiled and said without rising. 'Everything's played up these days to a bombastic, ridiculous level to sustain the public.' I waved aside the newspaper as if to kill the world's slowest fly.

'Ha, ha. You never did fancy other actors, the ones who're slightly—now how do I put it?—dramatic?'

And without breaking into any more pleasantries, Bolu Sarkar settled down in the chair opposite me, placing a moderately thick pile of papers on the table. 'Have you heard of Joe May?'

'No. Who is he?'

'You saw the UFA feature they showed the whole of last month at the Crown?'

'The German feature about the madman and the murderer?'

'Yes, that's it. *Hilde Warren and Death* it was called. Ran moderately well until they started playing *The Immigrant*. You know how Chaplin's getting popular these days. Well, UFA's boss is Joe May and Joe May wants to make a film in this country. He wants you in it. He's told me so himself. So, are you game, Abani-babu?'

Without waiting for any response, he swivelled around and clicked his fingers. I saw a waiter in the horizon look laconically at us and shake out of his torpor.

'Well, Abani-babu? Interested? Ha, ha,' he added unthinkingly.

'What's it about? What do I play?'

'Dear, dear Abani. What do you play? This is the script in front of me. These Germans actually have proper, detailed scripts, you know. And still they lost the war. Ha, ha.' He put the red cardboard-bound script before me. 'I want you to have a look at it. I'm supposed to pick up a copy for you. But right now, please, do have a quick look at it. It's all here. Once we get the contract out of the way, I'll get the copy delivered to you.' And he snapped his fingers again at the same man who had, it turned out, earlier moved, but not towards us.

The working title of the movie was typed in small, crisp letters. It said *The Indian Tomb* in English, the German title next to it in brackets with the name of its author, Thea van Harbou. I turned the page and there was a five-line synopsis. A German architect comes to India and falls in love with a temple dancer in the kingdom of Eschnapur. The king of Eschnapur's brother is scheming against him and plotting a coup. The king is also in love with the temple dancer, but it's the architect that the woman loves, not the king. This sets the otherwise able king to set his soldiers on the two lovers—thus giving his scheming brother an opportunity to plan a coup. The architect is thrown into prison while the dancer is forced to perform a deadly ritual. But the king—not a bad man at heart—intervenes just in time to save her life. The lovers escape just when the forces of the king's evil brother storm the palace.

The story sounded workable. There were elements of John Holwell. I could easily slip into my character of a lovestruck foreigner facing native hostility. With the right director and camera work, it could even be something nuanced and complex. I was finally going to act again.

A shadow arrived at our table. 'Two coffees and ... Now what do you have fresh? The pastries looked nice. Abani-babu, any pastry? Ha. Two chocolate pastries, with the chunky bits on the top. And don't forget the coffees. And extra milk.'

The waiter scribbled down the order as if reporting on a minor event.

'No milk for me, thank you,' I said, closing the pile that I was rummaging through. The direction notes seemed extensive, far more detailed than the ten-page handwritten 'scripts' that I had earlier worked from.

'Ah, yes. No milk in one coffee. And please, I'm in a bit of a hurry.'

'So it's a German film then?' I asked, trying and succeeding in not sounding excited.

'It's a European venture, Abani-babu. With this, the bioscopes will open up to new markets. To Europe, to England, to America!'

Our table had become bigger even as the morose waiter

with a Hapsburg jaw left two pastries and two coffees on it. The
newspaper and the thick script, fighting for space till a moment
ago, now seemed to be cohabiting fine in the presence of food
and beverage.

'Mr May is arriving here next Friday. He wants us to be
ready with everything well before the shooting starts. Mr May
requested that you be the first person I sound out, Abani-babu.
You are in, then? Ha, ha.' And as he munched on his pastry and
sipped on his coffee in the Tea Room, stalagmites and stalactites
formed and dissolved in his big mouth as he chewed and
breathed, chewed and breathed.

'Who else will be in it?'

There had to be a silent break between his audible chomping
and his reply.

'Well, Mr May has a German actor in mind for the role of
the architect. His name is Hans Marr, apparently a box-office
sure-fire in Germany. But there's no decision yet about who
plays the girl. There's some talk about his wife playing the
dancer. She was in *Hilde Warren* and she seems to be keen. But
Mr May is also toying with the idea of casting a genuine Indian
for the role. Too bad that she's gone, but Felicia Miller would
have been perfect, don't you think? Ha.'

Yes, Durga would have been good for the role. She always
was that little bit extra successful when playing a proper Indian.
As Lakshmibai, the warrior princess in *Rani of Jhansi*, for instance,
it was much more than the light piercing through her armour
that lent her near divinity. As Lakshmibai, she was what she
wasn't as the daughter of Sam Miller and as the newest addition
to the population of Australia—a woman who held the reins of
her destiny tightly in her own hands.

If there was a tone in Bolu-babu's voice that suggested a

faint wink and a nudge, I was too shocked to take note of it. If someone else was playing the lead, what did they want *me* to play? The effete king? The scheming brother? My enthusiasm had slipped even as Bolu went on to talk about scheduling and other minutiae of the shoot. And would I have to deal with this philistine, this loud man whose understanding of the bioscopes was limited to the people involved in their making and the money that would be generated? I would not allow that. If Joe May wanted me to act in his feature, especially if it was to be a minor role, I would deal only with Joe May.

I was looking at one of the three motionless fish that seemed to be recording the exchange taking place between Bolu-babu and me. Had it noticed the lizard that was levitating some distance away above it? Or did the refraction of light passing from air to water and then from fish eye to fish brain block the lizard from its view?

'Mr Sarkar, which character does Mr May have in mind for me?'

'Aah, now you're talking. Well, there's this fascinating character who's part-magician, part-kapalik and part-narrator. In fact, he's the one who keeps the whole story stitched together.'

An emptiness spread like firework from my innards. Another crummy part being offered to the quarantined.

'Bolu-babu, I'm interested. But when do I get to go through the script? I want to read it before I make up my mind.'

'Abani-babu, Abani-babu,' he said with mock-regret that was intended to camouflage real impatience and irritation. 'Of course, you need to go through the script. Which is why I'm carrying it now, so that in a few hours I can deliver a copy to you at home. But you don't know how glad I am that you've agreed to come on board . . .'

I reminded him that I had not made my final decision yet.

'Ah, of course. But you won't be disappointed. This is, Mr Chatterjee, your next step: world cinema.'

Saying which he snapped his fingers again. With pleasantries out of the way as quickly as they had been herded in, Bolu-babu paid the bill, squashed his face with a rings-bedecked hand to suggest a busy day ahead and stood up to leave. I also dragged my chair back to rise. As I took one last look, not at the immobile fish in the tank but at the lizard that was stuck a few fish-miles above them, I made out from the corner of my eyes two figures moving towards us. Without snapping my head in their direction, I casually turned my head to see a couple start-stop-starting towards me. They couldn't have been much older than I was, the man bearing that comfortable look which comes from a practised confidence of knowing that beauty is always close at hand. The two didn't even try to hide their rather infantile form of excitement and came up to me as I was turning to follow Bolu-babu out of the Tea Room door.

'Excuse me. Are you, aren't you . . . You are . . .'

She had a narrow forehead that seemed to not expand an inch even though she had her hair severely pulled back into a tight, small bun. Even the broken words that she had just uttered sounded refined, as if she was quoting a line in high Bengali. The kajol outlining her eyes served the same function that strong backlighting does when highlighting a face in a motion picture. And if her eyes hadn't caught me, I would have surely lingered on her mouth that was ever-so-slightly crooked as she spoke. She waved her hands as if trying to catch my name out of thin air, while the man looked intently around as if to search out the nearest ashtray despite actually also conducting the same activity of *placing* me.

'You were absolutely fantastic yesterday,' she gushed crookedly.

The man next to her nodded in furious agreement. He had suddenly lost all his sophistication and, instead of the dandy who was standing before me, there was now a wide-eyed, gleaming boy attempting to leave an impression on me.

I let out my trademark smile. It had worked in the past and there was no reason why it wouldn't protect me now from popular praise, the smoothest odourless poison that goes to one's head.

'Yes, I've got it now! Oof, I'm so bad with names. I'm so sorry. It's so embarrassing, Mr Bhaduri,' she spluttered. 'We went to see *Alamgir* yesterday. He had heard really good things from some of his friends. Oh, it was even better than we had thought it would be. And to think that this is your first stage appearance. It is your first stage production, is it not? We both go to the theatre quite often. But we haven't seen anything like *Alamgir* at the Cornwallis. I had no idea that anyone could be such a perfect Aurangzeb. Truly, Shishir-babu . . .'

The place suddenly seemed to erupt with lizards. The creature above the fish tank had been joined by another, and there had to be others raring to uncork themselves from the cold and take their rightful place in the light. There was no longer haughty numbness I felt. Bolu-babu sensing discomfort coming my way had moved on and disappeared out into the street. Was I in any position to tell the woman and the man that I was not the person they thought me to be? I could have pliered out a smile and cleared the confusion with a joke or a line of undetectable wit. But I didn't. If bioscope star Abani Chatterjee was being mistaken for theatre upstart Shishir Bhaduri, there must be a reason for it.

I nodded as I smiled, pulling myself out of the Tea Room as I conducted these more sophisticated motor nerve gestures. The door swung open and I managed my own escape. As I heard some agitated sentences swim their way outside, I could sense a whole contingent of heads turn and look at me—Abani in denial.

Outside, the grandest boulevard in the city greeted me half-heartedly. It was a much busier version of the cemetery on South Park Street, except that instead of the tangle of dignified-by-death greenery, there were stone, dust, hundreds of outsize hoardings, and several generations of traffic plying its way up and down this long street. The black automobiles moved like whirring giant ants, with very few drivers inside bothering *not* to use the horns—all of them sounding like collapsing lungs—lest their caste-importance as automobile drivers be diminished. The few carriages there were had already started to look out of date on this street, and as I stood outside the tea room I saw a traffic policeman, his wide belt strapped at chest level, shout in chaste Hindustani into the bewildered face of a two-horse carriage driver: 'Can't you see, fool, that this isn't a roundabout?' People had to look left and then right at least thrice before crossing the wide road. Accidents were common on Park Street.

And yet, despite all this stir and busyness, despite the fact that I was now armed with a possibility of clawing my way back to the life I knew best, I could see that the street, along with the city beyond, was preparing for decay.

The people were flowing like spittle from a faulty tubewell. The city was bathed in a purplish hue, strange for that time of the day, almost as if it was waiting to crack and creak. A man walked by briskly next to me, holding his dhuti-end just so that he could get a firm grip on himself. A gaggle of youngsters was haggling with a carriage driver while the nag was flapping his tail in the hopeless effort to drive away the flies feeding off a sore on its neck. An Englishwoman with a tiny umbrella that barely covered her hat-adorned head was raising her voice in consternation and a mangled mix of English, Bengali and Hindustani: 'Careful, now. Mr Messenji, please tell them to be careful. The table-end's scraping against the doorway!' And then there was a boy in bilious shorts who had latched on to the back of a stationary Ford, waiting for the vehicle to take him away to any place but here.

But as I turned the corner, bucketing out the memory of the mishap that had taken place inside the Tea Room, I saw the streets take on a different colour. The purple gave way to a muddier shade, a more liquid form of the yellow-grey that existed when everything was as it should be. In a side street, a small crowd had gathered. It was still gathering in force and numbers and was centring on a spot bang in the middle of the road.

'You can't see anything down there,' a voice from the human thicket said laconically as if replying to a query about directions.

'I doubt if you'll be able to *hear* anything from down there either,' said a portly man whom I could actually see.

'Has anyone called the corporation?' asked an Englishman in a shabby sort of waistcoat with his sleeves pulled up. No one seemed to register his presence even as the knot of humanity opened up just a little, making a path to the centre of whatever mysterious phenomenon was playing itself out. I entered the zone by walking through the remnants of this minutes-long human parting. The scene was, I noted with the smallest of pleasures, not too unlike an outdoor shoot.

As I reached very close to the epicentre, I noticed a young man, not older than a boy, really, generously covered in muck clamber out of a hole. The sinewy figure, with only its eyes and teeth blinking white, could have been one of those underworld demons I would worry about as a boy at the Chatterjee household.

So there I was confronting another Hole. This one was far from being the most private gateway to hell. It was a perfectly circular disk of emptiness and depth in the middle of the road near the centre of a city that only ten years ago had been the capital of the country. The boy had stepped out and was standing with a rope tied around his waist and covered with something dark and noxious that did not drip but clearly wanted to.

'Nothing,' he said shaking his head slowly, worried about spraying gunk on to others. 'There's no sign of anyone down there.' With a palm made rigid, he scraped a fearful layer off one arm as if he was sandpapering it at the same time.

In a crowd, there is always the explanator, the slightly unfortunate soul who gains whatever importance he can by explaining the proceedings to those who have just walked in. He looks like any other man, but suffers from the terrible vice of enjoying the self-righteous pleasure of being patient with others. Built into this arrogance is his ridiculous notion that every other man in the crowd is inferior to him, especially in the powers of observation and inference. It was such a man who—for lack of a better word—'explained'.

'There he was crossing the road and suddenly—"hoosh!"—he was gone. I was coming down that side of the street. He didn't even let out a cry. He was there and then not there. There was just a quick sound like a cycle tyre puncture as he fell through the manhole.'

As I stood there, waiting to see what people do when a person disappears as if by the draw of a lottery, I learnt that the unfortunate man had left no traceable signs of his vanishing. There were no belongings left behind—no upturned slipper, or blood from a scrape, or a file, a letter, a book. The explanator, who was also the sole eye-witness, described the man who vanished.

He was a large man with a moustache in white dhuti-panjabi. And he was sweating, something that was apparent even from a distance as 'he was constantly mopping his forehead with a white handkerchief. He was also carrying a thick red file or book or something in one hand'. I was still not sure that it was Balendranath Sarkar who had fallen through a manhole. But something inside me told me it was. There had been too many disruptions and falls in and around me for me not to know the signs.

The corporation authorities sent a two-member team 'down there' to investigate. I didn't stay till the investigation was done. But a week later, the *Basumati* carried a small report in one of its inside pages. It wasn't about a man falling into an uncovered manhole near Park Street never again to be seen, but about Balendranath Sarkar, a garment manufacturer, theatre owner and producer of motion pictures.

The police had conducted a search for Balu Sarkar after his son, Kamal Sarkar, sent a man to check a certain place (not elaborated in the report) two days after he had last seen his father and the man was told by the residents of this place—where Mr Sarkar would occasionally stay overnight—that they hadn't seen him for a full three days before his disappearance. That had been the last time he had made a nocturnal visit there. After duly conducting an investigation that involved people who had last met or seen him, the police declared Balendranath Sarkar 'permanently missing and/or probably demised'.

So. Did I contact the authorities about my midday meeting with Bolu-babu? Did I tell them that I was supposed to have got a call from him after receiving a copy of the script of the bioscope he wanted me to be in? No, I didn't. But I did keep telling myself for some time that a German by the name of Joe May would get in touch with me. I was so sure about this that I had even worked out my answer to the query, 'But didn't Mr Sarkar tell you about the feature?' I would show surprise with my voice if it was over the telephone, with my eyes if it was in person.

But even if I did know that there was an 'international' feature with the working title *The Indian Tomb* that was being planned, this knowledge was as useful to me as a glass of water is to a fish in the sea. There was no news of Joe May or *The Indian Tomb* or anything that would remotely suggest the return of Abani Chatterjee to the motion pictures.

So I kept quiet, while everything kept quiet back at me. The script never surfaced and neither did any offer.

In November that year, I saw a film called *The Indian Tomb*. I must admit that I was more drunk than I normally care to be when going to a picture theatre. My condition could have affected me when the lights went out and the orchestra started to scrape out notes. After the first two bars of the opening reel, I started snoring. Every once in a while, there were nudges from behind and the side accompanied by shush-es and more and more variations of 'What's happening, mister?' I believe the feature was about a German architect coming to an Indian kingdom and falling in love with a dancer whom the king secretly and then not so secretly loved. I knew by the hammer in my head the next day that utter despair is silent and is as brightly white as it is darkly black.

—

Which is why four years later when Charu Ray told me over the phone about the arrival of a European director keen to cast me in his bioscope, I chuckled into my Haig after nestling the instrument back on to its cradle. There was something fearful in this glass-echoed chuckle, a cheerful noise I generated to make the blood inside me lap around my body faster and with more vigour. I may have recognized the restless ghost of Bolu-babu's 'Ha, ha' in it.

## herr monocle

I had never seen a monocle on a man before. Actually, I had never seen a monocle before. It was the first thing I noticed about Fritz Lang. A concentrated pool of light bouncing off his face, which, on closer inspection, turned out to be the sun perched on his right eye. As he sat in the terrace of the Great Eastern like a bird, his fingers stitched into a bony knit, I noticed his large, rectangular face that was crowned by hair that looked like hot tar. His eyes were dark and large, almost without the white parts. Even as he was speaking to the people milling around him, his eyelids hung heavily in the sunlight, emitting a slight red glow that confirmed their thinness.

Initially, Charu Ray had been assigned as the assistant art director for the project. I learnt only a few minutes before my arrival at the Great Eastern Hotel that he had now been offered the job of assistant director. He was still flush with gratitude and excitement at the unexpected turn of events. It was audible in his voice.

'Abani, Abani, there you are. I was wondering what had happened to you. Mr Lang is over there. But grab a drink first. Or do you want to get one a bit later?'

He sounded as if he had been running laps around the seated figure in the middle. His sentences were punctuated by quick gasps of breath which exaggerated the smallness of his frame. As I spoke, he gently guided me towards the Monocle.

'Excuse me, Mr Lang. This is Abani Chatterjee.'

The Monocle clutched the sides of the cane sofa he was caved in, suggesting that he was about to get up and greet me. But there he sat, unclutching his hands, and using one of them to shield his face from the sun. It was the man sitting next to him who spoke and extended his hand.

'Ah, Mr Chatterjee, finally. It's a pleasure. Robert Palney.'

He was a tall, fleshy man in a beige suit and hat and seemed to have the singular job of being a buffer between Lang and anyone else in the vicinity. I could make out by his strong and stretched out accent that he was American. 'Fritz, this is Mr Chatterjee.'

The Monocle buckled and unbuckled his hands once again. Had the first round of hand movements not been to his satisfaction? Had he instinctively thought of responding to Charu's introduction and then corrected himself because of some rule that had been set up by Palney for a smoother interaction with people? Was the Monocle interested in responding at all?

I almost extended my hand, but then realized that it wasn't necessary.

He spoke with a thick European accent, looking at me as if I was a particularly ornate chandelier hanging from a mansion in the northern part of the city.

'Abani Chatterjee, hello.'

He didn't smile or employ any of those facial gestures that usually smoothen the process of introductions. There I stood awkwardly next to Charu Ray, who didn't quite know how to continue matters while the American and the Monocle fixed their gazes on me.

'I'll just get myself a drink.' That seemed to be an appropriate remark, considering that I got the feeling that the Monocle didn't talk much.

'Sure, the bar's over there,' Palney said, with his eyes still fixed on my face.

'Could you please get me a gin? No soda. Thank you, Herr Chatterjee.'

Lang spoke in a single pitch and tone, as if speaking was a more sinewy version of standing. The harsh plainness in his speech, however, was not annoying. There was a dramatic quality to it that suggested that his words were more interesting than they sounded.

'So Herr Chatterjee,' he said a while later, not having touched the drink I had got him from the bar. 'What do you think about acting in a German motion picture? I ask because my friend Herr Ray here finds it difficult, almost impossible, to believe that there can be any worthwhile bioscope outside America. And I think Robert encourages this view.'

Robert sniggered. He had a face that found sniggering comfortable. But instead of anything sinister issuing from his wide mouth after the snigger, I saw the American's shoulders shudder as he squeezed out a laugh to give me and Charu a signal that Lang was having a bit of fun.

'You were very competent in *The Black Hole of Calcutta*. I need competence, not acting. Robert invited me to the special screening of *The Black Hole* in Berlin. I have not seen any other Indian movie, but your approach appealed to me. You do not act and that is good. That is what is good.'

Both Palney and Charu waited for my reaction, the latter with a frown, the former looking up from his drink with a very slight raising of his eyebrows. Both of them seemed to confirm my belief that the Monocle was testing me in the balcony in lieu of a proper screen test. I sat down, taking a civilized sip of my gin. Then, without even hinting at a change of expression, Lang leaned forward, bridging the space between his chair and mine and spoke into my ear.

'I have reasons to believe that you will not understand my picture.'

'I'm sorry, Mr Lang?'

I was flustered and probably showed it. But I quickly corrected myself.

'Then why am I here?' I said, banishing any trace of irritation that may have reached the surface of my face and the tenor of my voice.

The Monocle had already slithered back, this time reclining into his seat quietly as if a long wait was finally over. There could be no uncomfortable slabs of silence here. There were too many people, some in the highly excitable stage that a production team is in before the business of shooting begins. And the alcohol was also making its own gurgling sound across the terrace.

'There is not enough gin in this drink. But that is nice. That is how this glass should be. Thank you, Herr Chatterjee. It's warm here. Robert, you look as deep-fried as a Wiener schnitzel already. Maybe we should move inside.'

Once again, his words didn't have any effect apart from giving flesh to sound. They seemed to be sophisticated objects strung together and left to hang from a coat hanger.

'So what brings you here, Mr Lang? Why an India picture?'

He drew a cigarette out of a case and let it dangle like a diver frozen in the act of diving off a board. Palney, after a small fumble, lit it with a lighter that was bigger than his hand.

'I don't know really, Herr Chatterjee. But why do you ask? Surely, you really don't want to know why. Or perhaps,' a long, feline drag on the cigarette and, 'you don't know what else to ask. Don't mind me saying this, but the story itself is banal and has nothing in it. Oh, forgive me, why should *you* mind? But see that spray of red over there?'

The Monocle barely turned his head in the direction of a fire escape of an adjoining building. But somehow I knew what he was pointing to. The wall next to the black metal twirl of stairs in the distance was, like the belly-high walls enclosing us at the Great Eastern's Terrace, neatly whitewashed. A streak of red, however, broke the whiteness with considerable violence. It was the sort of visual rupture usually associated with a force of nature. This one was a paan stain. The splatter's epicentre and the sparks that grew out of it seemed to be the beginnings of a process that would culminate in the making of a red wall—and ultimately a red hotel.

'Well, Herr Chatterjee. That is a mere stab of colour, somebody's unsavoury pugmarks that require to be removed. On the other hand, if that was on a canvas, a large white canvas, not a detail different from the way it is now, there on the wall, we would have something far more interesting, don't you think? It's the same thing with the story I will be filming. The story is banal as all stories are. It's when it is converted into a moving picture, an image for every word and for every gap between the words that it will become worth its existence. By the way, she's the writer of the story.'

This time, the Monocle actually raised a finger. The lady he pointed towards was busy talking to three men who were listening to her with rapt attention.

'That's Thea. She's the one who thinks that there's something wonderfully dark but anti-Gothic in the Asiatic way of life. She told me when she first wanted me to make an India feature quite some years ago that India is an animal, not a country. And that the English try to tame it, largely unsuccessfully—I'm not talking about political domestication, but aesthetically. What do you think, Herr Ray? Will there be shadows we can manufacture and capture in this heat and later let loose in cooler climates?'

Lang stood up, adjusted his shirt cuffs and looked down at the street below. 'It's an animal. Have you been to Europe, Herr Ray? Vienna? No? Well, Europe could have been Asiatic. It's just that we domesticated the animal long ago.'

The Monocle touched his collar as if to see whether his head was still attached to his body.

'There's something about this place that makes me sweat.'

'It's the heat, Franz,' Palney said with a broad smile.

'The heat, yes, that must be it. The heat.'

As he staggered back from the edge of the terrace, he looked at me, smiled while fixing another cigarette to its holder and said loudly for everyone to hear, 'No more drinks for me. Herr Chatterjee, let me introduce you to the others.'

He was sure-footed again. The clots of people standing all around registered his presence immediately. They faltered between their sentences or quickly destroyed any evidence of their conversations. I was being introduced to people in cinema after ages.

There was the art director Otto Hunte, a man with a bulging forehead and razor-thin lips who couldn't stop talking about the interiors of the Kali temple he had visited a few years ago with a Bengali stevedore and how they reminded him of a Siennese catacomb he had once visited. Then there was the cinematographer Carl Hoffman, a teetotaller from Tübingen, who had also visited this country some years ago and was keen that his friend, a young poet and novelist called Hermann Hesse, visit this country for 'a change of inspiration'.

'Paul, this is Abani Chatterjee, our Pandit. Herr Chatterjee, Paul Richter. Paul will be our William Jones. And this beautiful lady here is Margarete. Fräulein Schoen is delightful despite all the attention she's denying me.'

Margarete of the whimsical voice and flower-spattered cotton dress suddenly erupted like a mouse on fire, 'Fritz, Fritz, about my part, you know how I am about . . .' My lateral vision guided me to a corner where Mihir Das was listening to the tall lady whom the Monocle had earlier identified as Thea. So that was Thea von Harbou, the writer of the Joe May script that Bolu-babu had dangled above my head. Although I couldn't yet see her face very clearly, I did notice that the hard edges of it were being smoothened in the sun, transforming her into the embodiment of something pure and exotic and without passion.

'So you used to be in the theatre before, Mr Chatterjee?' the chiselled Paul Richter asked me before squashing his cigarette into the nearby ashtray.

'I've been in bioscopes some ten years. I never really had much exposure on the stage as I went straight to the pictures. Your first time in India?'

'Yes, first time for all of us actually, barring Carl and Otto. Carl's been interested in Buddhism for a long time. Thea has been to Ceylon. She came with Leni, another film friend of hers, to holiday next to the Indian Ocean. But she's never been up here to India. Have you met Thea?'

Richter led me to the spot where Mihir and Thea had been joined by another woman. The sari-clad woman and Mihir, who had avoided me for five years the way a dog avoids another dog's puddle, smiled at me nervously, looking quickly away when Richter nudged Thea and introduced me to her.

Thea did not look like an actress. As I had suspected from the distance, her face was too angular to be able to conduct any emotions barring the basic ones. It was a practised face. I smiled and told her that it was a pleasure to meet the writer and that she had done a wonderful job in capturing the mysterious communication between two civilizations and turning it into a tale of a personal voyage.

She turned around to face me properly, her face now rising more than a few inches above mine. I felt a warm scurry across the landscape of my body as she responded in perfect English. The terrace space suddenly tapered into a cluster of small rafts floating on a horizonless sea. I kept my emptied glass (I had forgotten whether I had stuck to gin or moved to schnapps or whisky) on the ledge, making sure that I did not lose my balance.

Encounters with women are more prevalent in my profession than in any other. Perhaps tailors meet more women. But actors, both in the bioscope and in the theatre, have to bear with this occupational hazard. There are only two kinds of women in this world—the predatory, and those who exist because they have to. The second kind are like air—only a bit more physical than a rumour, and far too absent to make their actual presence felt. The predator, on the other hand, need not always be a Mae West, planting her flag in landscapes and claiming territorial rights over people and the space they inhabit.

With this golden-haired woman who stretched out vertically in front me, I felt perturbed. She spoke in a manner that made her appear capable of tightening and loosening the iron bolts that hold up humans around her. Was she a predator?

'Ah, Mr Chatterjee, Mr Das was just telling me about you. Fritz saw one of your bioscopes at the UFA-Palast am Zoo last year and told me that he simply had to have you in this film. I'm afraid I haven't seen any of them yet. But Mr Das insists that I simply must.'

Mihir produced a weak smile that crumpled to the floor the moment it left his mouth. I acknowledged Thea's hand as she shook mine and registered a near firm grip in the touch. Her mouth was moving at a completely different speed from the sound that was coming out of it. I distinctly remember having to lip-read her. Her eyes were blue, not quite large enough to harbour clouds, but as bright as those hand-tinted reels in shorts, bursting with reds and blues and greens that made the reds and blues and greens of the real world look drained and colourless. They also made me think back to Shombhu-mama's old obsession about Kinemacolor cameras and projectors and his heartbreak over not meeting its prophet, Charles Urban.

(Incidentally, I was later disappointed with Kinemacolor. It turned out to be capable of depicting only wishy-washy colours. Just a few tints—mainly red and blue—would douse the running frames on the screen. One commentator in *Jugantar* even called the Kinemacolor experience 'a breakthrough, if depicting a desert in Rajasthan in jaundice yellow can be deemed a breakthrough'. Between Kinemacolor washouts and hand-coloured bioscopes, there never was any contest.)

Our encounter was terminated when, with a flick of her neck, she responded to a man standing next to the rubber plant on the other side. She excused herself with a smile and was gone. So there I stood, mortally afraid that I would now have no choice but to indulge Mihir Das with polite banter.

Five years ago, Mihir had been desperately trying to break

out of his standard stage roles as the brother of Ram, the son of Shivaji, the minister of Ashoka, the boot boy of Clive. He wanted to become a proper bioscope actor. I got to know him on the sets of *The Black Hole* in which he had a minor role as the adviser of Mir Jafar. He was one of the many people who had been there on the night I reportedly 'jumped' on Adela Heaslop née Quested. With each rendition of the incident, Mihir added his own colourful, verb-filled details. No wonder the man, one of the many responsible for turning me overnight from public darling to lumpen rapist, ultimately found success in bioscope direction rather than in acting.

Luckily, Paul Richter saved me.

'Thea is not only Lang's story-writer, collaborator and wife. She's also the only person who can control him. The only one,' he added in all seriousness, 'he's afraid of without having to be uncomfortable with.'

It had been the tiniest of introductions. But there I was, back in the whirring, chirping, hyper-emoting world of the bioscope, a toe returning inside its shoe-space. The Great Eastern terrace had already started to tilt in angles that were liberating despite it blocking off the view across the street. As I stood, momentarily by myself, squeezing the glass in my hand and feeling the Abani in me escape in bubbles, Lang rang the glass in his hand with a spoon. Standing next to a Victrola, which till a few minutes ago had been emitting sonorous music from inside its spacious, wooden bowels, the Monocle spoke.

'Ladies and gentlemen, a moment's attention please. As the director, I demand a moment's attention.'

A ripple of laughter aligned everyone like iron filings hypnotized by a horseshoe magnet. In clipped, hyperbolic understatements, Lang announced that he was looking forward to making his first 'movie about the Orient and its dark wonderments' and working with the cast and crew who were before him. Shooting would start next week and the budget required the feature to be completed in three weeks. There would be a meeting on Monday at nine in the morning in the hotel and he would like everyone to go through the script one more time before work started. I let out a loudish nod when he mentioned something about 'the new people who have come aboard'. But when I saw Charu and two other gentlemen nodding like horses waiting at the Maidan, I quickly transformed mine into a jerky movement signifying some sort of discomfort.

'Robert, I know you have to breathe over my shoulder to check whether we're putting Decla-Bioscop's money to any good use or not. You can let Herr Pommer sitting in his plush Berlin office know in the telegram you'll be sending today that Otto, Carl, Herr Ray and I went to the studios yesterday. Shooting begins next Tuesday. So Margarete and Paul, drink slowly, we have work to do the next few days.'

'Fritz, du diktator du!' Margarete Schoen shouted out from the front, her voice leaning over flirtily. Even the Monocle allowed himself a smile. Everyone laughed at that exchange. I didn't. By the time I realized that the moment for me to join in had passed, Lang had wrapped up his little speech and was moving away from the ominous Victrola, now being readied into action once again by a hotel staff.

But before he slipped away from the terrace, the Monocle theatrically pointed at the banner that the organizers had strung up above the doorway:

'A GAL A DAY! WELCOME FRITZ LANGE!'

'Well, that's the most inviting welcome I will ever receive anywhere. But where *are* the gals?' Lang said deadpan, a moment before the gathered worthies erupted into one dusty guffaw. My eyes were on Thea van Harbou towering next to a suited-booted Lalji. Once again I failed to join in the laughter. I was thinking of Durga. At the onset of my return to the bioscopes, I found myself afflicted with the worst possible problem that an actor can possibly have: bad timing.

—

Back home later that afternoon, I couldn't stop thinking of Thea. But in the new face, I kept seeing the old one. Thea and Durga looked nothing like each other. One had hair that was yellow as a mustard field and tied into a tight bun. The other had hair as black as any daughter-in-law from Nabakrishna Deb's family. One spoke English in an accent that would have not been out of place in any viceregal party. The other, I had heard speak only in heavy Bengali or, as was the case during scenes, not at all. And yet there was something more than the alabaster skin that brought the two together.

Thea was Lang's second wife. His first wife had allegedly found the Monocle in the arms of Thea one evening and had left him. Lang and Thea had been together ever since. I, for one, could see the virtue of being enmeshed in tall, white arms.

The drinks had left me with a dull head-throb. It wasn't quite an ache, but since no one has ever given the condition I was in a different name, I can only recall it as a headache. I sat down with my Haig and folded the script to the page where I made an appearance, somewhere deep inside the bundle. I was Pandit Ramlochan, the Sanskrit tutor of the great eighteenth-century Orientalist scholar Sir William Jones. The bioscope was about William Jones, his years in India, his decision to leave the successful and comfortable confines of London to undertake the task of reminding a forgetful country of its glorious past. But at the same time, it was about a man who, seeking an alibi for the failures in his personal life, finds the alibi, but to no avail.

The script of *The Scholar of Calcutta* was littered with detailed stage directions. It was almost as if Lang and Thea were not going to leave anything to chance or the whims of the actors. The script was full of typewritten lines like 'He moves next to the lamp and peers into the paper'; 'The look is more of a growl than a stare'; 'The hand is shown in close-up, so the crumpling must be done extra slowly'. As I kept reading, it became apparent to me that the camera and the sets were going to be the real actors in this bioscope.

Even the scene in which Richter as Jones staggers out of the Asiatic Society after a rousing reception to his groundbreaking paper on Sanskrit phonetics and fights the desire to throw himself into the river is more about what he *feels* rather than what he does. According to the script, the viewer sees a nor'wester raging, and Jones nearly blown into the Hugli. All because his wife, the patient Anne Maria, grows impatient with his life of scholarship and her own in a strange land.

Charu told me that what had drawn Lang and Thea to the story (written by an unknown Austrian lady by the name of Astrid Schenkl, who had studied Sanskrit in India and mysteriously disappeared while visiting Allahabad some eight years ago) was not only the matter of a European scholar losing himself in a world that he was trying to understand, but also the situation of the local Pandit, his tutor, who was thought by the rest of his peer group to be part of a secret cult. The fact that William Jones seeks out this Pandit, a non-Brahman in a world of Brahmans, to be his tutor makes the story a tale of twin souls, a fable about two conservative outlaws, both of whom are condemned to hanker after something they can never consider their own, and in the process neglect what is rightfully theirs. This 'explanation', typed out in double space unlike the rest of the script which was in single space, was on a smaller piece of paper, tied by a string right at the end.

'He's been working on this project ever since he completed the feature *Spiders*,' Charu explained. 'He calls it his attempt to capture the "Expressionism of the Asiatic".'

The more I read the script the more I realized that there was something awkward about it, something forcibly glued and yet not sticking. And yet, the real story, the real bioscope, stared at me as I held the slab of papers in my hand while resting my legs on the cane chair in my living room. For Pandit Ramlochan, it seemed to me, could be played—even within the tight prison that was the overwritten script—as a complex man fuelled by ambition and wracked by the guilt of being envious of a lesser, more fêted man. Dare I say, even at that stage and even with no guilt of envy harboured inside me, I saw the Pandit in me. Or perhaps, it was the other way round.

And yet, Lang had turned Ramlochan into a footstool of a character.

The Haig fuelled my thoughts farther afield. A shadow from the only light in the room was falling on the wall calendar depicting Kali in between the seated figures of Ramakrishna and Sharada. The three of them were shorn of their divinity and had the look of people in a hair-oil advertisement more at home on a Shyambazar billboard than on the wall of my room.

What was I to do? Creep up to the Monocle and tell him that his bioscope required a significant change of perspective? Tell him that the real story was not about the Englishman who wanted to unlock the past of a civilization but about the Pandit who was doomed to live his life out in an intellectual desert and only desired to move to a place where he would be finally appreciated by people like himself? Tell him that I saw myself in the man and the man in me?

But then, still young and with fireflies in my brain, I would rather have been consigned to the jatra than be mistaken as someone pleading for the role of my life. I grant you that when a man returns from an island-prison to the world that is not cordoned off, there is a sense of desperation that makes him willing to overlook acts of embarrassment that may be required to be committed. But my years in the wilderness hadn't quite purged me of that other, older desperation to protect myself from appearing like a complete fool before people, especially people like Lang. So under the shadow falling on the Ramakrishna–Kali–Sharada calendar, on which a lizard had now parked itself, I decided that I would hold my tongue. And to make me refrain from constantly returning to the thought of how holleringly obvious it was to make the story revolve around Pandit Ramlochan—and *not* around Sir William Jones— I pushed myself to think about Durga. Or was it Thea von Harbou?

—

'Paul, I need you to turn away from the camera when you hear the news of the new church being built. You don't like the idea of a church being built with the money of thieves and people whom you despise. So your body must show the contempt you feel for all of them.'

I was sitting through the shoots most days. The action

inside the studio was going on at breakneck speed, and I grudgingly admired Lang's stubbornness each time he crushed a long-stemmed cigarette and shouted 'Cut' and wanted a re-shoot and got it. I also understood why the Monocle had the habit of gridlocking his fingers. Behind the camera, it was either Carl Hoffman or Lang himself turning the handle. Unlike Shombhu-mama or the others at Alochhaya, neither of them counted out loud. But what Lang did was bob his head, as if goading on what was being performed in front of the camera to get inside the box. And with his left hand having nothing to do during these longish moments, it would fidget about as if with a life of its own. So Lang's clasping of fingers became understandable when he was not filming. The hands needed rest.

A day before my first scene, Richter invited me over to his hotel for a drink or two. We were only some hours away from becoming William Jones and Pandit Ramlochan and our bodies, the German insisted, needed to get used to each other.

'His *Dr Mabuse* was absolutely fantastical. It's about this man who controls minds and cheats, seduces and enthrals people with his powers. The sets, Herr Chatterjee! Oh, you should see the nightclub set that Otto designed. The walls tilt in and heave out around a gambling table and Lang plays the accordion with our eyes.'

Paul Richter's eyes shone like a pair of reflected spotlights as he sped on. He had played a playboy duped by the evil Mabuse in the film. Every time he spoke of the man who played Dr Mabuse, his voice dipped in veneration. 'Herr Klein-Rogge, oh . . . I don't know that a man can have such eyes. He had the same glaring, boring-into-the-air look throughout the shoot as he has in the film. Lang took two hours to shoot the playing cards scene to get the light falling just right on his eyes.'

Richter was slightly less enthusiastic about the mythological *The Nibelungen*, the last two-part feature that Lang had made before diving headlong into *The Scholar of Calcutta*. But the lack of hyperbole this time arose not so much out of aesthetic preference as out of awkwardness to gush on about a feature in which Richter himself played the lead role.

'Lang shot the scene in which I slay the dragon in a Zeppelin hangar that had been converted into a thirteenth-century forest,' he said, looking beyond a hoarding advertising Silver Clouds cigarettes.

Silver Clouds weren't bad at all. They tasted like trapped air before a thunderstorm—a quality endowed, I would learn, to the tobacco after a careful double-roasting. Rona, in his continuing attempts to be a sophisticate-husband, had switched from our regular brand to Silver Clouds, and I had tried them a few times. Launched as Gandhi Cigarettes, these were the country's first 'nationalist' cigarettes and were gaining more and more smokers for being healthier than other brands. Instead of being touched by the gesture, Gandhi wrote a whining article in *Young India* objecting to his name being used to sell cigarettes.

I have a strong feeling that this objection was because of the frustrating failure of a three-week fast that he thought would magically patch up the growing problems between Hindus and Muslims. This was a man who was worse than a bioscope starlet. If things didn't turn out the way he wanted them to, he would sulk and go on a fast. So the brand name 'Gandhi Cigarettes' was dropped and a new name given. It's another matter that the company had to fold up a few years later because of the change in nomenclature. Names still mattered a lot. I remember reading Pothan Joseph later in the *Bombay Chronicle*: 'Sales dropped and it melted like clouds in the silver sky.'

Silver Clouds was, however, still alive when I was on the balcony with Paul Richter that evening.

'Herr Chatterjee, can I ask you a personal question?' Richter turned around, leaning against the balcony wall. 'Do you think a German blacked up can play the role of an Indian? I mean, however good an actor he may be and with the necessary knowledge of Indian behaviour, can he convince the audience that he's an Indian?'

Aah! Richter was talking of the powers of convincing people and the need to be authentic.

'Mr Richter, what do you see in that cigarette hoarding there?'

'A man holding a cigarette . . . and the line "Every dark moment can have a . . . silver . . ." does it say "cloud"?'

'Yes, it does. It's advertising Silver Clouds cigarettes. They're not too expensive and are overwhelmingly smoked by Bengali gentlemen. The lower classes smoke cheaper cigarettes, while the English smoke Pall Malls.'

Richter blew a smoke ring that floated away in the hope that it would one day encircle the city below us.

'And so?'

'Well, that man on the billboard, does he look like me or like you? Do you think he's a Bengali, Richter?'

He turned around, took a good long look at the man illuminated by street light. The face was long, white, the beginnings of a dinner jacket peeping out around the shoulder region. His hair was fashioned in the style of Fairbanks, screeched to perfect combness, the billboard artist suggesting reflected light by a few streaks of white in the curve of black. The words next to his face, suggesting that his cigarette was his only true friend, were curled and a little fussy, almost effeminate in their effect. But the man's face was clearly that of a Charles, Peter, Edward or Albert—not that of Harish, Syed, Dijendra or Prabir.

'I must say that's the most Anglo-Saxon Bengali I've ever seen,' Richter said with a smile. His white shirt fluffed up in the evening breeze, making him look like a cricketer at the Eden Gardens in mid-run-up.

'If that European man on the billboard there can do his job, I don't see why any other European can't, with some deft make-up, pull it off as a screen Hindu.'

I, in my white shirt and brown trousers, remembered my stint as John Zepheniah Holwell, powder-dabbed and breeched, with a wig heavy with strands of manly blond curls straddling over my crow's nest hair. But more importantly, I recalled seeing myself as Holwell on the screen, as much of an Englishman as the Silver Clouds man was a Bengali. Had the people watching those climactic scenes fidgeted slightly in their seats, discomforted by the fact that it was Abani Chatterjee and not an Anglo playing the survivor of the Black Hole of Calcutta? Had they caught on to the fact that they were being fooled by bioscope actors with make-up? I don't think so.

'Ha! Well put, Herr Chatterjee. I ask because Lang seems to agree with you. It's only with you that he has made the exception.'

That was true. Till that moment I hadn't realized that, barring the scores of one-rupee extras, I was the only Indian in the cast. All the other characters in *The Scholar of Calcutta* were being played by consonant-munching Germans—not only William and Anna Maria Jones and the other Europeans, but also the Brahmans of Nadia, Raja Nabakrishna Deb, Pandit Ramlochan's helper Putu, and at least eight more non-firingis.

'Palney had suggested getting a few local actors apart from

you. It would, he said, make the film "genuine". Lang simply rejected the idea. I guess he has his reasons.'

With my mouth lined with a last drink, I left Richter to his devices, but not before I had picked up the fanciful phrase 'Auf wiedersehn'. In the backseat of a Studebaker, I looked at the streets outside. It was late and the electric lights made the city look like a running bioscope. We circled half around the place where the Holwell Monument, that giant non-Shaivite phallus at the corner of Dalhousie Square, had stood during my grandfather Bholanath Chatterjee's time. The driver and I then rolled along wide-screen surroundings with pastel coloured buildings that seemed always freshly painted. I heard a click the instant we entered Boro Bazar, the entry point into the inchoate. Instead of the seaside silence of Chowringhee, the old Black Town announced itself with night loudness. If it wasn't the sound of splashing water or snatches of a quarrel, there were the less subtle sounds of entangled and maddened dogs.

Just as the car turned a corner—for here was a particular stretch that was only made up of corners—the Klaxon horn erupted. Whether the man lit up by the arc lights of the Studebaker was shaking from the after-effects of a bone-crumbling hooter or because of the amount of alcohol he had consumed could not be confirmed. The driver had proceeded to stick his head out and spill forth a volley of words that referred to the man's pedigree and incestuous behaviour. But under the canopy of the car, I simply saw his face. It was bursting with a white light of its own and staring back at me.

'Gggghnaaaaaaaaa . . .' was the sound that erupted from his mouth, before he gnarled himself up again and shouted, 'The English are here! The English are here! Can anyone hear me? The English are here!'

I shook myself forward from my seat and barked at the driver in front.

'Just drive! Just get us out of here!'

With the arc lights falling one last time on the illuminated man in a white panjabi and dhuti and a thrice-wound garland of white flowers round his right wrist, the car quietly turned, sidestepping him. He was rooted to the ground even as he followed the car with his hub-cap eyes.

'Can anyone . . .' he had started again as his face receded through the window. But he was cut off by another burst of the Klaxon that left Boro Bazaar and its blackness jangling for minutes. I had crossed over to Lang's 'Asiatic side'. And this was where the city was, by civic and sensual order, supposed to provide me solace and an untrammelled feeling of belonging. Some twenty minutes later, I closed my eyes, no longer required to be in that day or hanker for tomorrow.

—

Ten minutes on the set, it became clear that Fritz Lang's bioscope was not going to be like those directed by Dhirendra Ganguli, Shishir Bhaduri and the other yodellers. As soon as I stepped out of the make-up room after getting myself into a greying dhuti and strapping on a gamchha across my shoulder, I was awash with a peculiar kind of happiness. After half a decade of not being allowed to be anyone else, I had almost forgotten what it was to step inside another skin, into a place where Abani Chatterjee disappeared.

I was Pandit Ramlochan Sharma. There had initially been a suggestion that I get my head shaved, leaving only a horse-tail strand of a tiki at the back. Then I reminded Lang that Ramlochan was no Brahman and my unshorn head would visually make me stand out from the Brahmans—played, of course, by shaved Germans whose heads were domes of skin bouncing off the powerful set lights. So I kept my hair, on which another longer pile was added.

In my heavy make-up, I was in my early sixties and I felt it. A head-rush of arrogance, like the first cigarette of the morning, greeted me as I walked towards the pool of light a few metres away from Lang and the camera. Otto Hunte was walking up and down the phalanx of arc lights, directing and redirecting positions.

'Ready?' the Monocle asked me with his hand resting on the camera handle. He could have been a zamindar, hand on elegant cane, posing before a slick-haired photographer.

Already, the machines, the railings, the criss-crossings that held up every part of the set had vanished. As I sat down at my position, next to a blacked-up Brahman and in front of a sweating William Jones, I was already thinking of how to impress the Englishman with my understanding of Kalidas and other gems from the Sanskrit language. The desire to catch his attention made the camera, the lights, the Monocle all sizzle and disappear. I was Pandit Ramlochan Sharma inside a courtroom in the company of people I despised.

Somewhere in the vague distance, I heard a voice shout out, 'Roll camera!' It could have been street noise.

Ramlochan meets William Jones for the first time. He is supposed to be intimidated and impressed by the man and the setting. I, however, feel neither. All I feel is the need to tell the man in the wig and jacket that I must be sent to his country to spread the knowledge of an ancient nation. I feel a good need to shake him by the collar and state that *I* am that person and no one else—certainly not any of those pompous, parroting Brahmans who pass themselves off as scholars discussing the exact number of asuras that died fighting the Goddess Chandi. But there is a stronger feeling: the desire to be fêted by the world and by those who truly value knowledge. Below that, the way the foundations of a building hold up its floors, lies another feeling, making itself felt like heartburn: to be in the place where it's not impossible to touch women with skin as white as salt.

'Don't act! I don't want acting. I want architecture! And for that you must stop acting, Herr Chatterjee. You read the script. So can we please stick to it! Okay, another take. Ready? I want you, Herr Chatterjee, to look into Jones's eye shiftily. Hold back the beginnings of a smile. Look at him the way a child looks at his father in army uniform for the first time. Okay, positions. Roll camera!'

I saw Richter and me and the other actors in the black and white of my eye. There was going to be a halo powdered all around Sir Williams's face looking on to the small multitude of scholars before him. He was to choose, in a cherry-pluck, one of them to teach him Sanskrit. Among the crowd, I would stand out as the only person without the caste marks—and still, in his magnanimity, the English scholar would choose me. That choice would be translated in a medium-shot on my face, a title card explaining who I was, my face explaining what I wished.

But as shooting continued, I grew increasingly uneasy with my Ramlochan. There were only three scenes to be shot in the entire shot with me in them. Later that evening, things came to a flashpoint. It was the scene when William Jones discovers that his Pandit is planning to sacrifice a child for the purpose of mastering a new science. Lang wanted Jones to drive sense into Ramlochan, making him give up his diabolical plan, with a momentous ray of light falling on my face inside my hut-room.

'I want the change to be fast,' he said, clearly with a detailed picture in mind. 'I want you to move as fast as good can change to evil.' He clapped his hands sharply to emphasize the point he was making.

The studio was hotter than the outside and the lights were making the Monocle sweat enough for his eyeglass to mist up from time to time. He kept rubbing away the moisture with an impeccably white handkerchief. But what started worrying everyone was that his normal aristocratic look had begun to change into something more dishevelled. There was a moment before the child-sacrifice scene that I noticed Paul shuffling over to Thea, who had arrived at some point, exchanging looks and words. It bothered me that Lang, in particular, and everyone, in general, were treating me as a child. Ramlochan was completely in their hands and the palpable feeling that I got was that there was a tussle under way between them and me.

Takes flew like garbage birds, picking on each scene and then shooed away until another take. The mumblings between Lang, Thea and Otto grew. Even as a man following a fixed script, placed inside the eighteenth-century and growing wary of not being able to think the way the Pandit was really supposed to think, I realized that there was something going deeply wrong. The film was turning out to be a joke. Despite my complete lack of reputation at that point, I feared for my reputation. I spoke about this to Charu at the Dilkhusha over mutton cutlets.

People were gently noticing me, with my unwigged hair cropped to a widow's mop. Certainly the regulars who had stopped noticing me since *The Black Hole of Calcutta* were now looking at me again, trying to place me, if not acknowledge me.

'Charu, how do you think the bioscope's going?' I asked

before glugging down some water so that I could listen to his response without any interruptions.

'Oh, this *is* an experience, Abani. I really sometimes wonder what would happen if our bioscopes were shown to regular audiences in Berlin, London, Paris, Chicago, New York.' And then he repeated 'Berlin' again without realizing it. 'All the places where performances are going hand in hand with the latest technologies, the latest tastes. Well, this is the big break, Abani. Don't worry about the takes. That's how Lang works with everyone.'

'What do you think about Lang?'

'Oh,' he said with a knowing double-shrug, 'he's different all right. Not at all like the Madhu Basus and the Jyotish Banerjis of the world. But that's the whole point. What he's capturing on film is distilled movement. I can't wait to see him on the cutting table.'

Clearly, Charu was not in any way perturbed by the way Lang conducted the making of the bioscope.

'Tell me something. You've seen any of his other films?'

Charu hollered for some water. He had bitten into a chilli. An answer was delayed for a while, as he sucked in air by the windful, hanging out his tongue to dry after each downpour of water. Breathing heavily, he finally said, 'Tea?'

'Sure. Have you seen any of Lang's movies?'

'No. But Franz Osten has.'

'Who's Franz Osten now? The man you met in London during that art course?'

'That's right. Osten's the brother of Peter Ostermayr the producer. Osten is getting into the bioscope business full-time and had mentioned something about the "Austrian Lang" to look out for. When he learnt that I was going to work with

Lang, Osten got all excited and wrote to me about how he had immensely enjoyed his *Dr Mabuse the Gambler* recently. An "incredible document of our time"—his words, not mine. And this isn't official yet, but with Lang making *The Scholar of Calcutta* here, Osten is already getting ready to make his own India feature. I smell a trend. And guess whose name I've recommended?'

He chuckled merrily, almost like a child, making me forget that he had been choking on his food just a few moments ago.

'I recommended you! I told him that Lang's got you in his feature. He's keen. But Abani, stick to the script, will you?' he added in case I had lost my powers of understanding.

'Listen Charu, maybe it's nothing to worry about and it'll be sorted out in the cutting room, but I'll be honest with you. Lang's idea of the film is all wrong. It's silly. And I know you'll think that just because I'm playing Ramlochan I'm saying this, but the Pandit's is the real story.' It was true. The more I thought about Ramlochan, the more I thought of my own condition. A man surrounded by the rabble and being mistaken for one of the rabble. I knew that there was a tuning fork that was ringing both of us, pretender and pretended, in the same pitch. The Pandit could not but be the real story. Anything else would be horrifying. Empty and horrifying for me.

Charu looked up, emitting a wan smile.

'Abani, listen. Correct me if I'm wrong: you've been out of the pictures for five years now. You remember how Lalji treated you? Not to mention the whole bioscope industry? You really want to throw it all away? For you to start nitpicking again . . . I don't know. What can I say? We're talking here about a rising European director. You are the only Indian actor he's chosen. For god's sake, Abani, why can't you take your costume off like other actors after a day's shoot? You have just another day's shoot a week later.'

'That's how I play a character, Charu. That's what I do, that's what I've done, for all bioscopes since *Prahlad*.'

Charu let out a wet guffaw. Squeezed it through his lips.

'Okay Ramlochan Pandit. I can't argue with that. So you're not drinking for a month either, eh?'

'Ramlochan isn't a Brahman, Charu. And I would certainly be drinking if I was as frustrated as he was living under the shadow of a fool who's a leech to boot,' I said, a glass of Haig flashing in my head.

Silence. I could see that Charu was getting impatient and upset.

'Charu, who is this Fritz Lang?'

I don't know why I asked him that question. The waiter had just plonked our change in a white plate pillowed with mouri and Charu took a sprinkleful with his fingers and threw back a pile into his mouth. After a few rounds of mastication, he pushed his chair back, stood up and replied as if I had asked him the time.

'I told you, Abani. He's a European director. What else can I say? You know, if you weren't interested, you could have told me right at the start ...'

I squeezed out of the chair. My eighteenth-century dhuti, which looked not a stitch different from a twentieth-century dhuti, may have planned on getting hitched to the chair leg. But I have always had a way of dealing with obtrusive furniture. I shift them around.

# the cabinet of kalibari

He wasn't whistling. It was more like a clucking sound. Actually, it wasn't even that. It was more like a finger running across the teeth of a comb, cutting the air into strips, while each stick that made a tooth snapped back into total attention.

'Oh, it's a dog,' Lang said with all the alarm that he could muster.

The mongrel had been trotting a few feet behind us and had finally crept up to the source of the sound that had got him interested. Unlike most street dogs, there was a firmness about this one, both in terms of body and character. It was grungy, rather than mangy, and the complete absence of abscesses or any flea-ravaged patches betrayed a pedigree that did not have its source in this part of town.

'He must have heard you making that sound.'

'What sound?'

'The sound you were just making.'

'Oh, this?' he said, before letting out another volley of wet clicks. He cracked open a smile, closed it as quickly and started walking briskly, this time picking up the pace a bit to gauge the dog's level of curiosity.

'It's from *Peer Gynt*, a piece called "In the Hall of the

Mountain King" by the Norwegian composer Grieg. I used to whistle this tune all the time when I first started shaving. It was quite the rage in Europe.'

Lang obviously couldn't whistle. The dog followed us for a while, leaving us when its attention got swayed by a woman ladling out a mish-mash of leftovers on the side of the street.

The Monocle had a flushed look about his face since we had left the Great Eastern and ventured out into the early evening parts of the city that he wanted 'a feel of'. There was less than a week left for shooting to be over and I, with no more scenes to look forward to—and the only one who actually lived in the part of the city that Lang was interested in having a look at— had volunteered to be his guide. Even Lang had looked up at me when I responded to this vague wish of his.

'If you're all right with it, I could take you to the Kalighat temple. It's not too far from here. That's if you want to go to the . . . how should I put it . . .?'

'You mean in the thick of it, eh? Yes. Absolutely. Palney will arrange a car for Friday. We have only two shoots in the morning. How does that sound, Herr Chatterjee? A temple we shall visit.'

'It would be my pleasure, Herr Lang,' I had said with a smile that befits a man seeking the world and getting to be part of a local town tour, a town in which he lives.

As you may well be asking, why had I gone out of my way and offered to escort Lang around town when I had begun to suspect that he was a charlatan scooping up the exotic the way Robert Flaherty did in his pictures, to serve his clientele back in Europe and America, a philistine who had no understanding of the powers of bioscope acting? There *was* a real reason for my forwardness, my servility, if you will. And it was the arrival of an envelope at home that finally convinced me that I had to act if I was to get my due.

—

It was a manila envelope. I used to once get envelopes of various sizes every single day. Useless notices, fawning letters, business missives and the occasional erotic declaration. (Shombhu-mama's letters had stopped long ago.) They would be penknifed open by my secretary, Swapan, and the bulk of it never came anywhere close to my eyes. But for some years now the mail had dried up. Even the anonymous hate mails that would come till three years ago, the ones that promised dire consequences if 'a pervert like you continues to live in the locality', didn't bother me any more.

So when Abala, the last of her kind in the Chatterjee household, walked up to where I was sitting and announced that I had a letter, I sat up, putting away *The Statesman*, in which a notice had made me chuckle more than once that evening. The small notice had read: 'Died William Jones (b. 1879) of enteric fever. Mourned by his family and colleagues at the British India Steam Navigation Company. He served as chief engineer and his last ship was the *Gazana*.' Chuckling, I had silently wished Paul Richter a long life before making the effort to reach for the dark-tinged small bottle before me.

Abala interrupted my time with *The Statesman*. The envelope only had my name on it, the 'Abanindranath' written with a greater flourish than the 'Chatterjee'. I turned to see whether there was the sender's name on the back. There was no name. Only a large '8' scrawled in the same ink as my name in front. It covered about an eighth of the space, beaming out from its

bottom-left corner. There was no confusion about what the '8'—
that twisted garland signifying the Bengali number four—stood
for. It was the same stand-alone, smooth-bottomed figure that I
had once seen on the back of Shombhu-mama's shirt. The '8'
stood stable, with extreme ease, never worrying for a moment
that it may roll over the finite space of paper and become a ∞.
It was the Char Murti insignia. This, after the authorities had
passed the Goonda Act only a year ago.

I hadn't seen the penknife for years. In fact, I didn't care if
there still was a penknife at all. But it was pretty obvious by
now that one of those gangs pretending to be part of the anti-
Britishwalas—and thought to have been either hounded out by
the authorities or sucked in by the cross-legged Congress Party—
had sniffed out the news that I was involved in a European
bioscope production. They must have sent a threatening letter,
the kind that usually says, 'Make a contribution for your
Motherland or face the consequences.'

Remembering the death of Jarasandha, the poor man who
was ripped right down his middle from one orifice to the other
for no fault of his, I tore the flap at a point and then pulled my
finger down the envelope's barely resisting spine. Something
was folded inside. It wasn't a letter. Instead, it was a hand-
coloured print.

As far as I could make out, it was a crude, modern rendition
of a Radha–Krishna tableau, the kind sold on the pavements
alongside those racy Bat-tala publications. I poured another
round of the vile but helpful fluid into my mouth. Everything
was garish about the picture. The besotted Radha had her head
resting on the delicate shoulder of Krishna ever-so-slightly as
the blue-skinned deity blew into his flute. There was nothing
remotely erotic or divine about the picture. It was just a gaudy

print conveying nothing but two iconic lovers in the most maudlin manner possible. Another belle, a flat-bellied gopi, was approaching the couple with a plate in her hand from the corner of the frame. Everything suggested a standard Radha–Krishna picture, something that I could pass on to Abala for her pleasure rather than crumple and lob into a corner behind me for her to sweep away the next morning.

But then I noticed it. Krishna and his small-breasted, tight-bloused lady friend sitting in the middle of a setting that was not their usual landscape. Instead of the usual cow lolling about with a mango tree and a small pond as backdrop, there was a sheep grazing in the foreground. Also, the paramours were seated not on a swing or under a tree in a standardized, mythical village but on a wooden bench outside a European-style cottage. To complete the picture of total dislocation, there was the tiniest of bridges spanning a gurgling brook on which the approaching gopi was positioned. In the background, there were snow-capped hills and pine forests and rooftops with chimneys and sloping thatches. It was Radha–Krishna in Switzerland.

I turned the picture around to read the accompanying message. There wasn't any. I picked up the ruptured envelope and inside, tucked away like a child hiding from marauding captors waiting to scrub him clean, there was a newspaper cutting dated 6 September 1918. Another quick swig and I read the piece of paper. The headline, in three decks, blotted print and diminishing size, read: 'Mr F.E. Langford. Well-known Artist Leaves for England.'

I kept reading this unsolicited cutting.

*'Lacking encouragement and patronage, Indian artists cannot raise the standard of indigenous painting in a manner*

*commensurate with the undoubted ability that exists among many of the younger school,' says Mr F.E. Langford, the well-known artist, who is leaving Calcutta for Liverpool on Wednesday. Mr Langford served Messrs. Johnston & Hoffman as an artist between the years 1908 and 1911, moving to Bombay in 1912 to practise upon his own account.*

*Born in Murree, he studied at the Charles School of Art, Ahmednagar, and won a scholarship to the prestigious South Kensington College of Art, in London. A number of his works were included in Academy exhibitions at a very early stage of his professional career. It is not generally known that during his earlier studies he explored the realms of stereoscopic photography, and though for various reasons he did not pursue his interest in this sphere, some effects of his early training are considered to have played on his mature works.*

*Mr Langford has executed the portraits of many Indian noblemen, that involved fairly extensive travel over the northern part of the country, and paintings based on Indian mythological studies. In recent years, he accompanied the Italian scholar F.D. Ascoli to venture into the Sunderbans, and his love of this marshland region resulted in three large landscapes which were exhibited in London. But among Indians the desire for possession of landscape works is almost negligible and during his experience, Mr Langford has received only one commission for a scenic canvas.*

*Last year he was engaged by the late Ameer of Afghanistan to organize, at Kabul, a School of Art of which he was to be the Principal. But while awaiting the firman to enter Afghanistan, news came announcing the assassination of the Ameer.*

And right at the bottom was a charcoalized picture of the man himself. F.E. Langford was a dead ringer for the Monocle, minus the monocle, that is. I took another look at the ghastly picture of the divine lovers on the other side of the table. As I placed the news cutting along with the garish reproduction, I could feel my heart racing like an automobile along the Strand. The rest of the evening and the night that followed were spent trying to understand why I, Abani Chatterjee, was being let into this damaging secret.

—

'Shall we, Herr Chatterjee?' I heard Lang say from the other room.

He was brimming with energy that pushed him into the car and then pulled him out of it when we reached the busy pathway that led to the temple. This was not the fingers-stitched Lang of the studio. His monocle had slipped off from its perch twice inside the car, and not once did he stop mid-sentence. Lang was keen to know about the distinguished resident of Kalighat. I cleared him of one misunderstanding.

'No, that's Nataraj you're talking about. He's the Destroyer, or Dissolver if you will. Technically, Kali is Nataraj's consort.'

'And both have more than one pair of arms?'

'Yes,' I told him, 'both are multi-armed,' adding the names of a few other deities who had this advantage over mortals. Some names, to be honest, I made up on the spot.

It turned out that Lang was introduced to the multifaceted charms of Kali by the artist Jeanne Mammen in Berlin. Mammen was fascinated by Indian art, especially the ones she thought were erotic in nature. Her favourite was the 'dancing Nataraja' or, as she might have informed Lang, the 'dancing Goddess Kali'.

'She finally dragged me to what would later become the Tingeltangel Club. And there for the first time I saw a girl, with two others hidden behind her, with only a slither of a garment covering her nether region and her eyes shot with kohl. She twirled her arms, and those borrowed from the girls behind her, like a puppet who was also the puppet-master. I was mesmerized, Herr Chatterjee, completely mesmerized.'

I could actually imagine the yet-to-be Monocle Monocle gazing with a religious fervour at this white Kali/Nataraja, dancing like a snake to some Negro tune.

Kalighat, one hoped, was miles away from Berlin. No fountains of champagne running into specially made gutters. Instead, I was helping Lang to negotiate and dodge the beggars who were approaching the shaheb fast and furious, sounding their clarion call even before they reached his earshot. The lane that we were walking down was low. That is what it was, low— a street cobbled out of various pieces of solidness, lined on both sides by the low roofs of numerous shacks and hovels and thickets of people. However, neither of us, being tall men, could sense our feet traversing at a level below normal ground. This notion, I must admit, may have been aggravated by the fact that nearly every step was really a wade through a very shallow pool of water.

'Herr Chatterjee,' Lang suddenly stopped on the wet street, barely missing a peel of some sort of ex-fruit. 'Hold this for a second.'

He handed me a silver box that he had taken out of his pocket while we had been walking. As I held it, I felt stupidly immobile. Everyone else on the street walked by, barely taking note of our presence in front of them and brushing against us as if we were permeable phantoms. The Monocle took out a crumpled handkerchief from his other pocket and gestured that I hand the box back to him.

'Nothing like an evening walk to a temple. How far is it?'

'Oh, we're nearly there. Barely another minute.'

'Try some of this.' He opened the box, took two pinches of a powder that was inside through his nostrils and ran the handkerchief across his nose as if he was polishing it. 'Go on, try some.'

It looked like chalk, except finer and whiter.

'Thank you, but I'm afraid I don't take snuff,' I replied politely.

'It's not snuff, my friend. It's catarrh powder. And of the finest quality too. Clears the mind, the nasal tract and the bronchial passage. Try it, Herr Chatterjee. It works in Berlin. It should work here.'

I never cared for snuff. I know Shombhu-mama had tried it a few times until he decided to stick to cigarettes. It was from one of his discarded containers that I had tried it and sneezed my nose out. The few other times that I did hold the infernal stuff in between my thumb and forefinger—most of it staying inside my nails for days—and snorted it up my nose, I had derived no pleasure at all.

But then, Lang insisted it was something else and that it would definitely not irritate me. Saying no at that stage was impossible. And if I wanted to carry out my plan, it would have been foolish to antagonize him just then. I took a pinch and sucked the white, dandruffy powder up my nose. There was no sneeze or cough, or any of the ill effects that I had expected nasally delivered substances to have on me. There was just a slight tingle.

We hadn't taken more than ten steps when the road and everything that lined it started to change. It was neither destroyed nor dissolved, but there was something that seemed to be curling up and down the road from the sides and in front. The bending was not gradual enough to remain unnoticed. Straight lines were bending and bent lines curled.

The shapes of the structures around me—the shacks selling flowers, the barely visible sweetshops on the sides, the moving heaps of people—had started to cut across each other. It seemed that I would have to carefully ply myself through the din, careful not to walk into one of the many objects and bring the whole road and its surroundings crashing down. A dog sitting rather regally next to a pitiful beggar woman appeared only as a silhouette, as if turned into a strange chiaroscuro by the talented Otto Hunte. I stared hard before leaving the dog and the beggar behind. Was the dog drained of colour and features because of sitting too close to the rag-woman? Or was it how it was at all times, wherever it sat?

'Is that the temple, Herr Chatterjee?' I heard Lang ask.

He had fallen behind me. Lights had started to pop up from the shacks, mangy orange bits that flickered like the eyes of jackals in a crematorium.

The temple was visible at last. The two-tiered curves that hung on the top made the structure look like a bloated corpse left floating in the Hugli. Cluttered around it were smaller structures, some of which were simple replicas of the temple itself. Wide-eyed, I noted the tiny temples within the miniature temples on the temple's surface. I hadn't ever noticed them before.

I had grown quiet for the last ten minutes or so. Nature abhors quietness. If people, out of weakness or otherwise, give silence an inch, this humped creature ends up gobbling whole expanses, leaving wastelands in its wake. I nearly burst out, 'Why are you here, F.E. Langford?' But I held my tongue as tightly as I would a slithering, flopping fish in the kitchen.

'After you.'

Lang was waiting for me to show him the way. Under the shadow of the temple, with its never-ending gush of crowds coming out, coming in, like a healthy blood-jet, I looked at the man next to me. His slick, combed-back hair was glowing in the fast-falling darkness.

One feature common to the interiors of all temples is their wetness. Even the driest of structures hold on to a moisture that makes them glisten in the dark. The frog's-back appearance adds only mould to the piling congregation—crowds entering the snake's gullet and coming out with an invisible slick coated all over their bodies and their minds. The ritual bathing of the divine dumbshows; the priestly doling out of charan amrita, that sickly sweet water-goulash that's hand-cupped and gulped like vodka shots; the constant displays of a hygiene fetish that even the most unclean of visitors show cannot fully explain the temple wetness. In the right frame of mind, one realized that one was in the belly of a beast that was sweating out its special secretions. As we took off our shoes and socks and stepped on to the stone floor of the Kalighat mandir, the temple's harmless mucus greeted us.

People were noticing Lang, some even panning him with their eyes as they briskly moved away on their own trajectories.

'How will we find our shoes when we come back?'

Lang was captivated by the shape-shifting nest of shoes, slippers, sandals that formed a brown, muddy glacier at the base of the temple steps. Many pairs found themselves distressingly separated and the distress seemed to be transmitted through Lang's chaos-attacked face.

'Oh don't worry, we'll find them. And your pair will be standing out in that crowd,' I said, briefly spotting a partially upturned woman's sandal that had shamelessly climbed on to an ordinary pair of men's shoes. Only a second ago I had spotted the sandal, with the same red alta mark on the surface where the foot rests, tidily lying like the gentlest of housewives next to its twin.

Stepping over this violence of leather, we moved up and then inside the temple. As I furrowed through the crowd, careful to create a pathway for my foreign companion, I tried to imagine how our surroundings would appear to the Monocle. An outdoor shot movie into a studio set? My catarrh-whirring brain saw the darkness inside just before it ate both of us whole.

We had to stop in our tracks almost immediately as a gentleman and a lady prostrated right in front of us, both muttering 'Ma, Ma . . .' And then, only a few wet steps later Lang saw *it*, as if its sole purpose was to surprise. Inside the cage-like cubicle in front was the geometrical figure almost hunchbacked by the weight of garlands and cloth.

'There she is.' A hump like a dark hill. A conch shell sounded melodramatically at that very moment.

Lang's jaw, forever tied mandible-to-maxilla by an invisible metal string, had creaked open. Glistening in a flickering pool of oil lamps, the solid river of gold that was the tongue bisected the figure that was before us. At the core lay the noseless black face pocked with three eyes with three red corneas staring back at us like a partially blinded spider. Three of the four hands were just about visible, one of them clutching the cutter as if it was a broom.

'She's like a machine, all metal,' Lang murmured.

More than just a few people were looking at the Monocle, some staring, some openly breaking into talk about a European Kali devotee. ('See the power of Kali? Even a shaheb has been seduced by her charms!') I made feeble attempts at pretending that I was not with him.

'That cutter in her hand, Herr Chatterjee,' he said with his eyes still fixed on the tongue with a body. 'I saw pictures being sold along the road outside. They showed a man holding the same weapon, in some pictures ready to bring it down on a woman, in others, her head already chopped and dangling from her neck like a door on a hinge.'

The Monocle was right. There were clusters of people sitting outside selling watercolours of various sizes, depicting various scenes—a man being thrashed by a woman with a broom, a seated woman having her hair braided by a maid, a seated woman smelling a rose, another one holding a peacock in one hand and a rose in another, a barber cleaning a lady's ear as she draws on a hookah. There were also religious paintings, not as popular as the other ones but still steady-sellers. But the watercolours that had caught Lang's eyes, and bore a vague resemblance, if only in tone, to the hunchbacked form of the goddess in front of him, were the ones that I had strenuously avoided to look at throughout my walk.

—

I had first seen Durga on the stage as Elokeshi in *What Is This That the Mahant Has Done!* The play itself had been a crowdpuller since the time it was first staged in 1874, a year after the infamous Tarakeshwar affair. By the time I saw it at the prebioscope Alochhaya, the story of the young and beautiful wife of Nabinchandra Banerjee being seduced/raped by the head priest of the Tarakeshwar shrine had been infused with all kinds of possibilities, some outrageous, some just patently untrue.

When Alochhaya decided to turn the play into a bioscope, I was still part-prompt-boy, part-bellboy, having only the yet-to-be-released *Prahlad* under my belt. The actor chosen to play the Mahant got the role because of his curling smile, a corrugated lower lip that made the women in the company uncomfortable. His high-pitched voice wouldn't have suited a hormonal predator on the stage. But in a bioscope, with only his heavy-lidded eyes, face-bending smile and clump of fake-beard to show, he was menacing even for strangers in the audience. The delicate Ramesh Pal, who would later go on to become moderately successful as Ram in *Laub-Kush*, played Nabinchandra.

Barring Durga, the acting was terrible. But with Pramanik Bhowmick as director and a master in the cutting room, *What Is This That the Mahant Has Done!* became a magical display of special effects and drama that the bioscope alone was capable of creating.

In the stage version, Durga, shining through her jewellery, had fallen at the feet of her husband, imploring him to forgive her. The whole stage had disappeared before my eyes as I stared at the sobbing woman who in a different scene, after being knifed by the deranged-by-heartbreak Nabinchandra, cried out: 'Lord, what I had thought would happen has finally happened; I am completely destroyed. If I die, I won't be unhappy; it will be the right punishment for me. But because of this lowly sinner, you too will die. I will be the reason for my Lord's death.' Two stabs later, the crumpled form of Durga was left abandoned under the spotlights.

In Pramanik's bioscope, the climactic scene, however, involved not Nabinchandra stabbing his wife Elokeshi repeatedly with a knife, but a full-throated decapitation.

Nabinchandra is ready to leave Tarakeshwar with Elokeshi for good. Bundles of clothes and goods have been packed and before leaving their blight behind, the couple is to have a reassuring paan before their journey. But after a desperate search for a carriage, Nabin finds no one willing to carry the couple away from the town, everyone fearing the chief priest's wrath. Even as Elokeshi reassures her husband that something will be managed and that he should just hold her instead of worrying, Nabinchandra has already made up his mind. If he can't take Elokeshi away from Tarakeshwar, he'll at least ensure that she never stays anywhere near the decrepit Mahant or any other man.

In front of the rolling camera, Ramesh Pal had brandished a bonti, the sort of cutter I had seen my mother and Abala use in the kitchen. Ramesh had brought down the blade in one looping arc passing *behind* Durga's head. Durga remained seated, with her paan still folded in her right hand, awaiting consumption.

In Alochhaya and other picture palaces, what audiences saw was less ordinary.

Elokeshi sits there, preserving her calmness and quietly wishing her husband would end his state of panic. Nabin, a few feet away, turns around with a bonti in his hand, moves forward and, before the woman in the frame can look up or utter a word, he raises the blade in a backswing and chops off Elokeshi's head, with her paan still visible in an unwavering right hand. I saw Elokeshi's head creak slowly towards the side, swivelling open from the neck like a trunk top being opened.

Her face was still visible and one could see, if one turned one's own head with hers, that it retained its living expression. And then, from the mouth of the neck erupted a dark smoke, coming out in swirls like when a blob of ink expands in curls in a glass of water.

This was only the second time I had seen bioscope blood. And it was Durga Devi's.

—

Lang stood still as if breathing wasn't mandatory.

'Herr Chatterjee, it's wunderbar. It's an object that has a human form. Actually, a human form that is an object. Wunderbar!' he said in the dank darkness.

I was only half-listening to him. My head was being washed away and a seaweed trail of thoughts left behind. I also seemed to be breathing in fresh, mint-like air that had just been created. All this while, devotees inside the smallish room kept walking in and out, clanging the bell and prostrating before Kali. There was a mechanical feel to everything that was taking place. The goddess, in her machine-like form, seemed to contain the engine while invisible cranks and chains and pulleys made the world and its people go about their specific seemingly unconnected ways.

It must have been the catarrh. But I was startled despite the knowledge of white granules playing inside both our heads when Lang asked me, 'Herr Chatterjee, can you see the light?'

It was a dull glow that had slowly turned bright and was now pouring out from that gigantic metal tongue. However, people around us, in the catacomb-like space we were standing in, didn't look in the least surprised or startled by the light. Did they, in their right minds, believe that the many flickering flames all around somehow travelled to the Tongue and then, like in a phlegm-thrower's throat, gush out in one spattering flow? Did they truly think this a normal phenomenon?

'Let's go, Mr Lang,' I said without betraying my growing confidence vis-à-vis the impostor.

I pushed myself against Lang/Langford. But instead of moving outwards towards the entrance that doubled as the exit, we found ourselves in a room, not larger than a large cupboard, practically next to the idol in its cage. There was no one here. The bells and the hum of human passage could be heard from outside. But nothing was visible. The room was empty except for smatterings of wet petals on the floor that resembled body parts too small for anyone to dispose of. But as my eyes adjusted to the dull non-darkness, I saw Lang holding up a brown stub. It looked like a three-fourth-smoked wet cigar.

'Herr Chatterjee, isn't this . . . it is, isn't it . . . a penis?'

He wasn't wrong. It did look like a shrivelled *thing*, wrinkly, odious and disembodied.

'Where did you find it?' I asked incredulously.

Bells were ringing, more conch shells blowing, as Lang pointed to the corner of the room, an armlength away, where an opened small box lay behind a grill. The stub, as far as I could now make out after a careful inspection, was *not* a penis. It had been resting on the red cloth inside the box when the curious Lang had picked it up.

'Look, that looks like a nail. A chipped nail,' I pointed to the barely visible dirty-white projection on the stub. As I held it between my four fingers, pressing it ever so slightly to gauge its texture, I knew what it was.

'It's a toe.'

'A toe?'

'A toe.'

'You mean a toe like on a foot?'

'Yes, I think so.'

We needed to get out of the temple, one room at a time. Lang was ready to step out when I matter-of-factly reminded him to put the toe back in its box. As he stared back at me, I calmly plucked the object from his fingers, walked towards the box and shut the grill. Pushing myself out, I carried the Monocle with me.

To not arouse any suspicion in the main room, I turned to face Lang as we walked forward.

'According to Hindu mythology, Sati, the consort of Shiv . . .' I started as we joined a passing crowd.

'But I thought Kali was Shiv's consort,' I heard Lang say from the region around my left shoulder.

'Oh, she's another incarnation of Kali. Anyway, according to Hindu mythology, Sati, the consort of Shiv . . .'

And I continued to play the guide to Lang's shaheb.

'Sati had jumped into a raging fire when her father insulted her husband for being a good-for-nothing, ganja-consuming wastrel. Shiv, on hearing of his beloved's death, rushed to his in-laws, picked up the burning corpse from the fire and in a rage that bends spoons and cracks tumblers, proceeded to dance the cosmic dance of destruction, all the while carrying Sati's body on his back.'

As we neared the entrance of the temple, I could see the nightlights outside.

'All the gods were worried at Shiv's hysteria. If he didn't stop, the universe would be destroyed. Which is where Lord Vishnu came into the picture. In order to get Shiv to stop dancing, Vishnu employed his fearful, whirring disc-weapon, the Sudarshan Chakra, and cut Sati's body into fifty-one pieces. With no load left on his back, Shiv stopped dancing.'

Incredibly both our shoes were there in the flat heap. Still unable to shake off the feeling of being watched, I continued my lecture while we curled up our socks and slipped on our shoes. Lang looked genuinely interested.

'Among the hacked pieces of Sati's body, her toe fell somewhere in the Bhagirathi river and was discovered by a devotee of Kali. It's generally believed that the toe had turned into stone and would take on its original form only from time to time, without any warning, without any schedule. The man who found the stone toe placed it in a shrine in the jungles nearby. Centuries later, the jungles were cleared to become part of this city. This temple was erected on the site of the old shrine.'

Disgorged from the temple, we were finally in the street again. Lang needed to say something. Instead he looked at me with a gaze that said, 'Take me away from here.' We walked past the side of the temple, across the pillared pavilion generously packed with people. It was only when we stepped on to the semi-solid quilt of stone, muck and wetness that I regained my composure. More importantly, I remembered what I had been preparing for since I had read the contents of the mysterious envelope. Along with the beggars, dogs and picture stalls, the street was now bordered with scavenging cats and rotund women.

'What, shaheb? Why don't you come inside for a while? Babu, don't you and your shaheb want to spend some time inside?'

She was hanging on to a wooden column of a two-storeyed

shed. There were two other women peering from the first floor, one of them already engaged in a half-hearted conversation with a man with the slimmest of moustaches and an umbrella. She kept swaying as if in a breeze that wasn't there.

'Is she . . .?'

'I think we'd better move along,' I said quickly, lighting a cigarette and offering Lang another.

'Herr Chatterjee? Did you see that? I just saw a man being led upstairs by a leash.'

And then without any warning, an incredibly large, scabby cat crawled past us with what seemed like a staring face in its mouth.

'That son of a bitch! It's taken the head! That son of a bitch has stolen my fish-head!'

The walking diphtheria disappeared into the crack of a bylane.

The cigarette was supposed to clear my head. Instead, as we walked with increasingly brisker steps, there were more figures emerging. Some of them swayed like the upstairs girl; some had only their faces visible, hatched with grilled windows. These were bodies, parts of bodies, parts of parts of bodies that were flashing and floating in the evening Kalighat air.

'Where is the car?' asked Lang. He seemed to be winded.

'Another two minutes,' I said, unsure of what I had just said. I told him to watch out for puddles. I don't think he heard me, which served my purpose of a final preparation that essentially meant choosing the exact moment when I would bring up the subject. I had practised what I would tell Lang-Langford. It had to be short and precise without any sort of vagueness. I walked next to him, turning my face, ready to start procedures. And that's when I saw Lang quivering. He threw away his cigarette and took out his powder box. He looked like a gangster in Raoul Walsh's *Regeneration* as he sniffed up his catarrh.

'Herr Chatterjee, how far?'

'Just round the corner, Mr Langford.'

The Monocle, without his monocle, looked as if he was about to be stomped into the ground by a giant foot descending from the sky. Everything that was Fritz Lang about him drained away in one gush.

'How . . .?'

'Never mind. Let me just say that you've been fooling a lot of people. I don't know why you've done it. I don't care. But clearly there is a reason and it must be important, Mr Langford.'

I was facing him as people squatted, sat and walked on either side of the road.

'Mr Chatterjee, please. Can we talk about this? It's . . .'

He was no longer speaking in the clipped, choppy English that was an endearing quality about the director of *The Scholar of Calcutta*. Instead, his accent at the Kalighat would have been not a dip out of place at the Carlton or other Anglo haunts.

'Does Thea know?' I asked, sensing with satisfaction how the earlier discomforts I had been experiencing had vanished completely.

'No. Abani-babu, you must . . .'

I cut him short with a short, stabbing 'Aa'.

'But . . .'

Another stab followed. I was going to do the talking.

As I talked and as he listened, everything started falling into place. I had no intention of exposing Frederick Ernest Langford or his ingenious business of miscegenated art. All I wanted was his help in reaching out to an international audience, or at least to American and European producers who would be free of petty and idiotic complexes. But as he talked and I listened, I realized that this was my chance to reclaim my position as a bioscope star in one swift step.

We entered the car, and as it coughed into life and trudged on to wider, brighter roads, Langford told me, blinking his eyes too hard and too many times, how he had left the country after being implicated in a 'misunderstanding over accounts' at the Government School of Art where he was teaching. He had been in touch with a German gentleman by the name of Oswald Spengler whom he had met during a brief visit to the university city of Halle. It was through Spengler that Langford had managed to go to Kabul after the scandal broke and was then hushed up. He had been recommended by Spengler to the Ameer to open an art college, but a palace intrigue involving Yousufzai raiders put an end to that.

'I boarded a ship to Europe with Spengler taking me in. But I had to change my identity. I didn't have a choice, Abani-babu. There could have been some people, even in Berlin, who may have met me during my first trip to Europe. Spengler suggested I take up the name Fritz Lang. It sounded Aryan and had a vague trace of me in it, he had said. My part of the deal was to establish contacts with artists here in Calcutta, buy artwork and sell it in Europe as genuine Hindu art. It became so successful that by the end of last year, there was a demand for commissioned works and I had to be here myself,' he said looking out of the rolled down window of the speeding car.

'Because of the war, London had made it impossible to make such enterprises in any way profitable. UFA and the rest of the German bioscope industry found a tiny window in exports of features. So . . .'

Spengler, it turned out, had known a real Fritz Lang, who had fought against the Russians and the Romanians in 1914. He was an arty, dreamy solider who had told Spengler in the barracks of his plans to 'make bioskops'. After the war, Langford explained, everyone in Europe, especially the losing side, wanted to recover their sanity by making 'bioskops'.

'By the time I reached Berlin, Lang had died of shrapnel wounds in an army hospital in Leipzig. Spengler knew people who could forge documents quickly—most of them going on to become art directors. My father was in the service of Prince Louis Alexander Battenberg before he moved to India after getting married. So I knew German well enough. A bit of training and fact-checking later, I became Fritz Lang, doing theatre work in Vienna until I was hired as a writer for Decla by Eric Pommer.'

Making this truth public at this point would destroy Langford's reputation. It would also end his contraband business in 'genuine fake Indian art'. That meant bad news not only for Langford but also for Spengler and some of his friends in the NSDAP, a rising political party, which had stakes in the whole enterprise.

As he spoke, I touched the object resting in my pocket. Without looking at Langford, I said, 'I understand. But you will have to do me a favour.'

The shrivelled toe in my black jacket tailored by M. Ali & Sons on Sukea Street was being tossed around by my dancing fingers. Did it bother me that the man next to me was drained of all the confidence I had seen in him till a few hours ago?

As I rolled my window up, instinctively protecting myself from the barking dog that tore its way alongside the moving car like a creditor scampering after a bankrupt, I told Langford that his secret was safe with me—as long as he scrapped the feature he had been making and made a new bioscope with a new storyline from scratch.

'But, but . . . you must understand Abani-babu! UFA won't allow me to junk the shoot and start another feature all over again! Berlin won't allow it! Too much money is at stake!'

I rolled down the window again. The mouth of the lane where I would be getting off was approaching fast. Before the driver closed the door of the car and stepped inside again, I looked at Langford and simply said, 'Herr Lang, it's up to you now whether you still want to remain yourself.'

My words bounced off the walls of the car before impaling him. Lang listened with a quivering mouth.

By the next month, three things happened: *The Scholar of Calcutta* remained unfinished while the shooting of *The Pandit & the Englishman* started; I was cast as Pandit Ramlochan Sharma, the protagonist of a story about ambition, recognition and longing in eighteenth-century Bengal; and Frederick Ernest Langford was allowed to disappear for the second time in one lifetime.

**\<interval\>**

*The words 'The Pandit & The Englishman', in white, elongated, appear on a black screen, followed by the squat, flattened words 'A Schoken Motion-Pictures Presentation'. A few seconds later, with the screen still bouncing off darkness, except for the intermittent white of words, the line 'A Tale of Desire, History & Longing from India' appears, then disappears to be replaced by 'Directed by Fritz Lang'.*

*From the illuminated rectangle of blackness a room shapes out. It's a wall in the room; a plain wall, pockmarked in certain areas, with a framed picture hanging on it. Next to the picture is a rack on which there are a few piles of paper curled up into rolls. The room, the wall, is lit up by a light whose source isn't visible immediately. A few seconds later, the light is seen to be an ironed-out flicker coming from a nearby oil lamp set on the floor.*

*The wall comes closer. The pockmarks reveal a smoothness of their own. The framed picture is no longer an indistinct rectangle. It is a standard picture of Kali, tongue out with a smile and a garland of mini-heads bearing moustaches. She is marching on an oblivious but wide awake Shiv. The picture of Kali remains in view for a few seconds longer. The first title comes on:*

*'1783, Krishnagar, a town near Calcutta. Pandit Ramlochan*

Sharma is a physician whose practice has been suffering because of his obsession with teaching the ancient Hindu language of Sanskrit. His dream is to teach the language to the English. For the purpose, he has, over the years, learnt the language of power: English.'

The text vanishes. A lizard crawls across the wall, stopping only when it reaches the picture of Kali and blocks the goddess's face with one of its webbed paws. The flame of the oil lamp comes into view.

The next title:

'To earn a livelihood, Ramlochan teaches local boys Sanskrit. He despises everyone—except for one person . . .'

A girl, not more than ten years old, approaches. Her face is lit up by the lamp light. She sits on the floor. After a brief exchange of looks with someone in the room, she starts reading out from a manuscript that had been lying open before her.

For the first time, Pandit Ramlochan Sharma is visible. He is a gaunt man of fair complexion. His eyes are like those of a bull, liquidly and exuding tenderness and self-pity. The girl sways back and forth, throwing her moving shadow on the wall beyond. The Pandit occasionally looks at her, in between patches of looking at the manuscript she is reading out aloud. He also keeps rubbing his bare back and chest with a wet cloth.

Ramlochan's face fills up the screen. His eyes, calm and moist, are surrounded by a face, the central point of which is a thin-lipped mouth that bends and stretches. The whole room comes into view—Ramlochan, the girl, the wall with its picture of Kali and the just about visible Shiv. Ramlochan stands up and gets a hand fan from the rack next to the wall. He fans, gently enough not to create a wind that will disturb the pile of manuscripts in front of the girl. One page, however, does fly away. The girl gets up to rescue it.

*She is wearing a white piece of cloth that is struggling to look like a sari. The girl is too young to have any soft, rounded edges. Her arms, her left shoulder, a considerable part of her legs are visible. Every part of skin on her that is visible gleams like dark rock-edges. While she recovers the page, Ramlochan stops fanning and wiping his body. He gazes at her with great intensity. This gaze turns into a brief second of muted terror when she turns to return to her assigned spot next to him. Ramlochan resumes his calm posture. But his chest is still rising and falling too fast.*

*The lizard now fills the screen. It slowly clambers away from the picture of Kali and flatfoots its way towards the rack. It disappears behind a pile of clothes.*

*The girl suddenly looks up at Ramlochan with a concerned look. Her face is oval and angelic. The lamp is flickering harder than before. The turbulence of the flame is reflected on the girl's face, especially on her black hair that is unnaturally long for a child her age.*

*Ramlochan stops fanning.*

*Another title card:*

*'Kuli, you didn't forgot the oil in the lamp again, did you?'*

*Ramlochan frowns. It is an exaggerated and therefore false frown. The girl looks ready to break into tears, when the lamp light splutters on their faces. Everything turns black.*

—

He heard the news of William's death and leaned forward. It was his way of registering the death of an old ally. Unfortunately, to the bearer of the news, Panchanan Karmakar, Ramlochan's movement was yet another confirmation of the Krishnagar scholar's rejection of social graces.

Six months ago, William had collapsed in his Garden Reach house with a fever. The doctors had detected rheumatism and then a tumour. That news too had come to Ramlochan, as he sat on the porch, courtesy the voluble Panchanan. But it had been winter, the dreary month of Aghran when the days end fast and thoughts slow down, and Ramlochan was beset with his own troubles.

'So you've lost your last pupils, eh?' Panchanan had asked, taking an elongated puff from Ramlochan's gargara, the hot bubbles fighting for space deep inside the pipe. The Pandit, wrapped in the safety of his old shawl, hadn't responded to his monthly friend from the city.

'Well, I can't really blame the parents,' Panchanan continued, waving away a diving, drunken mosquito. 'To be honest, I was surprised that you managed to carry on like this for so long. Your reputation hasn't been pure as ghee, you know.'

No, it hadn't, not in Aghran, and not now in the new year either. In the last six months, his precious reputation had evaporated. Living in Krishnagar was no longer an option. And with the death of William Jones, neither was moving to Calcutta. Being a Baidya teaching Sanskrit in a town bristling with Brahman scholars was bad enough. But somehow he had managed to keep those sanctimonious maggots at bay.

The sun was going down and the mosquitoes were coming out like an army of ghouls. Panchanan knew that with Jones's death, any hope that Ramlochan may still have had of being recognized and fêted had died. He had been buckling under frustration, the perpetually gnawing frustration of a talent being squashed.

Ramlochan had been feeling the burden of being hounded by those brain-dead Nadia Brahmans even before the scandal involving Kuli and himself forced his school to be closed. If there was one thing that had given him hope, it was his friendship with William Jones. But even that had frayed like a never-changed sacred thread.

It was Ramlochan who had been teaching Jones the finer points of the Sanskrit language for the last ten years. It was he who had made the Englishman learn Bengali after the latter wanted to do away with the translating middle-men in the courtrooms. And it was he who had pointed out to William the striking similarity between the river Hiranyabahu in a passage by Somdev and the river Erranaboas mentioned by Megasthenes, and that Sandrocottus and Samudragupta—and not Chandragupta, as the overexcited Jones had announced at the Society—were one and the same.

Ramlochan had asked little in return. The salary that the Englishman provided was good, but it wasn't money that he was after. It was something else—something that the Krishnagar Brahmans could only see as hollow pride and a shameful hankering for firingi applause. But he had brushed aside such mumblings and headshakings because he had hoped Jones would repay him properly one day.

He may not have told William his wish in so many words, but he had wanted to go to England and show his knowledge and expertise to an eager and appreciative people. He had hinted at this desire quite early on in their longstanding partnership by inquiring about life in London, its weather, its people and its scholars.

He had gained his own bits and pieces of information about England through his old friend I'tisam al-Din, who had, with his manservant and Captain Archibald Swindon, the representative of King George III in Bengal, sailed to England twenty-eight years ago. Like Ramlochan, I'tisam had also known all along that Nadia, with all its pitiful projections as the leading centre of culture and scholarship in the province, was a regurgitating cesspool, where the noise of constantly escaping gaseous bubbles was mistaken to be the chant of knowledge. He had trained as a scholar-official in the courts of the Nawab, rising to become Emperor Shah Alam's official liaison with the British monarch. It was from I'tisam that Ramlochan first got to know about courtly life in Allahabad, including the Emperor's wish to seek King George's help to return to his capital in Shahjahanabad. It was also while listening to his old friend during one of his visits to Krishnagar that Ramlochan realized that there was little point in seeking the favour of the Nawab's court. Instead, his future—and that of real scholarship in the country—lay with the firingis.

I'tisam returned to the country after spending three years in London. He was still wearing the same turban and shawl and robe and sticking to the same routine of daily Persian scholarship and nocturnal visits to his favourite ladies' quarters in Calcutta. But there was a new spring to his step. During his first meeting with Ramlochan after his return from England, he spoke enthusiastically about the hunger of the firingi to know more about Hindustan. He had been fêted several times in London as a Persian scholar of great renown, taking part in debates with Christian scholars, and the star of more than a couple of soireés in the university town of Oxford. It was from I'tisam that Ramlochan had first heard the name of William Jones—'his Persian grammar is weak, he has no clue of the phonetic structure of the language but he is a hungry learner'.

But what Ramlochan had tucked away in his head, not even daring to bring up the subject with himself except in moments of complete privacy and partial weakness, was his friend's detailed description of women in England.

'They are sexually depraved,' I'tisam had snorted out while sitting on the same porch that Ramlochan and Panchanan were now sitting on. 'Some of them don't even bother to cover their breasts while they're selling vegetables and meat. And they make kissing sounds and lewd gestures in their markets!'

Ramlochan remembered thinking that even Shabitri, Paramesh Brahman's daughter-in-law, would billow her breasts out each time she stretched to unfurl and rinse her hair while bathing in the Amrapara pond. Also, the middle-aged Tori, the physician Gangaram's wife, never bothered to cover herself properly each time her sari got hitched up, exposing her shuddering thighs as she husked the rice on their courtyard. But it was unthinkable for firingi women to behave this way. The Pandit knew that they danced with men in the halls and houses in Calcutta and even in the mansion parties thrown by the Bengali babus and zamindars. But that was different, it wasn't showcasing flesh. However, now, from what I'tisam had told him, about men and women kissing and groping each other in the open in England, it did sound like an invitation of flesh.

It was with I'tisam that Ramlochan had picked up the English language. While it was necessary for him, as the Nawab's emissary to the firingis and then as an employee of the firingis, to have a firm knowledge of the tongue, he saw it also as a window to escape from the mousetrap world of Krishnagar.

'So where did you learn English?' William had asked him during one of their first meetings. 'I have learnt English from my friends in Calcutta who know Englishmen at Fort William,' Ramlochan had answered in William's tongue. He had decided against mentioning I'tisam's name, considering that his opinion of William in Oxford had not been too kind. He also hadn't mentioned the written material—some printed, some copied—that he had collected over the years to help him learn the firingi's language. These were mostly translations, made by Englishmen before William, of Sanskrit slokas and poems.

One item in Ramlochan's collection stood apart from all the rest. It was an almanac that he had gathered from I'tisam. It was stuck inside a thick pile of notes about I'tisam's stay in England that would much later be used for his *Shigrif-namah-i Wilayat*, or The Wonder Book of Europe, which he had wanted the Pandit to translate into Bengali. (Ramlochan never did translate it, partly because it was tedious, and partly because he had hoped to write such a work himself one day.)

Right from the moment he had extricated the dog-eared pamphlet from the other papers, Ramlochan knew that it was special. On the cover was an illustration of a woman in a flowing European dress, not unlike the Hindustani ghagras worn by dancing girls but much more expansive. She was carrying a parasol and next to her there stood an Englishman, smiling at her. She was smiling back. Ramlochan would learn, by his own diligence, what the printed words on the cover said. It was the title of the pamphlet: *Harris's List of Covent Garden Ladies, or Man of Pleasure's Kalendar, 1767*.

There were other illustrations inside. His eagerness to unlock the secrets that accompanied these pictures made his progress in mastering the firingi's language much swifter. It was less than six months after *Harris's List* came his way that he hungrily read:

'Miss Smith, of Duke's Court in Bow Street . . . A well made lass, something under the middle-size, with dark, brown hair and a good complexion.'

Pages later:

'Mrs Hamblin, No. 1 Naked-Boy Court in the Strand . . . The young lady in question is not above 56. We know she must be particularly helpful to elderly gentlemen who are very nice in having their linen got up.'

That was when Ramlochan Pandit of Krishnagar had realized that he simply had to go to England one day. But now, with the news that Panchanan had brought from Calcutta, it had finally become impossible.

Anna Maria Jones looked out to the shoreline and then at her husband's placid, classical face. Standing next to her on the deck of the *Crocodile*, her husband of less than six months, William, was closer to her than ever before. And yet, he was already far away; much closer to the riverbank that the ship was now passing, than to the rustle of silk and the flutter of fans and the banter that had broken out on the deck all around them. He was already far from the courts of London, the corridors of Westminster, the halls of Oxford, and the long evening dinner discussions with other scholar gentlemen like Mr Gibbon and Mr Halhed. Even as the *Crocodile* entered the port of Calcutta, William Jones had the look of a man returning home.

'So this is it,' William said silently to himself. He clutched on to Anna's hand, careful to shift his precious book of Hindoo law into the other. 'This is the city that Mr Clive described as "one of the most wicked places in the Universe . . . Rapacious and Luxurious beyond concepcion".'

He couldn't quite make out what those brown bodies swathed in white were doing on the riverbank. But he sensed a charge of excitation, not unlike the tingling photovoltaic exhibitions that had become the rage in fashionable circles in Manchester and London.

This excitation had its roots not so much in the leap he was about to make in his professional life, as in the blind, exhilarating jump that he was going to make elsewhere. Let there be no doubt that it was his appointment as a Judge of the Supreme Court of Judicature at Fort William that enabled him to cross the seas and come here. And his subsequent knighthood *did* open up many doors that would have been shut otherwise. But it was the prospect of uncovering, peeling off a civilization, one layer at a time with the blunt knife of language that made the pacific Sir William betray his excitement and squeeze his wife's hand a little tighter than he would have done on ending any other sea journey.

The moment a stretch of white, flat-roofed mansions plotted by lines of tall trees came into view, the entire group of passengers out on the deck broke out in a loud hurrah and applause. No one, however, dared to throw his hat into the air. Who would retrieve it if it fell outside the ship?

'Sir William, your residence should be somewhere out there,' said Mr Rowland, the Company man with a bent smile. 'Welcome to Calcutta.'

William smiled back, patiently interrupting his thoughts to engage with the world of pointless Englishmen just for a moment. Rowland, returning to his job after his vacation in England, thankfully clipped back to join the boisterous others. All that the future founder of the Asiatic Society and unlocker of history's treasures could think of were lines from something he had committed to memory at the age of eleven:

'Now does my project gather to a head;

My charms crack not, my spirits obey; and time

Goes upright with his carriage.'

With the *Crocodile*'s crew now cranking into activity and a few catamarans with people appearing near the ship, Anna said over the noise, 'William, this is our new home then.'

Her husband looked at her lovingly. 'Now does my project gather to a head,' he said to himself silently not forgetting to squeeze Anna Maria's hand lovingly again.

Five months ago, they had set sail from Portsmouth and while she loved William with all her heart and put on a good show about their departure, Anna Maria was wracked with unease at the prospect of not only leaving England, but leaving England for such distant shores. Were there enough people there whom she would be able to speak to? But how many people even among those who could speak English would there be *not* from the merchant class or worse? There was William, of course.

When she was fourteen, her parents had taken her along with her sister to Siena. After a few days, she had started to react badly to the climate and the people. Calcutta was even farther away from London than Siena. And as during that terrible return journey from Italy years ago, this time too she forcibly tamed her nerves that were making her think a hundred thoughts all at the same time.

When the *Crocodile* had landed in the southern port of Madras a few days earlier, Anna had successfully pretended that this new land was what everybody back home had always been dreaming of. The mastery over a continent, the lavish comforts of such a mastery, the thrill of tearing away from the grey skies and the white chill of London. And yet, she wasn't always so confident about pulling off this game of self-deception.

After a fine evening of Drury Lane performance, William and she had been invited for dinner at Mr Jeremy Costwald's residence. Costwald, a man in his late fifties, had been an India man, and his heavy tan and loud manners showed for his years in Calcutta and Madras. Most importantly though, he was a proud survivor of the infamous Black Hole of Calcutta.

'Holwell's a blighter! He was there to be sure and he should know better than to make us who came out of it believe what he's written in the *Register*. Well of course we were all confined inside the Nabob's prison. And of course some of us didn't make it—twelve, to give you the exact number. But that was because of the musket injuries they suffered. The hakim—that's Hindustani for the court physician—actually tended to the injured, and there were three wounded Englishmen who recovered. But Holwell, total blighter that he is, wrote his thundering account. And who's going to say anything otherwise? Even the Crown has now taken his account seriously, some of His Majesty's insiders are even talking about setting up an imperial India policy. And all because of Holwell's rumbling prose!'

Sitting opposite Costwald, Anna Maria had tried to give her full attention to the splendid fowl she was enjoying. It was improper for the man to bring up a dark topic like the Black Hole at the dinner table. But Costwald, more than a few sherries down, was a horse that had burst through the stable gate.

'But dear sir, surely, you and the fortunate others can expose his untruth and paint a truer picture?' asked William, looking up from his plate.

'And contradict the official account of the East India Company as well as the second most powerful man in Bengal? No thank you, sir. I'd rather be telling my own stories.'

That night in London after the dinner, Anna was still brooding about all those tales about Calcutta that she had heard at the table. After closing the pages of *A Modest Proposal for Preventing the Children of Poor People from Being a Burden to Their Parents, or The Country and for Making Them Beneficial to the Public*, she had turned the lamp out and gone to the bedroom to sleep. William had, as was the case whenever he consumed even the smallest amount of alcohol, foregone his after-dinner hour in the library and was already asleep. All Anna could think of as she shut her eyes was the cruel brightness of a tropical sun suddenly blinking off in an overcrowded, swarmy prison cell.

The branches of the elm tree that cast striated shadows on the overlooking wall must have vanished at some point. Instead, there was a wild face wearing an enormous turban, exactly as described in a passage in Tavernier's book of travel, staring maliciously at her. He was speaking in some low, long-vowelled language that she could, remarkably, understand.

'Ah, Missus Jones, at last you can get what your heart desires, which is not too different from what your pretty, pale, smooth, blood-hiding body desires. Anna *Poorna*, you are not in London any more,' the face cackled, with lines breaking out on either side of its mouth, seamlessly changing into the ruddy countenance of Jeremy Costwald in full Company Army red-and-white regalia.

This uneasy dream—and variations of it—had revisited her throughout the *Crocodile*'s sojourn as it approached and entered the Indian Ocean. But not once had Anna mentioned anything about these confounding night images that were projected in her head to her husband. And why would she? William was embarking upon what could be the finest period in any man's life. In any case, the nightmares couldn't have been *that* terrible. William had not noticed anything in his wife to worry or upset him.

So when the *Crocodile* churned foam at its base as it anchored in the waters of the Hugli, she smiled to herself, hoping that William would notice her smile.

'So this is it,' said William Jones to the woman who would be sharing his life in Bengal as they both unblushingly strapped their hands around a shiny, hard, dog's-hair-brown torso. They were ferried across the shallows to the shore.

The light bathing the surroundings was very different from any other place William had ever been to. It wasn't blatantly bright and eager to turn to colour as it was in Morocco where the reds and yellows were embarrassingly exhibitionist. Neither was it as proudly clear as it was in many of the seaports in Europe. And it was definitely not washed in a veil of grey as it was in London, screening objects in the distance with a faint blue sheen that was the true colour of shadows.

In the Calcutta before him, the colours were domesticated, with only hints of its wild, junglee ancestry in the green around. For Anna Maria, however, the brown of the ground beneath her white summer shoes, the green of the trees and dense shrubberies lining it, and the dark blue-green of the waters she had just left behind didn't seem to be tame at all. Bengal lay there before them, a creature that was lazy and bearing some non-malignant, non-fatal disease. Both of them sensed it—one with hidden trepidation, the other with muffled excitement.

As they walked towards the carriage that was waiting for them—another had come only for their luggage—William couldn't help but think how their sense of belonging was now no longer in the hands of the loud-mouthed Captain Kershaw and his crew, or that of any of the philistine passengers.

William had been careful to carry two of his most precious possessions on his body. Just before he had clasped his hands around a stranger's neck, he had decided to move the two books by his friend Nathaniel Brassey Halhed—*Bodhaprakasám sabdasastram* . . . *A Grammar of the Bengal Language* and *A Code of Gentoo Laws, or Ordinations of the Pundits*—out of his spacious pockets into the safety of his own hands. He didn't think that this manoeuvre would make his carrier's task easier. But it was too great a risk to have either of the books fall out of his pockets and be damaged. Once inside the carriage, and after helping his wife into it, William placed the books on his lap and leant forward to quickly kiss Anna Maria on her cheek. When Mr Barker, the man who had come to receive the Joneses, joined them in the carriage, Anna was still emitting a blush. Mr Barker recognized it as the first effects of the Bengal heat on a just arrived English lady. He wasn't too wide of the mark.

—

Jones had gone stark, raving mad listening to the man sitting on his right. He had been jabbering away from the very minute he had arrived and showed no signs of quietening down. And yet, sitting in their hastily whitewashed bungalow overlooking the Jalangi river in Krishnagar, Jones did not regret travelling here for some respite. And he *had* found respite from the monkey life of Calcutta. It was one thing to be a Judge at the Fort, and quite another to be in contact with bearable company, the sort that not only froths on about financial scams but woodpecks constantly about the latest sexual scandal.

Jones had started his job on a sure enough footing. In his first ruling, he had cleared the long-pending dispositions of the amount of 23,00,000 rupees that the Company had seized from Chait Singh, the former raja of Benares, who had framed a serious charge of looting against Warren Hastings. His colleagues on the bench had not been helpful. Robert Chambers, good man that he was, had ruled that the East India Company should have the prize money. John Hyde, whose grasp of the law was impeccable, had said that this transfer was not lawful. Which is when Jones had stepped in and decreed that the 'plunder taken on the capitulation of besieged towns, belong to those who possess the power of making war and peace'.

It was Chambers who met Jones that very afternoon at the court and suggested they meet and discuss the formation of a club of sorts whose purpose would be to discuss, explore and understand the language and culture and tradition of the Hindus. Jones was always suspicious of clubs. But there was, this time, a strong reason for a group of like-minded Englishmen to meet regularly and do something that would benefit civilization and society. It was a shame that people like Alexander Dow had been the only providers of accounts of life in India. Jones had read Dow's abominable Drury House publication *Zingis*, a poetic tragedy that provided ample fodder for Dr Johnson's literary club. *Zingis* was astoundingly wrong in its description of life here, peppering only some basic pages with anything remotely looking or smelling like a fact. Somebody had to correct this picture of India for people back in England.

In any case, there was also a desperate need to understand the country for professional reasons.

'How should Hindus be examined in court? Can Brahmans give absolution for perjury? Should Hindus swear by the Ganges or any other holy thing or word? Chambers,' Jones had said while stirring his cup of tea, 'these are the questions we should resolve sooner rather than later.'

And then, there was the whole business of knowing this country. And such knowledge was certainly not going to be found in the deplorable chitter-chatter about Emma Wrangham and Madame Grand and the sooty bibis who seemed to be running the social life of the town. Knowing did not mean fanning fans more furiously to catch the latest news of the 'shocking case of William

Hunter and three mutilated maidens', or any other scandalous gossip peddled by the papers. Jones had let out a violent spurt of air through his nostrils when he came across the following item of news in the *Bengal Gazette*:

On Monday night, Rajah Nobkissen gave a nautch and magnificent entertainment to several persons of distinction in commemoration of Miss Wrangham's birthday. As the ladies arrived, they were conducted by the Rajah through a grand suite of apartments into the zenana, where they were amused until the singing began, which was so mellifluous as to give every face a smile of approbation. The surprising agility of one of the male dancers occasioned loud acclamations of applause.

'After supper there was a ball which was opened by Mr Livius and Miss Wrangham, who were dressed in the characters of Apollo and Daphne. When the minuets were ended, country dances struck up and continued till past three in the morning, when the company departed highly pleased with the elegant festival. And when the Rajah was attending Miss Wrangham to her carriage, he thanked her in very polite terms for having illuminated his house with her bright appearance.

Jones had thrown the *Gazette* on the floor, almost barking at the servant when he came to put it back in its rightful place. And to think that this was the place that he had desperately wanted to come to! It was the same Raja Nabakrishna Deb, the howling fool of Calcutta, who had donated land to build the new St John's Church. No one seemed to mind that the land had been used earlier for Christian burials, thus exposing the fact that the Raja's gesture was hardly the great act of charity that it was being made out to be. Jones knew that Calcutta needed a church. St Anne's had been destroyed by the mutineers and the city had been left practically churchless for the last thirty years. But to build a sacred house on a spot where till recently there was a gunpowder magazine yard and a burial ground was sacrilegious.

It seemed that the city was devoid of a single Christian soul. The moment Jones had heard about Nabakrishna's gesture, he had made his decision known: he was not going to contribute an anna to the St John's building fund. If he had any influence in the courtroom, he would see to it that no money was donated by any of his fellow Supreme Court Judges!

So, leaving the painted circus of Calcutta behind, if only for a few weeks at a time, meant a lot to Jones. Retreating to Krishnagar had also done a lot of good to Anna Maria's health, which hadn't been too good since she landed in the blood-boiling city nearly a year ago.

But as he sat here, waiting for Anna Maria to return from the garden where she was still drawing pictures of the various plants she had discovered, Jones couldn't help but think that there were monkeys even here, in Krishnagar. He was now in the company of Brahmans, hoping that one of the many scholars here would agree to give him lessons in Sanskrit grammar.

It had been Wilkins's idea that he seek out someone in this scholarly town in Nadia. Wilkins was one of the few people in Calcutta that Jones could actually talk to. He had also managed to get Jones a copy of the legal code of Manu, the starting point for any Englishman planning to understand Hindu law. But poor Wilkins was not suited for the wet heat of Bengal and had had to move northwards to Benares. The two of them continued to correspond with each other, but Jones sorely missed his fellow scholar's company. Wilkins was especially missed after the Asiatic Society was up and running. His contributions at the seven o'clock Thursday meetings in the Grand Jury Room would have been valued.

Even as he was thinking about all this, the man sitting on his right had not stopped talking. In fact, he hadn't even slowed down. His name, Jones had barely been able to make out in the clutter of the other introductions, was Pandit Gangaram. It had been obvious from the moment the Brahmans had arrived that this Gangaram was keen on making his point of view very clear: Sanskrit was not a language for firingis. He hadn't, of course, used the word 'firingi'; he had said 'Ingrej'. But the tone was very clear. For the last half-hour-or was it more?-Gangaram had been arguing how every language is specific to a people, 'like death rites and marriage ceremonies'. One could pick up 'the skin' of a language, but it would only rot when placed on the 'blood and bones of a different people'.

Jones had invited a dozen or so local scholars to his house. He had made his request plain. He would pay a handsome amount for his tuition. All he wanted was to learn the grammar and the literature in enough detail so he could make do without secondary material written by Europeans who clearly knew Sanskrit only very superficially. At one level, he didn't blame the Nadia scholars for believing that an Englishman learning Sanskrit was a hopeless task. But at another level, he was sure that, with the right help, he could correct that notion and unlock some secrets that remained hidden even to the Brahmans of this country.

Wilkins had mentioned the name of one Ramlochan Sharma. But upon gentle inquiry, Jones was told by the scholars that Ramlochan Sharma was not a Pandit, but a physician. In other words, he was a Baidya, a non-Brahman and therefore a non-scholar. And yet, Wilkins had brought up the name because the physician-Pandit had a reputation of being an outstanding, although unorthodox, interpreter of Sanskrit texts.

Apart from Wilkins' recommendation, Jones had heard the non-Brahman Pandit's name in the context of jurisprudence. It was Ramlochan Sharma who had created a ruckus some years ago when he, according to sources, helped the 'illiterate' widow of the Raja of Bardhaman take over her late husband's zamindari. It had reached Jones's ear even in London that the Permanent Settlement Act had been hurriedly passed so as to protect the Company and its native sympathizers from 'clever Hindu minds' like 'a Pundit Ramalocan'. It was even said at the Serjeants' that Warren Hastings had personally made a deal with this Krishnagar scholar.

But Ramlochan Sharma had not responded to his invitation. Instead, there were the Gangarams of the world, their nominal representative having proceeded at some point to read out one of his own works, a long poem he had written about the Maratha raids forty years ago. Jones vaguely caught the last line of the aural torture: 'So Bhaskar was killed at Monkora camp, and Gangaram has fulfilled his wish and told his story.'

He took a short bow and sat back on his low stool.

'I was there in Pandua when the Bargis raided Bardhaman. So everything I've written here is a historical account of what happened,' he said with his eyebrows arched.

Jones nodded.

'That's rubbish, Gangaram. That poem of yours is based on as much truth as a Mussalman bases his prayer on pork fat.'

The whole room looked up at the doorway from where the voice came. It was a voice that was not used to loudness and its edges were clearly strained. From where he was, Jones could only see a silhouette, a slight figure bordered and inked in with black. But as his eyes adjusted, he could see a small face suited to its small frame, frowning and smiling at the same time.

'And how do *you* know that, Ramlochan?' Gangaram responded, barely able to cover up the fact that his body was shaking like a leaf in a kalbaishakhi storm.

'You never set your foot anywhere near Bardhaman when the Bargis came, Gangaram, if people are to believe Raja Tilakchand. And your limping verse actually says that the Bargi raids were divine punishment for immorality and licentiousness becoming the norm among the people? Bah! And you've clearly stolen lines from Vidyalankara's *Chitracampu*. And if you could read Persian, I'm sure you wouldn't have hesitated to lift chunks from Ghulam Hussain Khan's *Siyar-ul-Mutakherin*.'

Jones's grasp of Bengali was weak, but he could understand the nature of the taunt being made. The whole room was now bursting with angry shouts and had become combustible.

'Now gentlemen,' Jones stood up and addressed the crowd in broken Bengali. 'I must remind you why I had invited all of you here. There is no need to lose . . .' he searched the word, he searched the Bengali word . . . 'control.'

A hush descended, but Jones knew that it was no use after this to sit down and hope for a civilized encounter. He waited for everyone to face him before he could make an announcement. Even the newcomer looked at him. He had no choice but to end the disastrous meeting. But Gangaram pre-empted his announcement.

'Thank you, William-saheb, for your hospitality. But I think my colleagues and I would rather go now. We have Durga pujo arrangements to attend to, unlike someone here. Shall we go, Chandi-pandit?'

They all namaskared Jones and filed out of the house one by one. Jones was slightly taken aback at the suddenness with which the proceedings had screeched to a halt. He didn't want to offend the learned men and saw them to the door. When he returned to the room, ready to put his feet up and gauge the damages, he heard the straggler speak.

'I apologize for driving your guests away. But it was a waste of time, truly,' he said in self-conscious English.

'Pandit Ramlochan Sharma, I presume? You don't get along too well with the folks in town, I see,' Jones said, not able to repress a small, tired smile.

'I'm willing to teach you. But will you learn here or will I have to be in Calcutta?'

'Here in Krishnagar. My wife and I plan to spend four months of the year here. I hope that suits you.'

'That would be better for me. I teach a few youngsters Sanskrit, Bengali and English here.'

The conversation meandered into matters at hand, the texts that the student would need to master as well as the schedule that suited both teacher and student. Jones sensed that there was more that the Pandit had in mind. But he restricted himself to recounting his scholastic background, his methods of teaching and the need to stay away from the works of the other scholars, 'to avoid the risks of becoming wrapped in empty theology'. That suited Jones. In fact, the man suited him more than he had bargained for.

It turned out that the Pandit had learnt his English from a John Andrews, who was known to the Bengali print-maker Panchanan Karmakar, who in turn was well acquainted with Charles Wilkins. It was with Panchanan's help that Wilkins had printed Halhed's *Bengali Grammar*, the first book using the

Bengali typeface. Surely, this was a sign that Pandit Ramlochan was the right man for the job. And what was the job that Jones had in mind? To go down into the very heart of the beast and peer into its soul by using the rope of language. The sinewy, strong rope that was Sanskrit.

Anna Maria had just walked into the house.

'Anna, I want you to meet Pandit Ramlochan Sharma. He will be my Sanskrit tutor.'

Neither Anna Maria nor her husband would have known what went through the Pandit's head as she set down her drawing book and dipped her head in acknowledgement of the guest's presence.

Bakulakalikâlalâlamani kalakanthîkalakalâkule kâle |
Kalayâ kalâvato 'pi hi kalayati kalitâstratâm madanah ||

If he had been able to hear the words darting inside the Pandit's head in one unbroken loop, Jones would have recognized the lines a few weeks later, when he learnt from Ramlochan the old grammarian's memory tool. Jones himself would go on to translate the lines a year later as:

Madan, the god of love, uses even the spots of the moon
as his beautiful weapon when the bakul plant shines with
new buds and the cuckoos and women with melodious
voices fill the air with their enchanting sounds.

William Jones was now dead, and there was no escape from the open hostility unleashed on Ramlochan by the Brahmans of Krishnagar. Before leaving, Panchanan had suggested that he move with him to Calcutta. There would be something he could manage—if not in the service of the Company then in the household of some knowledge-seeking babu. Ramlochan knew, of course, that things no longer allowed even that.

It had all started coming apart six months ago, when there had been a loud rap on his door accompanied by a louder string of abuse. It was Kuli's forever intoxicated father. Ramlochan, a late riser, took his time unhinging the bar from the door. Jadab, incredibly, wasn't tottering or letting off his characteristic fumes. Five or six people were standing behind him.

'What is it? I don't do visits any more. Go to another physician . . . is it an emergency?' Ramlochan was still bloated with sleep.

He should have recognized that there was something wrong in the faces of his early morning visitors. The air between him and the men outside was swirling, dancing about just that bit for an alert man to notice the violence building up in it. Not being the alert man he should have been, Ramlochan explained the shimmer in the air as a product of his gummy, clenched vision.

'Ramlochan, you better come out!'

Now that was an odd request—considering that Ramlochan had unbolted the door and was facing the irate Jadab-led mob. Perhaps they were referring to his position of having one foot inside and one foot outside the raised line of patted earth that was the threshold of his functional house. He crossed over sluggishly.

'Yes, what is it?'

Jadab, with his hay-munching face, was taken aback. He and the others had met in the courtyard of the Krishna temple just as the sun was dissolving the night, practising what they would say. Ishwar and Bhabani, two young strapping lads, had been chosen to drag Ramlochan out of the house in case he resisted.

'Well . . . I, we . . .' Kuli's father muttered. He then turned his head towards the others standing behind him.

Chandiprasad Gupta, one of the town's Brahmans who had always found Ramlochan teaching the sacred language outrageous, stepped forward. He touched one of Jadab's moderately broad farmer shoulders, giving the signal that he would do the talking. Chandi had the ability of conjuring up a pool of darkness around him when required. In the weak light of that morning, he had stepped out of the group, brought his bird nose within inches of Ramlochan's face and covered the immediate vicinity where both of them stood with his portable shadow.

'Ramlochan. What Kuli's father is trying to tell you is that you have been conducting the most shameful activities with his daughter. I had told Jadab not to send Kuli to your house. But this drunkard never did listen. Your filth has no place in this town. Leave us and conduct your firingi habits in the big city.'

'We *Pandits*,' Chandi continued, clenching his teeth to emphasize that the word meant different things to different people, 'had warned you, not once, not twice, but thrice about not making a fool of yourself by setting up a school here in Krishnagar. Don't think we didn't know why you had all those children come over to your *school*. Your sickness will not be tolerated, Ramlochan. Not after you've been caught preying on an innocent child. You have till the end of this month to get out of this town. Show your face in Krishnagar again and we'll use scriptural laws that judges in Calcutta have no inkling of.'

By now, Ramlochan was wide awake.

'There is nothing I have done to Kuli. What do you think I've done with her?'

He took a few steps forward as he spoke, careful to close the door shut as he faced Chandi Pandit.

Pandit Chandiprasad Gupta was an intelligent man. Unlike most of his fellow scholars in Krishnagar, he knew an intelligent man when he saw one. If he answered Ramlochan's challenging query and actually uttered the unspeakable crime that he was guilty of, he would be sinning himself. To describe, or even give a name to Ramlochan's lascivious activities before non-Brahmans was as shameful as the activities themselves. Also, describing his crime in Sanskrit—as was prescribed in situations like this, to keep smut out of untrained ears—would amount to acknowledging that the Baidya Ramlochan was indeed a Pandit.

So there he stood, phalanxed by a group of philistines that included Kuli's father. He narrowed his eyes to a pair of slits and hissed out words in high Bengali—a communicational compromise—that did the necessary job of hurling insults at Ramlochan, the purveyor of unspeakable crimes committed against a girl not more than ten years old.

'That is ridiculous! That is so ridiculous! Has the girl said that I have fucked her?' Ramlochan shouted at the top of his voice. 'Jadab, you actually heard your girl tell you that I fucked her?'

The single word had been unleashed from Ramlochan's quivering lips and there was nothing anyone, not even Chandi Pandit, could do about it except wince and mutter the Lord's name as an insulating device.

'You sick man! You think I'll make up stories about my own daughter?'

It was now Jadab's turn to let go. The hard, flat word that Ramlochan had used, and twice, had clearly scratched on the scab that Chandi Pandit had first allowed to fester in him. Visions of his little girl being ravished by the monster in front of him started to streak past him. Horribly, these recreated images were soon slowing down, giving him less time to escape them. They were a parody of all those pictures that flickered in his head every time he drank and reacted with guffaws to those bawdy songs sung by Pagla Gafoor about women stuck to their pitchers.

Jadab had to be held back by Ishwar and Bhabani, the two youngsters still training to be lathials, straining on each side of the man gone insane in the middle. It was Chandi Pandit who took the lead in turning around and leaving Ramlochan to himself. With the mob gone, he was suddenly a stranger on his own doorstep. He stood there blankly, until he simply sat down on the threshold like a bulging clothful of rice that had just been sickled.

That was half a year ago. With Panchanan on his way back to Calcutta, Ramlochan looked at the spot where he had crumpled. It seemed like years ago, weeks ago, days ago, moments ago, all in jumbling succession.

What had he done with Kuli? Nothing. What had he done to any child in the whole of Krishnagar? Nothing. It was true that along with Panini's, Katyayana's and Patanjali's grammar, the usual texts from *Astadhyayi*, *Vartikas* and *Mahabhasya*, and verses from *Kumarasambhava* and *Meghadutam*, he had also taught the basics of the English language to his students. The writings he taught these boys—and Kuli—were those that he had obtained during his trips to Calcutta. Towards the latter part of his tutorship, he had taken up William's offer of visiting him for three weeks in his residence at Garden Reach every three months. There were a few printed books that he had picked up during these sojourns from a circulating library in the Badamtala area. These were as instructive as they were delightful—Ossian's *Temora*, Oliver Goldsmith's *The Vicar of Wakefield*, Augustus Toplady's *Book of Hymns* and various collections of poetry, prose and drama.

Kuli was a bright girl and Ramlochan had spotted the spark in her very early on. So it was only natural that he ventured to teach her what he didn't teach the others—verses of his favourite firingi poet, the Earl of Rochester. He was so proud when Kuli was able to read out faultlessly for the first time one of his favourite verses, Rochester's *Song*:

> *By all love's soft, yet mighty powers*
> *It is a thing unfit*
> *That men should fuck in time of flowers*
> *Or when the smock's beshit.*
> *Fair nasty nymph, be clean and kind*
> *And all my joys restore*
> *By using paper still behind*
> *And sponges for before.*
> *My spotless flames can ne'er decay*
> *If after every close*
> *My smoking prick escape the fray*
> *Without a bloody nose.*

As Kuli would sway back and forth reading the delightful words in the lamplight, he would bathe in the sweet, light voice that would utter those rhyming, rocking words. She did not understand the meaning of the words she read, following only the letters and stringing them into sound. But he had told her meaningfully that he would teach her the meanings of firingi words later, once she had mastered their reading and their utterances. She not only became adept at reading out passages in English but was also able to write out Bengali words and whole passages in the Latin script, managing to even transpose the numbers of one language to the other. Confusion, however, would arise each time the number eight cropped up. She would unthinkingly change it to the English 'four'.

But had he even touched her once in all these years that she was seven, eight and nine? Never. Not even the time when she had spilled water on to his precious pile of notes on Joydeb. It had taken hours for them to dry on that monsoon day.

Ramlochan had been walking all this while and he found himself in front of William's bungalow. He had been unaware as he walked through the streets of Krishnagar, passing the shops and the houses, that people were no longer willing to let the eccentric Baidya Pandit go about his business of educating their children. Now inside the deserted growth of what was once a tidy garden under the charge of Anna Maria Jones, he walked through the tangle of green and soft ground right up to the muddy banks of the Jalangi.

Panchanan had told him that Anna Maria had left Calcutta for London weeks before William's death. It seemed apt that everyone was returning to their rightful places. Was it so long ago that Anna Maria, a broad hat on her head, had stood on this exact spot, looking into the horizon that was broken by boats gliding slowly? Ramlochan remembered being inside the house, facing the wigless William as he struggled with the various shades of 'ahamkara'. He had looked out, watching the whitest figure in all the green and brown, watching her hold down her hat in the warm river breeze.

How he had wanted to impress Anna Maria by speaking to her in English, perhaps quoting something meaningful from all those words that he had read and loved. But there had been far too few moments alone—two, to be exact: once when William had been caught up in the rain and he had to wait for less than ten minutes for his pupil to arrive, and the second time when she had rushed into the room holding a clay Krishna, and not finding her husband departed with a silent smile.

I'tisam al-Din had told him how he was advised, during his stay in England, to take up an English wife.

'But they were only thinking of someone from the lower classes. Now, why would I even consider one of those vulgar ladies as a wife, tell me?' he had said patting his beard down . . .

There was no point in thinking about all that any more. William Jones had died in Calcutta. He had already been fêted as 'the unlocker of the secrets of India' and had omitted any mention of Ramlochan Sharma. Never mind London, even the Asiatic Society in Calcutta had never thought it fit to invite Ramlochan for his discourse on the parallels between Sanskrit nouns and English root nouns, let alone on his study on the use of 'anustubh' and 'tristubh' in the *Bhagvat Gita*.

From the corner of his eye he could see a small group of girls playing on the banks of the river. None of them was Kuli. The brown waters of the Jalangi looked up to him and he returned the gaze. He vaguely heard the girls titter loudly to accompanying splashes. How he would have liked to hear right there and right then his dear old Ramprasad. The singer's voice would have dissolved easily in the waters below.

> *Tell me, brother, so what's after death?*
> *The whole world is arguing about it*
> *Some say you become a ghost*
> *Others that you go to heaven*
> *And some that you get close to God.*
> *The Vedas insist that you're a bit of sky*
> *Reflected in a jar*
> *Fated to shatter.*

Ramlochan held himself tightly just to know how real he was. Edging closer to the water, he could see the contours of a face looking at him, but with its form blurring, breaking and rippling into pieces. His grip around himself now hurt. But it was a confirmation that he was still there when Ramprasad's voice came back to answer a question that he had never bothered to ask.

> *Prasad says: you end, brother,*
> *Where you began, a reflection*
> *Rising in water, mixing with water*
> *Finally one with water.*

But it wasn't the singer's words that he last heard standing beside the Jalangi. It was his own voice, carefully, incorruptibly saying,

> *Greensleeves was all my joy*
> *Greensleeves was my delight*
> *Greensleeves was my heart of gold*
> *And who but my Ladie Greensleeves.*

# finally, the talkies

So why am I here? Why have I been left unsurrounded, unentertained, unnamed all these years? The answer to that is very simple. I have eluded the answer all this while, and the answer, in all its simplicity, has tried to track me down, bump into me as if in an unscripted collision. But some things are meant to be. Like Ramlochan playing my role in a long, stretched-out, twentieth-century chamber version of his gems-in-the-gutters life. Like my accepting why *The Pandit & The Englishman* did not push me back into the waters in which I belonged. Because *The Pandit & The Englishman* didn't see the light of the bioscope.

Fritz Lang, that is Frederick E. Langford, wrapped up the film here in this city and returned to Europe. The feature was supposed to be ready for release in two months. That's what Langford had told me in our final meeting in his room at the Great Eastern. But in early 1927, it wasn't a motion picture about an eighteenth-century Bengali scholar played by Abani Chatterjee that was released to the sound of Nagerbazar's famous tom-toms. Instead, it was a film about a mechanical woman set in the year 2026.

Needless to say, Lang's *Metropolis*, with all its cinematic trickery, got its director noticed around the world, especially in America. But can anyone who was there during the making of

*The Pandit & The Englishman* deny that it had all the ingredients of a fine film, a great bioscope? I did ask some people about what happened. Charu Ray, busy by then making features for none other than the Alochhaya Bioscope Company, didn't have answers. And Charu is the kind of person who doesn't mind it a bit if he is clueless. I even wrote letters to Lang, sending them to the UFA office in Berlin, the last one sent just before the war broke out. I didn't get a single reply. Like Shombhu-mama, he had vanished like a gypsy caravan. But unlike Shombhunath Lahiri—unlike, I daresay, Abani Chatterjee—Fritz Lang is remembered and celebrated everywhere, in your widescreened Los Angeles where you will read all this, in my curtaining Calcutta where I write it.

Lang's *Metropolis* discovered a star in Gustav Frölich, who I must admit impressed me. Frölich jumped from being an unknown, an extra in the movie, to becoming its main character—and all because Thea van Harbou reportedly had found him 'interesting'.

Both the story of Ramlochan Sharma and the duplicity of Langford have remained hidden. Which is why what I have been saying is not one bitter, self-pitying, woeful ramble of a rant. I'm approaching sixty, for god's sake, and I have finally learnt to live with injustice, intermittent running water, the noise made by loud Congress loafers in the locality whose existence Bidhan Roy pretends not to know about, and humiliation that would fill up the Maidan and still have bits and pieces of it spilling over on to Chowringhee. So for me to demand my rightful place in the history of bioscopes is pointless.

I have not been to a movie theatre for decades. The last time I entered a cinema, I was sick and had to be taken out of that dark hole. All that sound and talk in movies today leave me gasping for air. Perhaps we all become our fathers when we grow old.

As for daily life, Sumitra, Rona's daughter-in-law, brings me my three meals. Drinking is no longer an option. Bikash is too busy playing politics. But he had his fair share of anguish last month. The man he works for, the minister Harendranath Roy Choudhury, lost to a lanky, thirty-eight-year-old communist at the Baranagar constituency elections. So maybe he'll be dropping by more often now. Marriage, that easy outpost for companionship, never entered my mind until it was too late. What makes my colic worse is not so much that I could have had things differently, but that Langford, Lang, whatever you call him, is still out there, fêted and unexposed.

But then, when you stop pretending, you don't stop pretending. You just pretend something else. Is my present condition the result of lapsing into Abani Chatterjee? I don't think so. No one's interested in the character I've been playing for the last thirty years. I still don't think it was a bad choice, though. The people just don't care for it any more. Which is why I have to be careful even now. This city, which has been baring its teeth for far too long, will chew me up if I give in now to vulgar demand. In a way, my only companion in this totally unglamorous, non-nutritious, gnawing-away hole of obscurity is Ramlochan. Two figures in the footnotes. Two feetnote, hah! But I will not clamber out to be eaten by this city.

Which is why last September, after reading two letters that Sumitra had brought with my lunch, I tore up one and decided to act on the other. The first was from someone who introduced himself as an admirer. He was a young commercial artist at D.J. Keymer who had seen some of my old bioscopes, the ones that somehow survived the godowns with their dripping ceilings and lizard droppings. He wrote that he had plans of making a movie based on a story by Bibhuthibhushan Bandopadhyay. I had read a bit of the story, *Pather Panchali*, when it first came out in instalments in *Bichitra* during the Twenties. It was a melodramatic story and I hadn't cared much for it—it basically depicted the idiocy of rural life without actually identifying it as idiocy. He thought that I would be perfect for the role of a village grocer-teacher in the story. But he was also honest enough to tell me that it was a minor role ('but an important one'). After years of avoiding bit roles, I saw no sense in giving in now. So I never replied to the man.

The second letter was yours. I read it and it got me thinking. If you, sitting there in California, thought it worth the effort to want to know about me, my work and my life, there must be *something* in what I had done in those happy years in the bioscopes. It also gave me great relief that I hadn't succumbed to the temptations of whoring myself.

You mentioned in your letter that you are in the process of writing the biography of Sabu 'The Elephant Boy'. Apart from seeing him on the screen long ago in *The Thief of Baghdad* and *Cobra Woman*, I know nothing about him. But I know things about myself. Which is why I send you this.

# acknowledgements

Thanks to Ravi Singh, without whom this book would have remained the very untossed salad that it was. His editorial and vodka inputs have been at the core of the writing process of this book. I owe Jaishree Ram Mohan big time, not only for her extremely precious feedback but also for pretending to be drunk each time so that I never stood out.

The Charles Wallace Trust provided me the luxury that all writers crave: time. I got plenty of that in the two months I was a Writer-in-Residence at Stirling University, Scotland in 2005. Angela and Grahame Smith were terrific company, and many rounds of Highland Flings for the friends I made at Stirling.

Thanks also to Renuka Chatterjee, who read the manuscript and gave me valuable suggestions. A tip of the hat to my day job at *Hindustan Times*. Which other company would have put up with such nonsense?

Apologies to my father, who wanted me to go to film school ever since he took me to the cinema to see *2001: A Space Odyssey*. I was two years old.

And everything boils down to Diya. I'm still trying to impress her.